FIC   Narayan, R. K.,
Narayan 1906-

The grandmother's
tale and selected
stories.

The Grandmother's Tale

AND SELECTED STORIES

By the same author

The Grandmother's Tale

AND SELECTED STORIES

R. K. Narayan

VIKING

VIKING
Published by the Penguin Group
Penguin Books USA Inc., 375 Hudson Street, New York, New York 10014, U.S.A.
Penguin Books Ltd, 27 Wrights Lane, London W8 5TZ, England
Penguin Books Australia Ltd, Ringwood, Victoria, Australia
Penguin Books Canada Ltd, 10 Alcorn Avenue, Toronto, Ontario, Canada M4V 3B2
Penguin Books (N.Z.) Ltd, 182–190 Wairau Road, Auckland 10, New Zealand

Penguin Books Ltd, Registered Offices: Harmondsworth, Middlesex, England

First published in 1994 by Viking Penguin,
a division of Penguin Books USA Inc.

1   3   5   7   9   10   8   6   4   2

PUBLISHER'S NOTE: These are works of fiction. Names, characters, places, and incidents either are the product of the author's imagination or are used fictitiously, and any resemblance to actual persons, living or dead, events, or locales is entirely coincidental.

"The Grandmother's Tale," "Guru," and "Salt and Sawdust" originally appeared in *The Grandmother's Tale: Three Novellas*, published in Great Britain by William Heinemann Ltd.
Some of the selections previously appeared in the following books by Mr. Narayan published by Viking Penguin: "Emden," "An Astrologer's Day," "The Blind Dog," "Second Opinion," "Lawley Road," "Cat Within," and "The Edge" in *Malgudi Days*; "A Horse and Two Goats," "Annamalai," "A Breath of Lucifer," "Seventh House," and "Uncle" in *A Horse and Two Goats*; and "Annamalai," "A Horse and Two Goats," "A Breath of Lucifer," "Under the Banyan Tree," "Another Community," and "The Shelter" in *Under the Banyan Tree and Other Stories*.
"Second Opinion," "A Horse and Two Goats," "Seventh House," and "Uncle" originally appeared in *The New Yorker*; "Annamalai" in *Encounter*; "A Breath of Lucifer" in *Playboy*; and "Cat Within" and "The Edge" in *Antaeus*.

LIBRARY OF CONGRESS CATALOGING IN PUBLICATION DATA
Narayan, R. K.
The grandmother's tale and selected stories / R.K. Narayan.
p.   cm.
ISBN 0–670–85220–1
1. India—Fiction.   I. Title.
PR9499.3.N3G74   1994
823—dc20   94–4581

Printed in the United States of America • Set in Garamond #3 • Designed by Brian Mulligan

To the memory of my daughter, Hema, who selected the additional stories for this volume in order to give it stature: for half a century my companion, friend, philosopher and guide, enriching my life with a granddaughter and a grandson.

Contents

The Grandmother's Tale

I was brought up by my grandmother in Madras from my third year while my mother lived in Bangalore with a fourth child on hand after me. My grandmother took me away to Madras in order to give relief to an overburdened daughter.

My grandmother Ammani was a busy person. She performed a variety of tasks all through the day, cooking and running the house for her two sons, gardening, counseling neighbors and the tenants living in the rear portion of the vast house stretching away in several segments, settling disputes, studying horoscopes and arranging matrimonial alliances. At the end of the day she settled down on a swing—a broad plank suspended by chains from the ceiling; lightly propelling it with her feet back and forth, chewing betel, she was completely relaxed at that hour. She held me at her side and taught me songs, prayers, numbers and the alphabet till suppertime.

I mention "suppertime," but there was no fixed suppertime. My uncles returned home late in the evening. The senior uncle conducted a night school for slum children. (Some of them, later in life, attained eminence as pundits in the Tamil language and literature.) The junior uncle worked in the harbor as a stevedore's assistant and came home at uncertain hours. Suppertime could not be based on their homecoming but on my performance. My grandmother fed me only when I completed my lessons to her satisfaction. I had to repeat the multiplication table up to twenty but I always fumbled and stuttered after twelve and needed prodding and goading to attain the peak; I had to recite Sanskrit verse and slokas in praise of Goddess Saraswathi and a couple of other gods, and hymns in Tamil; identify six ragas when granny hummed the tunes or, conversely, mention the songs when she named the ragas; and then solve arithmetic problems such as, "If a boy wants four mangoes costing one anna per mango, how much money will he have to take?" I wanted to blurt out, "Boys don't have to buy, they can obtain a fruit with a well-aimed stone at a mango tree." I brooded, blinked without a word, afraid I might offend her if I mentioned the stone technique for obtaining a fruit. She watched me and then, tapping my skull, gently remarked, "Never seen a bigger dunce . . ." It was all very taxing, I felt hungry and sleepy. To keep me awake, she kept handy a bowl of cold water and sprinkled it on my eyelids from time to time.

I could not understand why she bothered so much to make me learned. She also taught me some folk songs which now, I realize, were irrelevant, such as the one about a drunkard sleeping indifferently while his child in the crib was crying and the mother was boiling the milk. The most unnecessary lesson, however, in my memory as I realize it now, was a Sanskrit lyric, not in praise of God, but defining the perfect woman—it said the perfect woman must work like a slave, advise like a Mantri (Minister), look like Goddess Lakshmi, be patient like Mother Earth and courtesan-like in the bed chamber—this I had to recite on certain days of the week. After the lessons she released me and served food. When I was six years old I was ceremoniously escorted to the Lutheran Mission School nearby and admitted in the "Infant Standard."

Later I grew up in Mysore with my parents, visiting my grandmother in Madras once a year during the holidays. After completing my college course, I frequently visited Madras to try my luck there as a free-lance author.

My junior uncle, no longer a stevedore's assistant but an automobile salesman for a German make, set out every morning to contact his "prospects" and demonstrate the special virtues of his car. He took me out with him, saying "If you want to be a writer, don't mope at home listening to grandmother's tales. You must be up and doing; your B.A. degree will lead you nowhere if you do not contact 'prospects.' Come out with me and watch. . . ." He drove me about, stopped here and there, met all sorts of persons and delivered his sales talk, making sure that I followed his performance intelligently. I avoided his company in the evenings, since he wined and dined with his "prospects" to clinch a sale. During his morning rounds, however, I went out with him to be introduced to men, who, he thought, were in the writing line. He left me in their company to discuss with them my literary aspirations. Most of them were printers, established in the highways and byways of the city, or publishers of almanacs, diaries, lottery tickets and race cards, who were looking for proofreaders on a daily wage of ten rupees.

My uncle urged me to accept any offer that came: "You must make a start and go up. Do you know what I was earning when I worked at the harbor? Less than twenty-five a month, in addition to occasional tips from clearing agents. That is how I learned my job. Then I moved on to a job at a bookshop in Mount Road, cycling up in the morning, carrying my lunch, and selling books till seven in the evening. It was hard work, but I was learning a job. Today do you know what I get? One thousand for every car I sell, in addition to expenses for entertaining the prospects. You will have to learn your job while earning, whatever the wages might be. That is how you should proceed."

After brooding over these suggestions, I began to ignore his advice and stayed at home, much to his annoyance: "Well, if you do not want to prosper, I will just say G.T.H. (go to hell). I have better things to do. . . ." (However, he relented subsequently after the publication of my first three novels, my first three in England.) In 1940, when I started a quarterly journal, "Indian Thought," in Mysore, he took it upon himself to help its circulation, applying his sales talk at high pressure. Carrying a sample copy of "Indian Thought" from door to door, he booked one thousand subscribers in Madras city alone in the first year. Unfortunately, "Indian Thought" ceased publication in the second year since I could not continue it single-handed.

Although aging, my grandmother was still active and concerned herself with other people's affairs, her domestic drudgery now mitigated by the presence of two daughters-in-law in the house. She sat as usual on the swing in the evenings, invited me to sit beside her, and narrated to me stories of her early days—rather of her mother's early life and adventures, as heard by her from her mother when she, Ammani, was about ten years old.

Day after day, I sat up with her listening to her account, and at night developed it as a cogent narrative. As far as possible, I have tried to retain the flavor of her speech, though the manner of her narrative could not be reproduced as it proceeded in several directions back and forth and got mixed up with asides and irrelevancies. I have managed to keep her own words here and there, but this is mainly a story-writer's version of a hearsay biography of a great-grandmother. She was seven when she was married, her husband being just ten years old. Those were the days of child marriages, generally speaking. Only widowers remarried late in life. It is not possible to fix the historical background by any clue or internal evidence. My grandmother could not be specific about the time since she was unborn at the beginning of her mother's story. One has to assume an arbitrary period—that is, the later period of the East India Company, before the Sepoy Mutiny. My grandmother could not specify the location of their beginning. It might be anywhere in the Southern Peninsula. She just mentioned it as "that village," which conjures up a familiar pattern: a hundred houses scattered in four or five narrow streets, with pillared verandas and pyols, massive front doors, inner courtyards, situated at the bend of a river or its tributary, mounds of garbage here and there, cattle everywhere, a temple tower looming over it all; the temple hall and corridor serving as a meeting ground for the entire population, and an annual festival attracting a big crowd from nearby hamlets—an occasion when a golden replica of the deity in the inner shrine was carried in a procession with pipes and drums around the village.

"What god was he?" I could not resist my curiosity; my grandmother knew as much as I did, but ventured a guess.

"Could be Ranganatha, an aspect of Vishnu, in repose in a state of yoga lying on the coils of the thousand-headed Adisesha. The god was in a trance, and watched and protected our village. They were married in that temple—my father and mother. Don't interrupt me with questions, as I have also only heard about these events. My mother told me that she was playing in the street with her friends one evening when her father came up and said, 'You are going to be married next week.'

" 'Why?' she asked and did not get an answer. Her father ignored her questions and went away. Her playmates stopped their game, surrounded and teased her. 'Hey, bride! Hey, bride!'

" 'Wait! You will also be brides soon!' she retorted. She rushed back home to her mother, crying, 'Whatever happens, I am not going to marry. My friends are making fun of me!' "

Her mother soothed her and explained patiently that she was old enough to marry, something that could not be avoided by any human being, an occasion when she would be showered with gifts and new clothes and gold ornaments. The girl, however, was not impressed. She sulked and wept in a corner of their home. After fixing the date of the wedding they kept her strictly indoors and did not allow her to go out and play. Her playmates visited her and whispered their sympathies.

On an auspicious day she was clad in a sari, decked in jewelry and taken to the pillared hall of the temple, where had gathered guests and relations and priests: a piper and drummer were creating enough noise to drown the uproar of the priests and chanting mantras and the babble of the guests. She was garlanded and made to sit beside a boy whom she had often noticed tossing a rubber ball in an adjoining street whenever she went out to buy a pencil, ribbon or sweets in a little shop. She felt shy to look at him now, sitting too close to him on a plank. The smoke from the holy fire smarted her eyes and also created a smoke screen blurring her vision whenever she stole a glance in his direction. At the auspicious hour the piper, drummer and the chanting priests combined to create the maximum din as Viswa approached the girl, seated on her father's lap, and tied the yellow thread around her neck, and they became man and wife from that moment.

In a week all celebration, feasting and exchange of ceremonial visits between the bride and bridegroom parties ceased. Viswanath the bridegroom went back to his school, run by a pedagogue on a brick platform under a banyan tree on the riverside. He was ragged by his class-fellows for getting married. He denied it and became violent till the pedagogue intervened and brought his cane down on the back of the teasing member.

The boy said between sobs, "He is lying. I was at the temple with my father and ate, along with the others, a big feast with four kinds of sweets. Viswanath wore new clothes, a gold chain and a big garland around his neck. If I am lying, let him take off his shirt and show us the sacred thread. . . ." He bared his chest and held up his sacred thread to demonstrate that he had only a bachelor's three-strand thread. The teacher was old, suffered from a sore throat and could not control his class of twenty-five children when a babble broke out on the subject of Viswa's marriage. A few cried, "Shame, shame," which was the usual form of greeting in their society.

The teacher tapped his cane on the floor and cried over the tumult, "Why shame? I was married when I was like Viswa. I have four sons and two daughters and grandchildren. My wife looks after those at home still, and runs the family; and they will also all marry soon. There is no shame in marriage. It's all arranged by that god in the temple. Who are we to say anything against his will? My wife was also small when we married. . . ."

The girl's life changed after her marriage. She could not go out freely, or join her friends playing in the street. She could not meet her husband, except on special occasions such as the New Year and other festival days when Viswa was invited to visit his wife's home with his parents. On those occasions the girl was kept aloof in a separate room and would be escorted to his presence by young women who would giggle and urge the young couple to talk and say something to each other and leave them alone for a little time. The couple felt embarrassed and shy and tongue-tied but took that opportunity to study each other's features. When they got a chance, the very first sentence the girl uttered was "There is a black patch under your ear." She made bold to touch his face with her forefinger. Apart from holding each other's right hand before the holy fire during their wedding ceremony this was their first touch. He found that her finger was soft and she found the skin under his left ear rough but pleasant. When she removed her finger she asked, "What is this patch?" She thrust her finger again to trace that black patch under his left ear. "Oh, that!" he said, pressing down her finger on the black patch. "It's a lucky sign, my mother says."

"Does it hurt?" she asked solicitously.

"No. They say it's lucky to have that mark," he said.

"How much luck?" she asked and continued, "Will you be-come a king?"

"Yes, that's what they say." And before they could develop this subject, others opened the door and came in, not wanting to leave the couple alone too long.

After that they discovered an interest in each other's company. But it was not easy to meet. It was impossible for the girl to go out, unless chaperoned by an elder of the family. Even such outings were limited to a visit to the temple on a Friday evening or to a relation on ceremonial occasions. Viswa wished he could be told when and where he could see her. Occasionally he found an excuse to visit her home on the pretext of wanting to meet his father-in-law on some business but it did not always work, as the man would be in his coconut grove far away. Viswa did not possess the hardihood to step into the house to catch a glimpse of his young wife. She kept herself in the deepest recess of their house for fear of being considered too forward, and he would turn back disappointed. But he soon found a way. He spied and discovered that she was more accessible at their back-yard, where she washed clothes at the well. There was only a short wall separating their backyard from a lane, which proved a more convenient approach since he could avoid a neighbor always lounging on the pyol and asking, "Ay! Visiting your wife? Insist upon a good tiffin . . ." It made him self-conscious. He would simper and murmur and hasten his steps only to be met by his mother-in-law at the door. Now, the backyard could be approached without anyone accosting him, but the lane was dirty and garbage-ridden; he did not mind it. On his way back from school if he took a diversion, he could approach the lane and the short wall. He placed a couple of bricks close to the wall, stood on the pile with his head showing up a few inches above it. It was a sound strategy though her back was turned to him, while she drew water from the well and filled a bucket and soaked her clothes. He watched her for a few moments and cried,

"Hey!" When she did not hear his call he clapped his hands, and she turned and stared at him. He said, "Hey, I am here."

Looking back watchfully into their house she asked, "Why?"

"To see you," he said.

"Come by the front door," she said.

And he said promptly, "I can't. It's no good. How are you? I came to ask," he said rather timidly.

"Why should you ask?" she questioned. He had no immediate answer. He just blinked. She laughed at him and said, "You are tall today."

"Yes," he said. "Is your name Balambal? It is too long."

"Call me Bala," she said, picked up her bucket and suddenly retreated into the house.

He waited, hoping she would come back. But the back door shut with a bang, and he jumped off muttering, "She is funny. I should not have married her. But what could I do? I was never asked whether I wanted to marry or not. . . ."

He ran down the lane and sought the company of his friend Ramu, who lived in a house next to the temple and who knew when the pujas at the temple were performed and when they would distribute the offerings—sweet rice and coconut pieces. If one stuck to Ramu one need not starve for snacks. He could take Viswa to see the god at the appropriate moment when the evening service was in progress and wait. After camphor flames were waved and cymbals and bells sounded, the offerings would be distributed. Piously standing on the threshold of the sanctum Ramu would whisper, "Viswa, shut your eyes and pray, otherwise they will not give you anything to eat!"

At the next session Viswa was more successful. Standing on the pile of bricks, he told her, "On Tuesday evening I went to the temple."

"Did you pray? What for?" she asked. Seeing his silence, she said, "Why go to temple if you don't pray?"

"I don't know any prayer."

"What did you learn at home?"

He realized she was a heckler and tried to ward off the attack. "I know some prayer, not all."

"Recite some," she said.

"No, I won't," he said resolutely.

"You will be sent to hell if you don't say your prayers."

"How do you know?" he asked.

"My mother has told me. She makes us all pray in the evenings in the puja room."

"Bah!" he said. "What do you get to eat after the prayers? At the temple if you shut your eyes and prostrate before the god, they give you wonderful things to eat. For that you must come with me and Ramu . . ."

"Who is Ramu?"

"My friend," Viswa said and jumped off the pile of bricks as there were portents of the girl's mother appearing on the scene. He was now satisfied that he had been able to establish a line of communication with Bala although the surroundings were filthy, and he had to tread warily lest he should put his foot on excreta, the lane serving as a public convenience.

They could not meet normally as husband and wife. Bala, being only ten years old, had to attain puberty and then go through an elaborate nuptial ceremony, before she could join her husband.

Viswa had other plans. One afternoon he stood on the brick pile and beckoned her. She looked up and frantically signaled to him to go away. "I have to talk to you," he said desperately and ducked and crouched while her mother appeared at the door for a moment.

After she had gone in, he heard a soft voice calling, "Hey, speak."

His head bobbed up again over the wall and he just said, "I am going away. Keep it a secret. . . ."

"Where are you going?"

"I don't know. Far away."

"Why?"

He had no answer. He merely said, "Even Ramu doesn't know."

"Who are you going with?"

"I don't know, but I am joining some pilgrims beyond the river."

"Won't you tell me why you are going away?"

"No, I can't . . . I have to go away—that is all."

"Can't you mention a place where you are going?"

"I don't know . . ."

She began to laugh. "Oh! Oh! You are going to 'I don't know' place. Is it?"

He felt irked by her levity and said, "I don't know, really. They were a group of pilgrims singing a *bhajan* about Pandaripura or some such place . . . over and over again."

"Are you sure?"

"You won't see me for a long time. . . ."

"But when will you come back?"

"Later . . . ," he said and vanished as he noticed her mother coming again, and that was the last the girl saw of him for a long time to come.

She remained indifferent for a week or ten days and then began secretly to worry. She thought at first Viswa was playing a joke and would reappear over the wall sooner or later. She wanted to tell her mother, but was afraid she might begin to investigate how she came to know Viswa had disappeared, and then proceed to raise the wall to keep him off. She suffered silently, toyed with the idea of seeking Ramu's help, but she had never seen him. Others at home did not bother. Her father was, as ever, interested only in his coconut garden, the price of coconut, coconut pests and so on. He left home at dawn after breakfasting on rice soaked overnight in cold water, packed a lunch and returned home at night tired and weary, leaving domestic matters to his wife's care.

*   *   *

Bala's mother noticed her brooding silence and gloom and asked one day, "What is ailing you?"

Bala burst into tears. "He . . . he . . . is gone," she said. "Who?"

Bala replied, "He . . . he . . . ," since a wife could not utter a husband's name.

When Bala's father returned home from the garden the lady told him, "Viswa has disappeared."

He took it lightly and said, "Must be playing with his friends somewhere. Where could he go? How do you know he has disappeared?"

"I have not seen him for a long time. He used to come up to see you, but as you were always away, he would turn back from the door."

"Poor boy! You should have called him in. Young people are shy!"

"Bala also shut herself in whenever he came . . ."

"She is also young and shy. I must take him with me to the garden sometime."

The lady persuaded the man to stay away from the coconut garden, and next morning they went over to Viswa's house. "After all they are our *sambhandis* [relations through matrimonial alliance] and we must pay them courtesy visits at least once in a while."

Viswa's parents lived in what was named Chariot Nook (where the temple chariot was stationed in a shed).

After a formal welcome and the courtesy of unrolling a mat for the visitors, both Viswa's father and Bala's asked simultaneously, "Where is Viswa?" When they realized no one knew the answer, Viswa's parents said, "We thought he was in your house. We were planning to come and see him."

Next they visited the schoolmaster, who said he had not seen Viswa for more than ten days.

It became a sensation in the village. Well-wishers of the family and others crowded in, speculating, sympathizing, and suggesting the next step, vociferous and excited and talking simultaneously. A little fellow in the crowd said, "I saw him with a group crossing the river . . ."

"When?"

"I don't remember."

"Didn't you talk to him?"

"Yes, he said he was going to Delhi." There was ironic laughter at this.

"Delhi is thousands of miles away . . ."

"More . . ."

"I hear sepoys are killing white officers."

"Who told you?"

"Someone from the town . . ."

"Who cares who kills whom while we are bothered about Viswa?"

Someone suddenly questioned Viswa's father. "Are you in the habit of beating him?"

"Sometimes you can't help it."

Viswa's mother said, "Whenever his teacher came and reported something, you lost your head," and burst into tears. "Teachers are an awful lot, you must pay no attention to what they say."

"But unless the teacher is strict young fellows can never be tamed."

Viswa's mother said, sobbing, "You thrashed him when that awful man came and said something."

"He had thrown cow dung on the master when he was not looking."

"You slapped him," said the mother.

"I only patted his cheek."

Everyone nursed a secret fear that Viswa had drowned in the river. Then the whole company trooped out, stood before the god in the temple hall, prayed and promised offerings if Viswa came back alive. If Bala could have opened her mouth to announce what she knew, it would have been a relief to everyone, but she remained dumb.

As time passed Bala found existence a sore trial. She was no longer the little girl with a pigtail, dressed in a cotton skirt and jacket. Now she had reached maturity—rather stocky with no pretensions to any special beauty except the natural charm of full-blown womanhood, she could not pass down the *agraharam* street without people staring at her, whispering comments at her back. Sometimes some friend of the family would stop her on her way to the temple and ask, "Any news? Do you hope he will come back?" She found it a strain to be inventing answers. She snapped at her questioners sometimes, but it made things worse. "Where is he?" people persisted in demanding.

She said one day, "In Kashmir, making a lot of money, and has sent a message to say he will be back soon."

"Who brought you the message?" She invented a name. Next time when they questioned her again about the messenger she just said, "He has gone there as a priest in some temple . . ." She soon tired of it all, and showed herself outside home as little as possible, but for a visit to the temple on Tuesday and Friday evening. She would gaze on the image in the sanctum when the camphor flame was waved to the ringing of the bells and pray, "O Lord. I don't even know whether my husband is alive. If he is alive help me to reach him. If he is dead, please let me die of cholera quickly." Other women looked at her strangely and asked among themselves, "Why is her mother not coming with her? There must be some reason. They are not on talking terms. She must be hiding something. He is no more but they are keeping it a secret. Instead of shaving her head and wearing white, she oils and combs her hair and decks flowers! And comes to the temple with *kumkum* on her brow pretending to be a Sumangali. A widow who pretends to be otherwise pollutes the temple precinct and its holiness is lost. She should be prohibited from entering the temple unless she shaves her head and observes the rules. Her mother must be a brazen woman to allow her out like this. We should talk to the priest."

The priest of the temple visited them one afternoon. Bala's mother was all excitement at the honor, unrolled a mat, seated him, offered him some fruits and milk and made a lot of fuss. The priest accepted it all and looked around cautiously and asked in a hushed voice, "Where is your daughter?" Bala generally retired to a back room when there was a visitor; but tried to listen to their talk. The priest was saying, "I remember Bala as a child, in fact I remember her wedding." He paused and asked, "Where is her husband, that boy who married her? I notice Bala at the temple some evenings."

Her mother was upset and not able to maintain the conversation. The priest said, "You know the old proverb 'You may seal the mouth of a furnace, but you cannot shut the mouth of gossip.' Till you get some proof to say he is living it is better that you don't send Bala to the temple. Its sanctity must be preserved—which is my duty, otherwise as a priest of the temple my family will face God's wrath."

At this point of their talk Bala rushed out like a storm, her face flushed. "You people think I am a widow? I am not. He is alive like you. I'll not rest until I come back with him some day, and shame you all. . . ." She threw a word of cheer to her mother and flounced out of the house.

Bala's mother tried to follow her down the street but Bala was too fast for her. People stood and stared at the mother–daughter chase. Bala halted. When her mother came up she whispered, "Go back home. . . . People are watching us. Keep well, I will come back. Remember that the priest is waiting there in our house. . . ." Mother was in a dilemma. She hesitated as Bala raced forward.

Bala dashed for a moment into the temple and prostrated

before the image, rose and hurried away before the priest or others should arrive and notice her. She rushed past all the gaping men and women, past all the rows of houses to Chariot Nook, to Viswa's house and knocked. Her mother-in-law opened the door and was aghast. "Bala! You look like Kali . . . what is the matter? Come in first. . . . You should stay with us . . ."

"Yes, when I come with my husband." She took a pinch of vermilion from a little bowl on a stool and pressed it on her brow, fell prostrate at her mother-in-law's feet, touched them reverently, sprang back and was off even as the lady was saying, "Your father-in-law will come back soon, wait . . ." Before her sentence was completed, Bala was gone.

Up to this point, my grandmother remembered her mother's narration. Beyond this, her information was hazy. She just said, "Bala must have gone to the village cart stand in the field beyond the last street, where travelers and bullock carts assembled." Bala must have paid for a seat in a carriage, traveled all night and reached a nearby town. Even in her hurry before leaving home, she did not forget to pack a small bag with a change of clothes, some money she had saved out of her birthday and other gifts, a few gold ornaments, and above all a knife in case she had to protect her honor and end her life. At the town she stayed in a choultry where an assortment of travelers and pilgrims was lodged. Her mind harped on a single word: "Pandaripur." She made constant inquiries of everyone she came across and set forth in that direction. After many false starts and retracing her steps, she got on the right track and joined travelers going on foot or by other modes of transport available, and reached Poona about a year later.

My grandmother's account had many gaps from this point onward. What Bala did after this, how she managed. What happened to her mother, where was her father all the while? What happened to Viswa's parents? Above all, why she went to Poona to search for her husband. What were the steps that led her steps to Poona? These were questions that never got an answer. My grandmother only snapped, "Why do you ask me? Am I a wizard to see the past? If you interrupt me like this, I'll never be able to complete the story, I can only tell you what I have heard from my mother. I just listened without interrupting her as you do now. If you don't shut your mouth and keep only your ears open, I'll never tell you anything more. You can't expect me to know everything. If you want all sorts of useless information about the past I cannot help you. Not my business. Whenever my mother felt like it, she would gather us around and tell her story—so that we might realize how strong and bold she was at one time. She would boast, 'You only see me as a cook at home feeding you and pampering your father's whims and moods, but at one time I could do other things which you, petted and spoilt children, could never even imagine . . . ,' she would remark from time to time."

By the time Bala reached Poona she had exhausted all her gold and cash and was left with nothing. She felt terrified and lonely. People looked strangely different and spoke a language she did not understand. She reached a public rest house, a charity institution where *roti* was distributed, and held out her hand along with the others, swallowed whatever she got in order to survive. She made the rest house the central point and wandered about studying the faces of passersby, hoping to spot Viswa. She feared that if he had grown a beard she would not be able to recognize him. All that she could remember was the head peeping over the wall, also the black patch under his left ear which he boasted would make him king—perhaps he was now the king of this town. She thought in her desperation of stopping some kindly soul to ask: "Who is the king here?" But they might take her to be a madcap and stone her.

The bazaars were attractive and she passed her time looking

at the display of goods. She was afraid to move about after dusk for fear of being mistaken for a loose woman soliciting custom. She returned to the rest house and stayed there. One day she was noticed by an elderly lady who asked in Marathi, "Who are you? I see you here every day. Where are you from? What is the matter?" Of course Bala could not understand her language, but felt it was all sympathy from a stranger and was moved to tears.

The old woman took her hand and led her out of the rest house, to a home nearby where there was a family. Men, women and children, who kept gazing on her like a strange specimen, surrounded her and joked and laughed. To their questions, all that she could answer was to take her fingers to the *thali* around her neck. They understood she was a married woman. When they questioned her further, she burst involuntarily into tears and uncontrollably into Tamil. She made up in gesticulation whatever she felt to be lacking in her Tamil explanation. She said, "My fate . . ."—she etched with her forefinger on her brow—"It's written here that I must struggle and suffer. How I have survived these months which I have lost count of, God alone knows. Here I have come, to this strange city, and I have to behave like a deaf-mute, neither understanding what you say nor making myself understood."

They listened to her lamentation sympathetically, without understanding a word, only realizing that it was a deeply felt utterance. Someone in the crowd, recognizing the sound of the language, asked, "Madarasi?"

"Must be so, she doesn't cover her head," said another. Bala could guess the nature of the query and nodded affirmatively.

"I can take you to a man who came here many years ago. He may understand you." He beckoned her to follow him. She indicated that she wanted a drink of water, feeling her throat parched and dry after her harangue.

A boy was deputed to guide her. She followed him blindly, not knowing or caring where she was going. The boy took her through the main street, past the bazaars and crowds, but proved too fast, running ahead. It was difficult to keep pace with him. She was panting with the effort. "Where are you taking me?" she asked again and again, but he only grinned and indicated some destination. Finally she found herself under an archway with a path leading to a big house. Leaving her there, the boy turned around and ran off before she could question him, perhaps feeling too shy to be seen with a woman.

She was puzzled, there was no one in sight. Beyond the archway and gate there was a garden. Presently a gardener appeared above a cluster of plants. He looked at her for a moment and stooped down again to resume his digging. Not knowing what to do next, she sat down on a sentry platform beside the arch, felt drowsy and shut her eyes. She woke up when she heard the sound of a horse trotting. She saw the rider pass under the arch and dismount in front of the house, helped by an attendant. He had thrown a brief glance at her in passing. He was dressed in breeches and embroidered vest and crowned with a turban—very much a man of these parts. Rather lean and of medium height. Could this be the man from the Tamil land? Seemed unlikely. She did not know what should be her next step. She continued to sit there. A little later, she noticed him again, coming out on his horse. She was all attention now, staring at him when he passed under the arch. She noticed his mustache curving up to his ears. He threw at her another brief glance and passed. She decided to sit through and wait indefinitely, hoping to find some identification mark next time. She invoked the god in their village temple and prayed, "Guide me, O Lord, I don't know what to do . . ." A couple of hours later the horse and the rider appeared, and once again he threw at her the briefest glance and passed.

An attendant in livery approached her from the house. He asked, "Who are you? Master has seen you sitting here. Go away, don't sit here. Otherwise he will be angry and call the kotwal. Go away . . ." She shook her head and sat immobile.

"Go away . . ." He gestured her to go. He kept saying, "Ko-

twal, kotwal, he will come and take you to prison . . ." She
would not move. The servant looked intimidated by her manner
and backed away. Ten minutes later he reappeared and asked her
to follow him. She felt nervous, wondering what sort of a man
she was going to encounter. The front steps seemed endless and
she felt weak at the knees and crossed the threshold expecting
the worst.

The man lounging on a couch watched her enter. She could
not understand whether this was the beginning or the end of
her troubles. She tried to study his face. There was not even a
remote resemblance between the head she last saw over the wall
and this man. He had no turban on and he was bald on top
though his whiskers reached up to his earlobes. Gazing at his
face she wondered what would happen if she made a dash for his
whisker and lifted it to look for the black patch below his left
ear: this might prove conclusive and the end of her quest. While
she toyed with the idea, he thundered in Marathi, "Who are
you? Why do you sit at my gate?"

She said, "They said that you speak Tamil . . ." Shaking his
head, he took out his purse, held out some money and tried to
wave her off. She refused the money. He summoned a servant to
show her out. She sat down on the floor and refused to move.

"They said you are from the South. Keep me here. I have
nowhere to go . . . I am an orphan. I will be your servant, cook
for you and serve you. Only grant me a shelter."

He gave an order to the servant, suddenly got up, went upstairs and shut himself in a room. She began to doubt her wisdom in depending upon the urchin who guided her. So far this
man had shown no sign of understanding Tamil, in which she
was addressing him. He had no identifiable feature except the
greenish color of his eyes, something that did not alter with
years. She felt it might be wiser to sneak away quietly.

The servant fetched two kotwals, who stood over her and commanded her to get up. She felt she was making a hideous mistake
in accosting a stranger and they were likely to think she was a
characterless blackmailer.

As the kotwals were trying to move her physically, she screamed in Tamil, "Don't touch me. I will reduce you to ashes . . ." (*Thodade unnai Posikiduven*). She looked fierce and the kotwals, though fiercer in a grotesque uniform and headgear, shrank back.

While this was going on, a woman entered, nearing middle age and authoritative. She scowled at the men and cried, "What are you doing? Leave her alone." They tried to explain, but she dismissed them instantly. She helped Bala to rise to her feet, seated her in a chair and asked, "Who are you? I heard you speak. Do you not understand our language?" Bala shook her head.

The other woman asked in Tamil, "Who are you?"

At this point, Bala had the shrewdness to conceal her purpose and just said, "I came with some pilgrims to fulfill a vow at Pandaripura, got stranded, separated from a group." And spun a story, which fell on sympathetic ears. "You are fortunate to live in a home like this, so comfortable and beautiful with its garden . . . ," said Bala.

"Yes, we love plants. . . ." She pointed upstairs. "He is a keen gardener himself. . . . When my father lived, he had no time left. All his hours he spent in his shop and came home late at night. After my husband joined us, my father got some relief. . . ."

Bala refrained from asking any question for fear of betraying her purpose but allowed the other to ramble on, gathering much information. She was on the point of asking his name but checked herself, as the woman referred to him only as "He" or "Bhatji."

Suddenly she cried, "Oh, how thoughtless of me to be sitting and talking like this without even asking if you are hungry. . . . Come in with me." She got up and led her to the kitchen. She lifted the lid of some vessels, bustled about, picked up a plate, set it on a little platform, put up a sitting plank and said, "Sit down and eat. I have something still left. We are both poor eaters. He is so busy outside in the shop and visiting the palace, he seldom eats at home—only at night. I make something for myself. I don't like to spend too much time cooking. I also sit in the shop part of the day, especially when he has to go on his rounds. He is an expert in judging diamonds and all gems. His advice and appraisal is sought by everyone in this city. We have a large collection of precious stones, apart from getting our supply from the mines in this country, we also import—he has to go to Bombay sometimes when ships arrive at the port."

She fed Bala, which revived her, since she had had nothing to eat after a couple of free *rotis* and a tumbler of water in the morning. She became loquacious and spirited. She washed the dishes at the backyard well and restored them to the kitchen shelf. The lady took her round the house and the garden. "My father built this in those days when we could engage many servants who kept the house clean, but now we have only ten. He always rests upstairs. Shall we go up and see the rooms there?"

Bala said, "Later, let us not disturb him now."

"Come, I'll show you your room. You should stay with us. Have you left your box in the rest house? Let us go and fetch it."

Bala said, "I came only with a small bag, but that was stolen on the way. Robbers set upon us and took away everything."

"My first glimpse of Bhatji was when he came into our shop one morning, long ago," said Surma. "My father was concentrating, with his eyeglass stuck on one eye, on selecting diamonds for a party. I was minding something else, bent over a desk. He was standing at the entrance, how long I could not say. When I looked up he was there. There were people passing in and out of the shop, he was unnoticed. When the shop was clear of the crowd, he was still there at the doorway. I asked, 'What do you want? Who are you?' There was something about his person that touched my heart. He was lanky and looked famished. My first impulse was to rush to his help in some way, but I held myself back—I was a young woman of eighteen years, he might be of my age . . . or a little more. Somehow I felt attracted to this lean boy with hair falling on his nape untended, covering his forehead and unshaven face. It must have been months and years since a barber came near him. 'Father!' I called suddenly. 'Here is a boy waiting since the morning.' It was a propitious moment since Father, instead of losing his temper, as was his habit whenever anyone stepped into the shop without any business (he was suspicious of youngsters particularly), somehow took off the eyeglass, and asked mildly, 'What do you want?' He answered promptly, 'I want to work . . .' in Marathi and then gave an account of himself. How he had started from a southern village, traveled up and about, visiting other parts of the country, working his way . . . 'How did you learn our language?' 'I was in Bombay and learned it.'

"Father took to him kindly. He asked him to step in and questioned him in detail. Father enjoyed the narration of the boy's adventures in other cities and his descriptions fascinated him. That a village boy from far off south should have had the courage to go out as far as Delhi (which was beyond Father's dreams) and survived seemed to my father a great achievement. He engaged him immediately as a handyman, gave him a room above our shop and arranged for his food and other comforts. Very soon he became my father's right-hand man, doing a variety of jobs in and out of the office and shop. He relieved Father of a lot of strain and understood not only the nature of the trade but a lot about gems, their qualities and value. Father was impressed with the boy's intelligence and the ease with which he could be trained. Within six months he left a lot of responsibilities to him, trusting him absolutely. At the earliest opportunity my father set a barber on him and made him presentable with his head shaved in the front, leaving an elegant little tuft on his top. Later, after we married, I induced him to grow whiskers so that he might have a weighty appearance.

"My father did not approve of our proposal to marry at first. He threatened to throw him out not only from our shop but from this country itself and ordered me not to talk to him and confined me at home. I had a miserable time. We eloped to Nasik and married in the temple of Triambaka—a sort of marriage, quiet and private. Eventually, Father reconciled himself to the situation. When he died the gem business and the house fell to my share."

Surma constantly expressed her admiration and love for Viswanath: "When I saw him first, he was so young and timid; now he manages our business and is often called to the court and high places for consultations and supply of gems."

The story-writer asked at this point, "Were they the only ones in that house?"

"Yes, must be so," said my grandmother.

"What happened to the rest of the family—there must surely have been other members of the family!"

"Why do you ask me? How do I know?" said my grandmother. "I can only tell the story as I heard it. I was not there as you know. This is about my father and mother, who were still apart though living under the same roof. . . ."

I asked the next question, which bothered me as a story-writer: "Did Surma Bai have no children?"

"I don't care if she had or had not or where they were, how is it our concern?"

"But you say they were living together for fifteen years!"

"What a question! How can I answer it? You must ask them. Anyway it is none of our business. My mother mentioned Surma, and only Surma and not a word about anyone else. If you want me to go on with the story you must not interrupt me. I forget where I was, I am only telling you what I know!" She stopped her narration at this point and left in a huff and went off to supervise her daughters-in-law in the kitchen.

Bala's opportune moment came when Surma said one evening, "I am joining some friends who perform *bhajans* [group singing] at the Krishna temple on Fridays. I will come back after it is over. You won't mind being alone?"

"Not at all," said Bala. "I'll look after the house and take care of everything . . ."

"He is in his room, he may come down if he wants anything."

"I'll take care of him, do not worry about him," said Bala reassuringly and saw her off in her tonga at the gate. The moment the tonga was out of sight she ran back into the house, shutting the front door, ran upstairs and entered Viswa's room. He was reclining on a comfortable couch reading a book. She shut the door behind her softly. He did not look up. He pretended to be absorbed in the book. She stood silently before him for a few moments, and then said, "What is the book that grips you so completely that you do not notice anyone entering your room?"

"What are you blabbering? Get out! You have no business to come up here!"

"Oh, stop that tone. Don't pretend. It's not good for you."

"Are you threatening me? I'll call the guard and throw you out."

"By all means. I know the guards. I am not what I was on the first day. I can speak to them myself. In fact I am closer to them than you. Call them and see what happens."

"Oh!" Viswa groaned. "Go away, don't bother me."

She said, "We must end this drama and how we are going to do it, I can't say now. But leave it at that . . ."

He pretended not to understand her language. But she said, "Your whiskers do not hide your face. If you lift the left one slightly, as you did the other day while washing your face, the black is still there, which proved correct my guess and also what you said years ago, when you peeped over the wall, that it was lucky and would make you a king. You are lucky, rich and favored at the court . . . I have waited long enough." She fingered her *thali* and said, "This can't lie. You knotted it in the presence of God."

He protested again, "No, no, I don't know what you are saying," but she was hammering her point relentlessly. Ultimately he was overwhelmed. "Be patient for some more time. Be as you are, Surma is a rare creature. We must not upset her."

"I will wait, but not forever . . ."

By the time Surma came back from the *bhajan* she found nothing unusual. Bala was at her post in the kitchen. Viswa was in the garden trimming a jasmine plant. Once again Viswa and Bala had resumed their aloofness. Bala was in no hurry. Now that she had established her stand, she just left him alone until the next *bhajan* day when Surma was away.

She said: "This can't go on much longer. We must go back."

"Go back where?" he asked in consternation.

"To our village, of course," she said calmly.

"Impossible!" he cried. "After all these years! I can't. I can't give up my trade!"

"You may take your share and continue the business any-where," she said calmly. She knew his weak point now, she could exploit it fully. Any excitement or anger would spoil her plan. She was very clear in her mind about how she should carry out her scheme. She had worked out the details of the campaign with care, timing it in minute detail. He knew it was going to be useless to oppose her.

He pleaded, "I'll tell her the truth and you may continue here as my wife, and not as a domestic."

"I want to get back to our own place and live there. I have set a time limit; beyond that I won't stay, I'll go back."

"Certainly, I will make any arrangement you want and send an escort to take you back home safely."

"You will be the escort, I'll not go with anyone else."

"Then stay here," he said.

At this stage, they had to stop the discussion, since they heard Surma return home. He was nervous to be alone with Bala and was terrified of her tactics.

"I can't live without Surma," he kept wailing.

"You will have to learn to live with your wife."

"Surma is also my wife."

"I know she is not. I know in this country it is not so easy. You have kept her, or rather she has kept you . . ."

He realized in due course that there was no escape. He said, "Give me time. I'll see how we can manage it."

"I've given you all the time . . . years and years. The trouble and the risk I have undergone to search you out, God alone is the witness! I am not going to allow it to go to waste. I am taking you back even if you kill me. I have set the date of our departure—not later than the next full moon."

At their next meeting he said, "I can't survive without Surma, she must also come with us. I don't know how to tell her."

"Try to persuade her to stay back. We will have to tell her the facts. After all you are going back to our legitimate home, to your real wife."

"No, I can't. You don't know her nature. She will commit suicide . . ."

"I will commit suicide if you are not coming away. Which of us shall it be?"

He felt desperate and said, "I can't live without her. Let her also come with us. We shall go away. Show some consideration to my feelings also."

"Very well, if she won't agree to go with us?"

"Please don't drive me mad. Who asked you to come all the way and torment me like this?" At this point she lost her patience and left him.

Surma asked him later, "You look rather tired and pale, shall I call the physician?" She lost no time in calling a physician, who said, "He is disturbed in mind. He must take medicine and rest. Something is troubling his mind."

Surma became agitated. "I have never seen him so sick at any time. What could it be! He was all right." She put him to bed and stayed by his side, leaving all household work to Bala; Viswa tossed and groaned in bed. Bala carried food to his bedside upstairs. She made it unnecessary for Surma to come down except for her bath and food and puja and then went up and sat by his side silently. The physician had given him some potion which acted as a sedative and put him to sleep.

Bala assumed an air of extreme gloom to match Surma's mood in sympathy. A week later she said, "Bhatji looks better. You should not fall sick moping at home. We will leave a guard at his side and go out for a little fresh air. Let us visit the temple and offer puja to Vitobha and stroll along the lake. You will feel refreshed."

"No, I can't leave him alone."

Four days later Bala repeated her suggestion, and added, "Ask him, he may like you to go out for your own good. I am sure he will have as much concern for your welfare."

Surma eventually agreed. Bala said, "You must think of the shop too. You must not leave it to Guru's care completely."

"Guru is a good man," Surma said. "He brings the accounts and reports every day, very dependable."

"Even then," Bala persisted. "You must go there or Bhatji can go as soon as possible. It'll also refresh him . . ."

"True, he is worrying about the shop silently. I do not know what to do . . . I have never been in this predicament before . . ."

When Guru came the next evening, they went out in the tonga, leaving him in charge of Viswa. They visited the temple first and then on to the lake. Strolling round the lake, which reflected the setting sun, Bala cried, "Oh, see how beautiful! See those birds diving in."

"I wish I could enjoy the scene and the breeze but my mind is troubled. How I wish Bhatji were well. If he was his normal self, riding his horse, sitting in the shop with his diamonds and customers, I could sit here and watch the lake with a free mind."

"He will benefit if he could travel and go for a change. We could leave for three or four months on a tour, the shop to be looked after by Guru and his son. That will make a new man of Bhatji."

"Where can we go?"

"We may go south, so many temples we could visit—especially I have in mind Gunasekaram where prayer to that god is specific for the kind of depression afflicting Bhatji. There are special pujas and offerings to be made to the god called Vaith-eeswaran, the cure is miraculous after a visit . . ."

"We can't, so far away and so long it'll take!"

Bala did not continue, but left the subject at that. But she repeated the suggestion whenever she found the chance. Surma thought it over and discussed the matter with Viswa and worked out the details and made preparations earnestly and settled for the journey after consulting their astrologer and physician.

"I remember," said Ammani, "my mother mention that they were carried in two palanquins and had a retinue of bearers who took over in relays at different stages, and many torch bearers and lancemen to protect them from robbers and wild animals when they crossed jungles in the mountain ghats. Arrangements for the journey were made by Surma, and Viswa, having influence at the court, also got the peshwa's support. I am sure the peshwa sent word to his vassals and subordinates along the route to protect and help the party. On the day fixed, Bala and party began their journey and arrived about a month later in Bangalore and camped in the rest house on a tank bund. I think from the description I had it is the same tank known as the Sampangi today."*

They camped for three days. All three were very happy: Bala, because she was on the way home, Viswa because they had suc-

---

* Actually, at present, it is the Nehru Stadium, the tank having been drained.

ceeded in persuading Surma to undertake the tour, and Surma because Viswa already looked better and eagerly anticipated the visit to the temples—he did not wish to think of the future beyond.

On the fourth day they wound up the camp, packed up and were ready to start onward. Bala however had made up her mind differently. From the rest house one set of steps led up to the highway where the palanquins were waiting. All other members of the party, the bearers and guards, Surma and Viswa, went up the steps. Bala however lagged behind, suddenly turned right about and went down the steps leading to the water's edge. At first they did not notice her. When they reached the road Surma asked, while climbing into their palanquin, "Where is Bala?"

Viswa said, "She seems to be taking her own time. Let us start. We should reach the next stage before nightfall. She will follow." The bearers lifted the palanquin containing Surma and Viswa. Viswa hesitated and said, "Stop! I see that she is going down the steps. Why? Probably a last minute wash? She is stepping down into the water."

Surma said, "It looks strange to me. . . . Oh, God, she has stepped into the water . . . Oh, stop!" she said in alarm when she heard Bala's scream:

"I'm drowning . . . Viswa come for a moment!"

Viswa jumped off the palanquin and reached the water's edge. By that time Bala stood neck-deep in water. Viswa shrieked in alarm, "What are you doing?"

She replied, with water lapping her chin, "I am not coming with you."

"Are you mad? Why this scene?" He made a move to go down and pull her up.

She said, "If you take another step, I'll go down. Stay where you are and listen. No, don't come near, you can hear me where you are."

"All right, I won't come forward. Don't stand in the water. Come up and speak."

"I won't come up until you turn Surma back to Poona."

Surma had meanwhile come down and was standing behind Viswa. "What! What have I done to you that you should say this?"

"You have been like a goddess to me, but I can't go home with you. Our village will not accept you. I am Viswa's wife. You see this *thali* was knotted by him. He is my husband, I can't share him with you."

Surma was shocked. "We were such good friends! Let me also drown with you."

At this Viswa held her back firmly. Bala said, "Viswa, take her with you and leave me alone. I am already shivering and will die of cold if you don't make up your mind quickly whether you want me or Surma. Send her back honorably home. Let the palanquins be turned around with her if you want to save me."

They pleaded, appealed and shed tears but the palanquins and the entourage had to turn around and head for Poona before Bala would come out. She did not want any of Surma's entourage to stay back.

"Ammani," I (this writer) said, "I can't find any excuse for the way your mother maneuvered to get rid of the other woman. Your mother was too deep and devious for the poor lady, who had shown so much trust in Bala whom she had sheltered and nourished when she was in desperate straits, not to mention the years she cared for and protected Viswa, who had after all strayed his way to Poona and was literally a tramp at the start . . ."

"Don't talk ill of your ancestors. Not right. He was not a tramp but a respected merchant and official at the peshwa's court," Ammani retorted.

"He had only been a lowly clerk in her father's shop, remember . . ."

"What of it? Whatever it is, he rose high because of his mettle."

"And mainly through Surma's support—he should have remembered it at the time he yielded to your mother's coercive tactics."

"What else could a poor woman like her do to recover her husband? Only a woman can understand it. To a woman, her husband is everything. She can't lose him. Remember in what condition Bala had left home and what trials she must have gone through to reach Poona and how much misery she faced before she could reach him? Everything is justified, all means are justified in her case. Did not Savitri conquer Yama himself and trap him into promising her a boon? And the boon she asked for was to have children and he gave her his blessing that she would have children. After accepting the boon, she asked how it would be possible when he, as the god of Death, was carrying away her husband's life, leaving his inert body in the forest, and then Yama had to yield back Satyavan's life. You could not imagine a greater woman than Savitri for austerity and purity of mind. . . ."

"Still, I am unable to accept your mother's tactics—she could have adopted some other method . . ."

"Such as?" she said, suppressing her irritation.

"She could have revealed that she was his wife on the first day itself."

"Surma would have bundled her off or got rid of her in some manner."

"Would not Viswa have protected her?"

"No, he was completely under her spell at that time."

"Was it necessary to drag the poor woman with false promises up to Bangalore? Could they not have managed it some other way?"

"Such as?" she asked again.

"I don't know. I'd have thought of more honorable ways . . ."

"You cannot manipulate people in real life as you do in a story," she said.

As my remarks incensed her, she refused to continue her story and abruptly got up with the excuse, "I have better things to do at this time than to talk to an argumentative fellow."

For nearly a week she ignored me while I followed her about with my notebook. She ignored me until I pleaded, "You must please complete the story. I want to hear it fully. You know why?"

"Why?"

"Otherwise I will be born a donkey in my next *janma*."

"How do you know?"

"The other day I attended a Ramayana discourse. A man got up in the middle of the narrative and tried to go out of the assembly but the pundit interrupted himself to announce, 'It's said in the Shastras that anyone who walks out in the middle of a discourse will be a donkey in his next birth,' and the man who was preparing to leave plumped back in his seat when he heard it. And so please . . ."

"Tomorrow evening, I'm going to be busy today."

Next evening after she had pottered around her garden and had her evening cold bath and said her prayers, she summoned me to the hall, took her seat on the swing, and continued her story.

At Bangalore the parting of ways was harrowing. Surma, always so assured, positive, and a leader, broke down and humbled herself to the extent of saying, "Let me only go with you. I have surrendered Viswa to you, only let me be near you. I have loved you as a friend. I'll come with you and promise to return to Poona after visiting the temples. Please show me this consideration. I accept with all my heart that he is your husband, I'll never ever talk to him again or look at him even. But let me be with you . . . Viswa, talk to her please . . ."

Viswa turned to Bala and said, "Let her come with us. She will visit the temples and go back. I promise."

Bala stood thinking for a while and wept a little, then controlled herself and said firmly to Surma, "No, it won't be possible, in our place we will be hounded out. I'll advise Viswa to go with you, anywhere, back to Poona or forward. Only leave me alone. You have got to choose."

It was pathetic and humiliating with their retinue and palanquin-bearers watching the scene. Bala put her arms around Surma, rested her head on her shoulder and then, sobbing, bowed down and prostrated at her feet, got up and moved away from her towards the tank again, whereupon Surma cried desperately, "Don't! Don't! I am leaving. May God bless you both." She hurried up her retinue and got into her palanquin and left while Bala stood on the last step of the tank and watched: and Viswa stood dumbstruck, not knowing what to do. That was the last they saw of Surma. She was not heard of again: whether she went back home to Poona or ended her misery by walking into the next available tank on the way, no one knew.

Viswa would have frantically raced behind the palanquins, but for the check of Bala's silent stare. They stayed in the same rest house for three more days waiting for travelers going south. Meanwhile, Bala summoned a barber and persuaded Viswa to shave off his whiskers, saying, "In our part of the country you will be taken for a ghoul and children will run away screaming at the sight of you." She stood away from him after the shave and observed, "Now I can recognize you better. The patch under the ear is intact. I am doubly assured now—the same features I knew, I used to see over the backyard wall, only filled up with age. Whatever made you hide such a fine face behind a wilderness of hair?"

"At the peshwa's court it was customary and considered necessary . . ."

At this point Ammani interrupted herself to warn me, "Don't ask me how long they took to reach their village. All I can say is ultimately they did reach their village, the river was there and the temple stood as solid as ever, but the old priest whose remarks had driven Bala out of her home and to whom she vowed to prove that her husband was alive was not there. The temple had a new priest, who did not remember the old families. All the same the very first thing Bala did was to enter the temple and stand before the god with her husband, praying for continued grace. She ordered an elaborate ritual of prayers and offerings and distributed food and fruits and cash to a large gathering of men, women and children. Viswa had left the place thirty years, and Bala about twenty years, before. Most of the landmarks were gone, also the people.

Bala went back to her old house in Fourth Street and found some strangers living in it, who said, "We bought this house from an old woman, who went to live her last days in Kasi after her husband's death. Their only daughter had run away from home and was not heard of again. . . ."

Viswa searched for his old house but could not locate it. That neighborhood had been demolished and Viswa could not find anyone to answer his questions, except a man grazing his cow, who just said, "Ask someone else. I know nothing." Viswa tried here and there, but could get no news of his parents or relatives. The village seemed to have been deserted by all the old families. Bala's main purpose to visit the temple and offer puja to Ranganatha accomplished, she saw no reason for staying in the village. They decided to move to a nearby town where Viswa could establish himself as a gem merchant and start a new life.

At this point I could not get my grandmother to specify which town it was. If I pried further, she only said, "I was not born then, remember."

"What was that town? Could it be Trichy?"

"Maybe," she said.

"Or Kumbakonam?"

"Maybe," she said again.

"Or Tanjore?"

"Why not?" she said mischievously.

"Or Nagapattinam?"

"I was not born. How could I know? I tell you again and again—but you question me as if I could see the past."

"From your village, the nearby town must have been within fifty or a hundred miles."

"You are again becoming argumentative."

"Have you not heard your mother mention any special landmark like a river or a temple?"

"She only mentioned that the river Kaveri was flowing and that it was a place with several temples: she mentioned that every evening she could visit a temple, a different one each day of the week."

"Let us take it as Kumbakonam. Where did your marriage take place?"

"On a hill temple, not far from where we lived."

"It must be Swami Malai in Kumbakonam. Were you so ignorant as not to notice where you were being married?"

"I was eleven and followed my parents."

"Extraordinary!" I said, which offended her and she threatened to stop her narration. But I pleaded with her to continue. I realized that she knew it was Kumbakonam but was only teasing me.

Viswanath established himself as a gem expert in Kumbakonam. He acquired a house not far from the river. He sat in a small room in the front portion of his house and kept his wares in a small bureau, four feet high, half glazed. (The heirloom is still with the family; when I was young I was given that little bureau for keeping my schoolbooks and odds and ends. I had inscribed in chalk on the narrow top panel of this bureau "R.K. Narayanaswami B.A.B.L. Engine Driver." My full name with all the honors I aspired to. I wonder if one can detect any trace of that announcement now. I have not seen the heirloom for many years.) Viswa's reputation spread as an expert appraiser of gems.

People brought him diamonds for evaluation and to check for flaws. Through an eyeglass he examined the stone and gave his verdict before they were handed over to the goldsmith for setting.

Bala turned out to be a model wife in the orthodox sense, all trace of her adventurous spirit or independence completely suppressed. One could hardly connect her with the young woman who had tramped all alone across hundreds of miles in search of her husband and succeeded in bringing him back home—dominating, devious and aggressive till she had attained her object. Now she was docile and never spoke to her husband in the presence of other people. Her tone was gentle and subdued. It was a transformation. She wore an eighteen-cubit length of silk sari in the orthodox style, instead of the twelve-cubit cotton wrap favored in Poona. She wore diamond earrings and decked herself in a heavy gold necklace and bangles, applied turmeric on her cheeks, and a large vermilion mark on her forehead. She rose at five in the morning, walked to the river, bathed and washed her saris, took them home for drying, filled a pitcher and carried it home, also drew several pails of water from the well in their backyard to fill a cauldron for domestic purposes. She circumambulated the sacred tulsi plant in the backyard and then sat down in the puja room with lamps lit and chanted mantras.

By the time Viswa woke up at six she had lit the kitchen fire and prepared his morning porridge or any other thing he needed for breakfast. She cooked for him twice a day; he went out on his work and they had their vegetables from a woman who brought them to their door in a basket for selection. In the evening she went to the temples with offerings and oil for the lamps in the shrines.

Their firstborn came two years later—a daughter, and then another daughter, and another daughter—"that is myself," said my grandmother. The fourth was a son.

The next twenty years, roughly, were years of prosperity. Viswa's business flourished. In proper time, he found bridegrooms
for his daughters and sent his son, Swaminathan, to study in
Madras at the medical college; he was in the first batch of Indians
to qualify for the medical profession.

Viswa was past sixty when he found himself isolated. His
daughters were married and gone. "I was the youngest and last
to leave home," said Ammani. "My husband, your grandfather,
was a submagistrate and posted to work in different villages of
our district, here, there and everywhere, until we came to rest
in Madras after his retirement. We bought this house in which
we find ourselves now, he also acquired a number of other houses
in this street, and bungalows in the western area on Kelly's Road,
agricultural lands somewhere, and a garden, and all his time
was taken up in managing his estates." (The garden, known as
"Walker Thottam," supplied vegetables to the wholesale market
at Kotawal Chavadi in George Town in "cart loads" according
to Ammani.)

"You said he was started on less than fifty rupees. How did
you manage to buy so many houses and lands?" I asked.

"We did not actually have to depend upon his pay . . ."

"Oh, I understand. I will not question you further."

"Even if you asked, I wouldn't be able to explain how a magistrate earned—money just poured in, I think. We had a
brougham and horse, a coachman and so much of everything.
My own family consisted of three daughters and two sons. The
eldest daughter was married and died in Madurai and my family
was reduced to four. Your mother was my second daughter. . . .

"I always felt that the kind of wealth your grandfather
amassed was illusory, because within six months of your grandfather's death, by a court decree all his property was lost through
a foolish business venture of his in steel. His trusted partner
declared insolvency and fled to Pondicherry and your grandfather's properties were attached and auctioned to make good a bank
loan; something to do with the notorious Arbuthnot Bank crash.
Even this house was nearly gone but for the help of a neighbor,

who loaned us five thousand rupees to redeem it at the last moment. Our creditors had already stuck notices of auction on our door, and by the beat of tom-toms and loud announcements were inviting bidders. Crowds gathered at our door. You were due to be delivered in a couple of weeks, but the bustle, crowd, and tom-tom beats, while we were cowering inside the house, were nerve-racking and affected your mother, who had come for her confinement and was in a delicate state of pregnancy; she became panic-stricken and got labor pains in that excitement. Your birth was rather premature. Only this house was saved of all your grandfather's property—thanks, as I mentioned, to the last-minute help of our neighbor Mr. Pillai, who lived in Number Two, Vellala Street."

(One morning, two years ago, I had a desire to revisit Number One, Vellala Street, in Purasawalkam, where all of us were born in one particular room. We habitually considered the house as the focal point of the entire family scattered in other districts, visiting it from time to time. My friend Ram [of *The Hindu*] was also curious to see the house and the environs as I described it in *My Days*. We drove down to Vellala Street in Purasawalkam, but found no trace of the old house. It was totally demolished, cleared and converted into a vacant plot on which the idea was to build an air-conditioned multistoried hotel. Among the debris we found the old massive main door lying, with ONE still etched on it. Ram made an offer for it on the spot and immediately transported it to his house, where he has mounted it as a showpiece.)

To go back to the main theme. Changes were coming in Viswa's life. His son, Dr. Swaminathan, was selected for the District Medical Officer's post at Kolar in Mysore State.

When Dr. Swaminathan left for Kolar, Viswa and Bala lived as a couple as at the beginning of their life. They missed their children and found life dull. Viswa, now nearing seventy, worked less, finding it tedious to continue his gem business. He felt irritated when customers came for advice and discouraged them. Gradually he stopped all business although his little bureau had a stock of precious stones.

Bala had become rather tired and engaged a cook, a woman, who brought along with her a twelve-year-old daughter. Bala found their company diverting. The woman, who had been destitute, now felt she had found a home and worked hard, relieving Bala of a lot of drudgery. Gradually, Bala preferred to lounge in bed, hardly stirring out, leaving the management of the house to the woman and her daughter. Viswa stationed himself all day in an easy chair on the verandah overlooking the street. Bala often implored him to go out and meet his cronies in the neighborhood who used to gather in the temple corridor, sit around and chat after a darshana of the god. But now he never went out, secretly worried about Bala's declining health. He sent for the *vaid,* who came every other day, studied her pulse and prescribed a medicine, a concoction of rare herbs, he claimed. Viswa wrote a letter to his son expressing anxiety, but official work kept Swaminathan busy. He could come only four weeks later. When he found his mother's condition serious, he struggled hard to retrieve her but with all the medicines and needles in his bag, he could not save her.

"When the obsequies were over, my brother and sisters returned to their respective places. My husband was a magistrate in Tindivanam. I had two daughters at that time and we also left."

Viswanath was persuaded to go to Kolar with his son. The house was practically locked up, with one or two rooms left open for the woman, with her daughter, to live there as a caretaker on a monthly salary.

Viswanath's life entered yet another phase: he had to live in Kolar with his son, whose family consisted of his wife and a daughter and a son, both under ten. At first Viswa had protested and resisted, but the doctor persuaded him to wind up his establishment in Kumbakonam.

At Kolar Dr. Swaminathan lived in a bungalow set in a spacious compound. Viswanath enjoyed an early morning walk in the compound and then inspected the kitchen garden in the backyard, and from the verandah watched the birds and trees, watched his two grandchildren going off to a nearby mission school, and his son leaving for the hospital in the morning. He turned in at noon for his bath, and then said his prayers in the puja room. His daughter-in-law, although reserved and formal, looked after his comforts and needs hour to hour. He had a room and he enjoyed his siesta after lunch. In spite of all the comfort and security he missed Bala and felt a vacuity at times. "No one can take her place," he often told himself. Sometimes he thought of Surma too but the intensity of feeling was gone, it was just a faded memory revived with effort, without any pangs of rec-ollection. His son, the doctor, was a busy man having to attend the government hospital, as well as administer medical services in the whole district and he had to be away on "circuits" fre-quently.

Viswa felt proud of his son, especially at the beginning when he brought his salary home and handed over the cash, about four hundred rupees, in a net bag. Viswa carried it in after counting the amount, and called his daughter-in-law, "Lakshmi, come and take charge of this cash. Count it properly and spend it wisely. You must also build up savings. I want nothing of this. I have no use for this cash. I have my own. This is all yours, keep it safely." This was a routine statement every month. He awaited the salary day month after month and the routine continued.

He was happy as long as it continued, but when the practice was gradually given up for practical reasons, and Swami began to hand his monthly salary directly to his wife, Viswa became resentful secretly, but tried to overcome it, hoping next time or the next time, Swami would resume the courtesy of recognizing his presence when he brought home the salary. This was probably a temporary aberration or an absent-minded lapse. He bore it for three months. At the end of it, he said to himself: "I'll intercept him tomorrow evening when he comes with the salary, I will not leave the verandah until he arrives; test whether he'll hand me the bag or still give it to his wife." Brooding over it he had magnified the situation and imparted an undue significance to it.

Next payday Swaminathan did not come in the evening but at noon suddenly, and was in a great hurry. Swaminathan did not enter the house but called from outside, "Lakshmi." When she emerged from the kitchen, he held out the salary bag from the verandah. "I can't come in now. . . . People are waiting. We are off to a nearby village where rat-falls are reported." He rushed back to the medical team waiting at the gate in a horse carriage. They were to go out and investigate a possible outbreak of bubonic plague and inoculate the population.

Viswa, who had been gathering coriander leaves in the kitchen garden, came in with a sprig for seasoning the lunch items. Lakshmi presented to him the money bag.

"What is this?"

"Salary. He brought it now."

Viswa glared at her, and asked, "Why at this hour? Why did he not call me?"

"He was in a hurry, people waiting at the gate . . ."

"Oh!" he said. "He is a big man, is he?" and ignored the bag, dropped the coriander on the floor, marched off to his room and bolted the door, came out at lunchtime, ate in grim silence, retired to his room again, sat on his bed and brooded: "He is becoming really indifferent. This morning he left without a word to me. All of them are behaving callously. Children go out and come in as they please. They don't notice me at all. Lakshmi thinks her duty done after feeding me as she would feed a dog, without a word. The last three days Swami never spoke to me more than three sentences. They think I am an orphan depending on their favors. This is the curse of old age. I will teach them a lesson. . . ."

He briskly made up a bundle of clothes, stuffed them in a small jute bag, wore his long gray shirt, seized his staff and started out. "Lakshmi," he called. She came out and was taken aback at the sight of him. He just said, "I am off . . . ," as he had said to Bala over the wall before absconding years ago. That tendency seemed to be ingrained in his blood.

"Where?" she asked timidly.

"Never mind where—did your husband tell me where he was going? That is all." He briskly got down the steps and was out, leaving the lady staring after him speechlessly. The children had gone out to school. He found his way to the railway station, waited for a train, got into it, changed trains and ultimately reached Kumbakonam and was back in his home in Salai Street, surprising the caretaker and her daughter.

My grandmother's actual words: "That was a disastrous step he took. What mad rage drove him to that extent no one could say. The caretaker and her daughter were not the kind he should have associated with. They were evil-minded, coming from a nearby village notorious for its evil practices such as fostering family intrigue, creating mischief and practicing black magic. When my father knocked, they were rather surprised but welcomed him with a great show of joy. They fussed over him. They consulted him on what he liked to eat, and cooked and fried things, and bought choice vegetables and fruits to feed him. Washed his feet whenever he came in after a short visit outside. They treated him like a prince, till he must have begun to think, 'My son and wife treated me like a tramp and hanger-on, not a day did anyone ask what I liked. They always restricted my eating with the excuse "You should not eat this or that at your age." My son thought that as a doctor, he was Brihaspathi himself! They denied me all delicacies, whereas this woman and her daughter know what I want. . . .' "

The house was filled all the time with the smell of frying—chips, *bondas, pakodas* and sweets. Viswa was a very contented man now. He had a sturdy constitution which withstood all the gluttony he was indulging in.

One fine day Ammani's family heard that he had married the caretaker's daughter in a quiet, simple ceremony conducted by

the woman, who managed to get a priest from her village. It
was a culmination of his rage against his son. He could think of
no better way to assert his independence. He was seventy-five
and the girl was seventeen. He married her convinced that it
would be the best way to shock and spite his family, all of whom
seemed hostile to him.

Now the woman had him under her control. In course of time,
she took further steps to consolidate her position. She began to
suggest that they were no longer mere caretakers of the house,
but his family, and that the young wife and her mother should
be made the owners of the house through a deed of transfer. She
found a pleader who prepared a document and presented it to
Viswa for his signature. At this point, he still had some sense
left. He hesitated and delayed while his mother-in-law kept up
her pressure, through persuasion, bullying, and even starving
him. He dodged the issue with some excuse or other, and began
to wonder if he should not have continued in Kolar. He was
losing his cheer; his second wife nagged him to sign the document. They had their eyes on his stock of precious stones, which
he always kept with him although he did no business now; he
also had enough cash left but took care to keep it with a banking
friend, drawing just the amount he needed at a time. This irked
his mother-in-law, who had aimed high, and now goaded her
daughter to sulk and nag him at night. He dodged her by taking
his bedroll to the pyol on the excuse that he found the room too
stuffy, thus evading his wife's pillow talk. He avoided her all
through the day too, while the mother-in-law murmured asides
and remarks. He was beginning to brood and plan a return to
Kolar. The thought of his son was exhilarating and Kolar seemed
a paradise and haven of peace.

The woman was shrewd and began to guess from his mood
that he might slip away. She told her daughter, "I have to go
to our village on some important work and will be back tomorrow, keep a watch on your husband. Keep him in and shut the
front door. . . ."

At their village the woman consulted the local wiseacre, explaining the difficulties her son-in-law was creating. The wiseacre's income was through his claims to magic, black or white, the exorcizing of spirits, and making potions, and amulets. He said, "You must tell me frankly what you want. Don't hide anything."

She explained that while she wanted her son-in-law to be friendly and amenable, he was becoming tough and hostile. She said tearfully, "Out of compassion for the fellow in dotage, I agreed to give him my daughter so tender and young. But he is becoming indifferent and illtreats her. You must help me."

The wiseacre pretended to note down points and said, "Come next week and bring two sovereigns . . . I'll have to acquire some ingredients and herbs, which will cost you something. I won't charge you for my service, that's my guru's command."

The woman went home thinking, "Only a week more . . ."

When she came back to the village a week later the wiseacre gave her a packet. "There are two pills in it. Give them both to him with his food. They are tasteless and will dissolve and when the pills get into his system, he'll follow his wife like a lamb and treat you as his guru."

The woman went back home gloating over the possibilities ahead, with the packet tucked in her sari at the waist. On the following Friday she prepared a special feast, explaining that this Friday was particularly sacred for some reason. She was secretive about the pills and did not mention it even to her daughter, but planned to get him to sign the document next day after the pill was completely assimilated in his system, with the document ready at hand. Viswa, a confirmed glutton these days, was pleased and seemed relaxed, bantered with his wife and mother-in-law in anticipation of the feast, saying, "This indeed is a pleasant surprise for me. What a lot of trouble you take!" The fragrance of delicacies emanating from the kitchen was overpowering. When the time came for lunch, the woman spread two long banana leaves side by side, saying that the couple must dine

together today, and heaped the leaves with item after item—the
high point of the feast being almond and milk *payasam* in a silver
bowl for him and in a brass cup for his wife. Before serving it,
the woman managed to dissolve the two pills in the silver bowl.

My grandmother concluded, "That was the end. My husband
was a submagistrate at Nagapattinam when we got information
that Viswa's end had come suddenly. I have nothing more to
add. Don't ask questions."

(My [this writer's] mother, Ammani's second daughter, who was
ninety-three at the time of her death, used to maintain that she
had a hazy recollection of being carried on the arms of her mother
at Kumbakonam and witnessing a lot of hustle and bustle following a funeral, people passing in and out of the house and
some boxes being locked and sealed by the police and a motley
crowd milling around.)

I asked my grandmother, "What happened to that woman
and your very young step-mother?"

"I don't know, I have no idea."

"No inquest, no investigation, no questioning of that
woman?"

"I don't know. We could not stay away from Nagapattinam
too long since the collector, an Englishman, was coming for
inspection and the magistrate was required to be present. We
had to leave. My brother, Dr. Swaminathan, came down from
Kolar, and took charge of the situation and Father's assets. I
can't tell you anything more about it. All I know is what I could
gather from my brother later. He spoke to our neighbors, who
mentioned to him the woman's schemes; the pleader had a lot
to say about that woman's ambition and maneuvers to grab the
wealth and property. My brother could not stay on for long
either, but before going back to Kolar he made some arrangement for the disposal of that house . . . that's all we know."

Guru

All alone in a big house he became a prey to a jumble of thoughts as he sat at the window overlooking Vinayak Street. Reclining on his ancient canvas chair, he gazed ahead at nothing in particular, an old raintree on which were assembled crows of the locality, passing clouds, bullock carts, cyclists, and uninteresting passersby. His wife had left him months ago, his two daughters seemed to have abandoned him too. His first daughter, Raji, the best of the lot, was in Trichy and his second in Lawley Extension only a couple of miles away but as far as he was concerned she might be on Mars or the Moon, displaying an indifference which was inhuman.

"I am past sixty and am orphaned though I slaved all my life to bring up the family . . . I have no craving for their company. Only I want them to realize that I do not need anyone's help, strong enough still, thank God, to look after myself. That Pankaja Lodge man sends me food in a brass container for four rupees a meal, enough quantity for two and I save a portion for the night meal too . . . if I feel hungry in between, a bun from the shops across the street costs only ten paise. In all I do not have to spend more than one hundred and fifty rupees a month, whereas my wife used to demand one thousand for housekeeping! I am surviving much to their surprise, a tiny portion of the self-generating interest from my savings is more than enough to keep me alive. And then there is the rent from the shops in Grove Street. Assets built up laboriously, risking my reputation and job.

"My family never cared to understand. How I wish they were appreciative and grateful! God is my only ally. He will never forsake me, I need no one else. I get up at six in the morning, bathe and worship the images in the puja room, read the *Ramayana* all afternoon. (I am not the sort to sleep in the afternoon.) I feel elated when I hold that ancient volume in my hand, the only treasure that could be named my ancestral property, which my brother claimed and gave up since I firmly told him that I would not tear out its pages in order to provide him a share; and in compensation he grabbed a copper bowl, a deer skin on which my father used to sit and meditate, and also a bamboo staff.

"I tell God, first thing in the day and again at night before sleep overcomes me, 'Sir, You have been extremely considerate, whatever others might say, You have been gracious although my colleagues and the public including my family talk ill of me. You know they speak out of jealousy and malign me, but You are All-Knowing and no thought can be hidden from You. You are my friend in a friendless world.'

"I have accepted only gifts and cash given out of good will by those whom I have served. Never demanded them. What one gives out of good will must be accepted with grace, say our Shastras, otherwise one will be hurting a good soul who wants to have the pleasure of giving.

"Apart from the *Ramayana*, I inherited from my father only common sense and the courage to face life under all circumstances. Through God's divine grace I rose from the smallest job in the revenue department to the present position in the red building occupying the tahsildar's seat."

The tahsildar's office was the focal point where peasants seeking various relief measures offered by the government and the government agencies met. Mr. Gurumurthi was the "agency." Peasants had to come to him for a variety of favors and present their applications for fertilizers, pesticides, spare parts for tractors, and cash loans. All applications had to be rubber-stamped on his desk and initialed by him, and for each touch of his seal on any paper he had to be paid a certain sum of money, depending on the value of the request, discreetly isolated from the quantum meant for the Treasury.

The isolated amount was propelled into the left-side drawer of his desk, only then did the applicant's paper become animated. When he closed the office for the day, Gurumurthi scooped out the contents of the drawer with loving fingers, and transferred them to a specially tailored inner pocket of his shirt, next to his skin where it gently heaved with his heart-throb. He enjoyed the feel of the wad nestling close to his heart.

He often reflected with satisfaction, "No pickpocket will have a chance. If everyone follows my method, pickpocketism will be eliminated, and those rogues will have to turn to honest jobs . . . perhaps to agriculture, and come to me for favors, who knows?"

A questioning mind might ask at this point, "Who is the real pickpocket?"

He was always the last to leave, after making sure there was no embarrassing presence lurking in any corner of the office except the old attender at the door wearing a red sash around his shoulder, displaying a badge announcing, PEON, TAHSILDAR'S OFFICE. He was a discreet man who had watched a succession of tahsildars in his career.

Gurumurthi's wife, Saroja, used to be a quiet-going, peace-loving sort, even-tempered and minding her business. But with years, she began to play the role of a better half, and became questioning, righteous, and argumentative. He noticed her transformation after the birth of their first daughter, Raji, who proved to be the best of the lot, the only one in the family who was at peace with herself and with the world.

She married the boy from a family who did not demand a dowry and were satisfied with a simple, inexpensive wedding. His wife, Saroja, suspected that the boy suffered from some deformity, and that his parents were anxious to marry him off anyhow. It was all an exaggeration, of course (Gurumurthi avoided too close a scrutiny). They turned out to be the happiest couple known, begetting three children in four years—twins at first and a single one later. They kept themselves, which was the best part of it.

Occasionally, Raji came down with her children; somewhat trying times those were, since her children were noisy and restless. Gurumurthi was not fond of grandchildren. Fortunately, the maximum time Raji could spare was one week, her husband needing her constant attention. Gurumurthi always felt relieved when she proposed to leave. Not so his wife, thoughtless woman, who would press her to stay on, until he put his foot down and said, "Leave her alone; after all Raji knows her responsibilities." He organized her departure with zest. He engaged a jutka to take her to the railway station, making sure that the girl had sufficient funds to pay the fare. At the ticket counter he held out his hand to her for money. He was in acute suspense till he bundled her and the children into a compartment within the five minutes' halt of the six o'clock Fast Express towards Trichy, and heaved a sigh of relief when the engine whistled and pulled out. He never permitted his wife to accompany them to the station, explaining, "I want to walk back, but if you come we may have to hire a jutka."

"Not at all necessary. I can also walk."

"Don't be argumentative," he sternly told her, and left her

behind to watch Raji's departure from the doorstep. At the railway platform when the train moved he became emotional, ran along with it, shouting, "Raji, take good care of yourself and the children, and convey my blessings to your husband."

His second daughter, Kamala, was married two years later. The family priest who generally carried a sheaf of horoscopes of eligible brides and grooms in his circuit was a busybody who, when not performing pujas, proposed marriage alliances among his clientele. One afternoon he sat down beside Gurumurthi's easy chair and asked, "Have you heard of Dr. Cheema of Lawley Extension?"

"Of course, who does not know him?" said Gurumurthi.

"His clinic is crowded all the time like a temple festival."

"I know, I know," said Gurumurthi. "What about him?" It was a Sunday, and he relaxed all day in his easy chair. The priest sat cross-legged on the floor as became an orthodox brahmin, who would not touch the leather covering on a sofa (though it might be only Rexine, resembling leather, who could be sure? He had two religious functions ahead and would have to take a bath if he touched leather and he avoided risk of pollution by sitting cross-legged on the floor, which also pleased his patrons who were wealthy).

The priest continued, "His son is twenty-one years old, and is studying for an auditor's job . . . I don't know what degree he will get. Very bright boy, whenever I see him I think of our Kamala, just a perfect match. I always keep in hand our Kamala's horoscope, I compared it with that boy's, just out of curiosity. The horoscopes match perfectly—perfectly means, I do not know how to say it—like—like," he quoted a sanskrit verse from the *Vedas* which said, "No power on earth or heaven could keep apart a couple whose stars are destined to merge." He concluded by asking, "May I show them our Kamala's horoscope?"

The priest's instinct turned out to be sound, as there never was a happier couple in the world. Only the alliance proved acrimonious, and continued long after Kamala had left her parents' home and was happily settled in Lawley Extension with her husband. The doctor realized when the wedding ceremonies were over that Gurumurthi was unreliable. The doctor had agreed to a simple, unostentatious wedding, as suggested by Guru. "Let us perform the ceremony at the hill temple and hold a reception in Malgudi. I don't believe in wasting money just for a show and in feeding a crowd. We could save that money and endow it as a fund for the young couple, so that they may have a good start in life." The doctor appreciated the idea, since his son planned to go to America for higher studies and could utilize the fund thus saved. The priest was a go-between for the negotiations. Gurumurthi kept his wife and daughter out of ear-shot when discussing financial matters with the priest. He told them from time to time, "Leave it to men to talk about these matters. Women should not interfere but mind their business."

After the wedding the doctor kept reminding him of his promise to give fifty thousand rupees saved from the wedding expenses. Gurumurthi prided himself secretly on managing to marry off both his daughters, without eroding his bank balance. Gurumurthi had simplified Kamala's marriage to such an extent that even Raji was not invited properly, and he spurned the idea whenever his wife reminded him to send them a formal announcement.

"All right, all right," he said, brushing her off. "Leave it to me. I know when to write." And he reflected, "Why should Raji be bothered to come with her crippled husband and the restless children, traveling all the way. Our outlook must change—a revolutionary change is needed in our society. Inviting a motley crowd for every wedding is senseless, I wonder whoever started this irrational practice?"

The doctor kept reminding him of the money due to his son, who was preparing to leave for America. Gurumurthi had perfected the art of dodging. He kept explaining that the delay was due to certain government bonds, which would mature soon. Gurumurthi had also promised the bridegroom two suits fit for

American wear, for which, he explained, he had ordered imported material from a firm in Madras, and as soon as it was received the young man could go straight to his tailor and get himself measured out. He added, "I know an excellent tailor who stitched suits for European planters settled in Mempi estates. His father also was a tailor to the British Governors." The proposal was gradually allowed to fade away.

Next, for the Deepavali festival, Guru had promised a solitaire diamond ring for his son-in-law. After waiting for three months, the doctor himself arrived one afternoon to remind him. Guru received him with a lot of fuss, summoned his wife and daughter to come out and do him obeisance. Kamala was counting the days before she could join her husband. Her father was putting it off on the plea that they were passing through an inauspicious part of the year. But his real motive was to avoid the expenses of an orthodox nuptial ceremony. Guru felt that our whole civilization was rotten and involved wasteful expenditure at every turn. There was no one to whom he could confide his thoughts. His wife was too narrow-minded and conventional and would not understand his philosophy of life. Best thing was to drift along without taking any decision, the inauspicious months giving him a sort of reprieve. The young couple met now and then and went out together; he was not so narrow-minded as to object to it—after all they were husband and wife. Once again it was his wife who displayed narrow prejudices—what would people say if a couple before the consummation ceremony met and roamed about? That was her upbringing, she was free to think as she liked, but he did not mind it, even hoped secretly that they would settle it between themselves and live happily ever after.

When the doctor on his present visit, after accepting all the snacks, broached the subject of the diamond ring, Guru hummed and hawed, "Eh, ring, ring, of course," he repeated reflectively. "That goldsmith is very, very slippery. What shall I do? Impossible man? Every day I go there and shout at him. But what's the use? He promised and swore by all the gods and his ancestors that he would give the ring before Deepavali. But you see . . ."

"Shall we both go and tackle him? He seems to be a crook. Why not tell the police? I know the superintendent," said the doctor.

"Yes, yes, of course, but only as a last resort. He has been our jeweler for generations. . . ."

The doctor got up and left. The lady of the house, who had been watching the scene from a corner, came out like a fury. "You are bringing shame on us. Is there no limit?"

"What limit?" Guru asked aggressively. "He is avaricious, thinks diamond rings grow on trees . . ."

At this point Kamala came out, her eyes swollen with tears. "Father, why did you promise it then?" she asked.

"Oh! Oh! You too! You should not be overhearing your elders talk."

"I am not a baby," she said. "You should keep your promise, it is awkward for me. I can't face them if you dodge like this."

"Oh, you have become their lawyer!" he said, laughing cynically. "I did not expect you to talk to me like this. You are more interested in those people—your father-in-law earns thousands every day. Why can't he buy a diamond ring for his son, if he cares so much for him?"

"My husband does not care for diamonds or anything."

"In that case why bother me? You will mind your business. Leave these matters to my judgement. Don't imitate your mother's manner. I'll see that you don't feel any embarrassment later. Be grateful I found you a husband—"

Her mother said, "It's no use talking to him," turned around and tried to take her daughter away.

But the girl stood firmly and persisted in saying, "He doesn't care for diamonds or any ring, it's *you* that offered and promised."

"Well, that's all an old story, such promises are a formality between in-laws during any Deepavali. One should not take such talk literally."

Kamala could find no words to express her indignation, but

burst into tears, and withdrew. Her mother came out again like a fury and shouted at Guru. He felt enraged and shouted back, "It's impossible to live in this house! Everyone heckles me." He briskly got up, put on his sandals, and walked out. He reached the corner of Vinayak Street, where he saw Rao the stamp vendor standing at his door. "These are bad days," said Guru. The other readily agreed with him and added, "What, with the prices going up, do you notice the price of brinjals? Impossible to buy vegetables, and such extravagant public expenditure by the government everywhere with no sort of consideration for the public."

"Even in private life so much extravagance we see, our women are old-fashioned and still continue old practices and ceremonials and presents, with Deepavali growing into a sort of trade—what with crackers, and fireworks, silks, and diamonds! Such a waste! The only solution is education. Our women must be educated," said Guru.

"When they get educated they become arrogant," said the other man. "Do you know how my brother's wife talks to him, because she is a B.A.? We are passing through hopeless days, on the whole. Even without a B.A. my wife insists on this and that and must have her own way in everything."

"It is bound to get worse if we don't do something about it."

"True, true," said the stamp vendor, feeling satisfied that he had sounded agreeable to a tahsildar, and did not contradict him in any manner. A tahsildar exercised his authority in several directions, and it was safer to be on agreeable terms with him. His seal on an application was indispensable especially to a stamp vendor whose livelihood depended on vending all denominations of special paper for legal documents.

When Guru reached home he found the street door ajar with no one in sight. He stood at the doorway and shouted, "What is the matter? Where is everybody hiding and why?"

His wife screamed back from an unseen corner, "Why do you get into the habit of shouting? No one is playing hide and seek here."

"Oh, you aren't? I am glad to hear that. Where is Kamala?"

"She was writing a letter, must have gone out to post it."

"Letters. Oh, letters! To whom?"

"She doesn't have to declare it to anyone."

"Oh, is that so? It was a mistake to have sent her to a college. Women become educated and arrogant."

His wife shouted back from her room, "What has come over you today?"

"That's what I want to ask you all. I made a mistake in staying away from the office today. You people don't seem to appreciate my company at home . . . I will go back to my work."

"Yes, do so. It's profitless to be away from your office table, I suppose!" she said, emerging from her room.

"But for my drudgery, you would not live in a house like this, or have those bangles and necklace . . ."

"Why this kind of talk?"

"Something has gone wrong, you have lost all sense of humor, you take everything literally and seriously like our Kamala's doctor-father-in-law, I only wanted to remind you that you came with a battered tin trunk . . . as a new bride, even the railway porter did not demand more than four annas to carry it on his head."

"And what did you bargain him down to actually?" she asked.

He laughed and said, "You have still got your sense of humor—I was wrong in saying that you had lost it. The trunk did not weigh much, I am sure, otherwise the porter would have demanded one rupee."

"The box had in it forty sovereigns only, which my father gave me, these bangles and a chain also . . . they don't weigh much inside a trunk. After that there was no addition in my box or on my person."

"What happened to the sovereigns?"

"Don't you remember that the two daughters are married but they could not be presented bare-necked and without bangles on their wrists at their wedding, and had to be provided with a minimum of jewelry."

"Why didn't you tell me?"

She spurned to answer his question and left his company. He kept looking in her direction and reflected, "Impossible to carry on any useful talk with women, always ready to squander and argue about it. Forty sovereigns to be squandered on tinsel to impress in-laws! After all, her father chose to give her a mere pittance but did not have the courtesy to tell me! What do I care what that battered tin box contained, so long ago? That box itself, where is it? Lost with all the junk when we moved here."

It was a provocative subject, revived whenever the lady wanted to score a point. "You have managed to bring along all your old things, particularly that unsightly, uncomfortable sofa in which no one could sit in peace," she would say.

"I did not bring it in, knowing what you would say," Guru replied.

"Not a word could I ever say about your treasures, although I wanted to keep my trunk and repair it—that would have made it new—"

"It was too battered, broken, rusty, discolored in patches, had only a single handle on the side, the other came off when the porter touched it. No wonder your father chose to put his forty sovereigns in it. He knew no one would be tempted to touch that tin trunk."

"Not worse than the sofa, your heirloom which you chose to bring all the way though it'd have saved money to break its legs and use them for heating water for a bath."

Guru explained, "I brought it along with other goods in that bullock cart—I didn't have to pay extra money for it. With a little polish and a pat here and there, it will fetch at least two hundred rupees."

"Then why don't you sell it?"

"Why does it bother you? After all, I have dumped it in the cowshed—"

"Cowshed! When are we buying the cow for the shed? If it

comes, the sofa will be in the next lane, I suppose, for any vagrant looking for trash or firewood."

"Aren't you terrified of the milk price today?" he asked, changing the subject.

"No need to worry about it, as you have successfully abolished coffee at home," she said.

"The smell of coffee is nauseating," he said.

"But I love coffee, I find it hard to do without it."

"No use thinking of it, you must have got used to being without it by now. It is not indispensable. I have brought up our daughters without coffee, they never had a craving for it. Two meals with good rice and vegetables will be sufficient to make one a giant."

"Our daughters have left this house because they didn't want to grow into giants under your care . . ."

"Why do you say *daughters?* Only Raji is gone, and in Trichy."

"Have you not noticed that Kamala who went out to post a letter has not returned, even after three hours? She won't come back. I promise it. She does not want to talk to you again."

"It's a conspiracy." He looked angry and upset. "When will she come back? Where is she?"

"She packed up her clothes and left for Lawley Extension in a jutka."

"I should not have left you both alone to hatch this plot."

"Don't call it a plot, she has only joined her husband. Thank God he loves her and could persuade his father not to bother about the gifts you promised."

"What about the formal nuptial ceremony?"

"They will manage it without public fuss, between themselves."

Guru let out a hearty laugh. "Very clever, without a paisa expense—"

"You know my father spent ten thousand rupees for our nuptials at our village, inviting a hundred guests for a three-day nuptial celebration. You welcomed it then."

"I was young and let my elders decide things."

"Also because the money they squandered was not yours."

He was in his seat transacting business as usual, with a crowd of villagers waiting for his favors. His badge-wearing doorkeeper who usually stood outside came in excitedly and whispered, "Collector is coming." Before he could complete his sentence the collector, the chief officer of the district, walked in, and Gurumurthi rose to his feet deferentially.

The peon tried to disperse the crowd of applicants, but the collector said, "Leave them alone." He said, "Sit down" to the tahsildar, who, however, kept standing since the collector himself did not sit but moved around inspecting the office, its furniture, and the load of files in a shelf at the back of the tahsildar. He asked, "Those are applications in front of you?"

"Yes, sir."

"Give me those papers."

With trepidation the tahsildar handed over the papers. The collector flicked through them still standing.

"Please take your seat, sir," Gurumurthi said offering his seat.

The collector went over and occupied the seat, spread out the papers on the table, and scrutinized them. "Why have you kept them pending so long?"

"Some details are awaited—some of the applications are incomplete."

The collector picked up a couple of applications, studied them, and asked, "Who are these applicants?" Before the tahsildar could find an answer, two men from the group came forward.

"They are our applications, your honor."

"When did you present them at this office?"

"Four months ago, sir."

"Why have you not sanctioned those loans yet?"

"They are not able to produce their birth certificates, sir."

The collector asked them, "Why have you failed to produce the certificates?"

"Our village Karnam is dead and the new man . . ."

The collector turned to Gurumurthi and said, "Very unsatisfactory. You could have taken their sworn statements and attested them."

"We have been coming here, your honor, every day—walking from our village, leaving our work—"

The collector summoned Gurumurthi to his office next day and said, "You may go on leave from tomorrow."

"May I know the reason, sir?"

"Not one reason, but several. I get reports and know what's going on."

"Oh, sir, there are gossipmongers and tale-bearers all around."

"Farmers come all the way to seek help and relief promised to them, and you delay and play with them some game."

"I am doing my best, sir, but they won't follow the procedure."

"I know what you are trying to say—excuses you are inventing. I don't want all that—I know what's going on in your office. You are a senior official—I don't want to be too hard on you. I could take disciplinary steps, but I'm giving you the choice of taking all the leave at your credit and seeking voluntary retirement at the end of it. If you don't want this choice, I'll have to recommend to the government an inquiry and further steps."

Gurumurthi was shaken at first, but survival seemed more important. He remembered a saying, "If the head is threatened, let the headgear be blown off." An inquiry would ruin him; they could withhold his pension and confiscate his property. Gurumurthi acted also as a money lender on the side, made possible by his delaying tactics when the villagers approached him for interest-free loans offered by the government.

He got over the initial shock in the course of time and adjusted himself to a retired life. He assured his wife, "We have enough to live on. Our daughters are married, and we have this house, the rents from those shops and my pension. What do I care? That young man, the collector, seems to be an upstart, I don't care. Everyone says he has been doing this sort of mischief in every district. He demanded certain explanations, but I firmly told him that I don't care to explain and am prepared to go. I demanded all the leave at my credit and then retirement. I told him that I have drudged for this ungrateful government long enough."

"What caste is he?" Saroja asked.

"I don't know. Whatever it may be, he is an upstart out to eliminate all the seniors in the service. When he found I was tough, he came down a step or two and tried to coax and cajole me to stay, but I was firm, made him understand that they do not deserve a conscientious hard-working man but only a hollow, showy scoundrel who would cringe for their favors."

"But it was rumored that you were not helpful to the villagers and so the collector—"

He cut her short. "Nonsense, don't listen to gossipmongers. You would not be living in this style if I didn't work hard. After all, your father was only a schoolmaster!"

"And yet you demanded a dowry from him!"

"Why do you bother about it now, so long ago! If he hadn't found the resources for a modest dowry, he'd have got a bankrupt son-in-law, not one who could support a family."

He organized his retired life satisfactorily. He left home every morning, went out and spent his time in the free reading room at the corner, a little den with newspapers old and new, piled on a small table at the center, and a shelf full of odd volumes discarded in the neighborhood. Some evenings he went and sat on a bench at the Jubilee Park, where pensioners like him were gathered, and Rao the stamp vendor would of course be there. They discussed the state of the nation and the problems of each other's health. From time to time he visited his banker on Mar-

ket Road to watch the savings burgeoning with monthly interest. Such moments away from home seemed to him beneficial,
as he could avoid his argumentative wife. Morning hours were
her worst time according to him, as she seemed too tense. After
lunch she mellowed, at about seven o'clock in the evening she
visited the temple. When she was away he relaxed in his canvas
chair and got absorbed in some odd volume picked up at the
free reading room. After dinner was a tranquil and peaceful time
unless she opened her gambit with "I met so and so in the
temple, do you know what she remarked?"

"You women seem to have no better business than gossiping."
It would start thus and then go on until both got tired and
sleepy.

Time passed. One day Gurumurthi brought out a proposition,
which sounded light at first but proved portentous. He had hesitated till he found his wife in a receptive mood, and then
brought out the proposition.

"Saroja, we must have a son."

She was taken aback. "What! At our age?" she exclaimed, and
was amused.

He explained, "Not that way. We can adopt." She still treated
it as a joke. Sitting on the pyol after dinner and enjoying the
night breeze and listening to the rustle of leaves of the raintree,
they were in a pleasant mood.

She asked, "Adopt? How? What do you mean?"

He elaborated. "We are old, our daughters live their own lives
away from us—"

"Why not?"

He fumbled on, "We are aged . . ."

"Nothing surprising. No one grows younger in this world—"
At this point she heard the rattle of vessels in the kitchen and
dashed away, muttering, "It's that cat again . . ."

He reflected, "I don't know how to talk to her. She either
laughs or gets angry and argues."

Next day he was determined to get it out of his system. He called suddenly, "Saroja, come here. I am serious about this." She was cleaning a corner of the hall with a broom and mop. He was sitting, as usual, in his canvas chair beside the window.

"I want to explain something." She dropped her broom and stood beside him. "Now listen—as we grow old, we need a son to look after us."

"Why this sudden decision? Are you serious?"

"I've told you I am serious. I can do many things without waiting for your opinion but now—"

"Yes, that's how I have lived. Even daughters' marriages, you never waited for my opinion, you were the one who made all the decisions. Women must not listen when you talk to the priest about financial matters. You are convinced that I don't know how to count cash over two rupees, I don't even know if you are rich or poor." Gurumurthi realized that he had started her off on a different track inadvertently. "You are the Supreme Lord and I am only a dependent not worth talking to," she concluded.

He realized that he had no chance to broach the subject which was obsessing his mind. Though normally he was the master of any situation, today he felt somewhat puzzled, yet decided to bully her to listen to him, the only way to get along in family affairs as he had known all his life.

He said firmly, "I want to adopt a son, and that is all there is to it."

She took a little time to understand the implications, stood silently awhile, and asked, "What do you expect me to say?"

"Show some interest, that's all." She turned round and went back to her corner. He felt infuriated, got up, followed her, caught her by the shoulder, turned her round to face him, looked into her eyes, and repeated firmly, "You must hear me fully."

Tears flowed down her cheeks as she shook herself free. "Do what you like, why should you bother me?"

"Adoption means by both parents—you have a part in the ceremony. Otherwise I do not have to ask you. You don't even ask who is the son?"

"I have said do what you please."

"Should you not know who is going to be the son? I'll tell you though, since it's my duty, even if you are indifferent. My brother Sambu's third son. He is ready to give him to us."

She said, "You mean Ragu! He is a monkey—I won't live in this house, if you bring him here!"

Gurumurthi shouted, "You are challenging me?" and went back to his chair, fretting. "She thinks she can order me about because I am gentle and considerate. I won't allow this sort of thing anymore and must put her in her place. I have refrained from mentioning why a son is needed to save her feelings, but I'll tell her even if it upsets her, I don't care."

He got up resolutely, went up to her, and shouted, "You know why? When I die, I want a son to light the funeral pyre and perform the rites, otherwise . . ."

"Otherwise what?" she asked. He glared at her speechlessly. She continued, "Life or death is not anyone's choice, we can't know."

He laughed ironically. "Oh, you are becoming a philosopher too, hm! You are listening too much to discourses in the evenings. Hereafter you had better stay away from those discourses at the temple . . ."

"You had better stay away from the stamp vendor at the corner house. Ever since you retired from service you have nothing better to do than listen to his advice and gossip at the reading room."

"Why do you talk ill of him! Shut up and don't talk of people you do not know!"

Now that she had got over the initial shock, she got into a taunting mood, and added, "Did that stamp vendor not mention also that if a son is not available your grandchildren can perform the rites? Anyway, why do you cultivate these unhappy thoughts?"

*   *   *

Gurumurthi pursued his plan methodically. He called his family priest and consulted him in whispers, while his wife ignored them and all their activity and minded her business. He wrote to his brother in Dindigul, a closely written postcard every day and awaited the arrival of the postman morning and evening, and kept talking about the arrangements as the date approached. What made him uneasy was that he was expected to buy new clothes for his brother and his wife and for himself and his wife too. He felt he could save on this item, as he had preserved the clothes presented to him and Saroja at festivals or other occasions by village applicants seeking his goodwill.

Saroja warned him, "They have been in storage for years and may have a musty smell."

He said, "Don't create problems, please put them out for airing. I'll get some naphthalene balls also . . . I don't mind the expense."

"You get a dozen for half a rupee," she said puckishly.

"You seem to know everything," he remarked.

The priest had explained, "Adoption is a very sacred matter, holier than all other activities. You must realize the sanctity of it. All gods and planetary deities must be satisfied with offerings in Homa through Agni the God of Fire. You will be acquiring a new entity, body and soul, and assume the responsibilities for his welfare. Your brother has five sons and it will be no loss to him to give one away; at the same time you will also gain merit by adopting a son. He must solemnly vow before the fire that he will be your dutiful son all his life and perform all the necessary rites when you join your revered ancestors."

Gurumurthi had also heard on the park bench a general statement from a member, "When you bring up a minor son in your custody, you can also demand a rebate on your tax."

With the arrival of Ragu, a lanky youth of twelve, Saroja made her exit, having remained monosyllabic and silent all through.

She had performed her duties mechanically, just obeying the directions of the priest, who had told her to sit beside her husband and join him in offering oblations in the holy fire. She prostrated at her husband's feet when directed, clasped his hand, received Ragu with open arms formally when told to, seated him on her lap and fed him with a piece of banana, sugar, honey and milk, sniffed his forehead, and touched it with sandal paste.

The smoke from the holy firehouse permeated every corner of the house, the smell of burnt faggots lingered in the air, irritating their eyes long after the ceremony, which ended at midday. The priest and four brahmins departed at three in the afternoon. After they left, Gurumurthi rested in his easy chair and fell asleep. Ragu sat on the pyol and watched the street. He would have loved to go out and wander about but his "father" had warned him not to go out alone, and so he sat there moping. His own parents had left soon after the ceremony.

When everybody was gone Saroja came out of her room carrying a small jute bag and a roll of bedding. A jutka stood at the door. She stepped out softly, after hesitating for a minute in front of her husband, unable to decide whether to wake him or not. She felt it would be unnecessary to take leave of him. She had already told him she was leaving after the adoption ceremony, explaining that she was going back to her village in Karur in order to take care of her old mother, who was lonely and helpless after her husband's death two years before.

Ragu lived as the son of the house for four days, greatly puzzled by his new life. He had never thought he would have to live permanently in the company of his uncle, who insisted upon being addressed as "Father." The boy felt uneasy in his grim company, and found it difficult to laugh at his jokes, listen to his observations, suggestions, obvious advices and moralizing, and above all his awkward storytelling. Gurumurthi depended on Pankaja Lodge for his sustenance, but the boy did not find that food adequate or acceptable. His "father" watched him all the time, he was never allowed to go out except in Gurumurthi's company, to sit on the park bench and listen to his cronies. The boy stood it for four days, secretly longing for his companions playing cricket in Dindigul streets, and one afternoon slipped away while his "father" was asleep.

Gurumurthi searched for the boy here and there and spent sleepless nights until a postcard arrived from Dindigul to say that the boy was back there and would soon join him after obtaining his school leaving certificate. Obviously it was never obtained. The boy kept away, and his father did not write to Gurumurthi again. Gurumurthi wrote once or twice, never got a reply, and decided not to waste money on postage anymore.

He reflected, "After all, it is all for the best, why should I keep that boy here? What for? Difficult to understand him. It has cost me less than seven hundred rupees and a hundred and fifty in rail fare for the parents to come for the ceremony and fifty rupees for feeding the priests; after all it made only a slight dent in my bank balance, that's all. And my brother's demand for a 'loan' of five thousand rupees, which I promised to consider though fully aware that it was a veiled price tag on the boy, need not be given now, that would have been another extravagance if that boy had stayed on. Also, the boy was too demanding, always wanting something to eat, frowning at Pankaja Lodge food. He was a glutton who could not be satisfied with a simple nutritious meal." It was also a strain to keep him amused or entertained, the fellow sticking to him all the time. Raji and Kamala as children were never like this fellow, they left him alone unless called to his side. Good riddance on the whole. He felt complacent, except when he was told by the stamp vendor, "The boy is only twelve, but when he attains majority he may legally demand a partition and a share of your property, especially if he should come over and perform the funeral rites when you die."

Gurumurthi felt uneasy at this prospect but comforted his mind with the proviso "*Only if* he performs my funeral ceremony, but why should I tell him or anyone of my death?"

Salt and
Sawdust

Being a childless couple Veena and Swami found their one-and-a-half-room tenement adequate. A small window opened on to Grove Street, a pyol beside the street door served for a sit-out, there was a kitchen to match and a backyard with access to a common well. The genius who designed this type of dwelling was Coomar of Boeing Silk Center, who had bought up an entire row of old houses adjoining his Silk Center, demolished them, and rebuilt them to house his staff working in the weaving factory beyond the river. It proved a sound investment and also enabled Coomar to keep his men under his thumb.

Swami left (on his bicycle) for his factory at seven-thirty a.m., but got up at five, while his wife was still asleep. He drew water from the common well, lit the stove, and prepared coffee and lunch for two, packing up a portion to carry. Veena got up late, gulped down the coffee kept on the stove, swept the floor, and cleaned the vessels. After her bath she lit an oil lamp before the image of a god in a niche.

After lunch, she sat on the pyol, watched the street with a

magazine in hand, and brooded over a novel she was planning to write, still nebulous. She felt she could start writing only when she got a proper notebook, which Swami had promised to bring this evening.

While returning home Swami stopped by Bari's Stationery Mart on Market Road, and announced, "My wife is going to write a novel. Can you give me a good notebook?"

"How many pages?" Bari asked mechanically.

Swami had no idea. He did not want to risk a conjecture. "Please wait. I'll find out and come back," he said and tried to leave.

Bari held him back. "I know what you want. We are supplying notebooks to novelists all the time. Take this home." He pressed into his hand a brown packet. "Two hundred pages Hamilton Bond, five rupees. Come back for more—our notebooks are lucky. Many writers have become famous after buying from us."

Veena was thrilled. She gazed on the green calico binding, flicked the pages, and ran her finger tenderly over the paper.

"Now I can really start writing. I have been scribbling on slips of paper—old calendar sheets and such things." She flicked the pages again, and cried, "Lined too!"

"Lined sheets are a great help. When you want another one, tell me, and I'll get it," he said.

"I want four hundred pages, but this will do for the present." She was so pleased that she felt she should do him a good turn; she hugged him and asked, "Shall I cook our dinner tonight?"

"No, no!" he cried desperately.

On earlier occasions when Veena cooked he had to swallow each morsel with difficulty, suppressing comment and silently suffering. He felt that they might have to starve unless he took over the kitchen duties. He realized that she was not made for it. Boiling, baking, spicing, salting, blending were beyond her understanding or conception. He was a good eater with taste and appetite. "A novelist probably cannot be a good cook," he concluded, "just as I cannot write a novel. She has not been taught to distinguish salt from sawdust." He quietly took over the kitchen, leaving her free to write whatever she fancied.

However, he would inquire from time to time, "What progress?"

She answered, "Can't say anything now, we have to wait."

Several days later, when he asked for progress, she said, "The heroine is just emerging."

"What do you call her?"

"Oh, names come very last in a novel."

"In that case how can a reader know who is who?"

"Just wait and see, it is my responsibility."

"I could write only two pages today," she said another day.

"Keep it up. Very soon you will fill four, eight, sixteen pages a day." His vision soared on multiples of four for some obscure reason. "I think I had better buy another two-hundred-page notebook before Bari's stock is exhausted. He said that the demand from novelists is rather heavy this season."

"Did he mention any novelist's name?"

"I will ask, next time I will find out."

Swami went to his room to change into a garb to suit his kitchen work. When he came out, changed to a knee-length dhoti and a towel over his shoulder, Veena said, "I was asking if he had met any novelist."

"Bari has met any number. I know only one novelist and she stands before me now." He then asked, "What kind of man is your hero?"

She replied, "What do you imagine him to be?"

"Tall, and powerful, not a fellow to be trifled with."

"So be it," she said, and asked, "Is he a fighting sort?"

"Maybe, if he is drawn to it."

She completed his sentence, "He won't hesitate to knock out the front teeth of anyone—"

Swami found the image of an adversary minus his teeth amusing, and asked, "What about the rest of his teeth?"

"He will deal with them when he is challenged next."

"You almost make him a dentist," he said.

"A Chinese dentist has opened a clinic at New Extension, and a lot of people sit before him open-mouthed."

"How have you come to know it?"

"Sometimes I lock the door and wander about till it is time to return home. Otherwise I cannot get ideas."

"When will you find time to write if you are wandering about?"

"Wandering about is a part of a writer's day. I also carry a small book and jot down things that interest me."

"Excellent plan," Swami said, and disappeared into the kitchen as he smelled burning oil from the frying pan.

Veena developed the idea further, and said when they settled down on the hall bench after supper, "I think a Chinese dentist is the hero, it is something original, no one has thought of him before. Chinese dentists are famous."

"But how can a girl of our part of the world marry a Chinese?"

"Why not?" she said and thought it over and said, "Actually, in the novel, he is not a Chinese. He only had his training in China."

"Why did he go to China?" asked Swami.

"When he was a boy he ran away from home."

"Why?"

"His schoolmaster caned him one day, and in sheer disgust he went and slept on a bench at the railway platform for two days and nights. When a train passed at midnight, he slipped into a carriage and finally joined some monks and sailed for Peking in a boat."

"Very interesting, very interesting," Swami cried. "How do you get these ideas?"

"When one writes, one gets ideas," Veena explained, and continued, "The monks left him at the port and vanished . . ."

"Were they supernatural beings? Could you explain their presence and help?"

"God must have sent them down to help the boy . . ."

"Why should God be interested?" Swami asked.

"God's ways are mysterious."

"True, God's ways are certainly mysterious," he endorsed her philosophy.

She continued, "And the young fellow wandered here and there in the streets of Peking, without food or shelter for a couple of days, and fainted in front of a dentist's clinic. In the morning when the dentist came to open the door, he saw the boy, and thought he was dead."

"What do they do in China with the dead?" he asked in genuine concern and added, "They probably bury."

"No, no, if he was buried that would end my story." She added, "Chinese are probably careful and cautious, unlike in our country, where they immediately carry away a body and dispose of it."

"Not always," Swami said, showing off his better knowledge of the situation. "Once, when I was working in a cloth shop, a body was found in the verandah and they immediately sent for a doctor."

"Why a doctor when he or she is already dead?"

"That's a routine in such circumstances," he generalized.

"I want you to find out from someone what the Chinese do when a body is found at the door. I must know before I proceed with the story."

"Since he becomes the Chinese dentist of your story later, he was not really dead—so why bother about it?" asked Swami.

"Of course," she agreed, "when he came back home, he knew how to work as a dentist, and became prosperous and famous."

"Readers will question you . . ."

"Oh, leave that to me, it is my business," Veena replied.

The story was taken one step further at the next conference. They had both got into the habit of talking about it every evening after dinner, and were becoming, unconsciously, collaborators.

"He fell in love with a girl, who had somehow lost all her teeth and come to have new ones fitted. . . . Day by day as he saw her with her jaws open to be fitted up, he began to love her, being physically so close to each other." Veena gloated over the vision of love blossoming in a dentist's chair.

Swami became critical. "With her jaws open and toothless gums, do you think it is possible for a man to be attracted? Is any romance possible in that state?"

"Don't you know that love is blind?"

Not wanting to appear to cross-examine or discourage her, he said, "Ah, now I understand, it is natural that a man who bends so close to a woman's face cannot help it, and it's his chance to whisper in her ears his passion, though if a toothless person came before me, I would not care for her."

Veena took offense at this point. "So that means if I lose my teeth, you will desert me?"

"No, no, you will always be my darling wife. But all that I am trying to say is, when the teeth are lost both the cheeks get sucked in and the mouth becomes pouchy, and the whole face loses shape."

Veena was upset at this remark, got up, and went away to the corner where her books were kept and started reading, ignoring him. By the time they sat down again the next night after dinner, she relented enough to say, "He need not be a dentist, I agree it's a difficult situation for lovers. Shall I say that he is something in a less awkward profession, a silk merchant or veterinary doctor?"

Swami was pleased that she had conceded his point, and felt that it was now his turn to concede a point and said, "No, no, let him be what he is, it's very original, don't change it—this is probably the first time a dentist comes into a story . . ." And on that agreeable note, peace was established once again. The dentist had to work on the heroine's gums for a long time, taking molds and preparing her denture, trying them out, filing, fitting and bridging; all the time Cupid was at work. It took the dentist several weeks to complete his task and beautify her face. When it was accomplished he proposed and they married, overcoming all obstacles.

As the notebook was getting filled, Veena took an afternoon off to spend time at the town hall library to browse through popular magazines on the hall table and romances on the shelves, desperately seeking ideas. Not a single book in the whole library on the theme of a dentist and a bare-gummed heroine. She returned home and remained silent all through the evening, leaving Swami to concentrate on his duties in the kitchen. She sat in her corner trying to go on with the story until Swami called from the kitchen, "Dinner ready."

One evening she confessed, "I have not been able to write even two lines today. I don't know in which language I should continue." She was suddenly facing a problem. She was good in English and always remembered her sixty percent in English literature in her B.A. At the same time she felt she should write in Tamil, that it was her duty to enrich her mother tongue so that all classes of people could benefit from her writing. It was an inner struggle, which she did not reveal even to her husband, but he sensed something was wrong and inquired tactfully, "Want anything?"

"What is our language?" she asked.

"Tamil, of course."

"What was the language of my studies at Albert Mission?"

"English."

"How did I fare in it?"

"You always got sixty percent."

"Why should I not write in English?"

"Nobody said you should not."

"But my conscience dictates I should write only in my mother tongue."

"Yes, of course," he agreed.

"You go on saying 'Yes' to everything. You are not helping me." Swami uttered some vague mumbling sounds. "What are you trying to say?" she asked angrily. He remained silent like a schoolboy before an aggressive pedagogue.

"Don't you realize that English will make my novel known all over India if not the whole world?"

"Very true," he said with a forced smile. "Why is she grilling me?" he reflected. "After all I know nothing about writing novels. I am only a weaving supervisor at Coomar's factory." He said to himself further, "Anyway, it's her business. No one compels her to write a novel. Let her throw it away. If she finds time hanging heavily, let her spin yarn on a charka."

He suddenly asked, "Shall I get you a charka?"

"Why?" she asked, rather alarmed at his irrelevancy.

"Mahatma Gandhi has advised every citizen of India to spin as a patriotic duty. They are distributing charkas almost free at Gandhi Center . . ."

By this time Veena felt that something was amiss; she abruptly got up and went over to her canvas chair in the corner, picking up a book from her cupboard. Swami sat in his wooden chair without moving or speaking. He began to feel that silence would be the safest course, fearing, as in a law court, any word he uttered might be used against him. He sat looking out of the window though nothing was happening there, except a donkey swishing its tail under the street lamp. "Flies are bothering it," he observed to himself, "otherwise it could be the happiest donkey." His neighbor was returning home with a green plastic bag filled with vegetables and passed him with a nod. Swami found the silence oppressive and tried to break it. "Mahatma Gandhi has advised that every individual should spin morning and evening and that'd solve a lot of problems."

"What sort of problems?" she asked gruffly, looking up from her book.

He answered, "Well, all sorts of problems people face."

"What makes you talk of that subject now?"

She was too logical and serious, he commented to himself. Has to be. Novelists are probably like that everywhere. He remained silent, not knowing how to proceed or in which direction. She sued for peace two days later by an abrupt announcement.

"I have decided to write both in Tamil and English, without bothering about the language, just as it comes. Sometimes I think in English, sometimes in Tamil. Ideas are more important than language. I'll put down the ideas as they occur to me, if in English, it'll be English, if the next paragraph comes in Tamil I'll not hesitate to continue in Tamil, no hard and fast rule."

"Of course there should be no hard and fast rule in such matters. To be reduced to a single language in the final stage, I suppose?"

"Why should I?" she said, slightly irritated. "Don't we mix English and Tamil in conversation?"

He wanted to say, "If you knew Hindi, you could continue a few paragraphs in Hindi too, it being our national language as desired by Mahatma Gandhi," but he had the wisdom to suppress it. Another mention of Gandhi might destroy the slender fabric of peace, but he asked solicitously, "Will you need another book for writing?"

"Yes," she said, "I'm abandoning this notebook and will make a fresh start on a new notebook. . . ." His mind got busy planning what to do with the blank pages of the present notebook. "I don't want to look at those pages again. I'll start afresh. You may do what you please with the notebook. Get me another one without fail tomorrow."

"Perhaps you may require two books, if you are writing two languages it may prove longer."

"Difficult to say anything about it now, but bring me one book—that will do for the present."

"I will tell Bari to keep one in reserve in any case," he said.

It went on like that. It became a routine for her to fill her notebook, adding to the story each day. They used to talk about it, until one day she announced, "They are married. It is a grand wedding since he was a popular dentist, and a lot of people in the town owed their good looks to him. His clinic was expanded and he engaged several assistants, and he was able to give his wife a car and a big house, and he had a farm outside, and they often spent their weekend at the farm."

"Any children?"

"By and by, inevitably."

"How many are you going to give them?"

"We will see," she said, and added, "At some point I must decide whether to limit their offspring to one or several."

"But China has the highest population," he said.

"True, but he is not a real Chinese, only trained there," she said, correcting him.

"Then he must have at least four children. Two sons and two daughters, the first and the third must be daughters," he said, and noticed that she looked annoyed; perhaps she felt he was interfering too much. He lapsed into silence.

"Suppose they also have twins?" he dared.

"We can't burden them that way, having no knowledge of bringing up a child ourselves."

"God will give us children at the appointed time."

"But you assume that we could recklessly burden a couple in the story!" she said.

She wrote steadily, filling up page after page of a fresh notebook . . . and with a look of triumph told Swami, "I won't need another notebook!" She held it up proudly. He looked through the pages, shaking his head in appreciation of her feat in completing the work; not entirely her work, he had a slight share in her accomplishment, of the two hundred pages in the book he had contributed ten pages, and was proud of it. In the story, at the dentist's wedding an elaborate feeding program was described for a thousand guests. The feast was very well planned —two days running they served breakfast, coffee and *idli* and *dosai* and *uppumav* and two sweets and fruit preparations, a heavy lunch with six vegetables and rice preparations, concluding with a light, elegant supper. Fried almonds and nuts were available in bowls all over the place, all through the day. The bridegroom, the dentist, had expressed a wish that a variety of eatables must be available for those with weak teeth or even no teeth; he had all kinds of patients, capable of different degrees of chewing and mastication.

Food had to be provided for them in different densities and caliber. Arrangements were made not only to provide for those who could chew hard food, masticate a stone with confidence, but also for those who could only swallow mashed, overripe banana. The doctor was saying again and again, "It is my principle that a marriage feast must be remembered—not only by those endowed with thirty-two teeth, but also by the unfortunate ones who have less or none."

At this stage Swami and Veena lost sight of the fact that it was a piece of fiction that they were engaged in but went on to chart every meal with tremendous zest. Swami would brook no compromise. It had to be the finest cuisine in every aspect.

"Why should you make it so elaborate and gluttonous?" Veena asked.

He answered, "The guests may have a wide choice, let them take it or leave it. Why should we bother? Anyway it is to cost us nothing. Why not make it memorable?" So he let himself go.

He explained what basic ingredients were required for the special items in the menu, the right stores which supplied only clean grains and pulses imported from Tanjore, and Sholapur, honey and saffron from Kashmir, apples from Kulu valley, and rosewater from Hyderabad to flavor sherbets to quench the afternoon thirst of guests, spices, cardamom, cinnamon and cloves from Kerala, and chillies and tamarind from Guntur. Swami not only knew where to get the best, but also how to process, dry, grind, and pulverize them before cooking. He also knew how to make a variety of sun-dried fritters, wafers, and chips. He arranged for sesamum from somewhere to extract the best frying oil, and butter from somewhere else to melt and obtain fragrant ghee.

Swami wrote down everything, including detailed recipes on the blank pages of the notebook that Veena had abandoned. When he presented his composition to Veena, she said, "Too long. I'll take only what is relevant to my story." She accepted only ten pages of his writing, rewrote it, and blended it into her narrative. Even with that Swami felt proud of his participation in a literary work.

Swami took the completed novel to Bari, who looked through the pages and said, "The lady, your missus, must be very clever."

"Yes, she is," said Swami, "otherwise how could one write so much? I could only help her with ideas now and then, but I am no writer."

Bari said, "I can't read your language or English very much, but I'll show it to a scholar I know, who buys paper and stationery from me. He is a professor in our college, a master of eighteen languages."

It took ten days to get an opinion. Ten days of suspense for Veena, who constantly questioned Swami at their night sessions after dinner, "Suppose the professor says it is no good?"

Swami had to reassure again and again, "Don't worry. He'll like it. If he doesn't, we will show it to another scholar." Every evening he stopped by at Bari's to ask for the verdict, while Veena waited anxiously for Swami's return.

"Wait, wait, don't be nervous. Scholars will take their own time to study any piece of work. We can't rush them."

One evening he brought her the good news. The scholar's verdict was favorable. He approved especially the double language experiment, which showed originality. Veena could not sleep peacefully that night, nor let her husband at her side sleep, agitated by dreams of success and fame as a novelist.

She disturbed him throughout the night in order to discuss the next step. "Should we not find a publisher in Madras? They know how to reach the readers."

"Yes, yes," he muttered sleepily.

"We may have to travel to Madras . . . can you take leave? If Coomar refuses to let you go, you must resign. If the novel is taken, we may not have to depend upon Coomar. If it becomes a hit, filmmakers will come after us, that'll mean . . ." Her dreams soared higher and higher. Swami was so frequently shaken out of sleep that he wondered why he should not take a pillow and move to the pyol outside.

Bari stopped their plan to visit Madras. "Why should you go so far for this purpose? I have paper and a friend has the best press . . ."

"Where?" asked Swami.

"You know Mango Lane just at the start of Mempi Hill Road?"

"No, never been there . . ."

"Once it was an orchard, where mangoes were cultivated and exported to Europe and America, till my friend bought the place, cleared the grove, and installed a press there; he prints and publishes many books, and also government reports and railway timetables. I supply all the paper he needs, he's a good customer—not always for our Hamilton Brand but he buys all sorts of other kinds. His name is Natesh, a good friend, he will print anything I want. Why should you wait upon publishers in Madras—they may not accept the novel, having their own notions, or if they take it they may delay for years. I know novelists who have aged while waiting and waiting."

"Impossible to wait," said Swami, recollecting his wife's anxiety and impatience to see herself in print.

Next day Bari had the printer waiting at his shop. He told Swami, "My friend came to order some thin paper for handbills, and I have held him back."

Natesh was a tall, lean, bearded person who wore a khadi *kurta* and dhoti, his forehead smeared with vermilion and holy ash. Natesh wished to see the manuscript. Swami produced the notebook for the printer's inspection next day. But when he suggested he'd take it with him to Mango Lane for estimating the printing charges, Swami felt embarrassed, not being sure if Veena would like to let it out of sight.

He said, "I'll bring it back later, the author is still revising."

Natesh went through the pages, counting the lines for about fifteen minutes, noting down the number of lines and pages, and declared, "I'll give an estimate for printing and binding in two days."

"I'll give an estimate for the papers required—that's my business," added Bari.

On this hopeful note they parted for the evening. Coming to brass tacks a couple of days later, Bari made a proposal. "I'll supply the paper definitely as a friend. Natesh has calculated that you will need twenty reams of white printing for the text, extra for covers. We will print five hundred copies at first. It would have cost less if the text had been in a single language but now the labor charges are more for two languages, and Natesh wants to print Tamil in black ink and English in red ink on a page, and that'll cost more. I can supply printing ink also. It would have been cheaper if your missus had written fewer pages and in her mother tongue only."

Swami said, being ignorant of the creative process, "I will tell her so—"

"No, no," cried Bari in alarm. "I'd not like to offend her, sir. Novelists must be respected and must be left to write in as many languages as they choose. Who are we to question?"

The printer at their next meeting said, "I can give a rough estimate, not the final one unless I go through the text for two days, and I won't undertake printing without going through the text to assure myself that it contains no blasphemy, treason, obscenity, or plagiarism. It's a legal requirement, if there is any of the above I'll be hauled up before a magistrate."

Swami became panicky, he had not read the manuscript; even if he had he could not say what offense Veena might have committed, but protested aloud, "Oh, no! Bari knows me and my family, and our reputation . . ."

Bari endorsed this sentiment. "Such offenses are unthinkable

in their family, they are very well known, of high class, otherwise
they can't be my customers. I would not sell Hamilton Bond
paper to anyone and everyone unless I am convinced that they
are lawful persons belonging to good families. If I gave my best
paper to all and sundry, where would I be?"

Swami had no answer to this question as he could not follow
the logic of Bari's train of thought. They were sitting around on
low aluminum stools and Swami's back ached, sitting erect and
stiff on a circular seat which had neither armrest nor a back. He
stood up.

Bari cried, "Sit, down, sit down. You must have tea." He
beckoned his servant, an urchin he had brought with him from
Aligarh, whom he never let out of sight. "Jiddu, three cups of
tea. Tell that man to give the best tea, otherwise I'll not pay."

While the boy dashed out for tea, Natesh said, "Apart from
other things I must guard against plagiarism."

Swami had heard of plague, but not plagiarism. "Please explain," he said.

When Natesh explained, he grew panicky. He wondered if
his wife visited the town hall library to lift passages from other
books. As soon as he went home, he asked his wife, "Did you
go to the town hall library?"

"Not today."

"But when you go there what do you generally do?"

"Why this sudden interest?" she asked.

He retreated into his shell again. "Just wanted to know if you
found any story as good as yours in the library . . ." She brushed
off his inquiry with a gesture.

He coaxed and persuaded her to give the novel for the printer's
inspection the next day. With many warnings she let him take
the notebook away with him, expressing her own doubt, "What
if he copies it and sells it?"

"Oh, no, he can't do that. We will hand him over to the
police, if he does. Bari will be our witness. We'll take a receipt."

Next day at Bari's Swami met Natesh and handed him the

notebook. Natesh took three days to complete his scrutiny of the novel and brought back the manuscript, safely wrapped in brown paper, along with the estimate. They conferred once again behind a stack of paper. They were silent while Jiddu went to fetch three cups of tea. After drinking tea Bari said, "Let us not waste time. Natesh, have you the estimate ready?"

"Here it is," said Natesh, holding out a long envelope.

Bari received it and passed it on to Swami with a flourish. Then he asked the printer, "How do you find the novel?"

"We will talk about it later . . ."

Bari said, "If you are not interested, Swami's missus will take it to the Madras printers."

"Why should she?" asked Natesh. "While we are here?"

"If so, come to the point. I'll supply the paper at less than cost price, when the book is sold you may pay . . ."

Swami felt rather disturbed. "But you said the other day, you would supply it . . ."

Bari said, "I am a businessman, sir, I said I'd supply the best paper at only cost price, and three months' sight."

"What is 'sight'?" asked Swami, now completely bewildered.

"Let us not waste time on technical matters," said Bari briefly. "When I said I'd supply, I meant I would supply, nothing more and nothing less."

At this point Natesh said, "You have not seen my estimate yet. Why don't you look through it first?"

Swami felt he was being crushed between heavyweights. He opened the estimate, took a brief look at the bewildering items, and then at the bottom line giving the total charges, felt dizzy, abruptly got up and rushed out into the street without a word, leaving the two agape.

Veena was standing at the door as usual. Even at a distance she could sense that something had gone wrong, judging from Swami's gait and downcast eyes. When he arrived and passed in without a word, she felt a lump in her throat. Why was he uncommunicative today? Normally he would greet her while coming up the steps. Today he was silent, could it be that the printer had detected some serious lapse, moral or legal, in her novel and threatened him with action? They ate in silence. When they settled down in their seats in the front room, she ventured to ask, "What happened?"

"Nothing," he said, "I have brought back the book."

"I see it. Are they not going to print it?"

"No, unless we sell ourselves and all that we have, to pay their bill. Even Bari has proved tricky and backed out though he had almost promised to supply the paper."

He went over to his cupboard and brought out the estimate. Veena studied it with minute attention, tried to understand the items in the bill, then let out a deep sigh, and showed symptoms of breaking down. Immediately Swami shed his gloom, assumed a tone of reckless cheer, and said, "You should not mind these setbacks, they are incidental in the career of any writer. I do not know very much about these things, but I have heard of authors facing disappointments all through life until a sudden break of good fortune occurred. Even Shakespeare. You are a first-class literary student, you must have read how downhearted he was till his plays were recognized."

"Who told you? I have never seen you read Shakespeare!"

Swami felt cornered and changed the subject. She did not press him further to explain his acquaintance with Shakespeare. This piece of conversation, however, diverted her attention, and she said, overcoming her grief, "Let us go away to Madras, where we will find the right persons to appreciate the novel. This is a wretched town. We should leave it."

Swami felt happy to see her spirit revive, but secretly wondered if she was going to force him to lose his job. Without contradicting her, he just murmured, "Perhaps we should write to the publishers and ask them first."

"No," she said. "It will be no use. Nothing can be done through letters. It will be a waste of time and money."

He felt an impulse to ask, "On reaching Madras are you going to stand outside the railway station and cry out, 'I have arrived with my novel, who is buying it?' Will publishers come tumbling over each other to snatch up your notebook?" He suppressed his thoughts as usual. She watched him for a while and asked, "What do you think?"

"I'll see Coomar and ask him for a week off."

"If he refuses, you must resign and come out."

This was the second time she had toyed with the idea of making him jobless, little realizing how they were dependent on Coomar for shelter and food. Somehow she had constituted herself Coomar's foe. This was not the time to argue with her. He merely said, "Coomar will understand, but this is a busy production season, lot of pressure at the moment."

She grumbled, "He wants to make more money, that is all, he is not concerned with other people's interests." Swami felt distressed at her notion of his boss, whom he respected, but he swallowed his words and remained silent.

Four days later, in the afternoon they had a visit from Bari and Natesh. It was a holiday and Swami was at home. He became fussy and drew the available furniture here and there, dashed next door and borrowed a folding chair, and managed seats for everybody. Veena threw a brief glance at the visitors, and walked past them unceremoniously and was off, while Swami fell into a state of confusion, torn between surprise at the arrival of visitors and an impulse to go after Veena. His eyes constantly wandered to the corner of the street while greeting and welcoming his visitors.

"Your missus going out in a hurry?" asked Bari.

"Yes, yes, she has an engagement in the Fourth Lane, busy all day . . ."

"Writing all the time?" asked the bearded man, whose bulging eyes and forehead splashed with holy ash and vermilion gave him a forbidding look.

"Yes, yes, she has to answer so many letters every day from publishers in Madras . . . before we go there . . ."

The two looked at each other in consternation. "No need, no need," they cried in unison, "while we are here."

"But she has definite plans to take her novel to Madras . . ."

When they said, "No sir, please, she will bring fame to Malgudi," Swami felt emboldened by their importunity, and said in a firm tone, "Your charges for printing will make me a bankrupt and a beggar." He looked righteous.

"But, sir, it was only a formality, estimates are only a business formality. You must not take it to heart, estimates are provisional and negotiable."

"Why did you not say so?" asked Swami authoritatively. He felt free to be rude.

"But you went away before we could say anything."

Swami gave a fitting reply as he imagined. Veena's absence gave him freedom. She would have controlled him with a look, or by a thought wave as he sometimes suspected, whenever a third person was present. He realized suddenly his social obligations. "May I offer you tea or coffee?"

After coffee and the courtesies, they came down to business. Natesh suddenly said, "I was in prison during the political struggle for Independence, and being a political sufferer our government gave me a pension, and all help to start my printing press—I always remind myself of Mahatmaji's words and conduct myself in all matters according to his commands." He doubtless looked like one in constant traffic with the other world to maintain contact with his Master. "Why am I saying this to you now?" he suddenly asked.

Bari had the answer for it, "To prove that you will always do your best and that you are a man of truth and nonviolence."

The other smiled in satisfaction, and then remarked to Swami, "Your wife has gone out, and yet you have managed to give us coffee, such good coffee!"

"Oh, that's no trouble. She keeps things ready at all times. I leave her as much time as possible for her writing too."

They complimented him on his attitude and domestic philosophy. Bari said, "We will not allow the novel to go out, we
will do it here."

Natesh said, "I am no scholar or professor, but I read the story
and found it interesting, and in some places I was in tears when
the young couple faced obstacles. I rejoiced when they married.
Don't you agree?" he asked, turning to Bari.

"Alas, I am ignorant of the language. If it had been in our
language I'd have brought it out famously, but you have told
me everything, and so I feel I have read it. Yes, it is a very
moving story, I'll supply the paper and Natesh will print it."

"Where?" asked Swami.

"In my press of course," replied Natesh. "At Madras I learned
the ins and outs of the publishing business. Under the British,
publishers were persecuted, especially when we brought out patriotic literature, and then I had to give up my job when Mahatmaji ordered individual Satyagraha. I was arrested for burning
the Union Jack, and went to prison. After I was released, the
Nehru government helped us to start life again. Now I am concentrating on printing . . . but if I find a good author, I am
prepared to publish his work. I know how to market any book
which seems good."

"So you think this novel will sell?" asked Swami, buoyed up.

"Yes, by and by, I know when it should be brought out. In
this case the novel should be published later as a second book,
we will keep it by. Your story portion stands by itself, but without spoiling it we can extract the other portion describing the
marriage feast as a separate part, and publish it as the first book,
with a little elaboration—perhaps adding more recipes of the
items served in the feast—it can then become a best-seller.
While reading it, my mouth watered and I felt hungry. It's so
successfully presented. With a little elaboration it can be produced as a separate book and will definitely appeal to the reader,
sort of an appetizer for the book to follow, that's the novel,
readers will race for it when they know that the feast will again
be found in the novel. If you accept the idea, we may immedi-

ately proceed. I know how to sell it all over the country. The author is at her best in describing food and feast. If you can give me a full book on food and feast, I can give you an agreement now, immediately. On signing it I'll give you one thousand and one thousand on delivery. We will bring it out at our own cost. When it sells, we will give you a royalty of ten percent, less the advance."

Later Swami explained to Veena the offer. Veena immediately said dolefully, "They want a cookery book, not a novel."

"I think so," Swami said, "but he will give a thousand rupees if you agree. Imagine one thousand, you may do many things."

"But the novel?"

"He will publish it as a second book, after your name becomes known widely with the first book."

"But I don't know any cookery . . ."

"It doesn't matter, I will help you."

"You have never allowed me in the kitchen."

"That should make no difference. You will learn about it in no time and become an authority on the subject . . ."

"Are you making fun of me?"

"Oh, no. You are a writer. You can write on any subject under the sun. Wait a minute." He went up to a little trunk in which he kept his papers, brought out the first green-bound notebook in which he had scribbled notes for the dentist's marriage feast. Veena went through it now carefully, and asked, "What do you want me to do?"

"You must rewrite each page of my notes in your own words—treat it as a basis for a book on the subject."

"What about the novel?"

"That will follow when you have a ready-made public." Veena sat silently poring over the pages which she had earlier rejected, now finding the contents absorbing. She thought it over and shook him again that night while he was sound asleep, and said, "Get me a new notebook tomorrow. I'll try."

Next evening on his way home, Swami picked up a Hamilton

notebook. Veena received it quietly. Swami left it at that till she herself said after three days, "I'll give it a trial first . . ."

That afternoon, after lunch Veena sat in her easy chair and wrote a few lines, the opening lines being: "After air and water, man survives by eating, all of us know how to eat, but not how to make what one eats." She wrote in the same tone for a few pages and explained that the pages following were planned to make even the dull-witted man or woman an expert cook . . .

She read it out to Swami that evening. He cried, "Wonderful! All along I knew you could do it, all that you have to do now is to elaborate the points from my notes in your own style, and that'll make a full book easily."

Swami signed a contract on behalf of Veena and received one thousand rupees advance in cash. Veena completed her task in three months and received one thousand rupees due on delivery of the manuscript. Natesh was as good as his word and Bari supplied the best white printing paper at concessionary rates. They called the book *Appetizer—A Guide to Good Eating.* Natesh through his contacts with booksellers sold out the first edition of two thousand copies within six months. It went through several editions and then was translated into English and several Indian languages, and Veena became famous. She received invitations from various organizations to lecture and demonstrate. Swami drafted her speeches on food subjects, traveled with her, and answered questions at meetings. They were able to move out of Grove Street to a bungalow in New Extension, and Veena realized her long-standing desire to see her husband out of Coomar's service. All his time was needed to look after Veena's business interests and the swelling correspondence, mostly requests for further recipes, and advice on minor problems in the kitchen.

Though Swami offered to continue to cook their meals, Veena prohibited him from stepping into the kitchen and engaged a master cook. In all this activity the novel was not exactly forgotten, but awaited publication. Natesh always promised to take it up next, as soon as the press was free, but *Appetizer* reprints kept the machines overworked, and there was no sign of the demand slackening. Veena, however, never lost hope of seeing her novel in print and Swami never lost hope that some day he would be allowed to cook, and the master cook could be secretly persuaded or bribed to leave.

Judge

∽

The Talkative Man said (to his usual evening audience lounging on the pedestal of Lawley Statue):

It was an unwise decision on my part to have accepted the
judgeship. I was forced into it by my well-wishers. God save us
from our well-wishers and relatives. Far too many of them all
around. I sometimes wish that I had been born in isolation in
some desert. Here Malgudi was swarming with kinsmen. Every
street housed a cousin, a roundabout nephew or a remote uncle,
so that unless I dashed past a door, I had no chance of reaching
my destination in time. "Hai! Don't go, I must tell you something," one or the other would cry at the sight of me. Baited by
such invitation, I would stop to listen to family gossip, discussion of national events and disasters, and when the speaker
paused for breath, picked up my bicycle and was on my way
again. I was a news reporter in those days, wandering all over
the town, ending up at the Boardless to recoup my energy with
coffee and snacks. Quite an active, happy life. Sheltered securely
in our ancestral home in Kabir Street, I was a contented man.

This perfect life threatened to come to an end once. While passing Grove Street one morning, an uncle of mine hailed me from his door—that horrible man spent his hours watching the street. He said to me, "Now listen to this attentively. Did you see in the morning paper an announcement calling young men with a law degree or journalistic experience to apply for a special judge's post—a new policy in order to clear the arrears in law courts? Why don't you present yourself for the interview at Madras? They will pay your rail fare."

I could not picture myself as a judge, sitting high, making pronouncements. The picture was too absurd. I suffered from severe short-sightedness—minus twelve being the strength of my glasses, which weighed down my nose and misshaped it. Without my glasses, I could not distinguish a mud wall from my mother-in-law, if I had one. So I said, "With such thick glasses one can't occupy a judge's seat." But my uncle brushed aside my objection, "Thick glasses add dignity to a man in high position." I was weak-minded enough to accept his advice. Not content with advising, he spread the news far and wide, and very soon I was overwhelmed with congratulations. I had not suspected that there could be so many in this world anxious to see me elevated to a judge's seat. I was getting tired of the advice I was receiving at every turn: "The important thing is the interview. Being a journalist you will get through creditably. We will arrange a grand celebration if you are selected. Do your best." Even our Varma, the level-headed proprietor of the Boardless, looked on me with awe, and murmured in an undertone, while I sat at his side sipping coffee, "The important thing is the interview. You must do your best."

Eventually, I appeared before an august body assembled in a chamber at the Madras High Court. Five men, two on each side of a chairman, gems culled from five corners of our country, were seated on a platform, while I was given a wooden stool to face them. They put me at my ease with some personal questions such as "Are you married or single?," "What is your weight?,"

"Do you like wheat or rice?" Then they put to me questions to plumb my general knowledge, intelligence, and judgment, such as "What is the average rainfall in northeast Somalia?," "Name a tenth-century ruler of Outer Mongolia," "Define in not more than four sentences the Loch Ness Monster." Finally, they asked why I wanted to be a judge and how I would handle a murder trial. I promptly said, "I would hang the murderer without any delay." The last mentioned question turned out prophetic, as I found myself, in course of time, sitting over a baffling murder case. Day after day, the case dragged on. I did my best to avoid a decision by postponement on flimsy grounds. "At the alleged time of the crime, Your Honor, A-three was at a post office."

"Which post office?"

"I'll find out, Your Honor."

"Look sharp. It is a crucial point. Till you are able to name the post office and file the report, hearing is adjourned."

And the court rose for the day, the seven poor souls in chains were marched off, and the lawyer and public prosecutor turned their attention to other miscreants in another court, while I grandly strode back to my chamber, shut the door, and stretched myself on a sofa and fell asleep.

I really had no idea how long I could go on postponing a decision. It was a complicated case. Some months before, on the highway between Kumbam and Malgudi, a man traveling in a bus was dragged out and hacked to death. The bus was full in addition to a conductor and the driver, but none saw it happen. The driver just said, "A blue Ambassador car blocked the road, and when I applied the brake, four men rushed into the bus, dragged away a passenger seated in the last row. I don't know what happened afterwards."

"Why could you not see what happened?"

"The four who entered the bus threw chilli powder in our eyes and dragged the man out."

"How many were seated in the bus?"

"About forty, Your Honor."

"How much chilli powder would be needed to blind forty pairs of eyes, and how many hands would be required to sprinkle the said powder simultaneously into all those forty pairs of eyes, not to mention the driver and the conductor, and how much powder was swept up from the floor of the bus after the event?"

This sounded to me an extremely subtle point from the defense lawyer. I noted it down ceremoniously. I was getting engrossed in the story and wished that I could be left alone to enjoy it without judging its merits. I asked now, "Did the police make any arrangement to collect the chilli powder from the bus, and if so, let the exhibit be marked, numbered, and filed." Thereby, I gained another term of irresolution. When the case came up again, the defending lawyer created a fresh problem. He objected to the post mortem report as being unconvincing. The description of the injuries on the deceased looked more like tooth and claw marks than those inflicted by blunt or sharp instruments, wounds that must have been inflicted by a tiger which was reported to be sighted off and on in that area, attacking cattle and men.

"Can you produce a certified report of the tiger's havoc?"

"Yes, Your Honor. I have the ranger's certificate, but it must be countersigned by the Conservator of Forests, who is away in Africa for a wildlife conference."

"When is he expected to return?"

"I will have to find out, your honor."

The prosecutor opposed this excuse for postponement as being vague, but I overruled his objection and posted the case for the fifteenth of the following month. The prosecution utilized the time to garnish and polish their story further so that they might present a convincing picture next time. The deceased and the accused were rival applicants for a license to sell arrack at a certain tavern. The deceased had his rival beaten up three days before the alleged incident and also threatened to molest his wife. The police had also registered a case against him at about that time. I made note of it but suddenly reverted to the tiger, which I thought was more interesting than the police.

"We will revert to the question of arrack license, later. But I must know now if pugmarks of the tiger were found at the scene of the crime."

"Yes, Your Honor."

"Were they measured and photographed?"

"They could be measured only partially, Your Honor, because a herd of buffalo was reported to have crossed the same track later; in spite of it, we did obtain certain photographs and measurements."

"Of the buffalo hooves?" I could not resist asking, which provoked laughter in the court. Encouraged by it, I added, "Possibly, the deceased came to a sorry end through getting mixed up among the stampeding buffalo." More laughter.

"Possibly, Your Honor, but it was also not unlikely that he was mauled by a tiger stalking the buffalo herd. He must have been knocked down senseless with a swing of its powerful paw, as is the habit with such beasts."

"Why did it not eat him off? The post mortem report makes no mention of any chewn-off bits from the body. No portion is missing?"

"Because at that very moment, a village procession passed with tom-toms and flares, and the tiger must have run away," said the defense lawyer.

"Can you get a sworn statement from the village *munsiff* about the procession?"

The prosecutor interrupted, "Your Honor, I submit that this court's valuable time is being sidetracked to listen to cock and bull stories."

"Rather buffalo and tiger story," I said, and there was laughter in the court. I was pleased with the way I was amusing them. Such entertainment could not last forever. I had to decide soon. Looking at the seven men accused of murder before me, I felt that if I sentenced to death any or all of them, I could be considered an eighth murderer. They had at least the excuse of rivalry, revenge, or resentment, while I would be only a cold-blooded hangman's partner, nothing less, if I pronounced a death sentence. I was obsessed with the feeling (like Roger de Coverley of Addison's *Essays*) that much might be said on both sides. When the defense lawyer argued, I nearly wept for the poor fellows arrayed before me. When the prosecutor dilated upon the nefariousness of the conspirators, I felt that without the formality of a trial they should be lined up and shot. One helpless man to be chased and butchered by seven with crowbars and hatchets and cycle chains while he was running for dear life. Oh! the thought was too horrible to contemplate. They were rakshasas. When inspired thus I seized my pen and drafted in a frenzy a model death sentence for most of them, except two youths who had only strayed into evil company. Those two boys looked tender and seemed incapable of any violence. But the prosecution had included them in a package—those boys were said to have, being energetic, raced along, overtaken their victim and, suddenly turning around, tripped him up, and held him down while the seniors dismembered him.

But in cross-examination they denied everything. The pair were from different villages, one working in a cycle repair shop and the other, a ragpicker, collecting scraps for a wastepaper merchant. While passing that way, each on his own business, they had stopped on seeing the dead body. When the police arrived, they were both bundled into the van and detained in a police lock-up till they put their thumb impressions on some papers put up before them. The prosecutor cross-examined till the boys messed up their own earlier versions, and entangled themselves in contradictions. Whatever it might be, I decided to give the young fellows the benefit of doubt. At this point, I received a warning from the chief justice not to prolong the case, in keeping with the government's new policy of abolishing law's delays. I had to submit immediately a report of my hearings and the adjournments up-to-date, whereupon the chief justice set a time limit for me to conclude and deliver judgement, giving me fifteen days, from the fifth of June to the twentieth. On the twenty-first, I must announce who was to hang. I felt desperate;

when I glanced out of the window I envied people who went about their business without a care, not having to judge a murder. I cursed the day I accepted this profession, and I cursed that busybody—my uncle of Grove Street—who had pushed me into it. I told myself devoutly, "Only God can help me."

Our family deity watched us from the temple on Tirupathi Hills; thither I went carrying a suitcase full of documents. I stood praying in the sanctum (being a judge, I was ushered into the presence of God through a special door though others had to wait in a long queue outside). The image of God Venkateswara decorated with flowers and gold and gems scintillated in the flickering oil lamps and camphor flame. I prostrated before the image and prayed, "Save me from making a fool of myself. From my analysis of the evidence, I feel accused one and three are to be hanged, numbers two, four, and five to be sentenced for life, for abettment and conspiracy. A-six and -seven—two years rigorous imprisonment, more as a corrective, being only youths found in bad company. I have not put pen to paper yet, waiting for a sign from the Almighty; I will sit down here for a moment and begin the first few lines in Your divine presence, work on it all night in my room and pronounce judgement on the twenty-first as ordered by the chief. Please guide me, my Lord!"

At this moment, I became aware of a slight pressure on my shoulder, followed by a blankness before my eyes. Everything vanished in a profound haze. The image of God which was scintillating a few moments ago was no longer visible. A devotee waiting outside cried, "Sir, there goes a monkey with your spectacles"; another man said, "Now it has gone out and is going up the other tower."

"If you throw a banana at him, he will catch the fruit and let go your glasses," said another.

Someone else suggested, "There must be a monkey trainer somewhere who can call it back if you give him five rupees."

I remembered the warning notices pasted on the temple pil-

lars: BEWARE OF MONKEYS! and GUARD YOUR SPECTACLES AND
HANDBAGS. Generations of monkeys flourished in the spacious
temple at various corners, perched on pillars and roofs, and were
in the habit of darting down and snatching away fruits from the
hands of pilgrims and also spectacles and other detachable articles on any person.

I had to be helped to get back home in the town. It took a
couple of days to get a new pair of glasses compounded. Till
then, I had to live the life of a blind man as an atonement for
the sin of accepting a judgeship without possessing a decisive
mind. I called my steno and dictated my judgement (when I got
a new pair of glasses), a verdict of not guilty, and ordered immediate release of all the seven accused. I viewed the monkey as
a bearer of a divine message in response to my prayer.

At this point, one of his listeners questioned the Talkative Man,
"We have been meeting you every day, when were you a judge
and where?"

"You demand an explanation! Do you? You won't get it. I
will only quote my friend Falstaff in Shakespeare's play. He was
asked to explain how or why of certain episodes. His reply was
a No sir, 'If reasons were as plentiful as blackberries, I would
give no man a reason upon compulsion'!"

Emden

When he came to be named the oldest man in town, Rao's age was estimated anywhere between ninety and one hundred and five. He had, however, lost count of time long ago and abominated birthdays; especially after his eightieth, when his kinsmen from everywhere came down in a swarm and involved him in elaborate rituals, and with blaring pipes and drums made a public show of his attaining eighty. The religious part of it was so strenuous that he was laid up for fifteen days thereafter with fever. During the ceremony they poured pots of cold water, supposedly fetched from sacred rivers, over his head, and forced him to undergo a fast, while they themselves feasted gluttonously. He was so fatigued at the end of the day that he could hardly pose for the group photo, but flopped down in his chair, much to the annoyance of the photographer, who constantly withdrew his head from under the black hood to plead, "Steady, please." Finally, he threatened to pack up and leave unless they propped up the old gentleman. There were seventy-five heads to be counted in the group—all Rao's descendants one way or another. The photographer insisted upon splitting the group, as otherwise the individuals would be microscopic and indistinguishable on a single plate. That meant that after a little rest Rao had to be propped up a second time in the honored seat. When he protested against this entire ceremony, they explained, "It's a propitiatory ceremony to give you health and longevity."

"Seems to me rather a device to pack off an old man quickly," he said, at which his first daughter, herself past sixty, admonished him not to utter inauspicious remarks, when everyone was doing so much to help.

By the time he recovered from his birthday celebrations and the group photo in two parts could be hung on the wall, the house had become quiet and returned to its normal strength, which was about twenty in all—three of his sons and their families, an assortment of their children, nephews and nieces. He had his room in the right wing of the house, which he had designed and built in the last century, judging by its appearance. He had been the very first to buy a piece of land beyond Vinayak Street; it was considered an act of great daring in those days, being a deserted stretch of land from which thieves could easily slip away into the woods beyond, even in daylight; the place, however, developed into a residential colony and was named Ratnapuri, which meant City of Gems.

Rao's earlier years were spent in Kabir Street. When he came into his own and decided to live in style, he sold off their old house and moved to Ratnapuri. That was after his second wife had borne him four daughters, and the last of them was married off. He had moved along with his first wife's progeny, which numbered eight of varying ages. He seemed to be peculiarly ill-fated in matrimony—his uncle, who cast and read the stars for the whole family, used to say that Rao had Mars in the seventh house, with no other planet to checkmate its fury, and hence was bound to lose every wife. After the third marriage and more children, he was convinced of the malevolence of Mars. He didn't keep a record of the population at home—that was not his

concern—his sons were capable of running the family and managing the crowd at home. He detached himself from all transactions and withdrew so completely that a couple of years past
the grand ceremony of the eightieth birthday he could not remember the names of most of the children at home or who was
who, or how many were living under his roof.

The eightieth birthday had proved a definite landmark in his
domestic career. Aided by the dimming of his faculties, he could
isolate himself with no effort whatever. He was philosophical
enough to accept nature's readjustments: "If I see less or hear
less, so much the better. Nothing lost. My legs are still strong
enough to take me about, and I can bathe and wash without
help . . . I enjoy my food and digest it." Although they had a
dining table, he refused to change his ancient habit of sitting on
a rosewood plank on the floor and eating off a banana leaf in a
corner of the dining hall. Everything for him went on automat-
ically, and he didn't have to ask for anything, since his needs
were anticipated; a daughter-in-law or niece or granddaughter or
a great-grand someone or other was always there to attend him
unasked. He did not comment or question, particularly not question, as he feared they would bawl in his left ear and strain their
vocal cords, though if they approached his right ear he could
guess what they might be saying. But he didn't care either way.
His retirement was complete. He had worked hard all his life to
establish himself, and provide for his family, each figure in the
two-part group photograph owing its existence to him directly
or indirectly. Some of the grandchildren had been his favorites
at one time or another, but they had all grown out of recognition, and their names—oh, names! they were the greatest impediments to speech—every name remains on the tip of one's
tongue but is gone when you want to utter it. This trick of
nature reduces one to a state of babbling and stammering without ever completing a sentence. Even such a situation was acceptable, as it seemed to be ordained by nature to keep the mind
uncluttered in old age.

He reflected and introspected with clarity in the afternoons—

the best part of the day for him, when he had had his siesta; got up and had his large tumbler of coffee (brought to his room exactly at three by one of the ministering angels, and left on a little teapoy beside the door). After his coffee he felt revived, reclined in his easy chair placed to catch the light at the northern window, and unfolded the morning paper, which, after everyone had read it, was brought and placed beside his afternoon coffee. Holding it close enough, he could read, if he wiped his glasses from time to time with a silk rag tied to the arm of his chair; thus comfortably settled, he half-read and half-ruminated. The words and acts of politicians or warmongers sounded stale—they spoke and acted in the same manner since the beginning of time; his eyes traveled down the columns— sometimes an advertisement caught his eye (nothing but an invitation to people to squander their money on all kinds of fanciful things), or reports of deaths (not one recognizable name among the dead). On the last page of the paper, however, half a column invariably gripped his attention—that was a daily report of a religious or philosophical discourse at some meeting at Madras; brief reports, but adequate for him to brush up his thoughts on God, on his incarnations and on definitions of Good and Evil. At this point, he would brood for a while and then fold and put away the paper exactly where he had found it, to be taken away later.

When he heard the hall clock chime four, he stirred himself to go out on a walk. This part of the day's routine was anticipated by him with a great thrill. He washed and put on a long shirt which came down to his knees, changed to a white dhoti, wrapped around his shoulder an embroidered cotton shawl, seized his staff and an umbrella and sallied out. When he crossed the hall, someone or other always cautioned him by bellowing, "Be careful. Have you got the torch? Usual round? Come back soon." He would just nod and pass on. Once outside, he moved with caution, taking each step only after divining the nature of the ground with the tip of his staff. His whole aim in life was to avoid a fall. One false step and that would be the end. Longevity was guaranteed as long as he maintained his equilibrium and verticality. This restriction forced him to move at snail's pace, and along a well-defined orbit every evening.

Leaving his gate, he kept himself to the extreme left of the street, along Vinayak Street, down Kabir Lane and into Market Road. He loved the bustle, traffic and crowds of Market Road —paused to gaze into shops and marvel at the crowd passing in and out perpetually. He shopped but rarely—the last thing he remembered buying was a crayon set and a drawing book for some child at home. For himself he needed to buy only a particular brand of toothpowder (most of his teeth were still intact), for which he occasionally stopped at Chettiar's at the far end of Market Road, where it branched off to Ellaman Street. When he passed in front of the shop, the shopman would always greet him from his seat, "How are you, sir? Want something to take home today?" Rao would shake his head and cross over to the other side of the road—this was the spot where his orbit curved back, and took him homeward, the whole expedition taking him about two hours. Before six-thirty, he would be back at his gate, never having to use his torch, which he carried in his shirt pocket only as a precaution against any sudden eclipse of the sun or an unexpected nightfall.

The passage both ways would always be smooth and uneventful, although he would feel nervous while crossing the market gate where Jayaraj the photo-framer always hailed him from his little shop, "Grand Master, shall I help you across?" Rao would spurn that offer silently and pass on; one had to concentrate on one's steps to avoid bumping into the crowd at the market gate, and had no time for people like Jayaraj. After he had passed, Jayaraj, who enjoyed gossiping, would comment to his clients seated on a bench, "At his age! Moves through the crowd as if he were in the prime of youth. Must be at least a hundred and ten! See his recklessness. It's not good to let him out like this. His people are indifferent. Not safe these days.

With all these lorries, bicycles and auto-rickshaws, he'll come to grief someday, I'm sure. . . ."

"Who's he?" someone might ask, perhaps a newcomer to the town, waiting for his picture to be framed.

"We used to call him Emden.* We were terrified of him when we were boys. He lived somewhere in Kabir Street. Huge, tall and imposing when he went down the road on his bicycle in his khaki uniform and a red turban and all kinds of badges. We took him to be a police inspector from his dress—not knowing that he wore the uniform of the Excise Department. He also behaved like the police—if he noticed anyone doing something he did not like, he'd go thundering at him, chase him down the street and lay the cane on his back. When we were boys, we used to loiter about the market in gangs, and if he saw us he'd scatter us and order us home. Once he caught us urinating against the school wall at Adam's Street, as we always did. He came down on us with a roar, seized four of us and shook us till our bones rattled, pushed us up before the headmaster and demanded, "What are you doing, Headmaster? Is this the way you train them? Or do you want them to turn out to be guttersnipes? Why don't you keep an eye on them and provide a latrine in your school?" The headmaster rose in his seat, trembling and afraid to come too close to this terrible personality flourishing a cane. Oh, how many such things in his heyday! People were afraid of him. He might well have been a policeman for all his high-and-mighty style, but his business was only to check the taverns selling drinks—and you know how much he collected at the end of the day? Not less than five hundred rupees, that is, fifteen thousand a month, not even a governor could earn so much. No wonder he could build a fancy house at Ratnapuri and bring up his progeny in style. Oh, the airs that family give themselves! He narrowly escaped being prosecuted—if a national

---

* A German warship that shelled Madras in 1916; ever since, the term indicates anyone who is formidable and ruthless.

award were given for bribe-taking, it would go to him: when he was dismissed from service, he gave out that he had voluntarily retired! None the worse for it, has enough wealth to last ten generations. Emden! Indeed! He married several wives, seems to have worn them out one after another; that was in addition to countless sideshows, ha! ha! When we were boys, he was the talk of the town: some of us stealthily followed and spied on his movements in the dark lanes at night, and that provided us a lot of fun. He had great appetite for the unattached female tribe, such as nurses and schoolmistresses, and went after them like a bull! Emden, really! . . ." Jayaraj's tongue wagged while his hands were cutting, sawing and nailing a picture frame, and ceased the moment the work was finished, and he would end his narrations with: "That'll be five rupees—special rate for you because you have brought the picture of Krishna, who is my family god. I've not charged for the extra rings for hanging. . . ."

Rao kept his important papers stacked in an almirah, which he kept locked, and the key hidden under a lining paper in another cupboard, where he kept his clothes and a few odds and ends, and the key of this second cupboard also was hidden somewhere, so that no one could have access to the two cupboards, which contained virtually all the clues to his life. Occasionally on an afternoon, at his hour of clarity and energy, he'd leave his easy chair, bolt the door and open the first cupboard, take out the key under the paper lining, and then open the other cupboard containing his documents—title deeds, diaries, papers and a will.

Today he finished reading the newspaper in ten minutes, and had reached his favorite column on the last page—the report of a discourse on reincarnations, to explain why one was born what he was and the working of the law of karma. Rao found it boring also: he was familiar with that kind of moralizing and philosophy. It was not four yet; the reading was over too soon. He found an unfilled half-hour between the newspaper reading and his

usual time for the evening outing. He rose from the chair, neatly
folded the newspaper and put it away on the little stool outside
his door, and gently shut and bolted the door—noiselessly, because if they heard him shut the door, they would come up and
caution him, "Don't bolt," out of fear that if he fell dead they
might have to break the door open. Others were obsessed with
the idea of *his* death as if they were all immortals!

He unlocked the cupboard and stood for a moment gazing at
the papers tied into neat bundles—all the records of his official
career from the start to his "voluntary retirement" were there on
the top shelf, in dusty and yellowing paper: he had shut the
cupboard doors tight, yet somehow fine dust seeped in and settled on everything. He dared not touch anything for fear of
soiling his fingers and catching a cold. He must get someone to
destroy them, best to put them in a fire; but whom could he
trust? He hated the idea of anyone reading those memos from
the government in the latter days of his service—he'd prefer
people not to know the official mess and those threats of inquiries
before he quit the service. The Secretary to the Government was
a demon out to get his blood—inspired by anonymous letters
and backbiters. Only one man had stood by him—his first assistant, wished he could remember his name or whereabouts—
good fellow; if he were available he'd set him to clean and arrange his almirah and burn the papers: he'd be dependable, and
would produce the ash if asked. But who was he? He patted his
forehead as if to jerk the memory-machine into action. . . . And
then his eyes roved down to the next shelf; he ran his fingers
over them lovingly—all documents relating to his property and
their disposal after his death. No one in the house could have
any idea of it or dare come near them. He must get the lawyer-
man (what was his name again?) and closet himself with him
someday. He was probably also dead. Not a soul seemed to be
left in town. . . . Anyway, must try to send someone to fetch
him if he was alive, it was to be done secretly. How? Somehow.

His eyes traveled to a shelf with an assortment of packets

containing receipts, bills and several diaries. He had kept a diary regularly for several years, recording a bit of daily observation or event on each page. He always bought the same brand of diary, called "Matchless"—of convenient size, ruled pages, with a flap that could be buttoned so that no one could casually open its pages and read its contents. The Matchless Stationery Mart off the main market manufactured it. On the last day of every December he would stop by for a copy costing four rupees—rather expensive but worth the price . . . more often than not the man would not take money for it, as he'd seek some official favor worth much more. Rao was not the sort to mind dispensing his official favors if it helped some poor soul. There was a stack of thirty old diaries in there (at some point in his life, he had abandoned the practice), which contained the gist of all his day-to-day life and thought: that again was something, an offering for the God of Fire before his death. He stood ruminating at the sight of the diaries. He pulled out one from the stack at random, wiped the thin layer of dust with a towel, went back to his chair and turned over the leaves casually. The diary was fifty-one years old. After glancing through some pages, he found it difficult to read his own close calligraphy in black ink and decided to put it back, as it was time to prepare for his walk. However, he said to himself, "Just a minute. Let me see what I did on this date, on the same day, so long ago . . ." He looked at the calendar on the wall. The date was the twentieth of March. He opened the diary and leafed through the earlier pages, marveling at the picture they presented of his early life: what a lot of activities morning till night, connected with the family, office and personal pursuits! His eyes smarted; he skipped longer passages and concentrated on the briefer ones. On the same day fifty-one years ago—the page contained only four lines, which read: "Too lenient with S. She deserves to be taught a lesson. . . ." This triggered a memory, and he could almost hear the echo of his own shouting at somebody, and the next few lines indicated the course of action: "Thrashed her soundly for her own good and

left. Will not see her again. . . . How can I accept the responsibility? She must have had an affair—after all a D.G.* Wish I
had locked her in before leaving." He studied this entry dispas-
sionately. He wondered who it was. The initial was not helpful.
He had known no one with a name beginning with *S*. Among
the ladies he had favored in his days, it could be anyone . . . but
names were elusive anyway.

With great effort, he kept concentrating on this problem. His
forehead throbbed with the strain of concentration. Of course,
the name eluded him, but the geography was coming back to
him in fragments. From Chettiar Stores . . . yes, he remembered
going up Market Road . . . and noted the light burning at the
shop facing him even at a late hour when returning home; that
meant he had gone in that narrow street branching off from
Market Road at that point, and that led to a parallel street . . .
from there one went on and on and twisted and turned in a maze
of bylanes and reached that house—a few steps up before tapping
gently on the rosewood door studded with brass stars, which
would open at once as if she was waiting on the other side; he'd
slip in and shut the door immediately, lest the neighbors be
watching, and retrace his steps at midnight. But he went there
only two days in the week, when he had free time. . . . Her
name, no, could not get it, but he could recollect her outline
rather hazily—fair, plump and loving and jasmine-smelling; he
was definite that the note referred to this woman, and not to
another one, also plump and jasmine-smelling somewhere not so
far away . . . he remembered slapping a face and flouncing out
in a rage. The young fellow was impetuous and hot-blooded . . .
must have been someone else, not himself in any sense. He could
not remember the house, but there used to be a coconut palm
and a well in the street in front of the house . . . it suddenly
flashed across his mind that the name of the street was Gokulam.

He rose and locked away the diary and secreted the key as

---

* Dancing Girl, a term denoting a public woman in those days.

usual, washed and dressed, and picked up his staff and umbrella and put on his sandals, with a quiet thrill. He had decided to venture beyond his orbit today, to go up and look for the ancient rosewood, brass-knobbed door, beside the coconut tree in that maze. From Chettiar Stores, his steps were bound to lead him on in the right direction, and if S. was there and happened to stand at the street door, he'd greet her . . . he might not be able to climb the four steps, but he'd offer her a small gift and greeting from the street. She could come down and take it. He should not have slapped her face . . . he had been impetuous and cruel. He should not have acted on jealousy . . . he was filled with remorse. After all, she must have shown him a great deal of kindness and given him pleasure ungrudgingly—otherwise, why would one stay until midnight?

While he tap-tapped his way out of his house now, someone in the hall inquired as usual, "Got your torch? Rather late today. Take care of yourself." He was excited. The shopman on the way, who habitually watched and commented, noted that the old man was moving rather jauntily today. "Oh, Respected One, good day to you, sir," said Mani from his cycle shop. "In such a hurry today? Walk slowly, sir, road is dug up everywhere." Rao looked up and permitted himself a gentle nod of recognition. He did not hear the message, but he could guess what Mani might be saying. He was fond of him—a great-grandson of that fellow who had studied with him at Albert Mission School. Name? As usual Mani's great-grandfather's name kept slipping away . . . he was some Ram or Shankar or something like that. Oh, what a teaser! He gave up and passed on. He kept himself to the edge as usual, slowed down his pace after Mani's advice; after all, his movement should not be noticeable, and it was not good to push oneself in that manner and pant with the effort.

At Jagan's Sweets, he halted. Some unknown fellow at the street counter. Children were crowding in front of the stall holding forth money and asking for this and that. They were blocking the way. He waited impatiently and tapped his staff noisily on the ground till the man at the counter looked up and asked, "Anything, Master?" Rao waved away the children with a flourish of his stick and approached the counter and feasted his eyes on the heaped-up sweets in different colors and shapes, and wished for a moment he could eat recklessly as he used to. But perhaps that'd cost him his life today—the secret of his survival being the spartan life he led, rigorously suppressing the cravings of the palate. He asked, "What's fresh today?" The man at the counter said, "We prepare everything fresh every day. Nothing is yesterday's . . ." Rao could only partly guess what he was saying but, without betraying himself, said, "Pack up *jilebi* for three rupees. . . ." He counted out the cash carefully, received the packet of *jilebi,* held it near his nostrils (the smell of food would not hurt, and there was no medical advice against it), for a moment relishing its rose-scented flavor; and was on his way again. Arriving at the point of Chettiar Stores, he paused and looked up at his right—yes, that street was still there as he had known it . . .

Noticing him hesitating there, the shopman hailed from his shop, "Oh, Grand Master, you want anything?" He felt annoyed. Why couldn't they leave him alone? And then a young shop assistant came out to take his order. Rao looked down at him and asked, pointing at the cross street, "Where does it lead?"

"To the next street," the boy said, and that somehow satisfied him. The boy asked, "What can I get you?"

"Oh, will no one leave me alone?" Rao thought with irritation. They seemed to assume that he needed something all the time. He hugged the packet of sweets close to his chest, along with the umbrella slung on the crook of his arm. The boy seemed to be bent on selling him something. And so he said, "Have you sandalwood soap?" He remembered that S., or whoever it was, used to be fond of it. The boy got it for him with alacrity. Its fragrance brought back some old memories. He had thought there was a scent of jasmine about S., but he realized now that it must have been that of sandalwood. He smelled it nostalgically before thrusting it into his pocket. "Anything else, sir?" asked the boy. "No, you may go," and he crossed Market Road over to the other side.

Trusting his instinct to guide him, he proceeded along the cross street ahead of Chettiar Stores. It led to another street running parallel, where he took a turn to his left on an impulse, and then again to his right into a lane, and then left, and then about-turn—but there was no trace of Gokulam Street. As he tap-tapped along, he noticed a cobbler on the roadside, cleared his throat, struck his staff on the ground to attract attention and asked, "Here, which way to Gokulam Street?" At first, the cobbler shook his head, then, to get rid of the inquirer, pointed vaguely in some direction and resumed his stitching. "Is there a coconut tree in this street?" The other once again pointed along the road. Rao felt indignant. "Haughty beggar," he muttered. "In those days I'd have . . ." He moved on, hoping he'd come across the landmark. He stopped a couple of others to ask the same question, and that did not help. No coconut tree anywhere. He was sure that it was somewhere here that he used to come, but everything was changed. All the generations of men and women who could have known Gokulam Street and the coconut tree were dead—new generations around here, totally oblivious of the past. He was a lone survivor.

He moved cautiously now, as the sun was going down. He became rather nervous and jabbed his staff down at each step, afraid of stumbling into a hole. It was a strain moving in this fashion, so slow and careful, and he began to despair that he'd ever reach the Market Road again. He began to feel anxious, regretted this expedition. The family would blame him if he should have a mishap. Somehow he felt more disturbed at the thought of their resentment than of his own possible suffering. But he kept hobbling along steadily. Some passersby paused to stare at him and comment on his perambulation. At some point, his staff seemed to stab through a soft surface; at the same moment a brown mongrel, which had lain curled up in dust, in perfect camouflage, sprang up with a piercing howl; Rao instinctively jumped, as he had not done for decades, luckily without falling down, but the packet of *jilebi* flew from his grip and landed in front of the mongrel, who picked it up and trotted away, wagging his tail in gratitude. Rao looked after the dog helplessly and resumed his journey homeward. Brooding over it, he commented to himself, "Who knows, S. is perhaps in this incarnation now. . . ."

An Astrologer's
Day

⌘

Punctually at midday he opened his bag and spread out his professional equipment, which consisted of a dozen cowrie shells, a square piece of cloth with obscure mystic charts on it, a notebook, and a bundle of palmyra writing. His forehead was resplendent with sacred ash and vermilion, and his eyes sparkled with a sharp abnormal gleam which was really an outcome of a continual searching look for customers, but which his simple clients took to be a prophetic light and felt comforted. The power of his eyes was considerably enhanced by their position— placed as they were between the painted forehead and the dark whiskers which streamed down his cheeks: even a half-wit's eyes would sparkle in such a setting. To crown the effect he wound a saffron-colored turban around his head. This color scheme never failed. People were attracted to him as bees are attracted to cosmos or dahlia stalks. He sat under the boughs of a spreading tamarind tree which flanked a path running through the town hall park. It was a remarkable place in many ways: a surging crowd was always moving up and down this narrow road morning till night. A variety of trades and occupations was represented all along its way: medicine sellers, sellers of stolen hardware and junk, magicians, and, above all, an auctioneer of cheap cloth, who created enough din all day to attract the whole town. Next to him in vociferousness came a vendor of fried groundnut, who gave his ware a fancy name each day, calling it "Bombay Ice Cream" one day, and on the next "Delhi Almond," and on the third "Raja's Delicacy," and so on and so forth, and people flocked to him. A considerable portion of this crowd dallied before the astrologer too. The astrologer transacted his business by the light of a flare which crackled and smoked up above the groundnut heap nearby. Half the enchantment of the place was due to the fact that it did not have the benefit of municipal lighting. The place was lit up by shop lights. One or two had hissing gaslights, some had naked flares stuck on poles, some were lit up by old cycle lamps, and one or two, like the astrologer's, managed without lights of their own. It was a bewildering crisscross of light rays and moving shadows. This suited the astrologer very well, for the simple reason that he had not in the least intended to be an astrologer when he began life; and he knew no more of what was going to happen to others than he knew what was going to happen to himself next minute. He was as much a stranger to the stars as were his innocent customers. Yet he said things which pleased and astonished everyone: that was more a matter of study, practice, and shrewd guesswork. All the same, it was as much an honest man's labor as any other, and he deserved the wages he carried home at the end of a day.

He had left his village without any previous thought or plan. If he had continued there he would have carried on the work of his forefathers—namely, tilling the land, living, marrying, and ripening in his cornfield and ancestral home. But that was not to be. He had to leave home without telling anyone, and he could not rest till he left it behind a couple of hundred miles. To a villager it is a great deal, as if an ocean flowed between.

He had a working analysis of mankind's troubles: marriage, money, and the tangles of human ties. Long practice had sharpened his perception. Within five minutes he understood what was wrong. He charged three paise per question, never opened his mouth till the other had spoken for at least ten minutes, which provided him enough stuff for a dozen answers and advices. When he told the person before him, gazing at his palm, "In many ways you are not getting the fullest results for your efforts," nine out of ten were disposed to agree with him. Or he questioned: "Is there any woman in your family, maybe even a distant relative, who is not well disposed towards you?" Or he gave an analysis of character: "Most of your troubles are due to your nature. How can you be otherwise with Saturn where he is? You have an impetuous nature and a rough exterior." This endeared him to their hearts immediately, for even the mildest of us loves to think that he has a forbidding exterior.

The nuts vendor blew out his flare and rose to go home. This was a signal for the astrologer to bundle up too, since it left him in darkness except for a little shaft of green light which strayed in from somewhere and touched the ground before him. He picked up his cowrie shells and paraphernalia and was putting them back into his bag when the green shaft of light was blotted out; he looked up and saw a man standing before him. He sensed a possible client and said, "You look so careworn. It will do you good to sit down for a while and chat with me." The other grumbled some reply vaguely. The astrologer pressed his invitation; whereupon the other thrust his palm under his nose, saying, "You call yourself an astrologer?" The astrologer felt challenged and said, tilting the other's palm towards the green shaft of light, "Yours is a nature . . ." "Oh, stop that," the other said. "Tell me something worthwhile. . . ."

Our friend felt piqued. "I charge only three paise per question, and what you get ought to be good enough for your money. . . ." At this the other withdrew his arm, took out an anna, and flung it out to him, saying, "I have some questions to ask. If I prove you are bluffing, you must return that anna to me with interest."

"If you find my answers satisfactory, will you give me five rupees?"

"No."

"Or will you give me eight annas?"

"All right, provided you give me twice as much if you are wrong," said the stranger. This pact was accepted after a little further argument. The astrologer sent up a prayer to heaven as the other lit a cheroot. The astrologer caught a glimpse of his face by the match light. There was a pause as cars hooted on the road, jutka drivers swore at their horses, and the babble of the crowd agitated the semidarkness of the park. The other sat down, sucking his cheroot, puffing out, sat there ruthlessly. The astrologer felt very uncomfortable. "Here, take your anna back. I am not used to such challenges. It is late for me today. . . ." He made preparations to bundle up. The other held his wrist and said, "You can't get out of it now. You dragged me in while I was passing." The astrologer shivered in his grip; and his voice shook and became faint. "Leave me today. I will speak to you tomorrow." The other thrust his palm in his face and said, "Challenge is challenge. Go on." The astrologer proceeded with his throat drying up, "There is a woman . . ."

"Stop," said the other. "I don't want all that. Shall I succeed in my present search or not? Answer this and go. Otherwise I will not let you go till you disgorge all your coins." The astrologer muttered a few incantations and replied, "All right. I will speak. But will you give me a rupee if what I say is convincing? Otherwise I will not open my mouth, and you may do what you like." After a good deal of haggling the other agreed. The astrologer said, "You were left for dead. Am I right?"

"Ah, tell me more."

"A knife has passed through you once?" said the astrologer.

"Good fellow!" He bared his chest to show the scar. "What else?"

"And then you were pushed into a well nearby in the field. You were left for dead."

"I should have been dead if some passerby had not chanced to peep into the well," exclaimed the other, overwhelmed by enthusiasm. "When shall I get at him?" he asked, clenching his fist.

"In the next world," answered the astrologer. "He died four months ago in a far-off town. You will never see any more of him." The other groaned on hearing it. The astrologer proceeded:

"Guru Nayak—"

"You know my name!" the other said, taken aback.

"As I know all other things. Guru Nayak, listen carefully to what I have to say. Your village is two days' journey due north of this town. Take the next train and begone. I see once again great danger to your life if you go from home." He took out a pinch of sacred ash and held it to him. "Rub it on your forehead and go home. Never travel southward again, and you will live to be a hundred."

"Why should I leave home again?" the other said reflectively. "I was only going away now and then to look for him and to choke out his life if I met him." He shook his head regretfully. "He has escaped my hands. I hope at least he died as he deserved." "Yes," said the astrologer. "He was crushed under a lorry." The other looked gratified to hear it.

The place was deserted by the time the astrologer picked up his articles and put them into his bag. The green shaft was also gone, leaving the place in darkness and silence. The stranger had gone off into the night, after giving the astrologer a handful of coins.

It was nearly midnight when the astrologer reached home. His wife was waiting for him at the door and demanded an explanation. He flung the coins at her and said, "Count them. One man gave all that."

"Twelve and a half annas," she said, counting. She was overjoyed. "I can buy some jaggery and coconut tomorrow. The child has been asking for sweets for so many days now. I will prepare some nice stuff for her."

"The swine has cheated me! He promised me a rupee," said the astrologer. She looked up at him. "You look worried. What is wrong?"

"Nothing."

After dinner, sitting on the pyol, he told her, "Do you know a great load is gone from me today? I thought I had the blood of a man on my hands all these years. That was the reason why I ran away from home, settled here, and married you. He is alive."

She gasped. "You tried to kill!"

"Yes, in our village, when I was a silly youngster. We drank, gambled, and quarreled badly one day—why think of it now? Time to sleep," he said, yawning, and stretched himself on the pyol.

The Blind
Dog

∽∾

It was not a very impressive or high-class dog; it was one of those commonplace dogs one sees everywhere—color of white and dust, tail mutilated at a young age by God knows whom, born in the street, and bred on the leavings and garbage of the marketplace. He had spotty eyes and undistinguished carriage and needless pugnacity. Before he was two years old he had earned the scars of a hundred fights on his body. When he needed rest on hot afternoons he lay curled up under the culvert at the eastern gate of the market. In the evenings he set out on his daily rounds, loafed in the surrounding streets and lanes, engaged himself in skirmishes, picked up edibles on the roadside, and was back at the market gate by nightfall.

This life went on for three years. And then occurred a change in his life. A beggar, blind of both eyes, appeared at the market gate. An old woman led him up there early in the morning, seated him at the gate, and came up again at midday with some food, gathered his coins, and took him home at night.

The dog was sleeping nearby. He was stirred by the smell of

food. He got up, came out of his shelter, and stood before the blind man, wagging his tail and gazing expectantly at the bowl, as he was eating his sparse meal. The blind man swept his arms about and asked, "Who is there?" At which the dog went up and licked his hand. The blind man stroked its coat gently tail to ear and said, "What a beauty you are. Come with me—" He threw a handful of food which the dog ate gratefully. It was perhaps an auspicious moment for starting a friendship. They met every day there, and the dog cut off much of its rambling to sit up beside the blind man and watch him receive alms morning to evening. In course of time observing him, the dog understood that the passersby must give a coin, and whoever went away without dropping a coin was chased by the dog; he tugged the edge of their clothes with his teeth and pulled them back to the old man at the gate and let go only after something was dropped in his bowl. Among those who frequented this place was a village urchin, who had the mischief of a devil in him. He liked to tease the blind man by calling him names and by trying to pick up the coins in his bowl. The blind man helplessly shouted and cried and whirled his staff. On Thursdays this boy appeared at the gate, carrying on his head a basket loaded with cucumber or plantain. Every Thursday afternoon it was a crisis in the blind man's life. A seller of bright-colored but doubtful perfumes with his wares mounted on a wheeled platform, a man who spread out cheap storybooks on a gunnysack, another man who carried colored ribbons on an elaborate frame—these were the people who usually gathered under the same arch. On a Thursday when the young man appeared at the eastern gate one of them remarked, "Blind fellow! Here comes your scourge—"

"Oh, God, is this Thursday?" he wailed. He swept his arms about and called, "Dog, dog, come here, where are you?" He made the peculiar noise which brought the dog to his side. He stroked his head and muttered, "Don't let that little rascal—" At this very moment the boy came up with a leer on his face.

"Blind man! Still pretending you have no eyes. If you are

really blind, you should not know this either—" He stopped, his hand moving towards the bowl. The dog sprang on him and snapped his jaws on the wrist. The boy extricated his hand and ran for his life. The dog bounded up behind him and chased him out of the market.

"See the mongrel's affection for this old fellow," marveled the perfume vendor.

One evening at the usual time the old woman failed to turn up, and the blind man waited at the gate, worrying as the evening grew into night. As he sat fretting there, a neighbor came up and said, "Sami, don't wait for the old woman. She will not come again. She died this afternoon—"

The blind man lost the only home he had, and the only person who cared for him in this world. The ribbon vendor suggested, "Here, take this white tape"—he held a length of the white cord which he had been selling—"I will give this to you free of cost. Tie it to the dog and let him lead you about if he is really so fond of you—"

Life for the dog took a new turn now. He came to take the place of the old woman. He lost his freedom completely. His world came to be circumscribed by the limits of the white cord which the ribbon vendor had spared. He had to forget wholesale all his old life—all his old haunts. He simply had to stay on forever at the end of that string. When he saw other dogs, friends or foes, instinctively he sprang up, tugging the string, and this invariably earned him a kick from his master. "Rascal, want to tumble me down—have sense—" In a few days the dog learned to discipline his instinct and impulse. He ceased to take notice of other dogs, even if they came up and growled at his side. He lost his own orbit of movement and contact with his fellow creatures.

To the extent of this loss his master gained. He moved about as he had never moved in his life. All day he was on his legs, led by the dog. With the staff in one hand and the dog lead in the other he moved out of his home—a corner in a choultry verandah a few yards off the market: he had moved in there after the old woman's death. He started out early in the day. He found that he could treble his income by moving about instead of staying in one place. He moved down the choultry street, and wherever he heard people's voices he stopped and held out his hands for alms. Shops, schools, hospitals, hotels—he left nothing out. He gave a tug when he wanted the dog to stop, and shouted like a bullock driver when he wanted him to move on. The dog protected his feet from going into pits, or stumping against steps or stones, and took him up inch by inch on safe ground and steps. For this sight people gave coins and helped him. Children gathered around him and gave him things to eat. A dog is essentially an active creature who punctuates his hectic rounds with well-defined periods of rest. But now this dog (henceforth to be known as Tiger) had lost all rest. He had rest only when the old man sat down somewhere. At night the old man slept with the cord turned around his finger. "I can't take chances with you—," he said. A great desire to earn more money than ever before seized his master, so that he felt any resting a waste of opportunity, and the dog had to be continuously on his feet. Sometimes his legs refused to move. But if he slowed down even slightly his master goaded him on fiercely with his staff. The dog whined and groaned under this thrust. "Don't whine, you rascal. Don't I give you your food? You want to loaf, do you?" swore the blind man. The dog lumbered up and down and round and round the market place on slow steps, tied down to the blind tyrant. Long after the traffic at the market ceased, you could hear the night stabbed by the far-off wail of the tired dog. It lost its original appearance. As months rolled on, bones stuck up at his haunches and ribs were reliefed through his fading coat.

The ribbon seller, the novel vendor, and the perfumer observed it one evening, when business was slack, and held a conference among themselves: "It rends my heart to see that poor dog slaving. Can't we do something?" The ribbon seller remarked, "That rascal has started lending money for interest—I heard it from that fruit seller— He is earning more than he needs. He has become a very devil for money—" At this point the perfumer's eyes caught the scissors dangling from the ribbon rack. "Give it here," he said and moved on with the scissors in hand.

The blind man was passing in front of the eastern gate. The dog was straining the lead. There was a piece of bone lying on the way and the dog was straining to pick it up. The lead became taut and hurt the blind man's hand, and he tugged the string and kicked till the dog howled. It howled, but could not pass the bone lightly; it tried to make another dash for it. The blind man was heaping curses on it. The perfumer stepped up, applied the scissors, and snipped the cord. The dog bounced off and picked up the bone. The blind man stopped dead where he stood, with the other half of the string dangling in his hand. "Tiger! Tiger! Where are you?" he cried. The perfumer moved away quietly, muttering, "You heartless devil! You will never get at him again! He has his freedom!" The dog went off at top speed. He nosed about the ditches happily, hurled himself on other dogs, and ran round and round the fountain in the market square barking, his eyes sparkling with joy. He returned to his favorite haunts and hung about the butcher's shop, tea stall, and the bakery.

The ribbon vendor and his two friends stood at the market gate and enjoyed the sight immensely as the blind man struggled to find his way about. He stood rooted to the spot waving his stick; he felt as if he were hanging in midair. He was wailing. "Oh, where is my dog? Where is my dog? Won't someone give him back to me? I will murder it when I get at it again!" He groped about, tried to cross the road, came near being run over by a dozen vehicles at different points, tumbled and struggled and gasped. "He'd deserve it if he was run over, this heartless blackguard—," they said, observing him. However, the old man struggled through and with the help of someone found his way back to his corner in the choultry verandah and sank down on his gunnysack bed, half faint with the strain of his journey.

He was not seen for ten days, fifteen days, and twenty days. Nor was the dog seen anywhere. They commented among themselves. "The dog must be loafing over the whole earth, free and happy. The beggar is perhaps gone forever—" Hardly was this sentence uttered when they heard the familiar tap-tap of the blind man's staff. They saw him again coming up the pavement—led by the dog. "Look! Look!" they cried. "He has again got at it and tied it up—" The ribbon seller could not contain himself. He ran up and said, "Where have you been all these days?"

"Know what happened!" cried the blind man. "This dog ran away. I should have died in a day or two, confined to my corner, no food, not an anna to earn—imprisoned in my corner. I should have perished if it continued for another day— But this thing returned—"

"When? When?"

"Last night. At midnight as I slept in bed, he came and licked my face. I felt like murdering him. I gave him a blow which he will never forget again," said the blind man. "I forgave him— after all, a dog! He loafed as long as he could pick up some rubbish to eat on the road, but real hunger has driven him back to me, but he will not leave me again. See! I have got this—" and he shook the lead: it was a steel chain this time.

Once again there was the dead, despairing look in the dog's eyes. "Go on, you fool," cried the blind man, shouting like an ox driver. He tugged the chain, poked with the stick, and the dog moved away on slow steps. They stood listening to the tap-tap going away.

"Death alone can help that dog," cried the ribbon seller, looking after it with a sigh. "What can we do with a creature who returns to his doom with such a free heart?"

Second
Opinion

I stole in like a cat, unlocked my door, struck a match and lit a kerosene lantern. I had to make sure that I did not wake up my mother. Like a hunter stalking in a jungle, who is careful not to crackle the dry leaves underfoot, I took stealthy steps along the front passage to my room at the other end past a window in the hall. The moment I shut the door of my cubicle, I was lord of my own universe—which seemed to me boundless, although enclosing a space of only eight feet by ten. The sloping roof tiles harbored vermin of every type, cobwebs hung down like festoons, lizards ensconced behind ancient calendars on the walls darted up and down ambushing little creatures that crawled about, urging them on their evolutionary path. Every gnat at death was reborn a better creature, and ultimately, after a series of lives, became an ape and a human being, who merged ultimately in a supreme indivisible godhood. With such an outlook, a result of miscellaneous, half-understood reading, there could be no place for a spray or duster! I never allowed anyone to clean my room.

I never touched the brass vessel left outside my door, containing my supper, unless I felt hungry. How could I ever feel hunger while all day I had been sipping coffee at the Boardless —although I didn't have to spend a paisa on it. It just flowed my way. Varma generally ordered a cup for himself every two hours to make sure that his restaurant's reputation was not being unmade in the kitchen. Invariably, he ordered for me, too, not only as an act of hospitality, but as a means of obtaining a "second opinion," to quote my doctor. I'll deviate a little to describe Dr. Kishen of the M.M.C. (Malgudi Medical Center). Those days when I believed in being useful at home, I used to take my mother, off and on, to see the doctor. Whatever disadvantage we might have had in inheriting that rambling old house, its location was certainly an asset. Kabir Street, running parallel to Market Road, had numerous connecting lanes; and one could always step across to reach the doctor or the vegetable market. M.M.C. was centrally situated, as Dr. Kishen never failed to mention while examining your tongue or chest, when you couldn't enter into an argument. "Do you see why there is greater rush here than at other places? It's because if you measure, you will find this is equidistant from anywhere in this city . . ."

After his equidistant observation, he'd invariably conclude an examination with ". . . such is my diagnosis, go for a second opinion if you like . . ." Varma was also likeminded, I suppose. He seemed to be very unsure of the quality of his own coffee even after tasting it, and always wanted my confirmation. And then in the course of the day others dropped in, the six o'clock group, which occupied a corner in the hall and over coffee exchanged all the town gossip, and always insisted that I join them, with the result that when I came home at night, I had no appetite for the contents of the brass tiffin-box.

Early morning a young servant came to take away the vessel for washing. She was about ten years old, with sparkling eyes set in tan-colored rotund cheeks, with whitest teeth, and a pigtail terminating in a red ribbon. I was fond of her, and wished I were a painter and could execute a world's masterpiece on canvas. She knew that she was my favorite and could approach my room with impunity. She would lift the vessel and cry out, "Oh, untouched?"

"Hush," I'd say, "not so loudly. . . ." She would smile mischievously and say, "Oh, oh!" and I knew the next minute it would become world news. In a short while my mother would appear at my door to demand an explanation, and to say, "If this sort of thing goes on, I don't know where it is going to take us . . . I sliced cucumber specially for you, and you don't hesitate to throw it away. . . . At least mention your likes and dislikes. You won't do even that, but just reject." I didn't mind what she said as long as she remained on the threshold and did not step into my room. I sat on my mat, leaning back on the wall and listened impassively to whatever she said, reflecting how difficult it was to practice one's philosophy of detachment; Siddhartha did wisely in slipping away at midnight when others were asleep, to seek illumination. In my own way I, too, was seeking illumination, but continued to remain in bondage. The common roof, the married state (ultimately, of course), every kind of inheritance and every bit of possession acted as a deadly tentacle. Following this realization, the first thing I abandoned was furniture and, in a manner of speaking, also the common roof of the main house, since my cubicle was detached. It was not at all easy.

Our father's house had many mansions and apparently was designed for a milling crowd. Our front door opened on Kabir Street and our back door on the Sarayu River, which flowed down rather tamely at some distance from our house although you could hear it roaring along wildly in spate when it rained on Mempi Hills. It was all right as a vision to open the little door at our backyard, and sit at the edge of the flowing river to listen to its music; but now the back door had practically sealed itself firmly along the grooves with the dust and rust of decades, and the river had become inaccessible, owing to thorns and wild vegetation choking the path. I have heard my mother describe how in her younger days they had treated the river as a part of the home, every house in Kabir Street having access to it through a back door, how they bathed and washed and took water in pots, and how the men sat on its sandbank at dusk and dawn for their prayers. That was before wells were dug in every house. "The river used to be much nearer to us in those days," she would assert; "it's somehow moved away so far out. When wells were dug people became lazy and neglected the river; and no wonder she has drawn herself away; though in those days you could touch the water if you stretched your arm through the back door. But have you noticed how at Ellaman Street, even today, the river nestles closer to the houses, since they care for it and cherish it. They have built steps and treat her with respect. They never fail to light and float the lamps in Karthik month . . . whereas in our street people are lazy and indifferent. In those days, I begged your father not to dig a well, which encouraged others also . . ." She could never forgive the well diggers.

"But, Mother, it's the same water of the river that we are getting in the well . . ."

"What does that mean? How?" And then I had to explain to her the concept of the underground water table; carried away by its poetry and philosophy, I would conclude, "You see, under the earth it's all one big sheet of water, perhaps hundreds or even thousands of cubic feet, all connected; a big connected water sheet, just as you say Brahman is all-pervading in this form and that in the universe—" She would cut me short with "I don't know what has come over you, I talk of a simple matter like water and you go on talking like a prophet . . ."

In those days I spent a great deal of my time sitting in the back portion of our home, which had an open courtyard with a corridor running along the kitchen, store and dining room, where my mother spent most of her time. In those days I had nothing much to do except sit down, leaning on the pillar, and attempt to enlighten my mother's mind on modern ways. But she was impervious to my theories. We were poles apart. Not only on the river, but on every question, she held a view which, as a rational being, I could never accept.

Sometimes I felt harassed. Mother would not leave me in peace. I had my little cubicle in the western wing of the house across the hall. At the other end used to be my father's room. He would sit there all day, as I thought, poring over books, of philosophy, one would suspect, considering the array of volumes on the shelves around him along the wall, in Sanskrit, Tamil and English; the *Upanishads,* with commentaries and interpretations by Shankara, Ramanuja and all the "world teachers." There were books on Christianity and Plato and Socrates in gilt-edged volumes. I had no means of verifying how much use he made of them. His room was out of bounds to me. He always sat cross-legged on the floor, before a sloping teakwood desk, turning over the leaves of an enormous tome; in my state of ignorance, I imagined that the treasury of philosophy at his elbow was being exploited. But it was only later in life that I learned that the mighty tomes on his desk were ledgers and all his hours were spent in adding, subtracting and multiplying figures. He had multifarious accounts to keep—payments to men from the village cultivating our paddy fields; loans to others on promissory notes; trust funds of some temple or a minor. All kinds of persons sat patiently on the pyol of the house, and entered his room when summoned; there would follow much talking, signing of papers and counting of cash taken out of the squat wrought-iron safe with imposing handles and a tricky locking system. It stood there three-foot high, and seemed to have become a part of my father's personality. Out of it flowed cash and into it went documents. It was only after my father's death that I managed to open the safe, after a good deal of trial and error. While examining the papers I discovered that the library of philosophy had been hypothecated to him by some poor academic soul who could never redeem it. But Father had never disturbed the loaded shelves, except for dusting the books, since he wanted them to be in good condition when redeemed by their hapless owner. However, it was a godsend for me. I always sneaked into his room to look at their titles when he was away at the well for his bath, which kept him off long enough for me to examine the books. For a long time he would not let me handle them. "You wouldn't know what they say," he said. . . . At a later stage he relented, and allowed me to take one book at a time, with warnings and admonitions. "Don't fold the covers back, but only half-open them, so that their backs are not creased—the books have to be returned in good condition, remember."

I selected, as he ordered, one book at a time. I loved the weight, feel and scent of every volume—some of them in a uniform series called the "Library of World Thought." I sat up in my room leaning on a roll of bedding and pored over each volume. I cannot pretend that I understood everything I read. I had had no academic training or discipline, not having gone beyond Matriculation, which I never passed, even after three attempts. After Father's death, I gave up, realizing suddenly it was silly to want to pass an examination. Who were they to test and declare me fit or unfit—for what? When this thought dawned, I stopped in my tracks in my fourth effort. I bundled and threw up into the loft all my class notes and examination books.

The loft was in the central hall, a wide wooden panel below the ceiling. From a proper distance, aimed correctly, you could fling anything into it, to oblivion. One had to go up a ladder to reach it, and then move around hunchback fashion to pick up something or for spring cleaning. But for years no one had been up in the loft, even though it continued to get filled from time to time. In those days, my mother could always find some sturdy-limbed helper ready to go up to sweep and dust or pick up a vessel (all the utensils of brass and bronze she had brought in as a young bride decades ago were stored in the loft). Besides these, there were ledgers, disused lamps, broken furniture pieces, clothes in a trunk, mats, mattresses, blankets and what not. I dreaded her cleaning-up moods, as she always expected my participation. For some time I cooperated with her, but gradually began to avoid the task. She would often complain within my hearing, "When *he* was alive, how much service he could command within the twinkling of an eye . . . I had to breathe ever so lightly what I needed and he would accomplish it." When she stood there thus, with her arms akimbo and lecturing, I generally retreated. I shut the door of my room and held my breath until I could hear her footsteps die away. She was too restless to stay in one place, but moved about, peeping into various corners of the house. She would suddenly suspect that the servant girl might have fallen asleep somewhere in that vast acreage and go on a hunt for her. She was in a state of anxiety over one thing or another; if it was not the servant, it would be about the well in the backyard; she must run up to it and see if the rope over the pulley was properly drawn away and secured to the post, or whether it had slipped into the well through the girl's carelessness. "If the rope falls into the well . . . ," and she would go into a detailed account of the consequences; how there was no one around, as they had had in the old days, who would run up and get a new rope or fetch the diver with his hooks and harpoons to retrieve the rope.

It was a sore trial for me each day. I could not stand her. Her voice got on my nerves while she harangued, reprimanded or bawled at the servant girl. I shut and bolted the door of my room. I wanted peace of mind to go through the book in hand, *Life of Ramakrishna*, passages from Max Müller, Plato's *Republic* —it was a privilege to be able to be a participant in their thoughts. I felt thrilled to be battling with their statements and wresting a meaning out of them. Whatever they might have meant, they all seemed to hold forth the glory of the soul, which made me survey myself top to toe and say, "Sambu, who are you? You are not the creature with a prickly stubble on the chin,

scar on the kneecap, with toenail splitting and turning blue . . .
you are actually made of finer stuff." I imagined myself able to
steer my way through the traffic of constellations in the firmament, in the interstellar spaces, and along the Milky Way; it
enabled me to overlook the drab walls around me and the un-
inspiring spectacles outside the window opening on Kabir Street.
Into this, shattering my vision, would come hard knocks on my
door. Mother would be standing there crying, "Why do you have
to close this door? Who is there in this house to disturb you or
anyone? Not like those days . . . Whom are you trying to shut
out?" I could only look on passively. I was aware that she was
ready for a battle, but I had not based my life on a war-footing
yet. She looked terrifying with her gray unkempt hair standing
like a halo around her head, her eyes spitting fire. I felt nervous,
the slightest wrong move could spark off a conflagration.

I don't know what came over her six months after her husband's death. At the first shock of bereavement she remained
subdued. For months and months she spoke little, spent much
of her time in the puja room, meditating and chanting holy verse
in an undertone. She went about the business of running the
house without any fuss, never noticing anything too closely. She
left me very much alone, though hinting from time to time that
I should study and pass my B.A. In those days, some of the
flotsam and jetsam who had been thriving indefinitely on my
father's hospitality were still occupying various portions of my
house. As long as they were all there, Mother kept herself in the
background and behaved like a gentle person. Probably she had
a code as to how she should behave in the presence of hangers-
on. When I got the last of them out—that was the mad engineer, who had sought shelter from his brothers scheming to
poison him and who finally had to be bundled off with the help
of neighbors and the driver of the ambulance van—she began
to breathe freely and probably felt that the stage had been
cleared for her benefit. Following it, her first hostile act was to
shut my father's room and put a lock on the door. I was aghast

when I realized that access to the books was cut off. As she spent most of her time in the middle block of the house, I had to be running after her, begging for the key if I wished to see a book. At first, she would not yield. "Read your schoolbooks first and pass your examination," she said. "Time enough for you to read those big books, after you get your degree. Anyway, you won't understand them. Do you know what your father used to say? He said that he could not make them out himself! What do you say to that?"

"I don't doubt it. Did he at any time try? He always sat with his back to them." She grew angry at this remark. "Don't laugh at your elders, who have nurtured you," she would say and move off dramatically to end the conversation. I had to follow her, begging, "The key, please, Mother . . ." I was young enough in those days not to feel discouraged. Finally she would say, "Don't mess up the books. You are so persistent—if you could have shown half this persistence in your studies!" I hated her at such moments. Why should she attach importance to examinations and degrees? Traditional and habitual manner of thought. Her sister's sons at Madras were all graduates, and she felt humiliated in family circles when they compared my performance. Before I finally gave up studies, whenever the Matriculation results were announced she would scream, "You have failed again! You fool! You are a disgrace . . ."

I would shout back, "What can I do? You think marks are to be bought in the market?"

After some more exchanges of the same kind, she would break down and have a quiet cry in a corner, abandoning for the day her normal activities, not even lighting the lamp in the puja room in the evening. A deadly gloom would descend on the house, everything still and silent, no life stirring even slightly. We would become petrified figures in that vast house. I would feel upset and oppressed in this atmosphere and leave without a word, to seek some bright spots such as the town library, the marketplace, the college sports ground, and, more than any other place, the Boardless Hotel, to pass the time in agreeable company.

Instead of the dark house to which I usually sneaked back, today when I returned from the Boardless I found the light in the hall burning. I was puzzled. I went up a few steps in the direction of my room and stopped. I heard voices in the hall and a lot of conversation. My mother's voice was the loudest, sounded as spirited as in her younger days. She was saying, "He is not a bad boy, but likes to sound so. If we talk to him seriously, he'll certainly obey me." The other one was gruff-voiced and saying, "You should not have let him go his way at all; after all, young persons do not know what is good for them, it is for the elders to give them the necessary guidance." I was hesitating, wondering how to reach the door to my room, unlock it without being noticed. If they heard the click of the key, they were bound to turn their attention on me. My door was at the end of the verandah, and I could not possibly go past the window without being seen. I felt hunted. I could not go back to the Boardless. I quietly sat down on the pyol of the house, leaning against the pillar supporting the tiled roof, stretched my legs and resigned myself to staying there all night, since from the tenor of the dialogue going on, there was no indication it would ever cease. The gruff voice was saying, "What keeps him out so late?" My mother was saying, "Oh, this and that. He spends a lot of time at the library, reads so much!" I appreciated my mother for saying this. I never suspected that she had such a good opinion of me. What secret admiration she must be having—never showing any sign of it outside. It was a revelation to me. I almost felt like popping up and shouting, "Oh, Mother, how nice of you to think so well of me! Why could you not say so to me?" But I held myself back.

He asked, "What does he plan to do?"

"Oh!" she said, "he has some big plans, which he won't

talk about now. He is very deep and sensitive. His ambition is to be a man of learning. He spends much time with learned persons . . ."

"My daughter, you know, is also very learned. She reads books all the time . . ."

"Sambu has read through practically all the volumes that his father left for him in that room. Sometimes I just have to snatch the books from him and lock them away so that he may bathe and eat! I don't think even an M.A. has read so much!"

"I really do not worry what he will do in life, though holding some position or an office is the distinguishing mark of a man." He recited a Sanskrit line in support of this. "Let him not strain in any manner except to be a good husband. My daughter's share of the property . . ." Here he lowered his voice and they continued to talk in whispers.

At dawn my mother caught me asleep on the pyol when she came out to sweep the front steps and wash the threshold as others before her had been doing for one thousand years. She was aghast at seeing me stretched out there. At some part of the night I must have fallen asleep. I think they were passing on to some sort of reminiscences far into the night, and they were both convulsed with laughter at the memory of some ancient absurdity. I had never heard my mother laughing so much. She seemed to have preserved a hidden personality especially for the edification of her old relatives or associates, while she presented to me a grim, serious, director-general aspect. It was foolish and thoughtless of me to have lain there and got caught so easily. Luckily her guest had gone to the backyard for a bath and had not seen me. Otherwise he'd have suspected that I had come home drunk, and been abandoned by undesirable companions at our door. Ah, how I wish he had seen me in this condition, which would have been a corrective to all the bragging my mother had been indulging in about me. She hurriedly woke me up. "Sleeping in the street! What'll people think! Why didn't you go into your room? Did you return so late? What were you doing all the time?" There was panic in her tone, packed with suspicion that I must have been drinking and debauching—the talk of the town was the opening of a nightclub called Kismet somewhere in the New Extension, where the youth of the city were being lured. Someone must have gossiped about it within her hearing. I was only half-awake when she shook me and whispered, "Get into your room first—"

"Why?" I asked, sitting up.

"I do not want you to be seen here . . ."

"I found you talking to someone and so I . . ." I had no rational conclusion to my sentence.

She gripped my arm and pulled me up, probably convinced that I needed assistance. I made a dash for my door, shut myself in and immediately resumed my sleep, a part of my mind wondering whether I should not have said, "I was at Kismet . . ." I got up later than usual. There was no trace of the visitor of the night, which made me wonder if I had been having nightmares. "He left early to catch the bus," explained Mother when I was ready for coffee. I accepted her explanation in silence, refraining from asking further questions. I felt a premonition that some difficult time was ahead. We met at the middle courtyard as usual, where I accepted my coffee after a wash at the well. Normally we would exchange no words at this point; she would present a tumbler of coffee when I was seen at the kitchen door. There our contact would stop on most days, unless she had some special grievance to express, such as a demand for house tax or failure on the part of the grocer or the milk supplier. I'd generally listen passively, silently finish the coffee and pass on, bolt myself in, dress and make my exit by the verandah as unobtrusively as possible. But today, after coffee, she remarked, "The servant girl hasn't come yet. Of late she is getting notions about herself." I repressed my remarks, as my sympathies were all on the side of that cheerful little girl, who had to bear a lot of harsh treatment from her mistress. After this information Mother said, "Don't disappear, stay in . . ." and she allowed herself a mild smile; she seemed unusually affable; this combined with all the good things she had been saying last night bewildered me. Some transformation seemed to be taking place in her; it didn't suit her at all to wear a smile; it looked artificial and waxwork-like and toothy. I wished I could fathom her mind; the grimness and frown and growl were more appropriate for her face. I said, "I have some work to do and must go early."

"What work?" she asked with a mischievous twinkle in her eyes. I felt scared. There were a dozen excuses I could give; should I tell her about Varma's treasure hunt (on Mondays he brought a sheaf of planchette messages purporting to give directions for a buried treasure in the mountains and sought my interpretation of them), or the little note I had promised a college student on Jaina philosophy, or apt quotations for a municipal councillor's speech for some occasion. I was afraid my mother would pooh-pooh them, and so I just said, "I have many things to do—you wouldn't understand." Normally she would burst out, "Understand! How do you know? Have you tried? Your father never kept anything from me." But today she just said, "Very well, I don't want to bother you to tell me," with a mock-sadness in her voice. It was clear that she was continuing the goodwill she had exhibited last night before the stranger. I felt uneasy. She was playacting, for what purpose I could not guess.

Presently she followed me into my room and said, "You may go after listening to me. Your business can wait for a while." She sat down on my mat and invited me to sit beside her to listen attentively. I felt nervous. This was not her sitting hour; she'd be all over the place, sweeping, washing, cleaning and driving the girl about. But today what could be the important item of business, suspending all else?

It was not long in coming. "Do you know who has come?" I knew I was being pushed to the wall. Sitting so close to her made me uneasy. I felt embarrassed, especially when I noticed a strand of white beard on her chin. Was she aware of its existence? Ridiculous if she was going about, behaving as if it weren't there.

"Gray-beard loon . . ." A phrase emerged now out of the miasma of assorted reading of hypothecated property. I recollected her boasts before the visitor about my studious habits. After waiting for me to say something (luckily I was brooding over Shakes-peare's line—or was it Coleridge's?—otherwise I would have promptly said, "Some dark, hook-nosed fellow with a tuft—I couldn't care less who," every word of which would have irritated her), she explained, "The richest man in our village: a hundred acres of paddy, coconut garden—from the coconut garden alone his income would be a lakh of rupees, and from cattle. . . . They are distantly related to us . . ." She went into genealogical details explaining the family alliances of several generations and drop-ping scores of names. She was thorough. I was amazed at the amount of information stored in her mind; she knew also where every character lived, scattered though they were between the Himalayas in the north and the tip of Cape Comorin in the south. I was fascinated by the way she was piling up facts in order to establish the identity of the man with the tuft. I felt like the Wedding-Guest in "The Ancient Mariner." I could not break away. Here was another line floating up from the literary scrap acquired from my hypothecated property: "Hold off!" the Wedding-Guest wailed, "unhand me," but the Ancient Mariner gripped his wrist and said with a faraway look, "With my cross-bow I shot the Albatross." While my head buzzed with these irrelevant odds and ends, my mother was concluding a sentence: "The girl has studied up to B.A. and is to be married in June —he is keen that it should be gone through without any delay. She is his last issue and he is anxious to settle her future . . . and the settlement he has proposed is very liberal . . ." I re-mained silent. I could now understand the drift of her conver-sation. She mentioned, "The horoscopes match very well. He came here only after the astrologers had approved."

"Where did he get my horoscope?" I asked.

"They took it from your father many, many years ago; they were such good friends and neighbors in our village." She added again, "They were such good friends that they vowed on the day the girl was born to continue the friendship with this alliance. On the very day she was born, you were betrothed," she said calmly, as if it were the normal thing.

"What are you saying? Do you mean to say you betrothed to me a child only a few hours old?"

"Yes," she said calmly.

"Why? Why?" I asked, unable to comprehend her logic. "Don't you see how absurd it is?"

"No," she said. "They are a good family, known and attached to us for generations."

"It's idiotic," I cried. "How can you involve me in this manner? What was my age then?"

"What does it matter?" she said. "When I was married I was nine and your father thirteen, and didn't we lead a happy life?"

"That's irrelevant, what you have done with your lives. How old was I?"

"Old enough, about five or six, what does it matter?"

"Betrothed? How? By what process?"

"Don't question like that. You are not a lawyer in a court," she said, dropping her mask of friendliness.

"I may not be a lawyer, but remember that I am not a convict either," I said, secretly wondering if it was a relevant thing to say.

"You think I am a prisoner?" she asked, matching my irrelevancy.

I remained silent for a while and pleaded, "Mother, listen to me. How can any marriage take place in this fashion? How can two living entities possessing intelligence and judgement ever be tied together for a lifetime?"

"How else?" she said, and picking up my last word, "What lifetime? Of course, every marriage is for a lifetime. No one marries anew every month."

I felt desperate and cried, "Idiotic! Don't be absurd, try to understand what I am saying . . ."

She began to wail loudly at this. "Second time you are hurling an insulting word. Was it for this I have survived your father? How I wish I had mounted the funeral pyre as our ancients decreed for a widow; they knew what a widow would have to face in life, to stand abusive language from her own offspring." She beat her forehead with such violence that I feared she might crack her skull. Face flushed and tears streaming down her cheeks, she glared at me; I quailed at her look and wished that I could get up and escape. At close quarters, unaccustomed as I was, it was most disturbing. While she went on in the same strain, my mind was planning how best to get away, but she had practically cornered me and was hissing and swaying as she spoke. I began to wonder if I had thoughtlessly used some bad word and was going over our conversation in a reverse order. My last word was "idiotic," nothing foul and provocative in such a word. Most common usage. "Idiot" would have been more offensive than "idiotic." "Idiotic" could be exchanged between the best of friends under any circumstance of life and no one need flare up. Before this word she had said, "No one marries anew every month." I never said that they did. What a civilization, "A Wounded Civilization," a writer had called it. I could not help laughing slightly at the thought of the absurdity of it all. It provoked her again. Wiping her eyes and face with the tip of her sari, she said, "You are laughing at me! Yes, I've made a laughingstock of myself bringing you up, tending you, nursing you and feeding you, and keeping the house for you. You feel so superior and learned because of the books your father has collected laboriously in the other room . . ."

"But they weren't his . . . only someone's property mortgaged for a loan . . . ," I said, unable to suppress my remark.

And she said, "With all that reading you couldn't even get a B.A.! While every slip of a girl is a graduate today." Her voice sounded thick and hoarse due to the shouting she had indulged in.

I abruptly left, snatching my *kurta* and the upper cloth which were within reach, though I generally avoided this dress as it made one look like a political leader. I preferred always the blue bush shirt and dhoti or pants, but they were hanging by a hook on the wall where Mother was leaning. As I dashed out I heard her conclude, ". . . any date we mention, that man will come and take us to see the girl and approve . . ." So, she was imagining herself packing up, climbing a bus for the village with me in tow, to be received at that end as honored visitors and the girl to be paraded before us bedecked in gold and silk, waiting for a nod of approval from me. "Idiotic," I muttered again, walking down our street.

Going down Market Road, I noticed Dr. Kishen arrive on a scooter at the M.M.C., already opened by his general assistant, named Ramu, who fancied himself half a doctor and examined tongue and pulse and dispensed medicine when the doctor's back was turned. The doctor did not mind it, as Ramu was honest and rendered proper account of his own transactions. The doctor on noticing me said, "Come in, come in." A few early patients were waiting with their bottles. He was one who did not believe in tablets, but always wrote out a prescription for every patient, and Ramu concocted the mixture and filled the bottles. The doctor always said, "Every prescription must be a special composition to suit the individual. How can mass-produced tablets help?" He wrote several lines on a sheet of paper and then turned the sheet of paper and wrote along the margin, too; he challenged anyone to prove that his prescriptions were not the longest: "I'll give free medicine to anyone who can produce a longer prescription anywhere in this country!" And his patients, mostly from the surrounding villages, sniggered and murmured approval. When he hailed me I just slowed down my pace but did not stop. "Good morning, Doctor. I'm all right . . ." He cut me short with, "I know, I know, you are a healthy animal of no worth to the medical profession, still I want to speak to you. . . . Come in, take that chair, that's for friends who are in good health; sick people sit there." He flourished his arm in the di-

rection of a teakwood bench along a wall and a couple of iron
folding chairs. He went behind a curtain for a moment and came
out donning his white apron and turned the hands of a sign on
the wall which said DOCTOR IS IN, PLEASE BE SEATED. He briefly
glanced through a pile of blotters and folders advertising new
infallible drugs and swept them away to a corner of his desk.
"Of value only to the manufacturers, all those big companies and
multinationals, not to the ailing population of our country. I
never give these smart canvassing agents in shirtsleeves and tie
more than five minutes to have their say, and one minute to pick
up their samples and literature and leave. While there are other
M.D.s in town who eat out of their hands and have built up a
vast practice with physician samples alone!" Ramu went round
collecting the bottles from those occupying the bench. "Why
don't you give me a check?" asked the doctor.

I thought he was joking and said, "Yes, of course, why not?"
to match what I supposed was his mood, and added, "How
much? Ten thousand?"

"Not so much," he said. "Less than that . . ." He took out a
small notebook from the drawer and kept turning its leaves. At
this moment an old man made his entry, coughing stentoriously.
The doctor looked up briefly and flourished his hand towards
the bench. The old man didn't obey the direction but stood in
the middle of the hall and began, "All night . . ." The doctor
said, "All right, all right . . . sit down and wait. I'll come and
help you to sleep well tonight." The man subsided on the bench,
a sentence he had begun trailing away into a coughing fit.

The doctor said, "Two hundred and forty-five rupees up to
last week . . . none this week." I now realized that this was more
than a joke. I was aghast at this demand. He thrust his notebook
before me and said, "Twenty visits at ten rupees a visit. I have
charged nothing for secondary visits, and the balance for medicine . . ." The cough-stricken patient began to gurgle, cleared
his throat and tried to have his say. The doctor silenced him
with a gesture. A woman held up a bawling kid and said, "Sir,

he brings up every drop of milk . . ." The doctor glared at her and said, "Don't you see I'm busy? Am I the four-headed Brahma? One by one. You must wait."

"He brings up . . ."

"Wait, don't tell me anything now." After this interlude he said to me, "I don't generally charge for secondary visits—I mean a second call, which I can respond to on my way home. I charge only for visits which are urgent. In your case I've not noted the number of secondary visits."

I was mystified and said, "You have yourself called me a healthy brute, so what's it all about?"

"Don't you know? Has your mother never spoken to you?"

"No, never, I never thought . . . Yes, she spoke about my marrying some girl, worried me no end about it," I said, and added, "Doctor, if you can think of some elixir which'll reduce her fervor about my marriage . . ."

"Yes, yes, I'm coming to it. It's a thing that is weighing on her mind very much. She feels strongly that there must be a successor to her when she leaves." The doctor seemed to be talking in conundrums. The day seemed to have started strangely. "Has she not discussed her condition with you?" Before I could answer him or grasp what he was saying, the man with the cough made his presence felt with a deafening series, attracting the doctor's attention, and as the doctor rose, the woman lifted the child and began, "He doesn't retain even a drop . . ." The doctor said to me, "Don't go away. I'll dispose of these two first." He took the squealing baby and the cougher, one by one, behind the curtain, and came back to his table and wrote a voluminous prescription for each, and passed them on to Ramu through a little window. Presently he resumed his speech to me, but was interrupted by his patients, who wanted to know whether the mixture was to be drunk before or after a meal and what diet was to be taken. He gave some routine answer and muttered to me, "It's the same question again and again, again and again— whether they could have buttermilk or *rasam* and rice or bread and coffee, and whether before or after—what does it matter? But they want an answer and I have to give it, because the medical profession has built up such rituals! Ha! ha!"

At this moment two others approached his desk, having waited on the bench passively all along. He gestured them to return to their seats, and rose saying, "Follow me, we will have no peace here . . ." I followed him into his examination room, a small cabin with a high table, screened off and with a lot of calendar pictures plastered on the wall. He asked me to hoist myself on the examining table as if I were a patient, and said, "This is the only place where I can talk without being interrupted." I had been in suspense since his half-finished statements about my mother. He said, "Your mother is in a leave-taking mood . . ." I was stunned to hear this. I could never imagine my mother in such a mood. No one seemed to have her feet more firmly planted on the earth, with her ceaseless activities around the house, and her strident voice ringing through the halls. The doctor had said "leave-taking." How could she ever leave her universe? It was inconceivable. My throat went dry and my heart raced when I tried to elicit further clarification from him. I said weakly, "What sort of leave-taking? Thinking of retiring to Benares?"

"No, farther than that," said the doctor, indicating heaven, after lighting a cigarette. The little cabin became misty and choking. I gently coughed out the smoke that had entered my lungs without my striking a match. The smoke stung my eyes and brought tears, observing which the doctor said sympathetically, "Don't cry. Learn to take these situations calmly; you must think of the next step to take, practically and calmly." He preached to me the philosophy of detachment, puffing away at his cigarette, and not minding in the least the coughing, groaning and squealing emanating from the bench in the hall. I felt bad to be holding up the doctor in this manner. But I had to know what he was trying to say about my mother through his jerky half-statements. He asked suddenly, "Why hasn't she been talking to you?" I had to explain to him that I came home late

and left early, and we met briefly each day. He made a depre-
catory sound with his tongue and remarked, "You are an un-
dutiful fellow. Where do you hide yourself all day?"

"Oh, this and that," I said, feeling irritated. "I have to see
people and do things. One has to live one's own life, you know!"

"What people and what life?" pursued the doctor relentlessly.
I couldn't explain to him really how I spent the day. He'd have
brushed aside anything I said. So I thought it best to avoid his
question and turn his thoughts to my mother. Here he had created a hopeless suspense and tension in me, and was wandering
in his talk, puffing out smoke and tipping the ash on the cement
floor. What an untidy doctor—the litter and dust and ash alone
was enough to breed disease and sickness—he was the most
reckless doctor I'd ever come across. As more patients came into
the other room, Ramu parted the curtain and peeped in to say,
"They are waiting." This placed some urgency into the whole
situation and the doctor hastily threw down the cigarette,
crushed it under his shoe and said, "For four months I have been
visiting your home off and on, some days several times—that
little girl would come running and panting to say, 'Come, Doctor, at once, Amma is very ill, at once.' When such a call is
received I never ignore it. I drop whatever I may have on hand
and run to the patient. Giving relief to the suffering is my first
job. . . . Sometimes the girl would come a second time, too."

"What was it?" I asked, becoming impatient.

"Well, that's what one has to find out; I'm continuously
watching and observing. It's not in my nature to treat any com-
plaint casually and take anything for granted. . . ." He was
misleading himself, according to what I could observe of his
handling of his patients. After a lot of rambling, he came to the
point: "She is subject to some kind of fainting, which comes on
suddenly. However, she is responding to treatment; I think it
must be some kind of cardiac catch, if I may call it so, due to
normal degenerative process. We can keep her going with medicines, but how long one cannot say. . . ."

"Does she know?" I asked tremblingly.

"Yes, I had to call to her about it in a way, and she has understood perfectly. She has a lot of philosophy, you know. Perhaps you don't spend any time with her . . ." I remained dumb. The doctor's observations troubled my conscience. I had not paid any attention to my mother, to her needs or her wants or her condition, and had taken her to be made of some indestructible stuff. "The only thing that bothers her now is that you will be left alone; she told me that if only you could be induced to marry . . ."

So that was it! I understood it now. She must have been busy all afternoon sending the little girl to the post office to buy postcards, and then writing to her relations in the village to find a bride for me, and she had finally succeeded in reviving old relationships and promises and getting the tufted man down with his proposals. What a strain it must have been to organize so much in her state of cardiac degeneration, performing her daily duties without the slightest slackening. In fact, she seemed to have been putting on an exaggerated show of vitality when I was at home, probably suffering acutely her spells of whatever it was while I sat listening or lecturing at the Boardless till midnight! I felt guilty and loathed myself and my self-centered existence. Before I left, the doctor uttered this formula: "Well, such is my finding. Take a second opinion if you like. I'd not at all mind it. Can you let me have your check tomorrow?"

When I emerged from the anteroom, the waiting patients looked relieved. Outside in the street I hesitated for a moment and turned my feet homeward instead of, as was my invariable custom, to the Boardless.

When I opened the door of my room and appeared before my mother, she was taken aback, having never seen me home at this hour. I was happy to find her as active as ever, impossible to connect it with the picture conjured by the doctor's report, although I seemed to note some weak points in her carriage and under her eyes. I kept staring at her. She was puzzled. I wanted to burst out, "How do you feel this morning? All right? Possibility of falling into a faint?" I swallowed my words. Why should I mention a point which she had kept from me? That might upset her, better not show cognizance of it. She wanted to ask, perhaps, "Why are you at home now?" But she didn't. I felt grateful to her for her consideration. We looked at each other for some time, each suppressing the question uppermost in our minds. Only the little servant girl opened her eyes wide and cried, "You never come at this time! Are you going to eat? Amma has not prepared any food as yet . . ." "Hey, you keep quiet," Mother ordered her; she turned to me. "I'm about to light the oven. This girl arrived so late today! Is there anything you'd like?" What a change was coming over us all of a sudden. I could hardly believe my ears or eyes—remembering the tenor of our morning conversation. I went back to my room, wondering what I should do if she had her attack while I was here. She seemed to be all right; still, I'd a feeling of anxiety about leaving her there and going away to my room. Somehow I had an irrational anxiety that if I lost her from view for a moment anything might happen. I settled down in my room, leaving the door ajar, and tried to read; while my eyes scanned the lines, my thoughts were elsewhere. Suppose she had a seizure and suddenly passed away, without ever knowing that I was desperate to please her by agreeing to this frightful marriage. I hated it, but I had to do a thing I hated to please a dying mother. It was pathetic, her single-handed attempt in her condition to find me a bride. One had to do unpleasant things for another person's sake. Did not Rama agree to exile himself for fourteen years to please Dasaratha? My own hardship would be nothing compared to what Rama underwent, living like a nomad in the forests for fourteen years. In my case, at worst I'd have to suffer being wedded to a girl I didn't care for, which was nothing if one got used to it, and it'd help an old woman die in peace.

She had cooked some special items for me as if I were a rare guest. The lunch was splendid. She had put out a banana leaf for me in the corridor and arranged a sitting plank for me beside the rosewood pillar in the half-covered open court. She explained, "It's too stuffy with smoke in the kitchen. Your father did everything perfectly, but neglected the kitchen—never provided a chimney or window . . . if the firewood is not dry the smoke irritates my eyes till I think I'll go blind. One'd almost lose one's sight in the stinging smoke, but I've got used to it; even if I lose my sight it will not matter. But whoever comes after me . . ." This was the nearest hint of both her health and the successor to the kitchen. I absorbed the hint but had no idea what I should say; I felt confused and embarrassed. "We shall have to do something about it," I said, gratefully eating the rare curry with five vegetables she had prepared for me. I was amazed at her efficiency. I was an unexpected guest, but within a couple of hours she had managed to get the food ready. She must have been driving the little girl with a whip to run up and buy all the needed stuff for this lunch, all done quietly without giving a clue to the guest of honor lounging in his room with a book in hand. She must have been several times on the point of asking why I was back home at this hour, and I was on the point of asking for details of her symptoms; but both of us talked of other things. After lunch I retired to my room. I couldn't shut the door and rest. I frequently emerged from my shelter and paced the length of the house, up and down from the front door to the backyard, areas which I had not visited for months and months. I noticed without obviously watching how my mother was faring. She had eaten her lunch, and was chewing her betel nut and clove as had been her practice for years and years. That the shop was closed for the day was indicated by the faint aroma of cloves that hung about her presence, as I had noticed even as a child, when I trailed behind her at all hours, while my father sat counting cash in his room. She used to look like a goddess in her bright silk sari and straight figure, with diamonds sparkling in her ears.

She had unrolled a mat and was lying with her head resting on a plank in the corridor, which was her favorite spot. When she saw me pass, she sat up and asked, "Want anything?"

"No, no, don't disturb yourself. Just a glass of water, that's all." I went into the kitchen and poured a tumbler of water out of the mud jug, took a draught of unwanted cold water and went back to my room. This was an unaccustomed hour at home and I could not overcome the feeling of strangeness. She seemed all right and I felt relieved. She produced a tumbler of coffee when I reappeared in her zone, after an afternoon nap. I began to feel bored and wanted to go out to my accustomed haunts, the public library, the town hall, the riverside at Nallappa's grove and finally the Boardless. Normally I'd start the day at the Boardless, finish my rounds and end up there again.

When I was satisfied she was normal, I had a wash at the well, dressed, and started out. I went to the back portion, where she was scrubbing the floor, to tell her I was going out, casually asking, "Where is that girl? Why are you doing it yourself?"

"That girl wanted the day off. The floor is so slippery. Nothing like doing things yourself if your limbs are strong enough . . . ," she said.

I said very calmly and casually, "If you like, you may tell that man to come for a talk and arrange our visit to the village. You may write to him to come anytime," and without further talk, I briskly left.

All evening my mind was preoccupied. I was not the sort to explain my personal problems to anyone, and so when I sat beside Varma at the Boardless and he asked me, "Anything wrong? You have come so late," I gave some excuse and passed on to other subjects. The six o'clock group arrived—the journalist whom we called the universal correspondent, since he couldn't name any paper as his, an accountant in some bank, a schoolmaster and a couple of others whose profession and background were vague—and assembled in its corner. The talk was all about Delhi politics as usual—for and against Indira Gandhi—with considerable heat but in hushed tones, because Varma threw a hint that walls have ears. I'd normally participate in this to the extent of contradicting everyone and quoting Plato or Toynbee. But today I just listened passively, and the journalist said,

"Where has your sparkle gone?" I said I had a sore throat and a cold coming.

After an hour I slipped out. I crossed Ellaman Street and plodded through the sands of Sarayu and walked down the bank listening to the rustling of leaves overhead and the sound of running water. I was deeply moved by the hour and its quality in spite of my worries. People sat here and there alone or in groups, children were gamboling on the sands. I said to myself, "Oh, the lovely things continue, in spite of the burdens on one's soul. How I wish I could throw off the load and enjoy this hour absolutely. Most people here are happy, chatting and laughing because they are not bothered about a marriage or a mother. . . . God! I wish I could see a way out." I sat on the river parapet and brooded hard and long. Marriage seemed to me most unnecessary, just to please a mother. Supposing the M.M.C. doctor had not spotted me in the morning, I'd have gone my way, leaving marriage and mother to take their own course, that tufted man to go to the devil. I could welcome neither marriage nor my mother's death. They spoke of the horns of dilemma; I understood now what it meant. I felt hemmed in, with all exits blocked—like a rat cornered who must either walk into the trap or get bashed. I was getting more and more confused. No one told me that I should marry or otherwise I'd lose my mother. Mother's health was not dependent on me: the degenerative process must have started very early. I had decided to marry only because it'd make her die peacefully, a purely voluntary decision—no dilemma in any sense of the term. After this elaborate analysis I felt a little lighter in mind. I abandoned myself to the sound of the river and leaves, of the birds chirping and crowing in the dark while settling on their perches for the night.

Two men sitting nearby got up, patting away the sand from their seats. They were engaged in a deep discussion, and as they passed me one was saying, "I'd not rely on any single opinion so fully and get nose-led; one must always get a second opinion before deciding the issue." They were old men, probably pensioners reminiscing on family affairs or official matters. The expression "second opinion" was a godsend and suddenly opened a door for me. My doctor himself constantly recommended a "second opinion." I'd not rely only on the M.M.C. I'd get my mother examined by Dr. Natwar, who was a cardiologist and neurosurgeon, as he called himself, who had his establishment at New Extension. Everyone turned to that doctor at desperate moments. He had acquired many degrees from different continents, and sick persons converged there from all over the country. I was going to ask him point-blank if my mother was to live for some more years or not, and on his judgement was going to depend my marriage. I only prayed, as I trudged back home oblivious of the surroundings, that my mother had taken no action on my impulsive acceptance of the morning. I was confident that she couldn't have reached postal facilities so quickly.

I got up early next morning and met the M.M.C. doctor at his home. He hadn't yet shaved or bathed; with his hair ruffled and standing up he looked more like a loader of rice bags in the market than a physician. "To think one hangs on this loader's verdict on matters of life and death!" I reflected, while he led me in and offered me a cup of coffee. His tone was full of sympathy as he presumed that something had gone wrong with my mother; he was saying, "Oh, don't be anxious, I'll come, she'll be all right, must be another passing fit . . ." I had to wake up from my reverie as he concluded, "I won't take more than forty minutes to get ready, and the first call will be at your house, although a case of bronchitis at the Temple Street is in a critical stage." Never having practiced the art of listening to others, he went on elaborating details of the bronchitis case. When he paused for breath, I butted in hastily to ask, "May I seek a second opinion in my mother's case?"

"Why not? Just the right thing to do. I'm after all as human as yourself—not a Brahma. No one could be a Brahma . . . Just wait . . ." He gave me the morning paper and disappeared for forty minutes and reappeared completely transformed into the

usual picture of the presiding deity of the M.M.C. He handed
me a letter for Dr. Natwar, saying, "He is a good chap, though
you may find him rather brusque. Take this letter and get an
appointment for your mother and then see me."

I had to spend the whole morning at Dr. Natwar's consulting
room in New Extension. A servant took my letter in, and after
I had glanced through all the old illustrated magazines heaped
on a central table again and again, I sat back resigned to my
fate. A half-door kept opening and shutting as sick persons with
their escorts passed in and out. After nearly two hours the servant
brought back my letter, marked "Tuesday, 11 a.m." Tuesday
was still five days away. Suppose the tufted man came before
that? I asked the servant, "Can't I see the doctor and ask for an
earlier date?" He shook his head and left. This unseen healer was
like God, not to be seen or heard except when he willed it. The
demigods were equally difficult to reach.

In her present mood it was not difficult to persuade my
mother to submit herself to a second opinion, although I still
had to pretend that I knew nothing of the test performed by Dr.
Kishen. I had to explain that one had to make sure, at her age,
of being in sound condition and what a privilege it would be to
be looked over by Dr. Natwar. I didn't tell her that it cost me
a hundred rupees for this consultation. Gaffur's taxi was available
for fifteen rupees (the old Gaffur as well as the Chevrolet were
no more, but his son now sat on the dry fountain, looking like
him as I remembered him years ago, with an Ambassador car
parked in the road) to take her over to Dr. Natwar's clinic.

Dr. Natwar's electronic and other medical equipment was fitted up in different rooms. I caught a glimpse of my mother as
she was being wheeled about from section to section. She looked
pleased to be the center of so much attention and to be put
through so many gadgets. She looked gratefully at me every time
she passed the hall, as if to say that she had never suspected that
I was such a devoted son. The demigod who had taken my letter
on the first day appeared and beckoned me to follow him. All

the rest had vanished—the trolley, the attendants, as well as my
mother—had vanished completely, as if they had been images
on the screen of a magic-lantern show. I followed him, marveling
at the smooth maneuvering of the puppets in this institution.
On the doctor's word depended my future freedom. I was ushered
into the presence of Dr. Natwar, who seemed quite young for
his reputation, a man of slight build and a serious face and small,
tight lips which were hardly ever opened except to utter precise
directions. His communication with his staff was managed with
a minimum of speech—with a jerk of his head or the wave of a
finger.

"Mr. Sambu, nothing wrong with your mother." He pushed
towards me a sheaf of documents and photographs and paper
scrolls in a folder. "Keep these for reference: absolutely nothing
to warrant this check-up. Blood contents, urine and blood pressure, heart and lungs are normal. Fainting symptoms might have
been due to fatigue and starvation over long periods. No medi-
cation indicated. She must eat at more frequent intervals, that's
all." Getting up, I muttered thanks, but hesitated. He was ready
to press the bell for the next case. I shuffled my feet as if to
move, but turned round to ask, "How long will she live?" A
wry smile came over his face as he rang the bell and said, "Who
can answer that question? . . ." As the next visitor was ushered
in, he said simply, "I'd not be surprised if she outlived you
and me."

If she was going to outlive me and the doctor, I reflected on
the way home, why could I not tell her straightaway that the
time had come for us to dismiss her tufted cousin and his daughter from our thoughts. But I found her in such a happy mood
as we traveled homeward, I didn't have the heart to spoil it. She
had already begun to talk of the wedding preparations. "The
only thing that bothered me all along was that I might not have
the strength to go through it all. Now I can; oh, so many things
to do!" I looked away, pretending to watch the passing scenes,
cattle grazing in the fields, bullock-cart caravans passing and so

forth. What a monomania, this desire to see me wedded! She was saying, "I must write to my brother and his wife to come ahead and help us: invitation letters to be printed and distributed, clothes and silver vessels . . . oh, so much to do . . . I don't know, but my brother is a practical man . . ." She went on chattering all the way. I was indifferent. Time enough to throw the bombshell. The drive and the air blowing on her face seemed to have stimulated her. With her health assured, she was planning to plunge into matrimonial activities with zest. I couldn't understand what pleasure she derived from destroying my independence and emasculating me into a householder running up to buy vegetables at the bidding of the wife or changing baby's napkin. I shuddered at the prospect.

The moment we got out of the taxi, the little girl came running, holding aloft a postcard. "The postman brought this letter."

"Oh, the letter has come," Mother cried, thrilled, and read it standing on the house steps and declared, "He is coming by the bus at one o'clock—never thought he'd come so soon . . ."

"Who, the tuft?" I asked.

She looked surprised at my levity. "No, you must not be disrespectful. What if someone has a tuft? In those days everyone was tufted," she said, suppressing her annoyance. She went up the steps into the house, while I paid off the taxi. When she heard the car move off, she came to the street and cried, "Why have you sent the car away? I thought you should meet him at the bus stand and bring him home, that would have been graceful. Anyhow, hurry up to the bus stop; you must not keep him waiting, better if you are there earlier and wait for the bus— they are such big people, you have no notion how wealthy and influential they are, nothing that they cannot command; if you went there, they could command big cars for your use, you have no idea. They grow everything in their fields, from rice to mustard, all grains and vegetables, don't have to buy anything from a shop except kerosene. Before you go, cut some banana leaves,

large ones from the backyard garden." I cut the banana leaves as
she ordered, went up to the corner shop and bought the groceries
she wanted for the feast. I put down the packages while she
busied herself in the kitchen and was harrying the servant girl.
She was in high spirits, very happy and active. I hated myself
for dampening her spirits with what I was about to say. I stood
at the kitchen door watching her, wondering how to soften the
blow I was about to deliver. She turned from the oven to say,
"Now go, go, don't delay. If the bus happens to come before
time, it'll be awkward to keep him waiting."

"Can't he find his way, as he did that night? No one went
out to receive him then."

"Now this is a different occasion; he is in a different
class now . . ."

"No, I don't agree with you. He is no more than a country
cousin of yours, and nothing more as far as I am concerned."

She dropped the vessel she had been holding in her hand,
and came up, noticing the change in my tone. "What has come
over you?"

"That tufted man is welcome to find his way here, eat the
feast you provide and depart. He will not see me at the bus stand
or here."

"He is coming to invite you to meet his daughter . . ."

"That doesn't concern me. I'm going out on my own business.
Feed him well and send him back to the village well fed, whenever you like; I'm off . . ."

I went into my room to change and leave by the other door
for the Boardless, haunted by the memory of pain on her face. I
felt sorry for her and hated myself for what I was. As I crossed
the pyol of the house and was about to reach the street, she
opened the front door and dashed out to block my way, im-
ploring tearfully, "You need not marry the girl or look at her,
only I beg you to go up and receive that man. After all, he is
coming on my invitation, we owe him that as a family friend,
otherwise it'll be an insult and they'll talk of it in our village

for a hundred years. I'd sooner be dead than have them say that a wretched widow could not even receive a guest after inviting him. Don't ruin our family reputation."

"Well, he came by himself the other evening."

"Today we've asked him." It was a strain for her to say all this in a soft voice, out of earshot of our neighbors. She looked desperate and kept wiping the tears with her sari and I suddenly felt the pathos of the whole situation and hated myself for it. After all, I had been responsible for the invitation. I wondered what I should do now. She begged, "Meet him, bring him home, eat with him, talk to him and then leave if you like. I'll see that he doesn't mention his daughter, you don't have to bother about the marriage. Do what you like, become a *sanyasi* or a sinner, I won't interfere. This is the last time. I'll not try to advise you as long as I breathe; this is a vow, though let me confess my dream of seeing grandchildren in this house is—" She broke down before completing the sentence. I felt moved by her desperation and secret dreams, pushed her gently back into the house and said, "Get in, get in before anyone sees us. I'll go to the bus stand and bring him here. I couldn't see him clearly the other day, but I'm sure to recognize him by the tuft."

A Horse and
Two Goats

Of the seven hundred thousand villages dotting the map of
India, in which the majority of India's five hundred mil-
lion live, flourish, and die, Kritam was probably the tiniest, indicated on the district survey map by a microscopic dot, the map
being meant more for the revenue official out to collect tax than
for the guidance of the motorist, who in any case could not hope
to reach it since it sprawled far from the highway at the end of
a rough track furrowed up by the iron-hooped wheels of bullock
carts. But its size did not prevent its giving itself the grandiose
name Kritam, which meant in Tamil "coronet" or "crown" on
the brow of this subcontinent. The village consisted of less than
thirty houses, only one of them built with brick and cement.
Painted a brilliant yellow and blue all over with gorgeous carvings of gods and gargoyles on its balustrade, it was known as
the Big House. The other houses, distributed in four streets, were
generally of bamboo thatch, straw, mud, and other unspecified
material. Muni's was the last house in the fourth street, beyond
which stretched the fields. In his prosperous days Muni had

owned a flock of forty sheep and goats and sallied forth every morning driving the flock to the highway a couple of miles away. There he would sit on the pedestal of a clay statue of a horse while his cattle grazed around. He carried a crook at the end of a bamboo pole and snapped foliage from the avenue trees to feed his flock; he also gathered faggots and dry sticks, bundled them, and carried them home for fuel at sunset.

His wife lit the domestic fire at dawn, boiled water in a mud pot, threw into it a handful of millet flour, added salt, and gave him his first nourishment for the day. When he started out, she would put in his hand a packed lunch, once again the same millet cooked into a little ball, which he could swallow with a raw onion at midday. She was old, but he was older and needed all the attention she could give him in order to be kept alive.

His fortunes had declined gradually, unnoticed. From a flock of forty which he drove into a pen at night, his stock had now come down to two goats, which were not worth the rent of a half rupee a month the Big House charged for the use of the pen in their backyard. And so the two goats were tethered to the trunk of a drumstick tree which grew in front of his hut and from which occasionally Muni could shake down drumsticks. This morning he got six. He carried them in with a sense of triumph. Although no one could say precisely who owned the tree, it was his because he lived in its shadow.

She said, "If you were content with the drumstick leaves alone, I could boil and salt some for you."

"Oh, I am tired of eating those leaves. I have a craving to chew the drumstick out of sauce, I tell you."

"You have only four teeth in your jaw, but your craving is for big things. All right, get the stuff for the sauce, and I will prepare it for you. After all, next year you may not be alive to ask for anything. But first get me all the stuff, including a measure of rice or millet, and I will satisfy your unholy craving. Our store is empty today. Dhal, chilli, curry leaves, mustard, coriander, gingili oil, and one large potato. Go out and get all this."

He repeated the list after her in order not to miss any item and walked off to the shop in the third street.

He sat on an upturned packing case below the platform of the shop. The shopman paid no attention to him. Muni kept clearing his throat, coughing, and sneezing until the shopman could not stand it anymore and demanded, "What ails you? You will fly off that seat into the gutter if you sneeze so hard, young man." Muni laughed inordinately, in order to please the shopman, at being called "young man." The shopman softened and said, "You have enough of the imp inside to keep a second wife busy, but for the fact the old lady is still alive." Muni laughed appropriately again at this joke. It completely won the shopman over; he liked his sense of humor to be appreciated. Muni engaged his attention in local gossip for a few minutes, which always ended with a reference to the postman's wife, who had eloped to the city some months before.

The shopman felt most pleased to hear the worst of the postman, who had cheated him. Being an itinerant postman, he returned home to Kritam only once in ten days and every time managed to slip away again without passing the shop in the third street. By thus humoring the shopman, Muni could always ask for one or two items of food, promising repayment later. Some days the shopman was in a good mood and gave in, and sometimes he would lose his temper suddenly and bark at Muni for daring to ask for credit. This was such a day, and Muni could not progress beyond two items listed as essential components. The shopman was also displaying a remarkable memory for old facts and figures and took out an oblong ledger to support his observations. Muni felt impelled to rise and flee. But his self-respect kept him in his seat and made him listen to the worst things about himself. The shopman concluded, "If you could find five rupees and a quarter, you will have paid off an ancient debt and then could apply for admission to *swarga*. How much have you got now?"

"I will pay you everything on the first of the next month."

"As always, and whom do you except to rob by then?"

Muni felt caught and mumbled. "My daughter has sent word that she will be sending me money."

"Have you a daughter?" sneered the shopman. "And she is sending you money! For what purpose, may I know?"

"Birthday, fiftieth birthday," said Muni quietly.

"Birthday! How old are you?"

Muni repeated weakly, not being sure of it himself, "Fifty." He always calculated his age from the time of the great famine when he stood as high as the parapet around the village well, but who could calculate such things accurately nowadays with so many famines occurring? The shopman felt encouraged when other customers stood around to watch and comment. Muni thought helplessly, "My poverty is exposed to everybody. But what can I do?"

"More likely you are seventy," said the shopman. "You also forget that you mentioned a birthday five weeks ago when you wanted castor oil for your holy bath."

"Bath! Who can dream of a bath when you have to scratch the tank bed for a bowl of water? We would all be parched and dead but for the Big House, where they let us take a pot of water from their well." After saying this Muni unobtrusively rose and moved off.

He told his wife, "That scoundrel would not give me anything. So go out and sell the drumsticks for what they are worth."

He flung himself down in a corner to recoup from the fatigue of his visit to the shop. His wife said, "You are getting no sauce today, nor anything else. I can't find anything to give you to eat. Fast till the evening, it'll do you good. Take the goats and be gone now," she cried and added, "Don't come back before the sun is down." He knew that if he obeyed her she would somehow conjure up some food for him in the evening. Only he must be careful not to argue and irritate her. Her temper was undependable in the morning but improved by evening time.

She was sure to go out and work—grind corn in the Big House, sweep or scrub somewhere, and earn enough to buy foodstuff and keep a dinner ready for him in the evening.

Unleashing the goats from the drumstick tree, Muni started out, driving them ahead and uttering weird cries from time to time in order to urge them on. He passed through the village with his head bowed in thought. He did not want to look at anyone or be accosted. A couple of cronies lounging in the temple corridor hailed him, but he ignored their call. They had known him in the days of affluence when he lorded over a flock of fleecy sheep, not the miserable gawky goats that he had today. Of course he also used to have a few goats for those who fancied them, but real wealth lay in sheep; they bred fast and people came and bought the fleece in the shearing season; and then that famous butcher from the town came over on the weekly market days bringing him betel leaves, tobacco, and often enough some bhang, which they smoked in a hut in the coconut grove, undisturbed by wives and well-wishers. After a smoke one felt light and elated and inclined to forgive everyone, including that brother-in-law of his who had once tried to set fire to his home. But all this seemed like the memories of a previous birth. Some pestilence afflicted his cattle (he could of course guess who had laid his animals under a curse), and even the friendly butcher would not touch one at half the price . . . and now here he was left with the two scraggly creatures. He wished someone would rid him of their company too. The shopman had said that he was seventy. At seventy, one only waited to be summoned by God. When he was dead what would his wife do? They had lived in each other's company since they were children. He was told on their day of wedding that he was ten years old and she was eight. During the wedding ceremony they had had to recite their respective ages and names. He had thrashed her only a few times in their career, and later she had the upper hand. Progeny, none. Perhaps a large progeny would have brought him the blessing of the gods. Fertility brought merit. People with fourteen

sons were always so prosperous and at peace with the world and
themselves. He recollected the thrill he had felt when he mentioned a daughter to that shopman; although it was not believed,
what if he did not have a daughter?—his cousin in the next
village had many daughters, and any one of them was as good
as his; he was fond of them all and would buy them sweets if
he could afford it. Still, everyone in the village whispered behind
their backs that Muni and his wife were a barren couple. He
avoided looking at anyone; they all professed to be so high up,
and everyone else in the village had more money than he. "I am
the poorest fellow in our caste and no wonder that they spurn
me, but I won't look at them either," and so he passed on with
his eyes downcast along the edge of the street, and people left
him also very much alone, commenting only to the extent, "Ah,
there he goes with his two goats; if he slits their throats, he may
have more peace of mind." "What has he to worry about anyway?
They live on nothing and have none to worry about." Thus people commented when he passed through the village. Only on the
outskirts did he lift his head and look up. He urged and bullied
the goats until they meandered along to the foot of the horse
statue on the edge of the village. He sat on its pedestal for the
rest of the day. The advantage of this was that he could watch
the highway and see the lorries and buses pass through to the
hills, and it gave him a sense of belonging to a larger world.
The pedestal of the statue was broad enough for him to move
around as the sun traveled up and westward; or he could also
crouch under the belly of the horse, for shade.

The horse was nearly life-size, molded out of clay, baked,
burnt, and brightly colored, and reared its head proudly, pranc-
ing its forelegs in the air and flourishing its tail in a loop; beside
the horse stood a warrior with scythe-like mustachios, bulging
eyes, and aquiline nose. The old image-makers believed in indicating a man of strength by bulging out his eyes and sharpening his mustache tips, and also decorated the man's chest with
beads which looked today like blobs of mud through the ravages

of sun and wind and rain (when it came), but Muni would insist that he had known the beads to sparkle like the nine gems at one time in his life. The horse itself was said to have been as white as a dhobi-washed sheet, and had had on its back a cover of pure brocade of red and black lace, matching the multicolored sash around the waist of the warrior. But none in the village remembered the splendor as no one noticed its existence. Even Muni, who spent all his waking hours at its foot, never bothered to look up. It was untouched even by the young vandals of the village who gashed tree trunks with knives and tried to topple off milestones and inscribed lewd designs on all walls. This statue had been closer to the population of the village at one time, when this spot bordered the village; but when the highway was laid through (or perhaps when the tank and wells dried up completely here) the village moved a couple of miles inland.

Muni sat at the foot of the statue, watching his two goats graze in the arid soil among the cactus and lantana bushes. He looked at the sun; it had tilted westward no doubt, but it was not the time yet to go back home; if he went too early his wife would have no food for him. Also he must give her time to cool off her temper and feel sympathetic, and then she would scrounge and manage to get some food. He watched the mountain road for a time signal. When the green bus appeared around the bend he could leave, and his wife would feel pleased that he had let the goats feed long enough.

He noticed now a new sort of vehicle coming down at full speed. It looked like both a motor car and a bus. He used to be intrigued by the novelty of such spectacles, but of late work was going on at the source of the river on the mountain and an assortment of people and traffic went past him, and he took it all casually and described to his wife, later in the day, everything he saw. Today, while he observed the yellow vehicle coming down, he was wondering how to describe it later to his wife when it sputtered and stopped in front of him. A red-faced foreigner, who had been driving it, got down and went around it,

stooping, looking, and poking under the vehicle; then he
straightened himself up, looked at the dashboard, stared in
Muni's direction, and approached him. "Excuse me, is there a
gas station nearby, or do I have to wait until another car
comes—" He suddenly looked up at the clay horse and cried,
"Marvelous," without completing his sentence. Muni felt he
should get up and run away, and cursed his age. He could not
readily put his limbs into action; some years ago he could outrun
a cheetah, as happened once when he went to the forest to cut
fuel and it was then that two of his sheep were mauled—a sign
that bad times were coming. Though he tried, he could not easily
extricate himself from his seat, and then there was also the problem of the goats. He could not leave them behind.

The red-faced man wore khaki clothes—evidently a policeman
or a soldier. Muni said to himself, "He will chase or shoot if I
start running. Some dogs chase only those who run—oh, Shiva
protect me. I don't know why this man should be after me."
Meanwhile the foreigner cried, "Marvelous!" again, nodding his
head. He paced around the statue with his eyes fixed on it. Muni
sat frozen for a while, and then fidgeted and tried to edge away.
Now the other man suddenly pressed his palms together in a
salute, smiled, and said, "*Namaste!* How do you do?"

At which Muni spoke the only English expressions he had
learned, "Yes, no." Having exhausted his English vocabulary, he
started in Tamil: "My name is Muni. These two goats are mine,
and no one can gainsay it—though our village is full of slan-
derers these days who will not hesitate to say that what belongs
to a man doesn't belong to him." He rolled his eyes and shuddered at the thought of evil-minded men and women peopling
his village.

The foreigner faithfully looked in the direction indicated by
Muni's fingers, gazed for a while at the two goats and the rocks,
and with a puzzled expression took out his silver cigarette case
and lit a cigarette. Suddenly remembering the courtesies of the
season, he asked, "Do you smoke?" Muni answered, "Yes, no."

Whereupon the red-faced man took a cigarette and gave it to Muni, who received it with surprise, having had no offer of a smoke from anyone for years now. Those days when he smoked bhang were gone with his sheep and the large-hearted butcher. Nowadays he was not able to find even matches, let alone bhang. (His wife went across and borrowed a fire at dawn from a neighbor.) He had always wanted to smoke a cigarette; only once did the shopman give him one on credit, and he remembered how good it had tasted. The other flicked the lighter open and offered a light to Muni. Muni felt so confused about how to act that he blew on it and put it out. The other, puzzled but undaunted, flourished his lighter, presented it again, and lit Muni's cigarette. Muni drew a deep puff and started coughing; it was racking, no doubt, but extremely pleasant. When his cough subsided he wiped his eyes and took stock of the situation, understanding that the other man was not an Inquisitor of any kind. Yet, in order to make sure, he remained wary. No need to run away from a man who gave him such a potent smoke. His head was reeling from the effect of one of those strong American cigarettes made with roasted tobacco. The man said, "I come from New York," took out a wallet from his hip pocket, and presented his card.

Muni shrank away from the card. Perhaps he was trying to present a warrant and arrest him. Beware of khaki, one part of his mind warned. Take all the cigarettes or bhang or whatever is offered, but don't get caught. Beware of khaki. He wished he weren't seventy as the shopman had said. At seventy one didn't run, but surrendered to whatever came. He could only ward off trouble by talk. So he went on, all in the chaste Tamil for which Kritam was famous. (Even the worst detractors could not deny that the famous poetess Avvaiyar was born in this area, although no one could say whether it was in Kritam or Kuppam, the adjoining village.) Out of this heritage the Tamil language gushed through Muni in an unimpeded flow. He said, "Before God, sir, Bhagwan, who sees everything, I tell you, sir, that we know nothing of the case. If the murder was committed, whoever did it will not escape. Bhagwan is all-seeing. Don't ask me about it. I know nothing." A body had been found mutilated and thrown under a tamarind tree at the border between Kritam and Kuppam a few weeks before, giving rise to much gossip and speculation. Muni added an explanation. "Anything is possible there. People over there will stop at nothing." The foreigner nodded his head and listened courteously though he understood nothing.

"I am sure you know when this horse was made," said the red man and smiled ingratiatingly.

Muni reacted to the relaxed atmosphere by smiling himself, and pleaded, "Please go away, sir, I know nothing. I promise we will hold him for you if we see any bad character around, and we will bury him up to his neck in a coconut pit if he tries to escape; but our village has always had a clean record. Must definitely be the other village."

Now the red man implored, "Please, please, I will speak slowly, please try to understand me. Can't you understand even a simple word of English? Everyone in this country seems to know English. I have gotten along with English everywhere in this country, but you don't speak it. Have you any religious or spiritual scruples against English speech?"

Muni made some indistinct sounds in his throat and shook his head. Encouraged, the other went on to explain at length, uttering each syllable with care and deliberation. Presently he sidled over and took a seat beside the old man, explaining, "You see, last August, we probably had the hottest summer in history, and I was working in shirtsleeves in my office on the fortieth floor of the Empire State Building. We had a power failure one day, you know, and there I was stuck for four hours, no elevator, no air conditioning. All the way in the train I kept thinking, and the minute I reached home in Connecticut, I told my wife, Ruth, 'We will visit India this winter, it's time to look at other civilizations.' Next day she called the travel agent first thing and told him to fix it, and so here I am. Ruth came with me but is staying back at Srinagar, and I am the one doing the rounds and joining her later."

Muni looked reflective at the end of this long oration and said, rather feebly, "Yes, no," as a concession to the other's language, and went on in Tamil, "When I was this high"—he indicated a foot high—"I had heard my uncle say . . ."

No one can tell what he was planning to say, as the other interrupted him at this stage to ask, "Boy, what is the secret of your teeth? How old are you?"

The old man forgot what he had started to say and remarked, "Sometimes we too lose our cattle. Jackals or cheetahs may sometimes carry them off, but sometimes it is just theft from over in the next village, and then we will know who has done it. Our priest at the temple can see in the camphor flame the face of the thief, and when he is caught . . ." He gestured with his hands a perfect mincing of meat.

The American watched his hands intently and said, "I know what you mean. Chop something? Maybe I am holding you up and you want to chop wood? Where is your axe? Hand it to me and show me what to chop. I do enjoy it, you know, just a hobby. We get a lot of driftwood along the backwater near my house, and on Sundays I do nothing but chop wood for the fireplace. I really feel different when I watch the fire in the fireplace, although it may take all the sections of the Sunday *New York Times* to get a fire started." And he smiled at this reference.

Muni felt totally confused but decided the best thing would be to make an attempt to get away from this place. He tried to edge out, saying, "Must go home," and turned to go. The other seized his shoulder and said desperately, "Is there no one, absolutely no one here, to translate for me?" He looked up and down the road, which was deserted in this hot afternoon; a sudden gust of wind churned up the dust and dead leaves on the roadside into a ghostly column and propelled it towards the mountain road. The stranger almost pinioned Muni's back to the statue and asked, "Isn't this statue yours? Why don't you sell it to me?"

The old man now understood the reference to the horse, thought for a second, and said in his own language, "I was an urchin this high when I heard my grandfather explain this horse and warrior, and my grandfather himself was this high when he heard his grandfather, whose grandfather—"

The other man interrupted him. "I don't want to seem to have stopped here for nothing. I will offer you a good price for this," he said, indicating the horse. He had concluded without the least doubt that Muni owned this mud horse. Perhaps he guessed by the way he sat on its pedestal, like other souvenir sellers in this country presiding over their wares.

Muni followed the man's eyes and pointing fingers and dimly understood the subject matter and, feeling relieved that the theme of the mutilated body had been abandoned at least for the time being, said again, enthusiastically, "I was this high when my grandfather told me about this horse and the warrior, and my grandfather was this high when he himself . . ." and he was getting into a deeper bog of reminiscence each time he tried to indicate the antiquity of the statue.

The Tamil that Muni spoke was stimulating even as pure sound, and the foreigner listened with fascination. "I wish I had my tape recorder here," he said, assuming the pleasantest expression. "Your language sounds wonderful. I get a kick out of every word you utter, here"—he indicated his ears—"but you don't have to waste your breath in sales talk. I appreciate the article. You don't have to explain its points."

"I never went to a school, in those days only Brahmin went to schools, but we had to go out and work in the fields morning till night, from sowing to harvest time . . . and when Pongal came and we had cut the harvest, my father allowed me to go out and play with others at the tank, and so I don't know the Parangi language you speak, even little fellows in your country probably speak the Parangi language, but here only learned men and officers know it. We had a postman in our village who could speak to you boldly in your language, but his wife ran away with someone and he does not speak to anyone at all nowadays. Who would if a wife did what she did? Women must be watched; otherwise they will sell themselves and the home." And he laughed at his own quip.

The foreigner laughed heartily, took out another cigarette, and offered it to Muni, who now smoked with ease, deciding to stay on if the fellow was going to be so good as to keep up his cigarette supply. The American now stood up on the pedestal in the attitude of a demonstrative lecturer and said, running his finger along some of the carved decorations around the horse's neck, speaking slowly and uttering his words syllable by syllable, "I could give a sales talk for this better than anyone else. . . . This is a marvelous combination of yellow and indigo, though faded now. . . . How do you people of this country achieve these flaming colors?"

Muni, now assured that the subject was still the horse and not the dead body, said, "This is our guardian, it means death to our adversaries. At the end of Kali Yuga, this world and all other worlds will be destroyed, and the Redeemer will come in the shape of a horse called 'Kalki'; this horse will come to life and gallop and trample down all bad men." As he spoke of bad men the figures of his shopman and his brother-in-law assumed concrete forms in his mind, and he reveled for a moment in the predicament of the fellow under the horse's hoof: served him right for trying to set fire to his home. . . .

While he was brooding on this pleasant vision, the foreigner utilized the pause to say, "I assure you that this will have the best home in the U.S.A. I'll push away the bookcase, you know I love books and am a member of five book clubs, and the choice and bonus volumes mount up to a pile really in our living room, as high as this horse itself. But they'll have to go. Ruth may disapprove, but I will convince her. The T.V. may have to be shifted too. We can't have everything in the living room. Ruth will probably say what about when we have a party? I'm going to keep him right in the middle of the room. I don't see how that can interfere with the party—we'll stand around him and have our drinks."

Muni continued his description of the end of the world. "Our pundit discoursed at the temple once how the oceans are going to close over the earth in a huge wave and swallow us—this horse will grow bigger than the biggest wave and carry on its back only the good people and kick into the floods the evil ones—plenty of them about—" he said reflectively. "Do you know when it is going to happen?" he asked.

The foreigner now understood by the tone of the other that a question was being asked and said, "How am I transporting it? I can push the seat back and make room in the rear. That van can take in an elephant"—waving precisely at the back of the seat.

Muni was still hovering on visions of avatars and said again, "I never missed our pundit's discourses at the temple in those days during every bright half of the month, although he'd go on all night, and he told us that Vishnu is the highest god. Whenever evil men trouble us, he comes down to save us. He has come many times. The first time he incarnated as a great fish, and lifted the scriptures on his back when the floods and sea waves . . ."

"I am not a millionaire, but a modest businessman. My trade is coffee."

Amidst all this wilderness of obscure sound Muni caught the word "coffee" and said, "If you want to drink 'kapi,' drive farther up, in the next town, they have Friday market, and there they open 'kapi-otels'—so I learn from passersby. Don't think I wander about. I go nowhere and look for nothing." His thoughts went back to the avatars. "The first avatar was in the shape of a little fish in a bowl of water, but every hour it grew bigger and bigger and became in the end a huge whale which the seas could not contain, and on the back of the whale the holy books were supported, saved and carried." Once he had launched on the first avatar, it was inevitable that he should go on to the next, a wild boar on whose tusk the Earth was lifted when a vicious conqueror of the Earth carried it off and hid it at the bottom of the sea. After describing this avatar Muni concluded, "God will always save us whenever we are troubled by evil beings. When we were young we staged at full moon the story of the avatars. That's how I know the stories; we played them all night until the sun rose, and sometimes the European collector would come to watch, bringing his own chair. I had a good voice and so they always taught me songs and gave me the women's roles. I was always Goddess Lakshmi, and they dressed me in a brocade sari, loaned from the Big House. . . ."

The foreigner said, "I repeat I am not a millionaire. Ours is a modest business; after all, we can't afford to buy more than sixty minutes of T.V. time in a month, which works out to two minutes a day, that's all, although in the course of time we'll maybe sponsor a one-hour show regularly if our sales graph continues to go up. . . ."

Muni was intoxicated by the memory of his theatrical days and was about to explain how he had painted his face and worn a wig and diamond earrings when the visitor, feeling that he had spent too much time already, said, "Tell me, will you accept a hundred rupees or not for the horse? I'd love to take the whiskered soldier also but no space for him this year. I'll have to cancel my air ticket and take a boat home, I suppose. Ruth can go by air if she likes, but I will go with the horse and keep him in my cabin all the way if necessary." And he smiled at the picture of himself voyaging across the seas hugging this horse. He added, "I will have to pad it with straw so that it doesn't break. . . ."

"When we played *Ramayana*, they dressed me as Sita," added Muni. "A teacher came and taught us the songs for the drama and we gave him fifty rupees. He incarnated himself as Rama, and He alone could destroy Ravana, the demon with ten heads who shook all the worlds; do you know the story of *Ramayana*?"

"I have my station wagon as you see. I can push the seat back and take the horse in if you will just lend me a hand with it."

"Do you know *Mahabharata?* Krishna was the eighth avatar of Vishnu, incarnated to help the Five Brothers regain their kingdom. When Krishna was a baby he danced on the thousand-hooded giant serpent and trampled it to death; and then he suckled the breasts of the demoness and left them flat as a disc though when she came to him her bosoms were large, like mounds of earth on the banks of a dug-up canal." He indicated two mounds with his hands. The stranger was completely mystified by the gesture. For the first time he said, "I really wonder what you are saying because your answer is crucial. We have come to the point when we should be ready to talk business."

"When the tenth avatar comes, do you know where you and I will be?" asked the old man.

"Lend me a hand and I can lift off the horse from its pedestal after picking out the cement at the joints. We can do anything if we have a basis of understanding."

At this stage the mutual mystification was complete, and there was no need even to carry on a guessing game at the meaning of words. The old man chattered away in a spirit of balancing off the credits and debits of conversational exchange, and said in order to be on the credit side, "O honorable one, I hope God has blessed you with numerous progeny. I say this because you seem to be a good man, willing to stay beside an old man and talk to him, while all day I have none to talk to except when somebody stops by to ask for a piece of tobacco. But I seldom have it, tobacco is not what it used to be at one time, and I have given up chewing. I cannot afford it nowadays." Noting the other's interest in his speech, Muni felt encouraged to ask, "How many children have you?" with appropriate gestures with his hands. Realizing that a question was being asked, the red man replied, "I said a hundred," which encouraged Muni to go into details. "How many of your children are boys and how many girls? Where are they? Is your daughter married? Is it difficult to find a son-in-law in your country also?"

In answer to these questions the red man dashed his hand into his pocket and brought forth his wallet in order to take immediate advantage of the bearish trend in the market. He flourished a hundred-rupee currency note and said, "Well, this is what I meant."

The old man now realized that some financial element was entering their talk. He peered closely at the currency note, the like of which he had never seen in his life; he knew the five and ten by their colors although always in other people's hands, while his own earning at any time was in coppers and nickels. What was this man flourishing the note for? Perhaps asking for change. He laughed to himself at the notion of anyone coming to him for changing a thousand- or ten-thousand-rupee note. He said with a grin, "Ask our village headman, who is also a money-lender; he can change even a lakh of rupees in gold sovereigns if you prefer it that way; he thinks nobody knows, but dig the floor of his puja room and your head will reel at the sight of the hoard. The man disguises himself in rags just to mislead the public. Talk to the headman yourself because he goes mad at the sight of me. Someone took away his pumpkins with the creeper and he, for some reason, thinks it was me and my goats . . . that's why I never let my goats be seen anywhere near the farms." His eyes traveled to his goats nosing about, attempting to wrest nutrition from minute greenery peeping out of rock and dry earth.

The foreigner followed his look and decided that it would be a sound policy to show an interest in the old man's pets. He went up casually to them and stroked their backs with every show of courteous attention. Now the truth dawned on the old man. His dream of a lifetime was about to be realized. He understood that the red man was actually making an offer for the goats. He had reared them up in the hope of selling them someday and, with the capital, opening a small shop on this very spot. Sitting here, watching towards the hills, he had often dreamed how he would put up a thatched roof here, spread a gunnysack out on the ground, and display on it fried nuts, col-

ored sweets, and green coconut for the thirsty and famished way-
farers on the highway, which was sometimes very busy. The
animals were not prize ones for a cattle show, but he had spent
his occasional savings to provide them some fancy diet now and
then, and they did not look too bad. While he was reflecting
thus, the red man shook his hand and left on his palm one
hundred rupees in tens now, suddenly realizing that this was
what the old man was asking. "It is all for you or you may share
it if you have a partner."

The old man pointed at the station wagon and asked, "Are
you carrying them off in that?"

"Yes, of course," said the other, understanding the transpor-
tation part of it.

The old man said, "This will be their first ride in a motor
car. Carry them off after I get out of sight, otherwise they will
never follow you, but only me even if I am traveling on the path
to Yama Loka." He laughed at his own joke, brought his palms
together in a salute, turned round and went off, and was soon
out of sight beyond a clump of thicket.

The red man looked at the goats grazing peacefully. Perched
on the pedestal of the horse, as the westerly sun touched off the
ancient faded colors of the statue with a fresh splendor, he ru-
minated, "He must be gone to fetch some help, I suppose!" and
settled down to wait. When a truck came downhill, he stopped
it and got the help of a couple of men to detach the horse from
its pedestal and place it in his station wagon. He gave them five
rupees each, and for a further payment they siphoned off gas
from the truck, and helped him to start his engine.

Muni hurried homeward with the cash securely tucked away at
his waist in his dhoti. He shut the street door and stole up softly
to his wife as she squatted before the lit oven wondering if by
a miracle food would drop from the sky. Muni displayed his
fortune for the day. She snatched the notes from him, counted

them by the glow of the fire, and cried, "One hundred rupees! How did you come by it? Have you been stealing?"

"I have sold our goats to a red-faced man. He was absolutely crazy to have them, gave me all this money and carried them off in his motor car!"

Hardly had these words left his lips when they heard bleating outside. She opened the door and saw the two goats at her door. "Here they are!" she said. "What's the meaning of all this?"

He muttered a great curse and seized one of the goats by its ears and shouted, "Where is that man? Don't you know you are his? Why did you come back?" The goat only wriggled in his grip. He asked the same question of the other too. The goat shook itself off. His wife glared at him and declared, "If you have thieved, the police will come tonight and break your bones. Don't involve me. I will go away to my parents. . . ."

Annamalai

The mail brought me only a postcard, with the message in Tamil crammed on the back of it in minute calligraphy. I was curious about it only for a minute—the handwriting, style of address, the black ink, and above all the ceremonial flourish of the language were well known to me. I had deciphered and read out to Annamalai on an average one letter every month for a decade and a half when he was my gardener, watchman, and general custodian of me and my property at the New Extension. Now the letter began: "At the Divine Presence of my old master, do I place with hesitancy this slight epistle for consideration. It's placed at the lotus feet of the great soul who gave me food and shelter and money in my lifetime, and for whose welfare I pray to the Almighty every hour of my waking life. God bless you, sir. By your grace and the grace of gods in the firmament above, I am in excellent health and spirits, and my kith and kin, namely, my younger brother Amavasai and my daughter, son-in-law, and the two grandchildren and my sister who lives four doors from me, and my maternal uncle and his children, who tend the coconut grove, are all well. This year the gods have been kind and have sent us the rains to nourish our lands and gardens and orchards. Our tanks have been full, and we work hard. . . ." I was indeed happy to have such a good report of fertility and joy from one who had nothing but problems as far as I could remember. But my happiness was short-lived. All the rosy picture lasted about ten closely packed lines, followed by an abrupt transition. I realized all this excellence of reporting was just a formality, following a polite code of epistle-writing and not to be taken literally in part or in whole, for the letter abruptly started off in an opposite direction and tone. "My purpose in addressing your honored self just today is to inform you that I am in sore need of money. The crops have failed this year and I am without food or money. My health is poor. I am weak, decrepit, and in bed, and need money for food and medicine. My kith and kin are not able to support me; my brother Amavasai is a godly man but he is very poor and is burdened with a family of nine children and two wives, and so I beg you to treat this letter as if it were a telegram and send me money immediately. . . ." He did not specify the amount but left it to my good sense, and whatever could be spared seemed welcome. The letter bore his name at the bottom, but I knew he could not sign; he always affixed his signature in the form of a thumb impression whenever he had to deal with any legal document. I should certainly have been glad to send a pension, not once but regularly, in return for all his years of service. But how could I be sure that he had written the letter? I knew that he could neither read nor write, and how could I make sure that the author of the letter was not his brother Amavasai, that father of nine and husband of two, who might have hit upon an excellent scheme to draw a pension in the name of a dead brother? How could I make sure that Annamalai was still alive? His last words to me before he retired were a grand description of his own funeral, which he anticipated with considerable thrill.

I looked at the postmark to make sure that at least the card had originated correctly. But the post office seal was just a dark smudge as usual. Even if it weren't so, even if the name of his village had been clearly set forth it would not have made any difference. I was never sure at any time of the name of his village, although as I have already said I had written the address for him scores of times in a decade and a half. He would stand behind my chair after placing the postcard to be addressed on the desk. Every time I would say, "Now recite the address properly."

"All right, sir," he would say, while I waited with the pen poised over the postcard. "My brother's name is Amavasai, and it must be given to his hand."

"That I know very well, next tell me the address precisely this time." Because I had never got it right at any time.

He said something that sounded like "Mara Konam," which always puzzled me. In Tamil it meant either "wooden angle" or "cross angle," depending on whether you stressed the first word or the second of that phonetic assemblage. With the pen ready, if I said, "Repeat it," he would help me by uttering slowly and deliberately the name—but a new one this time, sounding something like "Peramanallur."

"What is it, where is it?" I asked desperately.

"My village, sir," he replied with a glow of pride—once again leaving me to brood over a likely meaning. Making allowance for wrong utterance you could translate it as "Paerumai Nallur," meaning "town of pride and goodness" or, with a change of the stress of syllables, "town of fatness and goodness." Attempting to grope my way through all this verbal wilderness, if I said, "Repeat it," he generally came out with a brand-new sound. With a touch of homesickness in his tone and with an air of making a concession to someone lacking understanding, he would say, "Write clearly NUMTHOD POST," leaving me again to wrestle with phonetics to derive a meaning. No use, as this seemed to be an example of absolute sound with no sense, with no scope for an interpretation however differently you tried to distribute the syllables and stresses or whether you attempted a translation or speculated on its meaning in Tamil, Telugu, Kannada, or any of the fourteen languages listed in the Indian Constitution. While I sat brooding over all this verbiage flung at me, Annamalai waited silently with an air of supreme tolerance, only suggesting gently, "Write in English . . ."

"Why in English?"

"If it could be in Tamil I would have asked that chap who writes the card to write the address also; because it must be in English I have to trouble you"—a piece of logic that sounded intricate.

I persisted. "Why not in Tamil?"

"Letters will not reach in Tamil; what our schoolmaster has often told us. When my uncle died they wrote a letter and addressed it in Tamil to his son in Conjeevaram and the man never turned up for the funeral. We all joined and buried the uncle after waiting for two days, and the son came one year later and asked, 'Where is my father? I want to ask for money.'" And Annamalai laughed at the recollection of this episode. Realizing that I had better not inquire too much, I solved the problem by writing briskly one under another everything as I heard it. And he would conclusively ask before picking up the card, "Have you written via Katpadi?"

All this business would take its own time. While the space for address on the postcard was getting filled up I secretly fretted lest any line should be crowded out, but I always managed it somehow with the edge of my pen point. The whole thing took almost an hour each time, but Annamalai never sent a card home more than once a month. He often remarked, "No doubt, sir, that the people at home would enjoy receiving letters, but if I wrote a card to everyone who expected it, I would be a bankrupt. When I become a bankrupt will there be one soul among all my relatives who will offer a handful of rice even if I starve to death?" And so he kept his communications within practical limits, although they provided a vital link for him with his village home.

"How does one get to your village?" I asked.

"Buy a railway ticket, that's how," he answered, feeling happy that he could talk of home. "If you get into the Passenger at night paying two rupees and ten annas, you will get to Trichy in the morning. Another train leaves Trichy at eleven, and for seven rupees and four annas, it used to be only five fourteen before, you can reach Villipuram. One must be awake all night, otherwise the train will take you on, and once they demanded two rupees extra for going farther because I had slept over. I begged and pleaded and they let me go, but I had to buy another ticket next morning to get back to Katpadi. You can sleep on the station platform until midday. The bus arrives at midday and for twelve annas it will carry you farther. After the bus you may hire a jutka or a bullock cart for six annas and then on foot you reach home before dark; if it gets late bandits may waylay and beat us. Don't walk too long; if you leave in the afternoon you may reach Marakonam before sunset. But a card reaches there for just nine paise, isn't it wonderful?" he asked.

Once I asked, "Why do you have the address written before the message?"

"So that I may be sure that the fellow who writes for me does not write to his own relations on my card. Otherwise how can I know?" This seemed to be a good way of ensuring that the postcard was not misused. It indicated a rather strange relationship, as he often spoke warmly of that unseen man who always wrote his messages on postcards, but perhaps a few intelligent reservations in accepting a friendship improve human relations. I often questioned him about his friend.

"He has also the same name as myself," he said.

I asked, "What name?"

He bowed his head and mumbled, "My . . . my own name . . ." Name was a matter of delicacy, something not to be bandied about unnecessarily, a point of view which had not occurred to me at all until one day he spoke to me anent a signboard on the gate announcing my name. He told me point-blank when I went down to the garden, "Take away the name-board from that gate, if you will forgive my saying so."

"Why?"

"All sorts of people read your name aloud while passing down the road. It is not good. Often urchins and tots just learning to spell shout your name and run off when I try to catch them. The other day some women also read your name and laughed to themselves. Why should they? I do not like it at all." What a different world was his where a name was to be concealed rather than blazoned forth in print, ether waves, and celluloid!

"Where should I hang that board now that I have it?"

He just said, "Why not inside the house, among the pictures in the hall?"

"People who want to find me should know where I live."

"Everyone ought to know," he said, "otherwise why should they come so far?"

Digging the garden he was at his best. We carried on some of our choicest dialogues when his hands were wielding the pick-axe. He dug and kept digging for its own sake all day. While at work he always tied a red bandanna over his head, knotted above his ear in pirate fashion. Wearing a pair of khaki shorts, his bare back roasted to an ebonite shade by the sun, he attained a spontaneous camouflage in a background of mud and greenery; when he stood ankle-deep in slush at the bed of a banana seedling, he was indistinguishable from his surroundings. On stone, slope, and pit, he moved jauntily, with ease, but indoors he shuffled and scratched the cement floor with his feet, his joints creaked and rumbled as he carried himself upstairs. He never felt easy in the presence of walls and books and papers; he looked frightened and self-conscious, tried to mute his steps and his voice when entering my study. He came in only when he had a postcard to address. While I sat at my desk he would stand behind my chair, suppressing even his normal breath lest it should disturb my work, but he could not help the little rumbles and sighs emanating from his throat whenever he attempted to remain still. If I did not notice his presence soon enough, he would look in the direction of the gate and let out a drover's cry, "Hai, hai!" at a shattering pitch and go on to explain, "Again those cows, sir. Someday they are going to shatter the gate and swallow our lawn and flowers so laboriously tended by this old fellow. Many strangers passing our gate stop to exclaim, 'See those red flowers, how well they have come up! All of it that old fellow's work, at his age!' "

Annamalai might have other misgivings about himself, but he had had no doubt whatever of his stature as a horticulturist. A combination of circumstances helped him to cherish his notions. I did nothing to check him. My compound was a quarter acre in extent and offered him unlimited scope for experimentations. I had been living in Vinayak Street until the owner of a lorry service moved into the neighborhood. He was a relative of the municipal chairman and so enjoyed the freedom of the city. His lorries rattled up and down all day, and at night they were parked on the roadside and hammered and drilled so as to be made ready for loading in the morning. No one else in my street seemed to notice the nuisance. No use in protesting and complaining, as the relative of a municipal chairman would be beyond reproach. I decided to flee since it was impossible to read or write in that street; it dawned on me that the place was not meant for my kind anymore. I began to look about. I liked the lot shown by a broker in the New Extension layout, who also arranged the sale of my ancient house in Vinayak Street to the same lorry owner. I moved off with my books and writing within six months of making up my mind. A slight upland stretching away to the mountain road; a swell of ground ahead on my left and the railway line passing through a cutting, punctuated with a red gate, was my new setting. Someone had built a small cottage with a room on top and two rooms downstairs, and it was adequate for my purpose, which was to read and write in peace.

On the day I planned to move I requested my neighbor the lorry owner to lend me a lorry for transporting myself to my new home. He gladly gave me his lorry; the satisfaction was mutual as he could go on with all the repairs and hammerings all night without a word of protest from anyone, and I for my part should look forward to the sound of only birds and breeze in my new home. So I loaded all my books and trunks onto an open truck, with four loaders perched on them. I took my seat beside the driver and bade good-bye to Vinayak Street. No one to sigh over my departure, since gradually, unnoticed, I had become the sole representative of our clan in that street, especially after the death of my uncle.

When we arrived at New Extension the loaders briskly lifted the articles off the lorry and dumped them in the hall. One of them lagged behind while the rest went back to the lorry and shouted, "Hey, Annamalai, are you coming or not?" He ignored their call, and they made the driver hoot the horn.

I said to the man, "They seem to want you. . . ."

His brief reply was, "Let them." He was trying to help me put things in order. "Do you want this to be carried upstairs?" he asked, pointing at my table. The lorry hooted outside belligerently. He was enraged at the display of bad manners, went to the doorway, looked at them, and said, waving his arms, "Be off if you want, don't stand there and make donkey noise."

"How will you come back?"

"Is that your business?" he said. "Go away if you like, don't let that donkey noise trouble this gentleman."

I was touched by his solicitude, and looked up from the books I was retrieving from the packing cases, and noticed him for the first time. He was a thick-set, heavy-jowled man with a clean-shaven head covered with a turban, a pair of khaki shorts over heavy bow legs, and long arms reaching down to his knees; he had thick fingers, a broad nose, and enormous teeth stained red with betel juice and tobacco permanently pouched in at his cheek. There was something fierce as well as soft about him at the same time.

"They seem to have left," I remarked as the sound of the lorry receded.

"Let them," he said. "I don't care."

"How will you go back?" I asked.

"Why should I?" he said. "Your things are all scattered in a jumble here, and they don't have the sense to stop and help. You may have no idea, sir, what they have become nowadays."

Thus he entered my service and stayed on. He helped me to move my trunks and books and arrange them properly. Later he followed me about faithfully when I went round to inspect the garden. Whoever had owned the house before me had not bothered about the garden. It had a kind of battlement wall to mark off the backyard, and the rest was encircled with hedges of various types. Whenever I paused to examine any plant closely, Annamalai also stood by earnestly. If I asked, "What is this?" —"This?" he said, stooping close to it, "this is a *poon chedi* [flowering plant]," and after a second look at it declared what I myself was able to observe, "Yellow flowers." I learned in course of time that his classifications were extremely simple. If he liked a plant he called it "*poon chedi*" and allowed it to flourish. If it appeared suspicious, thorny, or awry in any manner he just declared, "This is a *poondu* [weed]," and, before I had a chance to observe, would pull it off and throw it over the wall with a curse.

"Why do you curse that poor thing?"

"It is an evil plant, sir."

"What kind of evil?"

"Oh, of several kinds. Little children who go near it will have stomachache."

"There are no children for miles around."

"What if? It can send out its poison on the air. . . ."

A sort of basement room was available, and I asked Annamalai, "Can you live in this?"

"I can live even without this," he said, and explained, "I am not afraid of devils, spirits, or anything. I can live anywhere. Did I have a room when I lived in those forests?" He flourished his arm in some vague direction. "That lorry keeper is a rascal, sir; please forgive my talking like this in the presence of a gentleman. He is a rascal. He carried me one day in his lorry to a forest on the hill and would never let me get away from there. He had signed a contract to collect manure from those forests, and wanted someone to stay there, dig the manure, and heap it in the lorries."

"What kind of manure?"

"Droppings of birds and dung of tigers and other wild animals and dead leaves, in deep layers everywhere, and he gave me a rupee and a half a day to stay there and dig up and load the lorry when it came. I lit a fire and boiled rice and ate it, and stayed under the trees, heaped the leaves around and lit them up to scare away the tigers roaring at night."

"Why did you choose this life just for one rupee and eight annas a day?" I asked.

He stood brooding for a few moments and replied, "I don't know. I was sitting in a train going somewhere to seek a job. I didn't have a ticket. A fellow got in and demanded, 'Where is your ticket?' I searched for it here and there and said, 'Some son of a bitch has stolen my ticket.' But he understood and said, 'We will find out who that son of a bitch is. Get off the train first.' And they took me out of the train with the bundle of clothes I carried. After the train left we were alone, and he said, 'How much have you?' I had nothing, and he asked, 'Do you want to earn one rupee and eight annas a day?' I begged him to give me work. He led me to a lorry waiting outside the railway station, handed me a spade and pickaxe, and said, 'Go on in that lorry, and the driver will tell you what to do.' The lorry put me down late next day on the mountain. All night I had to keep awake and keep a fire going, otherwise sometimes even elephants came up."

"Weren't you terrified?"

"They would run away when they saw the fire, and sometimes I chanted aloud wise sayings and philosophies until they withdrew . . . leaving a lot of dung around, just what that man required . . . and he sold it to the coffee estates and made his money. . . . When I wanted to come home they would not let me, and so I stayed on. Last week when they came I was down with the shivering fever, but the lorry driver, a good man, allowed me to climb on the lorry and escape from the forest. I will never go back there, sir, that lorry man holds my wages and asserts that he has given it all as rice and potato all these months. . . . I don't know, someday you must reckon it all up for me and help me. . . ."

He left early on the following morning to fetch his baggage. He asked for an advance of five rupees, but I hesitated. I had not known him for more than twenty-four hours. I told him, "I don't have change just at this moment."

He smiled at me, showing his red-tinted teeth. "You do not trust me, I see. How can you? The world is full of rogues who will do just what you fear. You must be careful with your cash, sir. If you don't protect your cash and wife . . ." I did not hear him fully as he went downstairs muttering his comment. I was busy setting up my desk, as I wished to start my work without any more delay. I heard the gate open, producing a single clear note on its hinges (which I later kept purposely on without oiling as that particular sound served as a doorbell). I peeped from my western window and saw him go down the road. I thought he was going away for good, not to return to a man who would not trust him with five rupees! I felt sorry for not giving him money, at least a rupee. I saw him go up the swell of ground and disappear down the slope. He was going by a shortcut to the city across the level-crossing gate.

I went back to my desk, cursing my suspiciousness. Here was one who had volunteered to help and I had shown so little grace. That whole day he was away. Next afternoon the gate latch clicked, and the gate hummed its single clear note as it moved on its hinges, and there he was, carrying a big tin trunk on his head, and a gunnysack piled on top of it. I went down to welcome him. By the time I had gone down he had passed around the house and was lowering the trunk at the door of the basement room.

He would stand below my window and announce to the air, "Sir, I am off for a moment. I have to talk to the mali in the other house," and move off without waiting for my reply. Sometimes if I heard him I said, as a matter of principle, "Why do you have to go and bother him about our problems now?"

He would look crestfallen and reply, "If I must not go, I won't go, if you order so."

How could I or anyone order Annamalai? It was unthinkable, and so to evade such a drastic step I said, "You know everything, what does he know more than you?"

He would shake his head at this heresy. "Don't talk so, sir. If you don't want me to go, I won't go, that is all. You think I want to take off the time to gossip and loaf?"

A difficult question to answer, and I said, "No, no, if it is important, of course . . ."

And he moved off, muttering, "They pay him a hundred rupees a month not for nothing . . . and I want to make this compound so good that people passing should say 'Ah' when they peep through the gate . . . that is all, am I asking to be paid also a hundred rupees like that mali?" He moved off, talking all the way; talking was an activity performed for its own sake and needed no listener for Annamalai. An hour later he returned clutching a drooping sapling (looking more like a shot-down bird) in his hand, held it aloft under my window, and said, "Only if we go and ask will people give us plants; otherwise why should they be interested?"

"What is it?" I asked dutifully, and his answer I knew even before he uttered it: "Flower plant."

Sometimes he displayed a handful of seeds tied to the end of his dhoti in a small bundle. Again I asked, "What is it?"

"Very rare seeds, no one has seen such a thing in this extension. If you think I am lying . . ." He would then ask, "Where are these to be planted?"

I would point out to a corner of the compound and say, "Don't you think we need some good covering there? All that portion looks bare. . . ." Even as I spoke I would feel the futility of my suggestion, it was just a constitutional procedure and nothing more. He might follow my instructions or his own inclination, no one could guess what he might do. He would dig up the earth earnestly at some corner and create a new bed of his own pattern, poke his forefinger into the soft earth and push the seed or the seedling in. Every morning he would stoop over it to observe minutely how it progressed. If he found a sprouting seed or any sign of life in the seedling, he watered it twice a day, but if it showed no response to his living touch, he looked outraged. "This should have come up so well, but it is the Evil Eye that scorches our plants. . . . I know what to do now." He dipped his finger in a solution of white lime and drew grotesque and strange emblems on a broken mud pot and mounted it up prominently on a stick so that those that entered our gate should first see the grotesque painting rather than the plants. He explained, "When people say, 'Ah, how good this garden looks!' they speak with envy and then it burns up the plants, but when they see the picture there, they will be filled with revulsion and our flowers will flourish. That is all."

He made his own additions to the garden each day, planting wherever he fancied, and soon I found that I could have no say in the matter. I realized that he treated me with tolerant respect rather than trust, and so I let him have his own way. Our plants grew anyhow and anywhere and generally prospered although the only attention that Annamalai gave them was an ungrudging supply of water out of a hundred-foot hose, which he turned on every leaf of every plant until it was doused and drowned. He also flung at their roots from time to time every kind of garbage and litter and called it manuring. By such assiduous efforts he created a generous, massive vegetation as a setting for my home. We had many rose plants whose nomenclature we never learned, which had developed into leafy menacing entanglements, clawing passersby; canna grew to gigantic heights, jasmine into wild undergrowth with the blooms maliciously out of reach although they threw their scent into the night. Dahlias pushed themselves above ground after every monsoon, presented their blooms, and wilted and disappeared, but regenerated themselves again at the next season. No one could guess who planted them originally, but nature was responsible for their periodic appearance, although Annamalai took the credit for it unreservedly. Occasionally I protested when *tacoma* hedges bordering the compound developed into green ramparts, shutting off the view in every direction. Annamalai, a prince of courtesy at certain moments, would not immediately contradict me but look long and critically at the object of my protest. "Don't think of them now, I will deal with them."

"When?" I asked.

"As soon as we have the rains," he would say.

"Why should it be so late?"

"Because a plant cut in summer will die at the roots."

"You know how it is with rains these days, we never have them."

This would make him gaze skyward and remark, "How can we blame the rains when people are so evil-minded?"

"What evil?"

"Should they sell rice at one rupee a measure? Is it just? How can poor people live?"

When the rains did come eventually it would be no use reminding of his promise to trim the hedges, for he would definitely declare, "When the rain stops, of course, for if a plant is trimmed in rain, it rots. If you want the hedge to be removed completely, tell me, I will do it in a few minutes, but you must not blame me later if every passerby in the street stares and watches the inside of the house all the time. . . ."

But suddenly one day, irrespective of his theories, he would arm himself with a scythe and hack blindly whatever came within his reach, not only the hedge I wanted trimmed but also a lot of others I preferred to keep. When I protested against this depredation, he just said, "The more we cut the better they will grow, sir." At the end of this activity, all the plants, having lost their outlines, looked battered and stood up like lean ghosts, with the ground littered green all over. At the next stage he swept up the clippings, bundled them neatly, and carried them off to his friend, namesake, and letter-writer, living in the Bamboo Bazaar, who had his cows to feed; in return for Annamalai's generosity, he kept his penmanship ever at Annamalai's service.

His gardening activities ceased late in the evening. He laid away his implements in a corner of his basement room, laboriously coiled up the hose, and locked it away, muttering, "This is my very life; otherwise how can an old fellow feed his plants and earn a good name? If some devil steals this I am undone, and you will never see me again." So much lay behind his habit of rolling up the rubber hose, and I fancied that he slept in its coils as an added safety. After putting it away he took off his red bandanna, turned on the tap, and splashed enormous quantities of water over himself, blowing his nose, clearing his throat, and grooming himself noisily; he washed his feet, rubbing his heels on a granite slab until they shone red; now his bandanna would be employed as a towel; wiping himself dry, he disappeared into the basement and came out later wearing a shirt and a white dhoti. This was his off hour, when he visited the gate shop at the level crossing in order to replenish his stock of tobacco and gossip with friends seated on a teak log. The railway gatekeeper who owned the shop (although for reasons of policy he gave out that it belonged to his brother-in-law) was a man of information and read out a summary of the day's news to this gathering out of a local news sheet published by the man who owned the Truth Printing Press and who reduced the day's radio broadcasts and the contents of other newspapers into tiny paragraphs on a single sheet of paper, infringing every form of copyright. He brought out his edition in the evening for two paise, perhaps the cheapest newspaper in the world. Annamalai paid close attention to the reading and thus participated in contemporary history. When he returned home I could spot him half a mile away from my window as his red bandanna came into view over the crest of a slope. If he found me near at hand, he passed to me the news of the day. That was how I first heard of John Kennedy's assassination. I had not tuned the radio the whole day, being absorbed in some studies. I was standing at the gate when he returned home, and I asked casually, "What is your news today?" and he answered without stopping, "News? I don't go hunting for it, but I overheard that the chief ruler of America was killed today. They said something like *Kannady* [which means "glass" in Tamil]; could any man give himself such a name?"

When I realized the import of his casual reference, I said, "Look, was it Kennedy?"

"No, they said 'Kannady,' and someone shot him with a gun and killed him, and probably they have already cremated him." When I tried to get more news, he brushed me off with "Don't think I go after gossip, I only tell you what approaches my ears . . . and they were all talking . . ."

"Who?" I asked.

"I don't know who they are. Why should I ask for names? They all sit and talk, having nothing else to do."

He would come into my study bearing a postcard in hand and announcing, "A letter for you. The postman gave it." Actually it would be a letter for him, which he'd never know until told, when he would suddenly become tense and take a step nearer in order to absorb all the details.

"What does he say?" he would ask irritably. His only correspondent was his brother Amavasai, and he hated to hear from

him. Torn between curiosity and revulsion, he would wait for
me to finish reading the postcard to myself first. "What does
that fellow have to say to me?" he would ask in a tone of disgust
and add, "As if I could not survive without such a brother!"

I'd read aloud the postcard, which always began formally with
a ceremonial flourish: "To my Godly brother and protector, this
insignificant younger brother Amavasai submits as follows. At
this moment we are all flourishing and we also pray for our
divine elder brother's welfare in one breath." All this preamble
would occupy half the space on the back of the card, to be
abruptly followed by mundane matters. "The boundary stone on
the north side of our land was tampered with last night. We
know who did it."

Pushing the tobacco on his tongue out of the way in order to
speak without impediment, Annamalai would demand, "If you
really know who, why don't you crack his skull? Are you bereft
of all sense? Tell me that first," and glare angrily at the postcard
in my hand.

I'd read the following line by way of an explanation: "But
they don't care."

"They don't? Why not?" The next few lines would agitate
him most, but I had to read them out. "Unless you come and
deal with them personally, they will never be afraid. If you keep
away, nothing will improve. You are away and do not care for
your kith and kin and are indifferent to our welfare or suffering.
You did not care to attend even my daughter's naming ceremony. This is not how the head of a family should behave."

The rest of the letter generally turned out to be a regular
charge sheet, but concluded ceremoniously, mentioning again
lotus feet and divinity. If I said, in order to divert his mind,
"Your brother writes well," he would suddenly grin, very pleased
at the compliment, and remark, "He to write! Oh, oh, he is a
lout. That letter is written by our schoolmaster. We generally
tell him our thoughts and he will write. A gifted man." He
would prepare to go downstairs, remarking, "Those fellows in

my village are illiterate louts. Do you think my brother could talk to a telephone?" One of his urban triumphs was that he could handle the telephone. In distinguishing the mouthpiece from the earpiece, he displayed the pride of an astronaut strolling in space. He felt an intimacy with the instrument, and whenever it rang he'd run up to announce, "Telepoon, sami," even if I happened to be near it. When I came home at night he'd always run forward to declare while opening the gate, "There was a telepoon—someone asked if you were in. . . ."

"Who was it?"

"Who? How could I know? He didn't show his face!"

"Didn't you ask his name?"

"No, what should I do with his name?"

One morning he waited at my bedroom door to tell me, "At five o'clock there was a telepoon. You were sleeping, and so I asked, 'Who are you?' He said, 'Trunk, trunk,' and I told him, 'Go away, don't trouble us. No trunk or baggage here. Master is sleeping.' " To this day I have no idea where the trunk call was from. When I tried to explain to him what a "trunk call" was (long-distance call) he kept saying, "When you are sleeping, that fellow asks for a trunk! Why should we care?" I gave up.

The only way to exist in harmony with Annamalai was to take him as he was; to improve or enlighten him would only exhaust the reformer and disrupt nature's design. At first he used to light a fire in the basement itself, his fuel consisting of leaves and all sorts of odds and ends swept up from the garden, which created an enormous pall of smoke and blackened the walls; also there was the danger of his setting fire to himself in that room without a chimney. I admonished him one day and suggested that he use charcoal. He said, "Impossible! Food cooked over charcoal shortens one's life, sir. Hereafter I will not cook inside the house at all." Next day he set up three bricks under the pomegranate tree, placed a mud pot over them, and raised a roaring fire. He boiled water and cooked rice, dal, onion, tomato, and a variety of greens picked from the garden, and created a stew whose fragrance rose heavenward and in its passage enticed me to peep over the terrace and imbibe it.

When the monsoon set in I felt anxious as to how he was going to manage, but somehow even when the skies darkened and the rains fell, between two bouts he raised and kept up the fire under the pomegranate shade. When it poured incessantly he held a corrugated iron sheet over the fire and managed, never bothering to shield his own head. He ate at night, and preserved the remnant, and on the following day from time to time quietly dipped his fingers into the pot and ate a mouthful, facing the wall and shielding his aluminum plate from any Evil Eye that might happen to peep in at his door.

There was not a stronger person in the neighborhood. When he stalked about during his hours of watch, tapping the ground with a metal rod and challenging in a stentorian voice, he created an air of utter intimidation, like a mastiff. God knows we might have needed a mastiff definitely in the early days, but not now. Annamalai did not seem to realize that such aggressive watch was no longer necessary. He did not seem to have noticed the transition of my surroundings from a lonely outpost (where I had often watched thieves break open a trunk and examine their booty by torchlight in a ditch a hundred yards from my bedroom window) into a populous colony, nor did he take note of the coming of the industrial estate beyond my house. If any person passing my gate dallied a minute, particularly at night after he had had his supper and the stars were out, Annamalai would challenge him to explain his presence. People passing my gate quickened their pace as a general policy. Occasionally he softened when someone asked for flowers for worship. If he saw me noticing the transaction, he would shout in rage, "Go away. What do you think you are? Do flowers come up by themselves? Here is the old fellow giving his life to tending them, and you think . . ." and charge threateningly towards the would-be worshiper; but if I remained indoors and watched through the window I could see him give a handful of flowers to the person at the gate, muting his steps and tone and glancing over his shoulder to make sure that I was not watching.

Annamalai was believed to earn money by selling my flowers, according to a lady living next door to me, who had constituted herself his implacable enemy. According to Annamalai, whenever I was away on tour she demanded of him the banana leaves grown in my garden, for her guests to dine on, and his steady refusal had angered her. Whenever I passed their compound wall she would whisper, "You are trusting that fellow too much, he is always talking to the people at the gate and always carrying on some transaction." A crisis of the first order developed once when she charged him with the theft of her fowls. She reared poultry, which often invaded my compound through a gap in the fence, and every afternoon Annamalai would be chasing them out with stones and war cries. When I was away for weeks on end, according to the lady, every other day she missed a bird when she counted them at night. She explained how Annamalai dazed the fowl by throwing a wet towel over its head, and carried it off to the shop at the level crossing, where his accomplices sold or cooked it.

Once feathers were found scattered around Annamalai's habitat when it was raided by a watchman of the municipal sewage farm who wore a khaki coat and pretended to be a policeman. Annamalai was duly frightened and upset. Returning home from a tour one afternoon, I found Annamalai standing on a foot-high block of stone, in order to be heard better next door, and haranguing, "You set the police on me, do you, because you have lost a fowl? So what? What have I to do with it? If it strays into my compound I'll twist its neck, no doubt, but don't imagine that I will thieve like a cheap rascal. Why go about fowl-thieving? I care two straws for your police. They come to us for baksheesh in our village; foolish people will not know that. I am a respectable farmer with an acre of land in the village. I grow rice. Amavasai looks after it and writes to me. I receive letters by post. If I am a fowl thief, what are those that call me so?

Anyway, what do you think you are? Whom do you dare to talk
to?" In this strain he spoke for about half an hour, addressing
the air and the sky, but the direction of his remarks could not
be mistaken. Every day at the same hour he delivered his harangue, soon after he had eaten his midday food, chewed tobacco,
and tied the red bandanna securely over his ears.

Sometimes he added much autobiographical detail. Although
it was beamed in the direction of the lady next door, I gathered
a great deal of information in bits and pieces which enabled me
to understand his earlier life. Mounted on his block of stone, he
said, "I was this high when I left home. A man who has the
stuff to leave home when he is only ten won't be the sort to steal
fowl. My father had said, 'You are a thief. . . .' That night I
slipped out of the house and walked. . . . I sat in a train going
towards Madras. . . . They threw me out, but I got into the next
train, and although they thrashed me and threw me out again
and again, I reached Madras without a ticket. I am that kind,
madam, not a fowl thief, worked as a coolie and lived in the
verandahs of big buildings. I am an independent man, madam,
I don't stand nonsense from others, even if it is my father. One
day someone called me and put me on the deck of a steamer and
sent me to a tea garden in Ceylon, where I was until the fever
got me. Do you think your son will have the courage to face
such things?"

At the same hour day after day I listened and could piece
together his life. "When I came back home I was rid of the
shivering fever. I gave my father a hundred rupees and told him
that a thief would not bring him a hundred rupees. I hated my
village, with all those ignorant folk. My father knew I was planning to run away once again. One day all of them held me down,
decorated the house, and married me to a girl. I and Amavasai
went to the fields and plowed and weeded. My wife cooked my
food. After my daughter appeared I left home and went away to
Penang. I worked in the rubber estates, earned money, and sent
money home. That is all they care for at home—as long as you
send money they don't care where you are or what you do. All

that they want is money, money. I was happy in the rubber plantations. When the Japanese came they cut off everybody's head or broke their skulls with their guns, and they made us dig pits to bury the dead and also ourselves in the end. I escaped and was taken to Madras in a boat with a lot of others. At home I found my daughter grown up, but my wife was dead. It seems she had fever every day and was dead and gone. My son-in-law is in a government job in the town. I am not a fowl thief. . . . My granddaughter goes to a school every day carrying a bag of books, with her anklets jingling and flowers in her hair. . . . I had brought the jewelry for her from Malaya." Whatever the contents of his narrative, he always concluded, "I am not a rascal. If I were a fowl thief . . . would a government officer be my son-in-law?"

I told him, "No one is listening. Why do you address the wall?"

"They are crouching behind it, not missing a word anyway," he said. "If she is a great person, let her be, what do I care? How dare she say that I stole her fowl? What do I want their fowl for? Let them keep them under their bed. I don't care. But if any creature ever strays here I'll wring its neck, that is certain."

"And what will you do with it?"

"I don't care what. Why should I watch what happens to a headless fowl?"

The postcard that most upset him was the one which said, after the usual preamble, "The black sheep has delivered a lamb, which is also black, but the shepherd is claiming it: every day he comes and creates a scene. We have locked up the lamb, but he threatens to break open the door and take away the lamb. He stands in the street and abuses us every day, and curses our family; such curses are not good for us." Annamalai interrupted the letter to demand, "Afraid of curses! Haven't you speech enough to outcurse him?" Another postcard three days later said, "They came yesterday and carried off the black sheep, the mother, when we were away in the fields."

"Oh, the . . ." He checked the unholy expression that welled up from the bottom of his heart. "I know how it must have happened. They must have kept the mother tied up in the back-yard while locking up the lamb. What use would that be?" He looked at me questioningly.

I felt I must ask at this point, "Whose sheep was it?"

"The shepherd's, of course, but he borrowed ten rupees and left me the sheep as a pledge. Give me my ten rupees and take away the sheep, that is all. How can you claim the lamb? A lamb that is born under our roof is ours." This was an intricate legal point, I think the only one of its kind in the world, impossible for anyone to give a verdict on or quote precedents, as it concerned a unique kind of mortgage which multiplied in custody. "I have a set of senseless dummies managing my affairs; it is people like my brother who made me want to run away from home."

This proved a lucky break for the lady next door as the following afternoon Annamalai left to seek the company of the level-crossing gateman and other well-wishers in order to evolve a strategy to confound the erring shepherd in their village. As days passed he began to look more and more serene. I sensed that some solution had been found. He explained that someone who had arrived from the village brought the report that one night they had found the black sheep being driven off by the butcher, whereupon they waylaid him and carried it back to the bleating lamb at home. Now both the sheep and the lamb were securely locked up, while his brother and the family slept outside on the pyol of the house. I couldn't imagine how long they could continue this arrangement, but Annamalai said, "Give me back my ten rupees and take away the sheep."

"What happens to the lamb?"

"It is ours, of course. The sheep was barren until it came to our house; that shepherd boy did not pledge a pregnant sheep."

It was the tailor incident that ended our association. The post-card from home said, "The tailor has sold his machine to another tailor and has decamped. Things are bound to happen when you sit so far away from your kith and kin. You are allowing all your affairs to be spoiled." Annamalai held his temples between his hands and shut his eyes, unable to stand the shock of this revelation. I asked no questions, he said nothing more and left me, and I saw him go up the slope towards the level crossing. Later I watched him from my window as he dug at a banana root; he paused and stood frozen in a tableau with his pickaxe stuck in the ground, arms akimbo, staring at the mud at his feet. I knew at that moment that he was brooding over his domestic affairs. I went down, gently approached him, pretended to look at the banana root, but actually was dying of curiosity to know more about the tailor story. I asked some casual horticultural questions and when he started to reply I asked, "Why are tailors becoming troublesome, unpunctual, and always stealing bits of cloth?"

My antitailor sentiment softened him, and he said, "Tailor or carpenter or whoever he may be, what do I care, I am not afraid of them. I don't care for them."

"Who is the tailor your brother mentions in his letter?"

"Oh, that! A fellow called Ranga in our village, worthless fellow, got kicked out everywhere," and there the narrative for the day ended because of some interruption.

I got him to talk about the tailor a couple of days later. "People didn't like him, but he was a good tailor . . . could stitch kerchief, drawers, banian, and even women's jackets . . . but the fellow had no machine and none of his relations would help him. No one would lend him money. I got a money order from Ceylon one day for a hundred rupees—some money I had left behind. When the postman brought the money order, this tailor also came along with him, at the same moment. How could he have known? After the postman left, he asked, 'Can't you give me a hundred rupees? I can buy a machine.' I asked him, 'How did you know that I was receiving a hundred rupees, who told you?' and I slapped his face, spat at him for prying into my affairs. The fellow wept. I was, after all, his elder, and so I felt sorry and said, 'Stop that. If you howl like that I will thrash you.' Then all our village elders assembled and heard both of us, and ordered that I should lend my hundred rupees to him.''

I failed to understand how anyone could order him thus. I asked naïvely, "Why should they have told you and what have they to do with it?"

He thought for a while and answered, "That is how we do it, when the elders assemble and order us . . . ."

"But you didn't call the assembly?"

"I didn't, but they came and saw us, when the tailor was crying out that I had hurt him. They then wrote a bond on government paper with stamp and made him sign it; the man who sold the paper was also there, and we gave him two rupees for writing the document.''

Later I got a picture of this transaction little by little. The tailor purchased a sewing machine with the loan from Anna-malai. Annamalai's brother accommodated the tailor and the machine on the pyol of his house; the tailor renewed the bond from time to time, paid the interest regularly and also a daily rent for occupying the pyol. This was a sort of gold-edged security, and Annamalai preserved the bond in the safety of a tin box in my cellar. When the time for its renewal came each year, he undertook a trip to the village and came back after a month with a fresh signature on the bond, attested by the village headman. But now the entire basis of their financial relationship was shaken. The original tailor had decamped, and the new tailor did not recognize his indebtedness, although he sat on the pyol of their house and stitched away without speaking to anyone.

"You never asked for your hundred rupees back?" I asked.

"Why should I?" he asked, surprised at my question. "As long as he was paying the interest, and renewing his signature. He might have been up to some mischief if I didn't go in person; that is why I went there every time." After all this narration, Annamalai asked, "What shall I do now? The rascal has decamped."

"But where is the machine?"

"Still there. The new tailor stitches everybody's clothes in our house but won't speak to us, nor does he go away from the machine. He sleeps under it every night."

"Why don't you throw him out?"

Annamalai thought for a while and said, "He will not speak to us and he will not pay us the rent, saying when pressed that he paid all the rent to the first tailor along with the price of the machine. . . . Could it be possible? Is it so in the letter you read?"

Very soon another postcard came. It started with the respected preamble, all right, but ended rather abruptly with the words "We have nowhere to sleep, the tailor will not move. Inside the house the sheep and the lamb are locked. As the elder of our family, tell us where we should sleep. My wives threaten to go away to their parents' houses. I am sleeping with all the children in the street. Our own house has no place for us. If you keep so far away from your kith and kin, such things are bound to happen. We suffer and you don't care."

At this point Annamalai indulged in loud thinking. "Nothing new, these women are always running off to their parents . . . if you sneeze or cough it is enough to make them threaten that they will go away. Unlucky fellow, that brother of mine. He has no guts to say, 'All right, begone, you *moodhevi,*' he is afraid of them."

"Why can't they throw out the tailor and lock up the machine along with the sheep? Then they could all sleep on the pyol . . ."

"I think he is the son of our wrestler—that new tailor, and you know my brother is made of straw although he has produced nine children." He considered the situation in silence for a while and said, "It is also good in a way. As long as he is not thrown out, the machine is also there. . . . God is helping us by keeping him there within our hold. If my brother has no place to sleep in, let him remain awake."

For the next three days I sensed that much confabulation was going on, as I saw the red bandanna go up the crest more often than usual. His adviser at the Bamboo Bazaar and the well-wishers at the gate shop must have attacked the core of the problem and discovered a solution. When he returned from the gate shop one evening he announced point-blank, "I must go to my village."

"Yes, why so suddenly?"

"The bond must be changed, renewed in the new tailor's name. You must let me go."

"When?"

"When? . . . Whenever you think I should go."

"I don't think you should go at all. I can't let you go now. I am planning to visit Rameswaram on a pilgrimage."

"Yes, it is a holy place, good to visit," he said patronizingly. "You will acquire a lot of merit. After you come back I will go." So we parted on the best of terms that day. As if nothing had been spoken on the subject till now, he came up again next day, stood behind my chair, and said without any preamble, "I must go."

"Yes, after I return from my pilgrimage."

He turned around and went down halfway, but came up again to ask, "When are you going?"

His constant questioning put me on edge; anyway I suppressed my annoyance and replied calmly, "I am waiting for some others to join me, perhaps in ten days."

He seemed satisfied with the answer and shuffled down. That night when I returned home he met me at the gate. Hardly had I stepped in when he said, "I will be back in ten days; let me go tomorrow. I will be back in ten days and I will guard the house when you are away on pilgrimage. . . ."

"Should we settle all questions standing in the street? Can't you wait until I am in?"

He didn't answer but shut the gate and went away to his room. I felt bad all that night. While I changed my clothes, ate, and read or wrote, there was an uneasiness at the back of my mind at the memory of my sharp speech. I had sounded too severe. I went down to his backyard first thing in the morning, earlier than usual. He sat under the tap with the water turned full blast on his head, and then went dripping to his basement room. He stuck a flower on a picture of God on his wall, lit an incense stick, stuck a flower over his ear, put holy ash on his forehead, knotted the bandanna over his ear, and, dressed in his shorts, emerged ready for the day, but there was no friendliness in his eyes. I spent the time pretending to examine the mango blooms, made some appreciative remarks about the state of the garden, and suddenly said, "You want to be away for only ten days?"

"Yes, yes," he replied eagerly, his mood softening. "I must renew the bond, or gather people to throw out that interloper and seize his machine . . . even if it means bloodshed. Someone has to lose his life in this business. I will come back in ten days."

It sounded to me a too ambitious program to be completed in ten days. "Are you sure that you want only ten days off?" I asked kindly.

"It may be a day more or less, but I promise to be back on the day I promise. Once I come back I won't go for two years, even then I won't go unless . . . I will leave the next renewal in my brother's hands."

I found myself irritated again and said, "I cannot let you go now," in a tone of extreme firmness, at which he came nearer and pleaded with his palms pressed together, "Please, I must renew the bond now; otherwise, if it is delayed, I will lose everything, and the people in my village will laugh at me."

"Get me the bond, I will have a look at it," I said with authority.

I could hear him open his black trunk. He came in bearing a swath of cloth, unwound it with tender care, and took out of its folds a document on parchment paper. I looked through it. The bond was worth a hundred rupees, and whoever had drafted it made no mention of a tailor or his machine. It was just a note promising repayment of a hundred rupees with interest from time to time, stuck with numerous stamps, dates, thumb impressions, and signatures. I really could not see how it was going to help him. I read it out to him and commented, with my fingers drumming effectively on the document, "Where is any mention of your tailor or his machine?"

"Surely there is the name 'Ranga' on it!"

"But there is no mention of a tailor. For all it says, Ranga could be a scavenger."

Annamalai looked panic-stricken. He put his eyes close to the document and, jabbing it with his finger, asked, "What does it say here?"

I read it word by word again. He looked forlorn. I said, "I will give you a hundred rupees and don't bother about the bond. What does it cost you to reach your village?"

He made loud calculations and said, "About ten rupees by passenger from . . ."

"Coming back, ten rupees. You have been going there for years now and you have already spent more than the principal in railway fare alone to get the bond renewed."

"But he pays interest," he said.

"Give me the bond. I will pay the amount and you stay on." I felt desolate at the thought of his going away. At various times I went out on journeys short and long. Each time I just abandoned the house and returned home weeks and months later to find even a scrap of paper in the wastebasket preserved with care. Now I felt desolate.

He brushed aside my economic arguments. "You won't know these things. I can always go to a court as long as the bond is there . . ."

"And involve yourself in further expenses? It will be cheaper to burn that bond of yours." He gave me up as a dense, impossible man whose economic notions were too elementary.

Next day and next again and again, I heard his steps on the stairs. "I will come back in ten days."

I said, "All right, all right, you have too many transactions and you have no peace of mind to do your duty here, and you don't care what happens to me. I have to change my plans for your sake, I suppose?"

All this was lost on him, it was gibberish as far as he was concerned. I was obsessed with flimsy, impalpable things while the solid, foursquare realities of the earth were really sheep and tailors and bonds. He stared at me pityingly for a moment as at an uncomprehending fool, turned, and went downstairs. The next few days I found him sulking. He answered me sharply whenever I spoke to him. He never watered the plants. He ignored the lady next door. More than all, he did not light the fire, as was his custom, in the shade of the pomegranate tree. He had taken off the red bandanna and hooded an old blanket over his head as he sat in a corner of the basement room, in a state of mourning. When I went out or came in, he emerged from the basement and opened the gate dutifully. But no word passed between us. Once I tried to draw him into a conversation by asking breezily, "Did you hear that they are opening a new store over there?"

"I go nowhere and seek no company. Why should you think I go about, gossiping about shops and things? None of my business."

Another day I asked, "Did anyone telephone?"

"Wouldn't I mention it if there had been telepoon?" he replied, glaring at me, and withdrew mumbling, "If you have no trust in me, send me away. Why should I lie that there was no telepoon if there was one? I am not a rascal. I am also a respectable farmer; send me away." He looked like someone else under his gray hood; his angry eyes peered at me with hostility. It seemed as if he had propped himself up with an effort all these years but now was suddenly falling to pieces.

A week later one morning I heard a sound at the gate, noticed him standing outside, his tin trunk and a gunnysack stuffed with odds and ends on the ground at his feet. He wore a dark coat which he had preserved for occasions, a white dhoti, and a neat turban on his head. He was nearly unrecognizable in this garb. He said, "I am going by the eight-o'clock train today. Here is the key of the basement room." He then threw open the lid of his trunk and said, "See if I have stolen anything of yours, but that lady calls me a fowl thief. I am not a rascal."

"Why do you have to go away like this? Is this how you should leave after fifteen years of service?" I asked.

He merely said, "I am not well. I don't want to die in this house and bring it a bad name. Let me go home and die. There they will put new clothes and a fresh garland on my corpse and carry it in a procession along all the streets of our village with a band. Whereas if I am dead in that basement room while you are away, I will rot there till the municipal scavengers cart me away with the garbage heap. Let me not bring this house an evil reputation. I will go home and die. All the garden tools are in that room. Count them if you like. I am not a thief." He waited for me to inspect his trunk.

I said, "Shut it, I don't have to search your trunk." He hoisted it on his head and placed over it the gunny bundle and was starting off.

"Wait," I said.

"Why?" he asked without stopping, without turning.

"I want to give you—" I began, and dashed in to fetch some money. When I returned with ten rupees, he was gone.

Lawley Road

The Talkative Man said:

For years people were not aware of the existence of a municipality in Malgudi. The town was none the worse for it. Diseases, if they started, ran their course and disappeared, for even diseases must end someday. Dust and rubbish were blown away by the wind out of sight; drains ebbed and flowed and generally looked after themselves. The municipality kept itself in the background, and remained so till the country got its independence on the 15th of August, 1947. History holds few records of such jubilation as was witnessed on that day from the Himalayas to Cape Comorin. Our municipal council caught the inspiration. They swept the streets, cleaned the drains, and hoisted flags all over the place. Their hearts warmed up when processions with flags and music passed through their streets.

The municipal chairman looked down benignly from his balcony, muttering, "We have done our bit for this great occasion." I believe one or two members of the council who were with him saw tears in his eyes. He was a man who had done himself well as a supplier of blankets to the army during the war, later spending a great deal of his gains in securing the chairmanship. That's an epic by itself and does not concern us now. My present story is different. The satisfaction the chairman now felt was, however, short-lived. In about a week, when the bunting was torn off, he became quite dispirited. I used to visit him almost every day, trying to make a living out of news reports to an upcountry paper which paid me two rupees for every inch of published news. Every month I could measure out about ten inches of news in that paper, which was mostly a somewhat idealized account of municipal affairs. This made me a great favorite there. I walked in and out of the municipal chairman's office constantly. Now he looked so unhappy that I was forced to ask, "What is wrong, Mr. Chairman?"

"I feel we have not done enough," he replied.

"Enough of what?" I asked.

"Nothing to mark off the great event." He sat brooding and then announced, "Come what may, I am going to do something great!" He called up an Extraordinary Meeting of the council, and harangued them; and at once they decided to nationalize the names of all the streets and parks, in honor of the birth of Independence. They made a start with the park at the market square. It used to be called The Coronation Park—whose coronation God alone knew; it might have been the coronation of Victoria or of Asoka. No one bothered about it. Now the old board was uprooted and lay on the lawn, and a brand-new sign stood up in its place declaring it henceforth to be HAMARA HINDUSTHAN PARK.

The other transformations, however, could not be so smoothly worked out. "Mahatma Gandhi Road" was the most sought-after name. Eight different ward councillors were after it. There were six others who wanted to call the roads in front of their houses "Nehru Road" or "Netaji Subash Bose Road." Tempers were rising and I feared they might come to blows. There came a point when, I believe, the council just went mad. It decided to give the same name to four different streets. Well, sir, even in the most democratic or patriotic town it is not feasible to have two roads bearing the same name. The result was seen within a fortnight. The town became unrecognizable with new names. Gone were the "Market Road," "North Road," "Chitra Road," "Vinayak Mudali Street," and so on. In their place appeared the names, repeated in four different places, of all the ministers, deputy ministers, and the members of the Congress Working Committee. Of course, it created a lot of hardship—letters went where they were not wanted, people were not able to say where they lived or direct others there. The town became a wilderness with all its landmarks gone.

The chairman was gratified with his inspired work—but not for long. He became restless again and looked for fresh fields of action.

At the corner of Lawley Extension and Market there used to be a statue. People had got so used to it that they never bothered to ask whose it was or even look up. It was generally used by the birds as a perch. The chairman suddenly remembered that it was the statue of Sir Frederick Lawley. The extension had been named after him. Now it was changed to "Gandhi Nagar," and it seemed impossible to keep Lawley's statue any longer there. The council unanimously resolved to remove it. The council with the chairman sallied forth triumphantly next morning and circumambulated the statue. They now realized their mistake. The statue towered twenty feet above them and seemed to arise from a pedestal of molten lead. In their imagination they had thought that a vigorous resolution would be enough to topple down the statue of this satrap, but now they found that it stood with the firmness of a mountain. They realized that Britain, when she was here, had attempted to raise herself on no mean foundation. But it made them only firmer in their resolve. If it was going to mean blasting up that part of the town for the purpose, they would do it. For they unearthed a lot of history about Sir Frederick Lawley. He was a combination of Attila, the scourge of

Europe, and Nadir Shah, with the craftiness of a Machiavelli. He subjugated Indians with the sword and razed to the ground the villages from which he heard the slightest murmur of protest. He never countenanced Indians except when they approached him on their knees.

People dropped their normal occupations and loitered around the statue, wondering how they could have tolerated it for so many years. The gentleman seemed to smile derisively at the nation now, with his arms locked behind and sword dangling from his belt. There could be no doubt that he must have been the worst tyrant imaginable: the true picture—with breeches and wig and white waistcoat and that hard determined look—of all that has been hatefully familiar in the British period of Indian history. They shuddered when they thought of the fate of their ancestors who had to bear the tyrannies of this man.

Next the municipality called for tenders. A dozen contractors sent in their estimates, the lowest standing at fifty thousand rupees, for removing the statue and carting it to the municipal office, where they were already worried about the housing of it. The chairman thought over it and told me, "Why don't you take it yourself? I will give you the statue free if you do not charge us anything for removing it." I had thought till then that only my municipal friends were mad, but now I found I could be just as mad as they. I began to calculate the whole affair as a pure investment. Suppose it cost me five thousand rupees to dislodge and move the statue (I knew the contractors were overestimating), and I sold it as metal for six thousand . . . About three tons of metal might fetch anything. Or I could probably sell it to the British Museum or Westminster Abbey. I saw myself throwing up the upcountry paper job.

The council had no difficulty in passing a resolution permitting me to take the statue away. I made elaborate arrangements for the task. . . . I borrowed money from my father-in-law, promising him a fantastic rate of interest. I recruited a team of fifty

coolies to hack the pedestal. I stood over them like a slave driver
and kept shouting instructions. They put down their implements
at six in the evening, and returned to their attack early next day.
They were specially recruited from Koppal, where the men's
limbs were hardened by generations of teak-cutting in Mempi
forest.

We hacked for ten days. No doubt we succeeded in chipping
the pedestal here and there, but that was all; the statue showed
no sign of moving. At this rate I feared I might become bankrupt
in a fortnight. I took permission from the district magistrate to
acquire a few sticks of dynamite, cordoned off the area, and
lighted the fuse. I brought down the knight from his pedestal
without injuring any limb. Then it took me three days to reach
the house with my booty. It was stretched out on a specially
designed carriage drawn by several bullocks. The confusion
brought about by my passage along Market Road, the crowd
that followed uttering jokes, the incessant shouting and instructions I had to be giving, the blinding heat of the day, Sir F.'s
carriage coming to a halt at every inconvenient spot and angle,
neither moving forward nor backward, holding up the traffic on
all sides, and darkness coming on suddenly with the statue nowhere near my home—all this was a nightmare I wish to pass
over. I mounted guard over him on the roadside at night. As he
lay on his back staring at the stars I felt sorry for him and said,
"Well, this is what you get for being such a haughty imperialist.
It never pays." In due course, he was safely lodged in my small
house. His head and shoulders were in my front hall and the rest
of him stretched out into the street through the doorway. It was
an obliging community there at Kabir Lane and nobody minded
this obstruction.

The municipal council passed a resolution thanking me for my
services. I wired this news to my paper, tacking on to it a ten-

inch story of the statue. A week later the chairman came to my house in a state of agitation. I seated him on the chest of the tyrant. He said, "I have bad news for you. I wish you had not sent up that news item about the statue. See these . . ." He held out a sheaf of telegrams. They were from every kind of historical society in India, all protesting against the removal of the statue. We had all been misled about Sir F. All the present history pertained to a different Lawley, of the time of Warren Hastings. This Frederick Lawley (of the statue) was a military governor who settled down here after the Mutiny. He cleared the jungles and almost built the town of Malgudi. He established here the first co-operative society for the whole of India, and the first canal system by which thousands of acres of land were irrigated from the Sarayu, which had been dissipating itself till then. He established this, he established that, and he died in the great Sarayu floods while attempting to save the lives of villagers living on its banks. He was the first Englishman to advise the British Parliament to associate more and more Indians in all Indian affairs. In one of his dispatches he was said to have declared, "Britain must quit India someday for her own good."

The chairman said, "The government have ordered us to reinstate the statue." "Impossible!" I cried. "This is my statue and I shall keep it. I like to collect statues of national heroes." This heroic sentiment impressed no one. Within a week all the newspapers in the country were full of Sir Frederick Lawley. The public caught the enthusiasm. They paraded in front of my house, shouting slogans. They demanded the statue back. I offered to abandon it if the municipality at least paid my expenses in bringing it here. The public viewed me as their enemy. "This man is trying to black-market even a statue . . . ," they remarked. Stung by it I wrote a placard and hung it on my door: STATUE FOR SALE. TWO AND A HALF TONS OF EXCELLENT METAL. IDEAL GIFT FOR A PATRIOTIC FRIEND. OFFERS ABOVE TEN THOUSAND WILL BE CONSIDERED. It infuriated them and made them want to kick me, but they had been brought up in a tradition of nonviolence and so they picketed my house; they lay across my door in relays holding a flag and shouting slogans. I had sent away my wife and children to the village in order to make room for the statue in my house, and so this picketing did not bother me—only I had to use the back door a great deal. The municipality sent me a notice of prosecution under the Ancient Monuments Act, which I repudiated in suitable terms. We were getting into bewildering legalities—a battle of wits between me and the municipal lawyer. The only nuisance about it was that an abnormal quantity of correspondence developed and choked up an already congested household.

I clung to my statue, secretly despairing how it was ever going to end. I longed to be able to stretch myself fully in my own house.

Six months later relief came. The government demanded a report from the municipality on the question of the statue, and this together with other lapses on the part of the municipality made them want to know why the existing council should not be dissolved and re-elections ordered. I called on the chairman and said, "You will have to do something grand now. Why not acquire my house as a National Trust?"

"Why should I?" he asked.

"Because," I said, "Sir F. is here. You will never be able to cart him to his old place. It'll be a waste of public money. Why not put him up where he is now? He has stayed in the other place too long. I'm prepared to give you my house for a reasonable price."

"But our funds don't permit it," he wailed.

"I'm sure you have enough funds of your own. Why should you depend upon the municipal funds? It'll indeed be a grand gesture on your part, unique in India. . . ." I suggested he ought to relieve himself of some of his old blanket gains. "After all . . . how much more you will have to spend if you have to fight another election!" It appealed to him. We arrived at a figure. He was very happy when he saw in the papers a few days later: "The Chairman of Malgudi Municipality has been able to buy back as a present for the nation the statue of Sir Frederick Lawley. He proposes to install it in a newly acquired property which is shortly to be converted into a park. The Municipal Council have resolved that Kabir Lane shall be changed to Lawley Road."

A Breath of
Lucifer

S am was only a voice to me, a rich, reverberating baritone.
His whispers themselves possessed a solid, rumbling quality.
I often speculated, judging from his voice, what he might look
like: the possessor of such a voice could be statuesque, with curls
falling on his nape, Roman nose, long legs able to cover the
distance from my bed to the bathroom in three strides although
to me it seemed an endless journey. I asked him on the very first
day, "What do you look like?"

"How can I say? Several years since I looked at a mirror!"

"Why so?"

"The women at home do not give us a chance, that is all. I
have even to shave without a mirror." He added, "Except once
when I came up against a large looking glass at a tailor's and
cried out absent-mindedly, 'Ah, Errol Flynn in town!' "

"You admired Errol Flynn?"

"Who wouldn't? As Robin Hood, unforgettable; I saw the
picture fifty times."

"What do you look like?"

215

He paused and answered, "Next week this time you will see for yourself; be patient till the bandages are taken off. . . ."

Sam had taken charge of my bodily self the moment I was wheeled out of the operation theater at the Malgudi Eye Clinic in New Extension with my eyes padded, bandaged, and sealed. I was to remain blindfolded for nearly a week in bed. During this confinement Sam was engaged for eight rupees a day to act as my eyes.

He was supposed to be a trained "male nurse," a term which he abhorred, convinced that nursing was a man's job and that the female in the profession was an impostor. He assumed a defiant and challenging pose whenever the sister at the nursing home came into my room. When she left he always had a remark to make, "Let this lady take charge of a skull-injury case; I will bet the patient will never see his home again."

Sam had not started life as a male nurse, if one might judge from his references. He constantly alluded to military matters, commands, campaigns, fatigue duties, and parades. What he actually did in the army was never clear to me. Perhaps if I could have watched his facial expressions and gestures I might have understood or interpreted his words differently, but in my unseeing state I had to accept literally whatever I heard. He often spoke of a colonel who had discovered his talent and encouraged and trained him in nursing. That happened somewhere on the Burma border, Indochina, or somewhere, when their company was cut off and the medical units completely destroyed. The colonel had to manage with a small band of survivors, the most active among them being Sam, who repaired and rehabilitated the wounded and helped them return home almost intact when the war ended. Which war was it? Where was it fought? Against whom? I could never get an answer to those questions. He always spoke of "the enemy," but I never understood who it was since Sam's fluency could not be interrupted for a clarification. I had to accept what I heard without question. Before they parted, the colonel composed a certificate which helped Sam in his career.

"I have framed it and hung it in my house beside Jesus," he said.

At various theaters of war (again, which war I could never know) his services were in demand, mainly in surgical cases. Sam was not much interested in the physician's job. He had mostly been a surgeon's man. He only spoke of incidents where he had to hold up the guts of someone until the surgeon arrived, of necks half severed, arms amputated, and all aspects of human disjointedness and pain handled without hesitancy or failure. He asserted, "My two hands and ten fingers are at the disposal of anyone who needs them in war or peace."

"What do you earn out of such service?" I asked.

He replied, "Sometimes ten rupees a day, five, two, or nothing. I have eight children, my wife, and two sisters and a niece depending on me, and all of them have to be fed, clothed, sent to schools, and provided with books and medicines. We somehow carry on. God gives me enough. The greater thing for me is the relief that I am able to give anyone in pain. . . . Oh, no, do not get up so fast. Not good for you. Don't try to swat that mosquito buzzing at your ear. You may jam your eye. I am here to deal with that mosquito. Hands down, don't put up your hand near your eyes." He constantly admonished me, ever anxious lest I should by some careless act suffer a setback.

He slept in my room, on a mat a few feet away from my bed. He said that he woke up at five in the morning, but it could be any time since I had no means of verifying his claim by a watch or by observing the light on the walls. Night and day and all days of the week were the same to me. Sam explained that although he woke up early he lay still, without making the slightest noise, until I stirred in bed and called, "Sam!"

"Good morning, sir," he answered with alacrity and added, "Do not try to get up yet." Presently he came over and tucked up the mosquito net with scrupulous care. "Don't get up yet," he ordered and moved off. I could hear him open the bathroom door. Then I noticed his steps move farther off as he went in to

make sure that the window shutters were secure and would not
fly open and hit me in the face when I got in and fumbled about.
After clearing all possible impediments in my way, he came back
and said, "Righto, sir, now that place is yours, you may go in
safely. Get up slowly. Where is the hurry? Now edge out of your
bed, the floor is only four inches below your feet. Slide down
gently, hold my hand, here it is. . . ." Holding both my hands
in his, he walked backward and led me triumphantly to the
bathroom, remarking along the way, "The ground is level and
plain, walk fearlessly. . . ."

With all the assurance that he attempted to give me, the
covering over my eyes subjected me to strange tricks of vision
and made me nervous at every step. I had a feeling of passing
through geological formations, chasms, and canyons or billowing
mounds of cotton wool, tarpaulin, or heaps of smithy junk or an
endless array of baffle walls one beside another. I had to move
with caution. When we reached the threshold of the bathroom
he gave me precise directions: "Now move up a little to your
left. Raise your right foot, and there you are. Now you do anything here. Only don't step back. Turn on your heel, if you must.
That will be fine." Presently, when I called, he re-entered the
bathroom with a ready compliment on his lips: "Ah, how careful
and clean! I wish some people supposed to be endowed with full
vision could leave a W.C. as tidy! Often, after they have been
in, the place will be fit to be burned down! However, my business in life is not to complain but to serve." He then propelled
me to the washbasin and handed me the toothbrush. "Do not
brush so fast. May not be good for your eyes. Now stop. I will
wash the brush. Here is the water for rinsing. Ready to go back?"

"Yes, Sam!"

He turned me around and led me back towards my bed. "You
want to sit on your bed or in the chair?" he asked at the end of
our expedition. While I took time to decide, he suggested, "Why
not the chair? You have been in bed all night. Sometimes I had
to mind the casualties until the stretcher bearers arrived, and I

always said to the boys, 'Lying in bed makes a man sick, sit up, sit up as long as you can hold yourselves together.' While we had no sofas in the jungle, I made them sit and feel comfortable on anything, even on a snake hole once, after flattening the top."

"Where did it happen? Did you say Burma?" I asked as he guided me to the cane chair beside the window.

He at once became cautious. "Burma? Did I say Burma? If I mentioned Burma I must have meant it and not the desert—"

"Which campaign was it?"

"Campaign? Oh, so many, I may not remember. Anyway it was a campaign and we were there. Suppose I fetch you my diary tomorrow? You can look through it when your eyes are all right again, and you will find in it all the answers."

"Oh! that will be very nice indeed."

"The colonel gave me such a fat, leather-bound diary, which cost him a hundred rupees in England, before he left, saying, 'Sam, put your thoughts into it and all that you see and do, and some day your children will read the pages and feel proud of you.' How could I tell the colonel that I could not write or read too well? My father stopped my education when I was that high, and he devoted more time to teach me how to know good toddy from bad."

"Oh, you drink?" I asked.

"Not now. The colonel whipped me once when he saw me drunk, and I vowed I'd never touch it again," he added as an afterthought while he poured coffee for me from the Thermos flask (which he filled by dashing out to a coffee house in the neighborhood; it was amazing with what speed he executed these exits and entrances, although to reach the coffee house he had to run down a flight of steps, past a verandah on the ground floor, through a gate beyond a drive, and down the street; I didn't understand how he managed it all, as he was always present when I called him, and had my coffee ready when I wanted it). He handed me the cup with great care, guiding my fingers around the handle with precision. While I sipped the coffee I could hear him move around the bed, tidying it up. "When the doctor comes he must find everything neat. Otherwise he will think that a donkey has been in attendance in this ward." He swept and dusted. He took away the coffee cup, washed it at the sink and put it away, and kept the toilet flush hissing and roaring by repeated pulling of the chain. Thus he set the stage for the doctor's arrival. When the sound of the wheels of the bandage trolley was heard far off, he helped me back to my bed and stationed himself at the door. When footsteps approached, the baritone greeted, "Good morning, Doctor, sir."

The doctor asked, "How is he today?"

"Slept well. Relished his food. No temperature. Conditions normal, Doctor, sir." I felt the doctor's touch on my brow as he untied the bandage, affording me for a tenth of a second a blurred view of assorted faces over me; he examined my eye, applied drops, bandaged again, and left. Sam followed him out as an act of courtesy and came back to say, "Doctor is satisfied with your progress. I am happy it is so."

Occasionally I thumbed a little transistor radio, hoping for some music, but turned it off the moment a certain shrill voice came on the air rendering "film hits"; but I always found the tune continuing in a sort of hum for a minute or two after the radio was put away. Unable to judge the direction of the voice or its source, I used to feel puzzled at first. When I understood, I asked, "Sam, do you sing?"

The humming ceased. "I lost practice long ago," he said, and added, "When I was at Don Bosco's, the bishop used to encourage me. I sang in the church choir, and also played the harmonium at concerts. We had our dramatic troupe too and I played Lucifer. With my eyebrows painted and turned up, and with a fork at my tail, the bishop often said that never a better Lucifer was seen anywhere; and the public appreciated my performance. In our story the king was a good man, but I had to get inside him and poison his nature. The princess was also pure but I had to spoil her heart and make her commit sins." He chuckled at the memory of those days.

He disliked the nurse who came on alternate days to give me a sponge bath. Sam never approved of the idea. He said, "Why can't I do it? I have bathed typhoid patients running one hundred and seven degrees—"

"Oh, yes, of course." I had to pacify him. "But this is different, a very special training is necessary for handling an eye patient."

When the nurse arrived with hot water and towels he would linger on until she said unceremoniously, "Out you go, I am in a hurry." He left reluctantly. She bolted the door, seated me in a chair, helped me off with my clothes, and ran a steaming towel over my body, talking all the time of herself, her ambition in life to visit her brother in East Africa, of her three children in school, and so forth.

When she left I asked Sam, "What does she look like?"

"Looks like herself all right. Why do you want to bother about her? Leave her alone. I know her kind very well."

"Is she pretty?" I asked persistently, and added, "At any rate I can swear that her voice is sweet and her touch silken."

"Oh! Oh!" he cried. "Take care!"

"Even the faint garlic flavor in her breath is very pleasant, although normally I hate garlic."

"These are not women you should encourage," he said. "Before you know where you are, things will have happened. When I played Lucifer, Marie, who took the part of the king's daughter, made constant attempts to entice me whenever she got a chance. I resisted her stoutly, of course; but once when our troupe was camping out, I found that she had crept into my bed at night. I tried to push her off, but she whispered a threat that she would yell at the top of her voice that I had abducted her. What could I do with such a one!" There was a pause, and he added, "Even after we returned home from the camp she pursued me, until one day my wife saw what was happening and gashed her face with her fingernails. That taught the slut a lesson."

"Where is Marie these days?" I asked.

He said, "Oh! she is married to a fellow who sells raffle tickets, but I ignore her whenever I see her at the market gate helping her husband."

When the sound of my car was heard outside, he ran to the window to announce, "Yes, sir, they have come." This would be the evening visit from my family, who brought me my supper. Sam would cry from the window, "Your brother is there and that good lady his wife also. Your daughter is there and her little son. Oh! what a genius he is going to be! I can see it in him now. Yes, yes, they will be here in a minute now. Let me keep the door open." He arranged the chairs. Voices outside my door, Sam's voice overwhelming the rest with "Good evening, madam. Good evening, sir. Oh! You little man! Come to see your grand-father! Come, come nearer and say hello to him. You must not shy away from him." Addressing me, he would say, "He is ter-rified of your beard, sir," and, turning back to the boy, "He will be all right when the bandage is taken off. Then he is going to have a shave and a nice bath, not the sponge bath he is now having, and then you will see how grand your grandfather can be!" He then gave the visitors an up-to-the-minute account of the state of my recovery. He would also throw in a faint com-plaint. "He is not very cooperative. Lifts his hands to his eyes constantly, and will not listen to my advice not to exert." His listeners would comment on this, which would provoke a further comment in the great baritone, the babble maddening to one not able to watch faces and sort out the speakers, until I im-plored, "Sam, you can retire for a while and leave us. I will call you later"—thus giving me a chance to have a word with my visitors. I had to assume that he took my advice and departed. At least I did not hear him again until they were ready to leave, when he said, "Please do not fail to bring the washed clothes tomorrow. Also, the doctor has asked him to eat fruits. If you could find apples—" He carried to the car the vessels brought by them and saw them off.

After their departure he would come and say, "Your brother,

sir, looks a mighty officer. No one can fool him, very strict he must be, and I dare not talk to him. Your daughter is devoted to you, no wonder, if she was motherless and brought up by you. That grandson! Watch my words, some day he is going to be like Nehru. He has that bearing now. Do you know what he said when I took him out for a walk? 'If my grandfather does not get well soon I will shoot you.' " And he laughed at the memory of that pugnacious remark.

We anticipated with the greatest thrill the day on which the bandages would be taken off my eyes. On the eve of the memorable day Sam said, "If you don't mind, I will arrange a small celebration. This is very much like New Year's Eve. You must sanction a small budget for the ceremony, about ten rupees will do. With your permission—" He put his hand in and extracted the purse from under my pillow. He asked for an hour off and left. When he returned I heard him place bottles on the table.

"What have you there?" I asked.

"Soft drinks, orange, Coca-Cola, this also happens to be my birthday. I have bought cake and candles, my humble contribution for this grand evening." He was silent and busy for a while and then began a running commentary: "I'm now cutting the cake, blowing out the candles—"

"How many?"

"I couldn't get more than a dozen, the nearby shop did not have more."

"Are you only twelve years old?"

He laughed, handed me a glass. "Coca-Cola, to your health. May you open your eyes on a happy bright world—"

"And also on your face!" I said. He kept filling my glass and toasting to the health of all humanity. I could hear him gulp down his drink again and again. "What are you drinking?"

"Orange or Coca-Cola, of course."

"What is the smell?"

"Oh, that smell! Someone broke the spirit lamp in the next ward."

"I heard them leave this evening!"

"Yes, yes, but just before they left they broke the lamp. I assured them, 'Don't worry, I'll clean up.' That's the smell on my hands. After all, we must help each other—" Presently he distributed the cake and burst into a song or two: "*He's a jolly good fellow,*" and then, "*The more we are together—*" in a stentorian voice. I could also hear his feet tapping away a dance.

After a while I felt tired and said, "Sam, give me supper. I feel sleepy."

After the first spell of sleep I awoke in the middle of the night and called, "Sam."

"Yes, sir," he said with alacrity.

"Will you lead me to the bathroom?"

"Yes, sir." The next moment he was at my bed, saying, "Sit up, edge forward, two inches down to your feet; now left, right, left, march, left, right, right turn." Normally, whenever I described the fantastic things that floated before my bandaged eyes he would reply, "No, no, no wall, nor a pillar. No junk either, trust me and walk on—" But today when I said, "You know why I have to walk so slowly—?"

"I know, I know," he said. "I won't blame you. The place is cluttered."

"I see an immense pillar in my way," I said.

"With carvings," he added. "Those lovers again. These two figures! I see them. She is pouting her lips, and he is trying to chew them off, with his arm under her thigh. A sinful spectacle, that's why I gave up looking at sculptures!"

I tried to laugh it off and said, "The bathroom."

"The bathroom, the bathroom, that is the problem. . . ." He paused and then said all of a sudden, "The place is on fire."

"What do you mean on fire?"

"I know my fire when I see one. I was Lucifer once. When I came on stage with fire in my nostrils, children screamed in the auditorium and women fainted. Lucifer has been breathing around. Let us go." He took me by my hand and hurried me out in some direction.

At the verandah I felt the cold air of the night in my face and asked, "Are we going out—?"

He would not let me finish my sentence. "This is no place for us. Hurry up. I have a responsibility. I cannot let you perish in the fire."

This was the first time I had taken a step outside the bedroom, and I really felt frightened and cried, "Oh! I feel we are on the edge of a chasm or a cavern, I can't walk." And he said, "Softly, softly. Do not make all that noise. I see the tiger's tail sticking out of the cave."

"Are you joking?"

He didn't answer but gripped my shoulder and led me on. I did not know where we were going. At the stairhead he commanded, "Halt, we are descending, now your right foot down, there, there, good, now bring the left one, only twenty steps to go." When I had managed it without stumbling, he complimented me on my smartness.

Now a cold wind blew in my face, and I shivered. I asked, "Are we inside or outside?" I heard the rustle of tree leaves. I felt the gravel under my bare feet. He did not bother to answer my question. I was taken through a maze of garden paths, and steps. I felt bewildered and exhausted. I suddenly stopped dead in my tracks and demanded, "Where are you taking me?" Again he did not answer. I said, "Had we better not go back to my bed?"

He remained silent for a while to consider my proposal and agreed, "That might be a good idea, but dangerous. They have mined the whole area. Don't touch anything you see, stay here, don't move, I will be back." He moved off. I was seized with panic when I heard his voice recede. I heard him sing *"He's a jolly good fellow, He's a jolly good fellow,"* followed by *"Has she got lovely cheeks? Yes, she has lovely cheeks,"* which was reassuring as it meant that he was still somewhere around.

I called out, "Sam."

He answered from afar, "Coming, but don't get up yet."

"Sam, Sam," I pleaded, "let me get back to my bed. Is it really on fire?"

He answered, "Oh, no, who has been putting ideas into your head? I will take you back to your bed, but please give me time to find the way back. There has been foul play and our retreat is cut off, but please stay still and no one will spot you." His voice still sounded far off.

I pleaded desperately, "Come nearer." I had a feeling of being poised over a void. I heard his approaching steps.

"Yes, sir, what is your command?"

"Why have you brought me here?" I asked.

He whispered, "Marie, she had promised to come, should be here any minute." He suddenly cried out, "Marie, where are you?" and mumbled, "She came into your room last night and the night before, almost every night. Did she disturb you? No. She is such a quiet sort, you would never have known. She came in when I put out the light, and left at sunrise. You are a good officer, have her if you like."

I could not help remarking, "Didn't your wife drive her away?"

Promptly came his reply: "None of her business. How dare she interfere in my affairs? If she tries . . ." He could not complete the sentence, the thought of his wife having infuriated him. He said, "That woman is no good. All my troubles are due to her."

I pleaded, "Sam, take me to my bed."

"Yes, sir," he said with alacrity, took my hand, and led me a few steps and said, "Here is your bed," and gave me a gentle push down until I sank at my knee and sat on the ground. The stones pricked me, but that seemed better than standing on my feet. He said, "Well, blanket at your feet. Call out 'Sam,' I am really not far, not really sleeping. . . . Good night, good night, I generally pray and then sleep, no, I won't really sleep. 'Sam,' one word will do, one word will do . . . will do . . ." I heard him snore, he was sound asleep somewhere in the enormous void.

I resigned myself to my fate. I put out my hand and realized that I was beside a bush, and I only hoped that some poisonous insect would not sting me. I was seized with all sorts of fears.

The night was spent thus. I must have fallen into a drowse, awakened at dawn by the bird noises around. A woman took my hand and said, "Why are you here?"

"Marie?" I asked.

"No, I sweep and clean your room every morning, before the others come."

I only said, "Lead me to my bed."

She did not waste time on questions. After an endless journey she said, "Here is your bed, sir, lie down."

I suffered a setback, and the unbandaging was postponed. The doctor struggled and helped me out of a variety of ailments produced by shock and exposure. A fortnight later the bandages were taken off, but I never saw Sam again. Only a postcard addressed to the clinic several days later:

"I wish you a speedy recovery. I do not know what happened that night. Some foul play, somewhere. That rogue who brought me the Coca-Cola must have drugged the drink. I will deal with him yet. I pray that you get well. After you go home, if you please, send me a money order for Rs. 48/—. I am charging you for only six days and not for the last day. I wish I could meet you, but my colonel has summoned me to Madras to attend on a leg amputation. . . . Sam."

Under the
Banyan Tree

The village Somal, nestling away in the forest tracts of
Mempi, had a population of less than three hundred. It was
in every way a village to make the heart of a rural reformer sink.
Its tank, a small expanse of water, right in the middle of the
village, served for drinking, bathing, and washing the cattle, and
it bred malaria, typhoid, and heaven knew what else. The cot-
tages sprawled anyhow and the lanes twisted and wriggled up
and down and strangled each other. The population used the
highway as the refuse ground and in the backyard of every house
drainwater stagnated in green puddles.

Such was the village. It is likely that the people of the village
were insensitive: but it is more than likely that they never noticed their surroundings because they lived in a kind of perpetual
enchantment. The enchanter was Nambi, the storyteller. He was
a man of about sixty or seventy. Or was he eighty or one hundred
and eighty? Who could say? In a place so much cut off as Somal
(the nearest bus stop was ten miles away) reckoning could hardly
be in the familiar measures of time. If anyone asked Nambi what

his age was he referred to an ancient famine or an invasion or
the building of a bridge and indicated how high he had stood
from the ground at the time.

He was illiterate, in the sense that the written word was a
mystery to him; but he could make up a story, in his head, at
the rate of one a month; each story took nearly ten days to
narrate.

His home was the little temple which was at the very end of
the village. No one could say how he had come to regard himself
as the owner of the temple. The temple was a very small struc-
ture with red-striped walls, with a stone image of the goddess
Shakti in the sanctum. The front portion of the temple was
Nambi's home. For aught it mattered any place might be his
home, for he was without possessions. All that he possessed was
a broom with which he swept the temple; and he had also a
couple of dhotis and upper cloth. He spent most part of the day
in the shade of the banyan which spread out its branches in front
of the temple. When he felt hungry he walked into any house
that caught his fancy and joined the family at dinner. When he
needed new clothes they were brought to him by the villagers.
He hardly ever had to go out in search of company; for the
banyan shade served as a clubhouse for the village folk. All
through the day people came seeking Nambi's company and
squatted under the tree. If he was in a mood for it he listened
to their talk and entertained them with his own observations and
anecdotes. When he was in no mood he looked at the visitors
sourly and asked, "What do you think I am? Don't blame me
if you get no story at the next moon. Unless I meditate how can
the goddess give me a story? Do you think stories float in the
air?" and moved out to the edge of the forest and squatted there
contemplating the trees.

On Friday evenings the village turned up at the temple for
worship, when Nambi lit a score of mud lamps and arranged
them around the threshold of the sanctuary. He decorated the
image with flowers, which grew wildly in the backyard of the

temple. He acted as the priest and offered to the goddess fruits
and flowers brought in by the villagers.

On the nights he had a story to tell he lit a small lamp and
placed it in a niche in the trunk of the banyan tree. Villagers as
they returned home in the evenings saw this, went home, and
said to their wives, "Now, now, hurry up with the dinner, the
storyteller is calling us." As the moon crept up behind the hillock, men, women, and children, gathered under the banyan tree.
The storyteller would not appear yet. He would be sitting in the
sanctum, before the goddess, with his eyes shut, in deep meditation. He sat thus as long as he liked and when he came out,
with his forehead ablaze with ash and vermilion, he took his seat
on a stone platform in front of the temple. He opened the story
with a question. Jerking his finger towards a vague, faraway
destination, he asked, "A thousand years ago, a stone's throw in
that direction, what do you think there was? It was not the
weedcovered waste it is now, for donkeys to roll in. It was not
the ashpit it is now. It was the capital of the king. . . ." The
king would be Dasaratha, Vikramaditya, Asoka, or anyone that
came into the old man's head; the capital was called Kapila,
Kridapura, or anything. Opening thus the old man went on
without a pause for three hours. By then brick by brick the
palace of the king was raised. The old man described the dazzling
durbar hall where sat a hundred vassal kings, ministers, and
subjects; in another part of the palace all the musicians in the
world assembled and sang, and most of the songs were sung over
again by Nambi to his audience; and he described in detail the
pictures and trophies that hung on the walls of the palace. . . .

It was story-building on an epic scale. The first day barely
conveyed the setting of the tale, and Nambi's audience as yet
had no idea who were all coming into the story. As the moon
slipped behind the trees of Mempi Forest, Nambi said, "Now,
friends, Mother says this will do for the day." He abruptly rose,
went in, lay down, and fell asleep long before the babble of the
crowd ceased.

The light in the niche would again be seen two or three days later, and again and again throughout the bright half of the month. Kings and heroes, villains and fairy-like women, gods in human form, saints and assassins jostled each other in that world which was created under the banyan tree. Nambi's voice rose and fell in an exquisite rhythm, and the moonlight and the hour completed the magic. The villages laughed with Nambi, they wept with him, they adored the heroes, cursed the villains, groaned when the conspirator had his initial success, and they sent up to the gods a heartfelt prayer for a happy ending. . . .

On the last day when the story ended, the whole gathering went into the sanctum and prostrated before the goddess. . . .

By the time the next moon peeped over the hillock Nambi was ready with another story. He never repeated the same kind of story or brought in the same set of persons, and the village folk considered Nambi a sort of miracle, quoted his words of wisdom, and lived on the whole in an exalted plane of their own, though their life in all other respects was hard and drab.

And yet it had gone on for years and years. And one moon he lit the lamp in the tree. The audience came. The old man took his seat and began the story. ". . . When King Vikramaditya lived, his minister was . . ." He paused. He could not get beyond it. He made a fresh beginning. "There was the king . . . ," he said, repeated it, and then his words trailed off into a vague mumbling. "What has come over me?" he asked pathetically. "Oh, Mother, great Mother, why do I stumble and falter? I know the story. I had the whole of it a moment ago. What was it about? I can't understand what has happened." He faltered and looked so miserable that his audience said, "Take your own time. You are perhaps tired."

"Shut up!" he cried. "Am I tired? Wait a moment; I will tell you the story presently." Following this there was utter silence. Eager faces looked up at him. "Don't look at me!" he flared up.

Somebody gave him a tumbler of milk. The audience waited patiently. This was a new experience. Some persons expressed their sympathy aloud. Some persons began to talk among themselves. Those who sat in the outer edge of the crowd silently slipped away. Gradually, as it neared midnight, others followed this example. Nambi sat staring at the ground, his head bowed in thought. For the first time he realized that he was old. He felt he would never more be able to control his thoughts or express them cogently. He looked up. Everyone had gone except his friend Mari the blacksmith. "Mari, why aren't you also gone?"

Mari apologized for the rest: "They didn't want to tire you; so they have gone away."

Nambi got up. "You are right. Tomorrow I will make it up. Age, age. What is my age? It has come on suddenly." He pointed at his head and said, "This says 'Old fool, don't think I shall be your servant anymore. You will be my servant hereafter.' It is disobedient and treacherous."

He lit the lamp in the niche next day. The crowd assembled under the banyan faithfully. Nambi had spent the whole day in meditation. He had been fervently praying to the goddess not to desert him. He began the story. He went on for an hour without a stop. He felt greatly relieved, so much so that he interrupted his narration to remark, "Oh, friends. The Mother is always kind. I was seized with a foolish fear . . . ," and continued the story. In a few minutes he felt dried up. He struggled hard: "And then . . . and then . . . what happened?" He stammered. There followed a pause lasting an hour. The audience rose without a word and went home. The old man sat on the stone brooding till the cock crew. "I can't blame them for it," he muttered to himself. "Can they sit down here and mope all night?" Two days later he gave another installment of the story, and that, too, lasted only a few minutes. The gathering dwindled. Fewer persons began to take notice of the lamp in the niche. Even these came only out of a sense of duty. Nambi realized that there was no use in prolonging the struggle. He brought the story to a speedy and premature end.

He realized what was happening. He was harrowed by the thoughts of his failure. "I should have been happier if I had dropped dead years ago," he said to himself. "Mother, why have you struck me dumb . . . ?" He shut himself up in the sanctum, hardly ate any food, and spent the greater part of the day sitting motionless in meditation.

The next moon peeped over the hillock, Nambi lit the lamp in the niche. The villagers as they returned home saw the lamp, but only a handful turned up at night. "Where are the others?" the old man asked. "Let us wait." He waited. The moon came up. His handful of audience waited patiently. And then the old man said, "I won't tell the story today, nor tomorrow unless the whole village comes here. I insist upon it. It is a mighty story. Everyone must hear it." Next day he went up and down the village street shouting, "I have a most wonderful tale to tell tonight. Come one and all; don't miss it. . . ." This personal appeal had a great effect. At night a large crowd gathered under the banyan. They were happy that the storyteller had regained his powers. Nambi came out of the temple when everyone had settled and said, "It is the Mother who gives the gifts; and it is She who takes away the gifts. Nambi is a dotard. He speaks when the Mother has anything to say. He is struck dumb when She has nothing to say. But what is the use of the jasmine when it has lost its scent? What is the lamp for when all the oil is gone? Goddess be thanked. . . . These are my last words on this earth; and this is my greatest story." He rose and went into the sanctum. His audience hardly understood what he meant. They sat there till they became weary. And then some of them got up and stepped into the sanctum. There the storyteller sat with his eyes shut. "Aren't you going to tell us a story?" they asked. He opened his eyes, looked at them, and shook his head. He indicated by gesture that he had spoken his last words.

When he felt hungry he walked into any cottage and silently sat down for food, and walked away the moment he had eaten. Beyond this he had hardly anything to demand of his fellow-beings. The rest of his life (he lived for a few more years) was one great consummate silence.

Another
Community

I am not going to mention caste or community in this story.
The newspapers of recent months have given us a tip which
is handy—namely the designation: "One Community" and "Another Community." In keeping with this practice I am giving
the hero of this story no name. I want you to find out, if you
like, to what community or section he belonged; I'm sure you
will not be able to guess it any more than you will be able to
say what make of vest he wore under his shirt; and it will be
just as immaterial to our purpose. He worked in an office which
was concerned with insurance business. He sat at a table, checked
papers and figures between eleven noon and five p.m. everyday,
and at the end of a month his pay envelope came to his hands
containing one hundred rupees. He was middle-aged now, but
his passage from youth to middle age was, more or less, at the
same seat in his office. He lived in a little house in a lane: it
had two rooms and a hall and sufficed for his wife and four
children, although he felt embarrassed when some guest or other
came down for a stay with him. The shops were nearby, the

children's school was quite close, and his wife had friends all
around. It was on the whole a peaceful, happy life—till the
October of 1947, when he found that the people around had
begun to speak and act like savages. Someone or a body of men
killed a body of men a thousand miles away and the result was
that they repeated the evil here and wreaked their vengeance on
those around. It was an absurd state of affairs. But there it was:
a good action in a far-off place did not find a corresponding echo,
but an evil one did possess that power. Our friend saw the tempers of his neighbors rising as they read the newspaper each day.
They spoke rashly. "We must smash them who are here," he
heard people say. "They don't spare even women and children!"
he heard them cry. "All right, we will teach those fellows a
lesson. We will do the same thing for them, here—that is the
only language they will understand." But he tried to say "Look
here—" He visualized his office colleague sitting on his right,
his postman, the fellow at the betel-leaves shop, and his friend
at the bank—all these belonged to another community. He had
not bothered about such a question all these days: they were just
friends—people who smiled, obliged, and spoke agreeably. But
now he saw them in a new light: they were of another community. Now when he heard his men talk menacingly, he visualized his post office friend being hacked in the street, or the
little girl belonging to that colleague of his, who so charmingly
brought him lemon squash whenever he visited them, and displayed the few bits of dance and songs she knew—he visualized
her being chased by the hooligans of his own community as she
was going to her school carrying a soap-carton full of pencils
and rubber! This picture was too much for him and he whispered
under his breath constantly, "God forbid!" He tried to smoothen
out matters by telling his fellowmen: "You see . . . but such
things will not happen here—" But he knew it was wishful
thinking. He knew his men were collecting knives and sticks.
He knew how much they were organizing themselves, with a
complete code of operations—all of which sounded perfectly

ghastly to his sensitive temperament. Fire, sword, and loot, and all the ruffians that gathered for instructions and payment at his uncle's house, who often declared, "We will do nothing by ourselves yet. But if they so much as wag their tail they will be finished. We will speak to them in the only language they will understand." Day by day life seemed to become intolerable. All straightforwardness seemed to have gone out of life suddenly. People seemed to him sneaky and secretive. Everyone seemed to him a potential assassin. People looked at each other as cannibals would at their prey. It seemed to him a shame that one should be throwing watchful, cautious looks over one's shoulder as one walked down a street. The air was surcharged with fear and suspicion. He avoided meeting anyone, for fear that they might gossip and spread wild stories. Someone or other constantly reported, "You know what happened? A cyclist was stabbed in ————Street last evening. Of course the police are hushing up the whole business." Or he heard someone say, "A woman was assaulted today" or "Do you know they rushed into the girls' school and four girls are missing. The police are useless; we must deal with these matters ourselves." Every such talk made his heart throb and brought a sickening feeling at his throat: he felt his food tasting bitter on his tongue. He could never look at his wife and children without being racked by the feeling: "Oh, innocent ones, what perils await you in the hands of what bully! God knows."

At night he could hardly sleep: he lay straining his ears for any abnormal sound that might burst out at night all of a sudden. Suppose they stole upon them and broke his door? He could almost hear the terrified screams of his little daughter and wife. And all night he kept brooding and falling off into half sleep and kept awake, awaiting the howl of riotous mobs. The howling of a distant dog seemed to him so much like mob-sound that a couple of times he got up and went up to the window to peep out, to see if any flames appeared over the skies far off. His wife woke up and asked sleepily, "What is it?" He answered casually,

"Nothing. You sleep," and returned to his bed. He was satisfied that nothing was happening. He secretly resolved that he'd fetch the woodchopper from the fuel room and keep it near at hand in case he had to defend his home. Sometimes the passage of a lorry or a cart pulled him out of his scant sleep and set him on his feet at the window: he stood there in the dark to see if it might be a police lorry going to a trouble spot. He spent almost every night in this anxious, agitated manner and felt relieved when day came.

Everyone mentioned that the coming Wednesday, the 29th of the month, was a critical day ahead. There was to be a complete showdown that day. It was not clear why they selected that date, but everybody mentioned it. In his office people spoke of nothing but the 29th. The activity in his uncle's house had risen to a feverish pitch. His uncle told him, "I'm glad we shall be done with this bother on the 29th. It is going to end this tension once for all. We shall clean up this town. After all they form only a lakh-and-a-half of the town population, while we . . ." He went into dizzying statistics.

Zero hour was approaching. He often wondered amidst the general misery of all this speculation how will they set off the spark: will one community member slap the cheek of another at a given moment in a formal manner? "Suppose nothing happens?" he asked, and his uncle told him, "How can nothing happen? We know what they are doing. They hold secret assemblies almost every night. Why should they meet at midnight?"

"They may not be able to gather everyone except at that hour," he replied.

"We don't want people to meet at that hour. We do not ask for trouble, but if anything happens, we will finish them off. It will be only a matter of a few hours; it will work like a push-button arrangement. But we will avoid the initiative as far as possible."

On the 29th most of the shops were closed as a precaution. Children stayed away from school, and said cheerfully, "No school today, Father—you know why? It seems there is going to be a fight today." The coolness and detachment with which his children referred to the fight made our friend envy them. His wife did not like the idea of his going to office. "It seems they are not going to office today," she said, referring to some neighbors. "Why should you go?" He tried to laugh off the question and while setting out, said, half-humorously, "Well, keep yourselves indoors, if you choose, that is, if you are afraid." His wife replied, "No one is afraid. As long as your uncle is near at hand, we have no fear—"

At the office, his boss was there, of course, but most of his colleagues were absent: all of them had written applying for casual leave. There seemed to be a sudden outbreak of "urgent private business" among his colleagues. The few that came wasted their time discussing the frightful possibilities of the day. Our friend's head had become one whirling mass of rumors and fears. He hated to hear their talk. He plunged himself in work. He worked at such speed and with such intensity that he found himself constantly exhausting the source of work. So much so, just to keep himself engaged, he excavated the files and accounts of four years ago for some minute checking. The result was that it was past seven-thirty when he was able to put away the papers and rise from his seat.

He suddenly fell into a feverish anxiety about reaching home. "My wife may feel anxious. God knows what the children will feel!" The figures at his office table had had a sort of deadening effect on his mind. He had felt all right as long as it lasted. But now he felt a sudden desire to reach home in the shortest time possible. The usual route seemed to him laborious and impossible. It seemed to his fevered mind that it might take hours and hours. He felt the best course would be to dash through the alley in front of his office and go home by a shortcut. It was a route which he favored whenever he was in a hurry although, under normal circumstances, he avoided it for its narrowness, gutters, and mongrels. He snatched a look at his watch and

hurried along the dark alley. He had proceeded a few yards when
a cyclist coming up halted his progress. The cyclist and the
pedestrian had difficulty in judging each other's moves, and they
both went off to the left or to the right together, and seemed to
be making awkward passes at each other, till the cyclist finally
ran his wheel between our friend's legs and fell off the saddle,
and both found themselves on the road dust. Our friend's nerves
snapped and he yelled out, "Why can't you ride carefully?" The
other scrambled to his feet and cried, "Are you blind? Can't you
see a cycle coming?" "Where is your light?"

"Who are you to question me?" said the other, shot out his
arm, and hit our friend in the face, who lost his head, and kicked
the other in the belly. A crowd assembled. Somebody shouted,
"He dares to attack us in our own place! Must teach these fellows
a lesson. Do you think we are afraid?" Shouts and screams in-
creased. It was deafening. Somebody hit our friend with a staff,
someone else with his hand; he saw a knife flashing out. Our
friend felt his end had come. He suddenly had an access of recklessness. He was able to view the moment with a lot of detachment. He essayed to lecture to the crowd on the idiocy of the
whole relationship, to tell them that they should stop it all at
once. But no sound issued from his voice—he found himself
hemmed in on all sides; the congestion was intolerable: everyone
in that rabble seemed to put his weight on him and claw at
some portion of his body. His eyes dimmed; he felt very light.
He mumbled to someone near, "But I will never, never tell my
uncle what has happened. I won't be responsible for starting all
the trouble. This city must be saved. I won't say the word that
will start all the trouble, that will press the button, so to say.
That'll finish up everybody, you and me together. What is it all
worth? There is no such thing as your community or mine. We
are all of this country. I and my wife and children: you and your
wife and children. Let us not cut each other's throats. It doesn't
matter who cuts whose: it's all the same to me. But we must
not, we must not. We must not. I'll tell my uncle that I fell

down the office staircase and hurt myself. He'll never know. He must not press the button."

But the button did get pressed. The incident of that alley became known within a couple of hours all over the city. And his uncle and other uncles did press the button, with results that need not be described here. Had he been able to speak again, our friend would have spoken a lie and saved the city; but unfortunately this saving lie was not uttered. His body was found by the police late next afternoon in a ditch in that wretched alley, and identified through the kerosene ration coupon in his breast pocket.

The Shelter

The rain came down suddenly. The only shelter he could run to was the big banyan tree on the roadside, with its huge trunk, and the spreading boughs above. He watched, with detachment, the rain patter down with occasional sprays coming in his direction. He watched idly a mongrel trotting off, his coat completely wet, and a couple of buffaloes on the roadside eating cast-off banana leaves. He suddenly became aware of another person standing under the tree, beyond the curve of the tree trunk. A faint scent of flower wafted towards him, and he could not contain his curiosity, he edged along the tree trunk, and suddenly found himself face to face with her. His first reaction was to let out a loud "Oh!," and he looked most miserable and confused. The lady saw him and suppressed a scream. When he had recovered his composure, he said, "Don't worry, I will go away." It seemed a silly thing to say to one's wife after a long separation. He moved back to his previous spot away from her. But presently he came back to ask, "What brought you here?"

He feared she might not give him a reply, but she said,

"Rain." "Oh!" He tried to treat it as a joke and tried to please her by laughing. "It brought me also here," he said, feeling idiotic. She said nothing in reply. The weather being an ever-obliging topic he tried to cling to it desperately and said, "Unexpected rain." She gave no response to his remark and looked away. He tried to drag on the subject further. "If I had had the slightest suspicion of its coming, I would have stayed indoors or brought my umbrella." She ignored his statement completely. She might be deaf for all it mattered. He wanted to ask, "Are your ears affected?" but feared that she might do something desperate. She seemed capable of doing anything when she became desperate. He had never suspected the strength of her feelings until that night of final crisis.

They had had several crises in their years of married life: every other hour they expressed differing views on everything under the sun; every question precipitated a crisis none too trivial to be ignored. It might be anything—whether to listen to Radio Ceylon or All-India Radio, whether one should see an English picture or a Tamil one, whether jasmine smell might be termed too strong or otherwise, a rose could be termed gaudy or not, and so forth; anything led to an argument and created tension, and effected a breach between the partners for a number of days, to be followed by a reconciliation and an excessive friendship lasting only for a while. In one such mood of reconciliation they had even drawn an instrument of friendship with elaborate clauses, and signed it before the gods in the puja room with a feeling that nothing would bother them again and that all their troubles were at an end, but it was short-lived and the very first clause of the contract, "We shall never quarrel hereafter," was the first to be broken within twenty-four hours of signing the deed, and all the other clauses, which covered such possible causes of difference as household expenses, criticism of food, budget discussions, references to in-laws (on all of which elaborate understanding had been evolved), did not mean anything.

Now standing in the rain he felt happy that she was cornered.

He had had no news of her after he had shut the door on her that night as it seemed so long ago. They had argued over the food as usual, and she threatened to leave the home, and he said, "Go ahead," and held the door open and she had walked out into the night. He left the door unbolted for a long time in the belief that she would return, but she didn't.

"I didn't hope to see you again," he ventured to say now and she answered, "Did you think I would go and drown myself?"

"Yes, that I feared," he said.

"Did you look for me in the nearby wells, or ponds?"

"Or the river?" he added. "I didn't."

"It would have surprised me if you had had so much concern."

He said, "You didn't drown yourself after all, how could you blame me for not looking for you?" He appealed to her pathetically. She nearly stamped her foot as she said, "That only shows you have no heart."

"You are very unreasonable," he said.

"Oh God, you have started giving a reading of my character. It is my ill fate that the rain should have come down just now and driven me over here."

"On the contrary I think it is a good rain. It has brought us together. May I now ask what you have been doing with yourself all this time?"

"Should I answer?" He detected in her voice a certain amount of concern and he felt flattered. Could he induce her to go back to him? The sentence almost formed itself on the tip of his tongue but he thrust it back. He merely asked, "Aren't you concerned with my own lot? Won't you care to know what I have been doing with myself all these months?" She didn't reply. She simply watched the rain pouring down more than ever. The wind's direction suddenly changed and a gust flung a spray of water on her face. He treated it as an excuse to dash up to her with his kerchief. She recoiled from his approach. "Don't bother about me," she cried.

"You are getting wet . . ." A bough above shook a few drops on her hair. He pointed his finger at her anxiously and said,

"You are getting drenched unnecessarily. You could move down a little this way. If you like I will stand where you are." He expected her to be touched by this solicitude. She merely replied, "You need not worry about me." She merely stood grimly looking at the rain as it churned up the road. "Shall I dash up and bring an umbrella or a taxi?" he asked. She merely glared at him and turned away. He said something else on the same lines and she asked, "Am I your toy?"

"Why do you say toy? I said no such thing."

"You think you can pick me up when you like and throw me out when you feel that way. Only toys are treated thus."

"I never told you to go away." he said.

"I am not listening to any of that again," she said.

"I am probably dying to say how sorry I am," he began.

"Maybe, but go and say that to someone else."

"I have no one else to say such things to," he said.

"That is your trouble, is it?" she asked. "That doesn't interest me."

"Have you no heart?" he pleaded. "When I say I am sorry, believe me. I am changed now."

"So am I," she said. "I am not my old self now. I expect nothing in others and I am never disappointed," she said.

"Won't you tell me what you are doing?" he pleaded. She shook her head. He said, "Someone said that you were doing Harijan work or some such thing. See how I am following your activities!" She said nothing in reply. He asked, "Do you live all the time here or . . . ?" It was plain that he was trying to get at her address. She threw a look at the rain, and then looked at him sourly. He said, "Well, I didn't order the rain anyway. We have got to face it together."

"Not necessarily. Nothing can hold me thus," she said and suddenly dashed into the rain and broke into a run. He cried after her, "Wait, wait. I promise not to talk. Come back, don't get drenched," but she was off, vanishing beyond the curtain of falling rain drops.

Seventh House

Krishna ran his finger over the block of ice in order to wipe away the layer of sawdust, chiseled off a piece, crushed it, and filled the rubber icebag. This activity in the shaded corner of the back verandah gave him an excuse to get away from the sickroom, but he could not dawdle over it, for he had to keep the icecap on his wife's brow continuously, according to the doctor's command. In that battle between ice and mercury column, it was ice that lost its iciness while the mercury column held its ground at a hundred and three degrees Fahrenheit. The doctor had looked triumphant on the day he diagnosed the illness as typhoid, and announced with glee, "We now know what stick to employ for beating it; they call it Chloromycetin. Don't you worry anymore." He was a good doctor but given to lugubrious humor and monologuing.

The Chloromycetin pills were given to the patient as directed, and at the doctor's next visit Krishna waited for him to pause for breath and then cut in with "The fever has not gone down," holding up the temperature chart.

The doctor threw a brief, detached look at the sheet and continued, "The municipality served me a notice to put a slab over the storm drain at my gate, but my lawyer said—"

"Last night she refused food," Krishna said.

"Good for the country, with its food shortage. Do you know what the fat grain merchant in the market did? When he came to show me his throat, he asked if I was an M.D.! I don't know where he learned about M.D.s."

"She was restless and tugged at her bedclothes," Krishna said, lowering his voice as he noticed his wife open her eyes.

The doctor touched her pulse with the tip of his finger and said breezily, "Perhaps she wants a different-colored sheet, and why not?"

"I have read somewhere the tugging of bedclothes is a bad sign."

"Oh, you and your reading!"

The patient moved her lips. Krishna bent close to her, and straightened himself to explain, "She is asking when you will let her get up."

The doctor said, "In time for the Olympics . . ." and laughed at his own joke. "I'd love to be off for the Olympics myself."

Krishna said, "The temperature was a hundred and three at one a.m. . . ."

"Didn't you keep the ice going?"

"Till my fingers were numb."

"We will treat you for cramps by and by, but first let us see the lady of the house back in the kitchen."

So Krishna found, after all, a point of agreement with the doctor. He wanted his wife back in the kitchen very badly. He miscooked the rice in a different way each day, and swallowed it with buttermilk at mealtimes and ran back to his wife's bedside.

The servant maid came in the afternoon to tidy up the patient and the bed, and relieved Krishna for almost an hour, which he spent in watching the street from the doorway: a cyclist passing, schoolchildren running home, crows perching in a row on the opposite roof, a street hawker crying his wares—anything seemed interesting enough to take his mind off the fever.

Another week passed. Sitting there beside her bed, holding the icebag in position, he brooded over his married life from its beginning.

When he was studying at Albert Mission he used to see a great deal of her; they cut their classes, sat on the river's edge, discussed earnestly their present and future, and finally decided to marry. The parents on both sides felt that here was an instance of the evils of modern education: young people would not wait for their elders to arrange their marriage but settled things for themselves, aping Western manners and cinema stories. Except for the lack of propriety, in all other respects the proposal should have proved acceptable; financial background of the families, the caste and group requirements, age, and everything else were correct. The elders relented eventually, and on a fine day the horoscopes of the boy and girl were exchanged and found not suited to each other. The boy's horoscope indicated Mars in the seventh house, which spelled disaster for his bride. The girl's father refused to consider the proposal further. The boy's parents were outraged at the attitude of the bride's party—a bride's father was a seeker and the bridegroom's the giver, and how dare they be finicky? "Our son will get a bride a hundred times superior to this girl. After all, what has she to commend her? All college girls make themselves up to look pretty, but that is not everything." The young couple felt and looked miserable, which induced the parents to reopen negotiations. A wise man suggested that, if other things were all right, they could ask for a sign and go ahead. The parties agreed to a flower test. On an auspicious day they assembled in the temple. The wick lamp in the inner sanctum threw a soft illumination around. The priest lit a piece of camphor and circled it in front of the image in the sanctum. Both sets of parents and their supporters, standing respectfully in the pillared hall, watched the image and prayed for guidance.

The priest beckoned to a boy of four who was with another group of worshipers. When he hesitated, the priest dangled a piece of coconut. The child approached the threshold of the sanctum greedily. The priest picked off a red and a white flower from the garland on the image, placed them on a tray, and told the boy to choose one.

"Why?" asked the boy, uneasy at being watched by so many people. If the red flower was chosen, it would indicate God's approval. The little boy accepted the piece of coconut and tried to escape, but the priest held him by the shoulder and commanded, "Take a flower!" at which the child burst into tears and wailed for his mother. The adults despaired. The crying of the child at this point was inauspicious; there should have been laughter and the red flower. The priest said, "No need to wait for any other sign. The child has shown us the way," and they all dispersed silently.

Despite the astrologers, Krishna married the girl, and Mars in the seventh house was, eventually, forgotten.

The patient seemed to be asleep. Krishna tiptoed out of the room and told the servant maid waiting in the verandah, "I have to go out and buy medicines. Give her orange juice at six, and look after her until I return." He stepped out of his house, feeling like a released prisoner. He walked along, enjoying the crowd and bustle of Market Road until the thought of his wife's fever came back to his mind. He desperately needed someone who could tell him the unvarnished truth about his wife's condition. The doctor touched upon all subjects except that. When Chloromycetin failed to bring down the fever, he said cheerfully, "It only shows that it is not typhoid but something else. We will do other tests tomorrow." And that morning, before leaving: "Why don't you pray, instead of all this cross-examination of me?"

"What sort of prayer?" Krishna had asked naïvely.

"Well, you may say, 'O God, if You *are* there, save me if You can!' " the doctor replied, and guffawed loudly at his own joke. The doctor's humor was most trying.

Krishna realized that the doctor might sooner or later arrive at the correct diagnosis, but would it be within the patient's lifetime? He was appalled at the prospect of bereavement; his heart pounded wildly at the dreadful thought. Mars, having lain dormant, was astir now. Mars and an unidentified microbe had combined forces. The microbe was the doctor's business, however confused he might look. But the investigation of Mars was not.

Krishna hired a bicycle from a shop and pedaled off in the direction of the coconut grove where the old astrologer lived who had cast the horoscopes. He found the old man sitting in the hall, placidly watching a pack of children climb over walls, windows, furniture, and rice bags stacked in a corner and creating enough din to drown all conversation. He unrolled a mat for Krishna to sit on, and shouted over the noise of the children, "I told you at the start itself how it was going to turn out, but you people would not listen to my words. Yes, Mars has begun to exercise his most malignant aspect now. Under the circumstances, survival of the person concerned is doubtful." Krishna groaned. The children in a body had turned their attention to Krishna's bicycle, and were ringing the bell and feverishly attempting to push the machine off its stand. Nothing seemed to matter now. For a man about to lose his wife, the loss of a cycle taken on hire should not matter. Let children demolish all the bicycles in the town and Krishna would not care. Everything could be replaced except a human life.

"What shall I *do?*" he asked, picturing his wife in her bed asleep and never waking. He clung to this old man desperately, for he felt, in his fevered state of mind, that the astrologer could intercede with, influence, or even apologize on his behalf to, a planet in the high heavens. He remembered the reddish Mars he used to be shown in the sky when he was a Boy Scout—reddish on account of the malignity erupting like lava from its bosom.

"What would you advise me to do? Please help me!" The old man looked over the rim of his spectacles at Krishna menacingly. His eyes were also red. "Everything is red," reflected Krishna. "He partakes of the tint of Mars. I don't know whether this man is my friend or foe. My doctor also has red eyes. So has the maid servant. . . . Red everywhere."

Krishna said, "I know that the ruling god in Mars is benign. I wish I knew how to propitiate him and gain his compassion."

The old man said, "Wait." He stood before a cupboard, took out a stack of palm-leaf strips with verses etched on them, four lines to a leaf. "This is one of the four originals of the *Brihad-Jataka,* from which the whole science of astrology is derived. This is what has given me my living; when I speak, I speak with the authority of this leaf." The old man held the palm leaf to the light at the doorway and read out a Sanskrit aphorism: " 'There can be no such thing as evading fate, but you can insulate yourself to some extent from its rigors.' " Then he added, "Listen to this: 'Where Angaraka is malevolent, appease him with the following prayer . . . and accompany it with the gift of rice and gram and a piece of red silk. Pour the oblation of pure butter into a fire raised with sandal sticks, for four days continuously, and feed four Brahmins.' . . . Can you do it?"

Krishna was panic-stricken. How could he organize all this elaborate ritual (which was going to cost a great deal) when every moment and every rupee counted? Who would nurse his wife in his absence? Who would cook the ritual feast for the Brahmins? He simply would not be able to manage it unless his wife helped him. He laughed at the irony of it, and the astrologer said, "Why do you laugh at these things? You think you are completely modern?"

Krishna apologized for his laugh and explained his helpless state. The old man shut the manuscript indignantly, wrapped it in its cover, and put it away, muttering, "These simple steps you can't take to achieve a profound result. Go, go. . . . I can be of no use to you."

Krishna hesitated, took two rupees from his purse, and held them out to the old man, who waved the money away. "Let your wife get well first. Then give me the fee. Not now." And as Krishna turned to go: "The trouble is, your love is killing your wife. If you were an indifferent husband, she could survive. The malignity of Mars might make her suffer now and then, mentally more than physically, but would not kill her. I have seen horoscopes that were the exact replica of yours and the wife lived to a ripe age. You know why? The husband was disloyal or cruel, and that in some way neutralized the rigor of the planet in the seventh house. I see your wife's time is getting to be really bad. Before anything happens, save her. If you can bring yourself to be unfaithful to her, try that. Every man with a concubine has a wife who lives long. . . ."

A strange philosophy, but it sounded feasible.

Krishna was ignorant of the technique of infidelity, and wished he had the slickness of his old friend Ramu, who in their younger days used to brag of his sexual exploits. It would be impossible to seek Ramu's guidance now, although he lived close by; he had become a senior government officer and a man of family and might not care to lend himself to reminiscences of this kind.

Krishna looked for a pimp representing the prostitutes in Golden Street and could not spot one, although the market gate was reputed to be swarming with them.

He glanced at his watch. Six o'clock. Mars would have to be appeased before midnight. Somehow his mind fixed the line at midnight. He turned homeward, leaned his bicycle on the lamppost, and ran up the steps of his house. At the sight of him the servant maid prepared to leave, but he begged her to stay on. Then he peeped into the sickroom, saw that his wife was asleep, and addressed her mentally, "You are going to get better soon. But it will cost something. Doesn't matter. Anything to save your life."

He washed hurriedly and put on a nylon shirt, a lace-edged dhoti, and a silk upper cloth; lightly applied some talcum and a strange perfume he had discovered in his wife's cupboard. He was ready for the evening. He had fifty rupees in his purse, and that should be adequate for the wildest evening one could want. For a moment, as he paused to take a final look at himself in the mirror, he was seized with an immense vision of passion and seduction.

He returned the hired cycle to the shop and at seven was walking up Golden Street. In his imagination he had expected glittering females to beckon him from their balconies. The old houses had pyols, pillars, and railings, and were painted in garish colors, as the houses of prostitutes were reputed to be in former times, but the signboards on the houses indicated that the occupants were lawyers, tradesmen, and teachers. The only relic of the old days was a little shop in an obscure corner that sold perfumes in colored bottles and strings of jasmine flowers and roses.

Krishna passed up and down the street, staring hard at a few women here and there, but they were probably ordinary, indifferent housewives. No one returned his stare. No one seemed to notice his silk upper cloth and lace dhoti. He paused to consider whether he could rush into a house, seize someone, perform the necessary act, shed his fifty rupees, and rush out. Perhaps he might get beaten in the process. How on earth was one to find out which woman, among all those he had noticed on the terraces and verandahs of the houses, would respond to his appeal?

After walking up and down for two hours he realized that the thing was impossible. He sighed for the freedom between the sexes he read about in the European countries, where you had only to look about and announce your intentions and you could get enough women to confound the most malignant planet in the universe.

He suddenly remembered that the temple dancer lived somewhere here. He knew a lot of stories about Rangi of the temple,

who danced before the god's image during the day and took
lovers at night. He stopped for a banana and a fruit drink at a
shop and asked the little boy serving him, "Which is the house
of the temple dancer Rangi?" The boy was too small to understand the purport of his inquiry and merely replied, "I don't
know." Krishna felt abashed and left.

Under a street lamp stood a jutka, the horse idly swishing its
tail and the old driver waiting for a fare. Krishna asked, "Are
you free?"

The driver sprang to attention. "Where do you wish to be
taken, sir?"

Krishna said timidly, "I wonder if you know where the temple
dancer Rangi lives?"

"Why do you want her?" the driver asked, looking him up
and down.

Krishna mumbled some reply about his wanting to see her
dance. "At this hour!" the driver exclaimed. "With so much silk
and so much perfume on! Don't try to deceive me. When you
come out of her house, she will have stripped you of all the silk
and perfume. But tell me, first, why only Rangi? There are others, both experts and beginners. I will drive you wherever you
like. I have carried hundreds like you on such an errand. But
shouldn't I first take you to a milk shop where they will give
you hot milk with crushed almond to give you stamina? Just as
a routine, my boy. . . . I will take you wherever you want to go.
Not my business anyway. Someone has given you more money
than you need? Or is your wife pregnant and away at her mother's house? I have seen all the tricks that husbands play on their
wives. I know the world, my master. Now get in. What difference does it make what you will look like when you come out
of there? I will take you wherever you like."

Krishna obediently got into the carriage, filling its interior
with perfume and the rustle of his silken robes. Then he said,
"All right. Take me home."

He gave his address so mournfully that the jutka driver, urging his horse, said, "Don't be depressed, my young master. You are not missing anything. Someday you will think of this old fellow again."

"I have my reasons," Krishna began, gloomily.

The horse driver said, "I have heard it all before. Don't tell me." And he began a homily on conjugal life.

Krishna gave up all attempts to explain and leaned back, resigning himself to his fate.

Cat
Within

A passage led to the backyard, where a well and a lavatory under a large tamarind tree served the needs of the motley tenants of the ancient house in Vinayak Mudali Street; the owner of the property, by partitioning and fragmenting all the available space, had managed to create an illusion of shelter and privacy for his hapless tenants and squeezed the maximum rent out of everyone, himself occupying a narrow ledge abutting the street, where he had a shop selling, among other things, sweets, pencils and ribbons to children swarming from the municipal school across the street. When he locked up for the night, he slept across the doorway so that no intruder should pass without first stumbling on him; he also piled up cunningly four empty kerosene tins inside the dark shop so that at the slightest contact they should topple down with a clatter: for him a satisfactory burglar alarm.

Once at midnight a cat stalking a mouse amidst the grain bags in the shop noticed a brass jug in its way and thrust its head in

256

out of curiosity. The mouth of the jug was not narrow enough to choke the cat or wide enough to allow it to withdraw its head. Suddenly feeling the weight of a crown and a blinker over its eyes at the same time, the cat was at first puzzled and then became desperate. It began to jump and run around, hitting its head with a clang on every wall. The shopkeeper, who had been asleep at his usual place, was awakened by the noise in the shop. He peered through a chink into the dark interior, quickly withdrew his head and cried into the night, "Thief! Thief! Help!" He also seized a bamboo staff and started tapping it challengingly on the ground. Every time the staff came down, the jar-crowned cat jumped high and about and banged its hooded head against every possible object, losing its sanity completely. The shopman's cry woke up his tenants and brought them crowding around him. They peered through the chink in the door and shuddered whenever they heard the metallic noise inside. They looked in again and again, trying vainly to make out in the darkness the shape of the phantom, and came to the conclusion, "Oh, some devilish creature, impossible to describe it." Someone ventured to suggest, "Wake up the exorcist." Among the motley crowd boxed in that tenement was also a professional exorcist. Now he was fast asleep, his living portion being at the farthest end.

He earned fifty rupees a day without leaving his cubicle; a circle of clients always waited at his door. His clients were said to come from even distant Pondicherry and Ceylon and Singapore. Some days they would be all over the place, and in order not to frighten the other tenants, he was asked to meet his clients in the backyard, where you would find assembled any day a dozen hysterical women and demented men, with their relatives holding them down. The exorcist never emerged from his habitation without the appropriate makeup for his role—his hair matted and coiled up high, his untrimmed beard combed down to flutter in the wind, his forehead splashed with sacred ash, vermilion and sandal paste, and a rosary of rare, plum-sized beads from the Himalayan slopes around his throat. He possessed an ancient palm-leaf book in which everyone's life was supposed to be etched in mysterious couplets. After due ceremonials, he would sit on the ground in front of the clients with the book and open a particular page appropriate to each particular individual and read out in a singsong manner. No one except the exorcist could make out the meaning of the verse composed in antiquated Tamil of a thousand years ago. Presently he would explain: "In your last life you did certain acts which are recoiling on you now. How could it be otherwise? It is karma. This seizure will leave you on the twenty-seventh day and tenth hour after the next full moon, this karma will end. . . . Were you at any time . . . ?" He elicited much information from the parties themselves. "Was there an old woman in your life who was not well-disposed to you? Be frank." "True, true," some would say after thinking over it, and they would discuss it among themselves and say, "Yes, yes, must be that woman Kamu. . . ." The exorcist would then prescribe the course of action: "She has cast a spell. Dig under the big tree in your village and bring any bone you may find there, and I'll throw it into the river. Then you will be safe for a while." Then he would thrash the victim with a margosa twig, crying, "Be gone at once, you evil spirit."

On this night the shopman in his desperation pushed his door, calling, "Come out, I want your help. . . . Strange things are going on; come on."

The exorcist hurriedly slipped on his rosary and, picking up his bag, came out. Arriving at the trouble spot he asked, "Now, tell me what is happening!"

"A jug seems to have come to life and bobs up and down, hitting everything around it, bang-bang."

"Oh, it's the jug-spirit, is it! It always enters and animates an empty jug. That's why our ancients have decreed that no empty vessel should be kept with its mouth open to the sky but always only upside down. These spirits try to panic you with frightening sounds. If you are afraid, it might hit your skull. But I can deal with it."

The shopman wailed, "I have lived a clean and honest life, never harmed a soul, why should this happen to me?"

"Very common, don't worry about it. It's karma, your past life. . . . In your past life you must have done something."

"What sort of thing?" asked the shopman with concern.

The exorcist was not prepared to elaborate his thesis. He hated his landlord as all the other tenants did, but needed more time to frame a charge and go into details. Now he said gently, "This is just a mischievous spirit, nothing more, but weak-minded persons are prone to get scared and may even vomit blood." All this conversation was carried on to the accompaniment of the clanging metal inside the shop. Someone in the crowd cried, "This is why you must have electricity. Every corner of this town has electric lights. We alone have to suffer in darkness."

"Why don't you bring in a lantern?"

"No kerosene for three days, and we have been eating by starlight."

"Be patient, be patient," said the house owner, "I have applied for power. We will get it soon."

"If we had electric lights we could at least have switched them on and seen that creature, at least to know what it is."

"All in good time, all in good time, sir, this is no occasion for complaints." He led the exorcist to the shop entrance. Someone flourished a flashlight, but its battery was weak and the bulb glowed like embers, revealing nothing. Meanwhile, the cat, sensing the presence of a crowd, paused, but soon revived its activity with redoubled vigor and went bouncing against every wall and window bar. Every time the clanging sound came, the shopman trembled and let out a wail, and the onlookers jumped back nervously. The exorcist was also visibly shaken. He peered into the dark shop at the door and sprang back adroitly every time the metallic noise approached. He whispered, "At least light a candle; what a man to have provided such darkness for yourself and your tenants, while the whole city is blazing with lights. What sort of a man are you!"

Someone in the crowd added, "Only a single well for twenty families, a single lavatory!"

A wag added, "When I lie in bed with my wife, the littlest whisper between us is heard on all sides."

Another retorted, "But you are not married."

"What if? There are others with families."

"None of your business to become a champion for others. They can look after themselves."

Bang! Bang!

"It's his sinfulness that has brought this haunting," someone said, pointing at the shopman.

"Why don't you all clear out if you are so unhappy?" said the shopman. There could be no answer to that, as the town like all towns in the world suffered from a shortage of housing. The exorcist now assumed command. He gestured to others to keep quiet. "This is no time for complaints or demands. You must all go back to bed. This evil spirit inside has to be driven out. When it emerges there must be no one in its way, otherwise it'll get under your skin."

"Never mind, it won't be worse than our landlord. I'd love to take the devil under my skin if I can kick these walls and bring down this miserable ramshackle on the head of whoever owns it," said the wag. The exorcist said, "No, no, no harsh words, please . . . I'm also a tenant and suffer like others, but I won't make my demands now. All in proper time. Get me a candle—" He turned to the shopman. "Don't you sell candles? What sort of a shopman are you without candles in your shop!" No one lost his chance to crucify the shopman.

He said, "Candles are in a box on the right-hand side on a shelf as you step in—you can reach it if you just stretch your arm . . ."

"You want me to go in and try? All right, but I charge a fee for approaching a spirit—otherwise I always work from a distance." The shopman agreed to the special fee and the exorcist cleared his throat, adjusted his coiffure and stood before the door of the shop proclaiming loudly, "Hey, spirit, I'm not afraid, I know your kind too well, you know me well, so . . .." He slid open the shutter, stepped in gingerly; when he had advanced a few steps, the jug hit the ventilator glass and shattered it, which aggravated the cat's panic, and it somersaulted in confusion and caused a variety of metallic pandemonium in the dark chamber; the exorcist's legs faltered, and he did not know for a moment what his next step should be or what he had come in for. In this state he bumped into the piled-up kerosene tins and sent them clattering down, which further aggravated the cat's hysteria. The exorcist rushed out unceremoniously. "Oh, oh, this is no ordinary affair. It seizes me like a tornado . . . it'll tear down the walls soon."

"*Aiyo!*" wailed the shopman.

"I have to have special protection . . . I can't go in . . . no candle, no light. We'll have to manage in the dark. If I hadn't been quick enough, you would not have seen me again."

"*Aiyo!* What's to happen to my shop and property?"

"We'll see, we'll see, we will do something," assured the other heroically, he himself looking eerie in the beam of light that fell on him from the street. The shopman was afraid to look at him, with his grisly face and rolling eyes, whose corners were touched with white sacred ash. He felt he had been caught between two devils—difficult to decide which one was going to prove more terrible, the one in the shop or the one outside. The exorcist sat upright in front of the closed door as if to emphasize, "I'm not afraid to sit here," and commanded, "Get me a copper pot, a copper tumbler and a copper spoon. It's important."

"Why copper?"

"Don't ask questions . . . All right, I'll tell you: because cop-

per is a good conductor. Have you noticed electric wires of copper overhead?"

"What is it going to conduct now?"

"Don't ask questions. All right, I'll tell you. I want a medium
which will lead my mantras to that horrible thing inside."

Without further questioning, the shopman produced an aluminum pot from somewhere. "I don't have copper, but only
aluminum . . ."

"In our country let him be the poorest man, but he'll own a
copper pot. . . . But here you are calling yourself a sowcar, you
keep nothing; no candle, no light, no copper . . . ," said the
exorcist.

"In my village home we have all the copper and silver . . ."

"How does it help you now? It's not your village house that
is now being haunted, though I won't guarantee this may not
pass on there. . . . Anyway, let me try." He raised the aluminum
pot and hit the ground; immediately from inside came the sound
of the jug hitting something again and again. "Don't break the
vessel," cried the shopman. Ignoring his appeal the exorcist hit
the ground again and again with the pot. "That's a good sign.
Now the spirits will speak. We have our own code." He tapped
the aluminum pot with his knuckles in a sort of Morse code. He
said to the landlord, "Don't breathe hard or speak loudly. I'm
getting a message: I'm asked to say it's the spirit of someone
who is seeking redress. Did you wrong anyone in your life?"

"Oh, no, no," said the shopman in panic. "No, I've always
been charitable . . ."

The exorcist cut him short. "Don't tell me anything, but talk
to yourself and to that spirit inside. Did you at any time handle
. . . wait a minute, I'm getting the message . . ." He held the
pot's mouth to his ear. "Did you at any time handle someone
else's wife or money?"

The shopman looked horrified. "Oh, no, never."

"Then what is it I hear about your holding a trust for a
widow . . . ?"

He brooded while the cat inside was hitting the ventilator, trying to get out. The man was in a panic now. "What trust? May I perish if I have done anything of that kind. God has given me enough to live on . . ."

"I've told you not to talk unnecessarily. Did you ever molest any helpless woman or keep her at your mercy? If you have done a wrong in your childhood, you could expiate . . ."

"How?"

"That I'll explain, but first confess . . ."

"Why?"

"A true repentance on your part will emasculate the evil spirit." The jug was hitting again, and the shopman became very nervous and said, "Please stop that somehow, I can't bear it." The exorcist lit a piece of camphor, his stock-in-trade, and circled the flame in all directions. "To propitiate the benign spirits around so that they may come to our aid . . ." The shopman was equally scared of the benign spirits. He wished, at that pale starlit hour, that there were no spirits whatever, good or bad. Sitting on the pyol, and hearing the faint shrieking of a night bird flying across the sky and fading, he felt he had parted from the solid world of men and material and had drifted on to a world of unseen demons.

The exorcist now said, "Your conscience should be clear like the Manasaro Lake. So repeat after me whatever I say. If there is any cheating, your skull will burst. The spirit will not hesitate to dash your brains out."

"Alas, alas, what shall I do?"

"Repeat after me these words: I have lived a good and honest life." The shopman had no difficulty in repeating it, in a sort of low murmur in order that it might not be overheard by his tenants. The exorcist said, "I have never cheated anyone."

". . . cheated anyone," repeated the shopman.

"Never appropriated anyone's property . . ."

The shopman began to repeat, but suddenly stopped short to ask, "Which property do you mean?"

"I don't know," said the exorcist, applying the pot to his ear.
"I hear of some irregularity."

"Oh, it's not my mistake . . . ," the shopman wailed. "It
was not my mistake. The property came into my hands, that's
all . . ."

"Whom did it belong to?"

"Honappa, my friend and neighbor, I was close to his family.
We cultivated adjoining fields. He wrote a will and was never
seen again in the village."

"In your favor?"

"I didn't ask for it; but he liked me . . ."

"Was the body found?"

"How should I know?"

"What about the widow?"

"I protected her as long as she lived."

"Under the same roof?"

"Not here, in the village . . ."

"You were intimate?"

The shopman remained silent. "Well, she had to be protected . . ."

"How did she die?"

"I won't speak a word more—I've said everything possible; if
you don't get that devil after all this, you'll share the other's fate
. . ." He suddenly sprang on the exorcist, seized him by the
throat and commanded, "Get that spirit out after getting so
much out of me, otherwise . . ." He dragged the exorcist and
pushed him into the dark chamber of the shop. Thus suddenly
overwhelmed, he went in howling with fright, his cry drowning
the metallic clamor. As he fumbled in the dark with the shopman mounting guard at the door, the jug hit him between his
legs and he let out a desperate cry, "Ah! Alas! I'm finished," and
the cat, sensing the exit, dashed out with its metal hood on,
jumped down onto the street and trotted away. The exorcist and
the shopman watched in silence, staring after it. The shopman
said, "After all, it's a cat."

"Yes, it may appear to be a cat. How do you know what is inside the cat?"

The shopman brooded and looked concerned. "Will it visit us again?"

"Can't say," said the exorcist. "Call me again if there is trouble," and made for his cubicle, saying, "Don't worry about my *dakshina* now. I can take it in the morning."

The Edge

∽

When pressed to state his age, Ranga would generally reply, "Fifty, sixty or eighty." You might change your tactics and inquire, "How long have you been at this job?"

"Which job?"

"Carrying that grinding wheel around and sharpening knives."

"Not only knives, but also scythes, clippers and every kind of peeler and cutter in your kitchen, also bread knives, even butcher's hatchets in those days when I carried the big grindstone; in those days I could even sharpen a maharaja's sword" (a favorite fantasy of his was that if armies employed swords he could become a millionaire). You might interrupt his loquaciousness and repeat your question, "How long have you been a sharpener of knives and other things?" "Ever since a line of mustache began to appear here," he would say, drawing a finger over his lip. You would not get any further by studying his chin now overlaid with patchy tufts of discolored hair. Apparently he never looked at a calendar, watch, almanac or even a mirror. In such a blissful state, clad in a dhoti, khaki shirt and turban, his was a familiar figure in the streets of Malgudi as he slowly passed in front of homes, offering his service in a high-pitched, sonorous cry, "Knives and scissors sharpened."

He stuck his arm through the frame of a portable grinding apparatus; an uncomplicated contraption operated by an old cycle wheel connected to a foot-pedal. At the Market Road he dodged the traffic and paused in front of tailor's and barber's shops, offering his services. But those were an erratic and unreliable lot, encouraging him by word but always suggesting another time for business. If they were not busy cutting hair or clothes (tailors, particularly, never seemed to have a free moment, always stitching away on overdue orders), they locked up and sneaked away, and Ranga had to be watchful and adopt all kinds of strategies in order to catch them. Getting people to see the importance of keeping their edges sharp was indeed a tiresome mission. People's reluctance and lethargy had, initially, to be overcome. At first sight everyone dismissed him with "Go away, we have nothing to grind," but if he persisted and dallied, some member of the family was bound to produce a rusty knife, and others would follow, vying with one another, presently, to ferret out long-forgotten junk and clamor for immediate attention. But it generally involved much canvassing, coaxing and even aggressiveness on Ranga's part; occasionally he would warn, "If you do not sharpen your articles now, you may not have another chance, since I am going away on a pilgrimage."

"Makes no difference, we will call in the other fellow," someone would say, referring to a competitor, a miserable fellow who operated a hand grinder, collected his cash and disappeared, never giving a second look to his handiwork. He was a fellow without a social standing, and no one knew his name, no spark ever came out of his wheel, while Ranga created a regular pyrotechnic display and passing children stood transfixed by the spectacle. "All right," Ranga would retort, "I do not grudge the poor fellow his luck, but he will impart to your knife the sharpness of an egg; after that I won't be able to do anything for you. You must not think that anyone and everyone could handle steel. Most of these fellows don't know the difference between a knife blade and a hammerhead."

Ranga's customers loved his banter and appreciated his work, which he always guaranteed for sixty days. "If it gets dull before then, you may call me son of a . . . Oh, forgive my letting slip such words. . . ." If he were to be assailed for defective execution, he could always turn around and retort that so much depended upon the quality of metal, and the action of sun and rain, and above all the care in handling, but he never argued with his customers; he just resharpened the knives free of cost on his next round. Customers always liked to feel that they had won a point, and Ranga would say to himself, "After all, it costs nothing, only a few more turns of the wheel and a couple of sparks off the stone to please the eye." On such occasions he invariably asked for compensation in kind: a little rice and buttermilk or some snack—anything that could be found in the pantry (especially if they had children in the house)—not exactly to fill one's belly but just to mitigate the hunger of the moment and keep one on the move. Hunger was, after all, a passing phase which you got over if you ignored it. He saw no need to be preoccupied with food. The utmost that he was prepared to spend on food was perhaps one rupee a day. For a rupee he could get a heap of rice in an aluminum bowl, with unexpected delicacies thrown in, such as bits of cabbage or potato, pieces of chicken, meat, lime-pickle, or even sweet *rasagulla* if he was lucky. A man of his acquaintance had some arrangement with the nearby restaurants to collect remnants and leftovers in a bucket; he came over at about ten in the night, installed himself on a culvert and imperiously ladled out his hotchpotch—two liberal scoops for a rupee. Unless one looked sharp, one would miss it, for he was mobbed when the evening show ended at Pearl Cinema across the street. Ranga, however, was always ahead of others in the line. He swallowed his share, washed it down at the street tap and retired to his corner at Krishna Hall, an abandoned building (with no tangible owner) which had been tied up in civil litigations for over three generations, with no end in sight. Ranga discovered this hospitable retreat through sheer luck on the very first day he had arrived from his village in search of shelter. He occupied a cozy corner of the hall through the goodwill of the old man, its caretaker from time immemorial, who allotted living space to those whom he favored.

Ranga physically dwelt in the town no doubt, but his thoughts were always centered round his home in the village where his daughter was growing up under the care of his rather difficult wife. He managed to send home some money every month for their maintenance, particularly to meet the expenses of his daughter's schooling. He was proud that his daughter went to a school, the very first member of his family to take a step in that direction. His wife, however, did not favor the idea, being convinced that a girl was meant to make herself useful at home, marry and bear children. But Ranga rejected this philosophy outright, especially after the village schoolmaster, who gathered and taught the children on the pyol of his house, had told him once, "Your child is very intelligent. You must see that she studies well, and send her later to the Mission School at Paamban" (a nearby town reached by bus).

Originally Ranga had set up his grinding wheel as an adjunct to the village blacksmith under the big tamarind tree, where congregated at all hours of the day peasants from the surrounding country, bringing in their tools and implements for mending. One or the other in the crowd would get an idea to hone his scythe, shears or weeding blade when he noticed Ranga and his grinding wheel. But the blacksmith was avaricious, claimed twenty paise in every rupee Ranga earned, kept watch on the number of customers Ranga got each day, invariably quarreled when the time came to settle accounts and frequently also demanded a drink at the tavern across the road; which meant that Ranga would have to drink, too, and face his wife's tantrums when he went home. She would shout, rave and refuse to serve him food. Ranga could never understand why she should behave so wildly—after all, a swill of toddy did no one any harm; on the contrary, it mitigated the weariness of the body at the end of a day's labor, but how could one educate a wife and improve her understanding? Once, on an inspiration, he took home a bottle for her and coaxed her to taste the drink, but she retched at the smell of it and knocked the bottle out of his hand, spilling its precious contents on the mud floor. Normally he would have accepted her action without any visible protest, but that day, having had company and drunk more than normal, he felt spirited enough to strike her, whereupon she brought out the broom from its corner and lashed him with it. She then pushed him out and shut the door on him. Even in that inebriate state he felt relieved that their child, fast asleep on her mat, was not watching. He picked himself up at dawn from the lawn and sat ruminating. His wife came over and asked, "Have you come to your senses?" standing over him menacingly.

After this crisis Ranga decided to avoid the blacksmith and try his luck as a peripatetic sharpener. Carrying his grinding gear, he left home early morning after swallowing a ball of ragi with a bite of raw onion and chillies. After he gave up his association with the blacksmith, he noticed an improvement in his wife's temper. She got up at dawn and set the ragi on the boil over their mud oven and stirred the gruel tirelessly till it hardened and could be rolled into a ball, and had it ready by the time Ranga had had his wash at the well. He started on his rounds, avoiding the blacksmith under the tamarind tree, crisscrossed the dozen streets of his village, pausing at every door to announce, "Knives and cutters sharpened." When he returned home at night and emptied his day's collection on his wife's lap, she would cry greedily, "Only two rupees! Did you not visit the weekly market at . . . ?"

"Yes, I did, but there were ten others before me!"

His income proved inadequate, although eked out with the

wages earned by his wife for performing odd jobs at the Big House of the village. Now she began to wear a perpetual look of anxiety. He sounded her once if he should not cultivate the blacksmith's company again, since those who had anything to do with iron gathered there. She snarled back, "You are longing for that tipsy company again, I suppose!" She accused him of lack of push. "I suppose you don't cry loud enough, you perhaps just saunter along the streets mumbling to yourself your greatness as a grinder!" At this Ranga felt upset and let out such a deafening yell that she jumped and cried, "Are you crazy? What has come over you?" He explained, "Just to demonstrate how I call out to my patrons when I go on my rounds, a fellow told me that he could hear me beyond the slaughteryard. . . ."

"Then I suppose people scamper away and hide their knives on hearing your voice!" And they both laughed at the grim joke.

The daughter was now old enough to be sent to the Mission School at Paamban. Ranga had to find the money for her books, uniform, school fee and, above all, the daily busfare. His wife insisted that the girl's schooling be stopped, since she was old enough to work; the rich landlords needed hands at their farms, and it was time to train the girl to make herself useful all around. Ranga rejected her philosophy outright. However meek and obedient he might have proved in other matters, over the question of his daughter's education he stood firm. He was convinced that she should have a different life from theirs. What a rebel he was turning out to be, his wife thought, and remained speechless with amazement. To assuage her fears he asked, "You only want more money, don't you?"

"Yes, let me see what black magic you will perform to produce more money."

"You leave the girl alone, and I will find a way. . . ."

"Between you two . . . well, you are bent upon making her a worthless flirt wearing ribbons in her hair, imitating the rich folk. . . . If she develops into a termagant, don't blame me, please. She is already self-willed and talks back."

Presently he undertook an exploratory trip to Malgudi, only twenty-five miles away. He came back to report: "Oh, what a place, it is like the world of God Indra that our pundits describe. You find everything there. Thousands and thousands of people live in thousands of homes, and so many buses and motorcars in the streets, and so many barbers and tailors flourishing hundreds of scissors and razors night and day; in addition, countless numbers of peeling and slicing knives and other instruments in every home, enough work there for two hundred grinders like me; and the wages are liberal, they are noble and generous who live there, unlike the petty ones we have around us here."

"Ah, already you feel so superior and talk as if they have adopted you."

He ignored her cynicism and continued his dream. "As soon as our schoolmaster finds me an auspicious date, I will leave for the town to try my luck; if it turns out well, I will find a home for us so that we may all move there; they have many schools and our child will easily find a place." His wife cut short his plans with "You may go where you like, but we don't move out of here. I won't agree to lock up this house, which is our own; also, I won't allow a growing girl to pick up the style and fashions of the city. We are not coming. Do what you like with yourself, but don't try to drag us along." Ranga was crestfallen and remained brooding for a little while, but realized: "After all, it is a good thing that's happening to me. God is kind, and wants me to be free and independent in the town. . . . If she wants to be left behind, so much the better."

"What are you muttering to yourself?" she asked pugnaciously. "Say it aloud."

"There is wisdom in what you say; you think ahead," he replied, and she felt pleased at the compliment.

*   *   *

In the course of time a system evolved whereby he came home to visit his family every other month for three or four days. Leaving his grinding apparatus carefully wrapped up in a piece of jute cloth at Krishna Hall, he would take the bus at the market gate. He always anticipated his homecoming with joy, although during his stay he would have to bear the barbed comments of his wife or assuage her fears and anxieties—she had a habit of hopping from one anxiety to another; if it was not money, it was health, hers or the daughter's, or some hostile acts of a neighbor, or the late hours his daughter kept at school. After three days, when she came to the point of remarking, "How are we to face next month if you sit and enjoy life here?" he would leave, happy to go back to his independent life, but heavy at heart at parting from his daughter. For three days he would have derived the utmost enjoyment out of watching his daughter while she bustled about getting ready for school every morning in her uniform—green skirt and yellow jacket—and in the evening when she returned home full of reports of her doings at school. He would follow her about while she went to wash her uniform at the well and put it out to dry; she had two sets of school dress and took good care of them, so that she could leave for school each day spick-and-span, which annoyed her mother, who commented that the girl was self-centered, always fussing about her clothes or books. It saddened Ranga to hear such comments, but he felt reassured that the girl seemed capable of defending herself and putting her mother in her place.

At the end of one of his visits to the family he stood, clutching his little bundle of clothes, on the highway beyond the coconut grove. If he watched and gesticulated, any lorry or bus would stop and carry him towards the city. He waited patiently under a tree. It might be hours but he did not mind, never having known the habit of counting time. A couple of lorries fully laden passed and then a bus driven so rashly that his attempt to stop it passed unnoticed.

"Glad I didn't get into it. God has saved me, that bus will

lift off the ground and fly to the moon before long," he reflected as it churned up a cloud of sunlit dust and vanished beyond it. Some days, if the time was propitious, he would be picked up and deposited right at the door of Krishna Hall; some days he had to wait indefinitely. His daughter, he reflected with admiration, somehow caught a bus every day. "Very clever for her age." He prayed that his wife would leave her alone. "But that girl is too smart," he said to himself with a chuckle, "and can put her mother in her place." He brooded for a moment on this pleasant picture of the girl brushing off her mother, rudely sometimes, gently sometimes, but always with success, so that sometimes her mother herself admired the girl's independent spirit. That was the way to handle that woman. He wished he had learned the technique, he had let her go on her own way too long. But God was kind and took him away to the retreat of Krishna Hall; but for the daughter he would not be visiting his home even once in three years. The girl must study and become a doctor—a lady doctor was like an empress, as he remembered the occasions when he had to visit a hospital for his wife's sake and wait in the corridor, and noticed how voices were hushed when the "lady" strode down that way.

He noticed a coming vehicle at the bend of the road. It was painted yellow, a peculiar-looking one, probably belonging to some big persons, and he did not dare to stop it. As it flashed past, he noticed that the car also had some picture painted on its side. But it stopped at a distance and went into reverse. He noticed now that the picture on the car was of a man and a woman and two ugly children with some message. Though he could not read, he knew that the message on it was TWO WILL DO, a propaganda for birth control. His friend the butcher at the Market Road read a newspaper every day and kept him well informed. The man in the car, who was wearing a blue bush-shirt, put his head out to ask, "Where are you going?"

"Town," Ranga said.

The man opened the door and said, "Get in, we will drop you

there." Seated, Ranga took out one rupee from his pocket, but the man said, "Keep it." They drove on. Ranga felt happy to be seated in the front; he always had to stand holding on to the rail or squat on the floor in the back row of a bus. Now he occupied a cushioned seat, and wished that his wife could see and realize how people respected him. He enjoyed the cool breeze blowing on his face as the car sped through an avenue of coconut trees and came to a halt at some kind of a camp consisting of little shacks built of bamboo and coconut thatch. It seemed to be far away from his route, on the outskirts of a cluster of hamlets. He asked his benefactor, "Where are we?"

The man replied breezily, "You don't have to worry, you will be taken care of. Let us have coffee." He got off and hailed someone inside a hut. Some appetizing eatable on a banana leaf and coffee in a little brass cup were brought out and served. Ranga felt revived, having had nothing to eat since his morning ragi. He inquired, "Why all this, sir?"

The man said benignly, "Go on, you must be hungry, enjoy."

Ranga had never known such kindness from anyone. This man was conducting himself like a benign god. Ranga expected that after the repast they would resume their journey. But the benign god suddenly got up and said, "Come with me." He took him aside and said in a whisper, "Do not worry about anything. We will take care of you. Do you want to earn thirty rupees?"

"Thirty rupees!" Ranga cried. "What should I do for it? I have not brought my machine."

"You know me well enough now, trust me, do as I say. Don't question and you will get thirty rupees if you obey our instruction; we will give you any quantity of food, and I'll take you to the town . . . only you must stay here tonight. You can sleep here comfortably. I'll take you to the town tomorrow morning. Don't talk to others, or tell them anything. They will be jealous and spoil your chance of getting thirty rupees. . . . You will also get a transistor radio. Do you like to have one?"

"Oh, I don't know how to operate it. I'm not educated."

"It is simple, you just push a key and you will hear music."

He then took Ranga to a secluded part of the camp, spoke to him at length (though much of what he said was obscure) and went away. Ranga stretched himself on the ground under a tree, feeling comfortable, contented and well fed. The prospect of getting thirty rupees was pleasant enough, though he felt slightly suspicious and confused. But he had to trust that man in the blue shirt. He seemed god-like. Thirty rupees! Wages for ten days' hard work. He could give the money to his daughter to keep or spend as she liked, without any interference from her mother. He could also give her the radio. She was educated and would know how to operate it. He wondered how to get the money through to her without her mother's knowledge. Perhaps send it to her school—the writer of petitions and addresses at the post office in the city would write down the money order for him and charge only twenty-five paise for the labor. He was a good friend, who also wrote a postcard for him free of charge whenever he had to order a new grinding wheel from Bangalore. Ranga became wary when he saw people passing; he shut his eyes and fell into a drowse.

The blue bush-shirt woke him up and took him along to another part of the camp, where inside a large tent a man was seated at a desk. "He is our chief," he whispered. "Don't speak until he speaks to you. Answer when he questions. Be respectful. He is our officer." After saying this, he edged away and was not to be seen again.

Ranga felt overawed in the presence of the officer. That man had a sheet of paper in front of him and demanded, "Your name?" He wrote it down. "Your age?"

Ranga took time to comprehend, and when he did he began to ramble in his usual manner, "Must be fifty or seventy, because I . . ." He mentioned inevitably how a thin line of mustache began to appear when he first sharpened a knife as a professional. The officer cut him short. "I don't want all that! Shall I say you are fifty-five?" "By all means, sir. You are learned and you know best."

Then the officer asked, "Are you married?"

Ranga attempted to explain his domestic complications: the temper of his present wife, who was actually his second one; how he had to marry this woman under pressure from his relatives. He explained, "My uncle and other elders used to say, 'Who will be there to bring you a sip of gruel or hot water when you are on your deathbed?' It's all God's wish, sir. How can one know what he wills?" The officer was annoyed but tried to cover it up by going on to the next question: "How many children?"

"My first wife would have borne ten if God had given her long life, but she fell ill and the lady doctor said . . ." He went into details of her sickness and death. He then went on to some more personal tragedies and suddenly asked, "Why do you want to know about all this sorrowful business, sir?" The officer waved away his query with a frown. Ranga recollected that he had been advised not to be talkative, not to ask, but only to answer questions. Probably all this formality was a prelude to their parting with cash and a radio. The officer repeated, "How many children?"

"Six died before they were a year old. Do you want their names? So long ago, I don't remember, but I can try if you want. Before the seventh I vowed to the goddess on the hill to shave my head and roll bare-bodied around the temple corridor, and the seventh survived by the goddess's grace and is the only one left, but my wife does not understand how precious this daughter is, does not like her to study but wants her to become a drudge like herself. But the girl is wonderful. She goes to a school every day and wants to be a lady doctor. She is a match for her mother."

The officer noted down against the number of children "Seven" and then said commandingly, "You must have no more children. Is that understood?" Ranga looked abashed and grinned. The officer began a lecture on population, food production and so forth, and how the government had decreed that no one should have more than two children. He then thrust forward the sheet of paper and ordered, "Sign here." Ranga was nonplussed. "Oh! if I had learned to read and write . . . !"

The officer said curtly, "Hold up your left thumb" and smeared it on an inking pad and pressed it on the sheet of paper. After these exertions, Ranga continued to stand there, hoping that the stage had arrived to collect his reward and depart. He could cross the field, go up to the highway and pay for a bus ride, he would have money for it. But the officer merely handed him a slip of paper and cried, "Next!" An orderly entered, pushing before him a middle-aged peasant, while another orderly propelled Ranga out of the presence of the officer to another part of the camp, snatched the slip of paper from his hand and went away, ignoring the several questions that Ranga had put to him. Presently Ranga found himself seized by the arm and led into a room where a doctor and his assistants were waiting at a table. On the table Ranga noticed a white tray with shining knives neatly arrayed. His professional eye noted how perfectly the instruments had been honed. The doctor asked, "How many more?" Someone answered, "Only four, sir." Ranga felt scared when they said, "Come here and lie down," indicating a raised bed. They gently pushed him onto it. One man held his head down and two others held his feet. At some stage they had taken off his clothes and wrapped him in a white sheet. He felt ashamed to be stripped thus, but bore it as perhaps an inevitable stage in his progress towards affluence. The blue bush-shirt had advised him to be submissive. As he was lying on his back with the hospital staff standing guard over him, his understanding improved and his earlier suspicions began to crystallize. He recollected his butcher friend reading from a newspaper how the government was opening camps all over the country where men and women were gathered and operated upon so that they could have no children. So this was it! He was seized with panic at the prospect of being sliced up. "Don't shake, be calm," someone whispered softly, and he felt better, hoping that they would let him off at the last minute after looking him over thoroughly. The blue-shirt had assured him that they would never hurt or harm an old man like him. While these thoughts were flitting across his mind, he noticed a hand reaching for him with a swab of cotton. When the wrap around him was parted and fingers probed his genitals, he lost his head and screamed, "Hands off! Leave me alone!" He shook himself free when they tried to hold him down, butted with his head the man nearest to him, rolled over, toppling the white tray with its knives. Drawing the hospital wrap around, he stormed out, driven by a desperate energy. He ran across the fields screaming, "No, I won't be cut up . . . ," which echoed far and wide, issuing from vocal cords cultivated over a lifetime to overwhelm other noises in a city street with the cry "Knives sharpened!"

Uncle

I am the monarch of all I survey, being the sole occupant of this rambling ancient house in Vinayak Street. I am five-ten, too huge for the easy chair on which I am reclining now. But I remember the time when I could hardly reach the arm of this easy chair. I remember the same chair at the same spot in the hall, with some ancient portrait hanging on a nail over it, with my uncle comfortably lounging and tormenting me by pushing his glittering snuffbox just out of my reach. While trying to reach for it I tumbled down again and again; he emitted a loud guffaw each time I lost my balance and sprawled on the floor. I felt frightened by his loud laughter and whined and cried. At that moment my aunt would swoop down on me and carry me off to the kitchen, set me down in a corner, and place before me a little basin filled with water, which I splashed about. I needed no further attention except a replenishment of water from time to time. I also watched with wonderment the smoke curling up from the oven when the lady puffed her cheeks and blew on the fire through a hollow bamboo pipe. The spell would suddenly be broken when she picked me up again, with a bowl of rice in her hand, and carried me off to the street door. She would carefully seat me on the pyol of the house, my back supported against the slender pillars, and try to feed me. If I averted my head she gripped my neck as in a vise and forced the rice between my lips. If I howled in protest she utilized the chance to thrust more rice into my open mouth. If I spat it out she would point at a passerby and say, "See that demon, he will carry you off. He is on the lookout for babies who won't eat." At that stage I must have faced the risk of dying of over- rather than underfeeding. Later in the day she would place a dish of eatables before me and watch me deal with it. When I turned the dish over on the floor and messed up the contents, Uncle and Aunt drew each other's attention to this marvelous spectacle and nearly danced around me in joy. In those days my uncle, though portly as ever, possessed greater agility, I believe.

My uncle stayed at home all day. I was too young to consider what he did for a living. The question never occurred to me until I was old enough to sit on a schoolbench and discuss life's problems with a class fellow. I was studying in the first year at Albert Mission School. Our teacher had written on the blackboard a set of words such as Man, Dog, Cat, Mat, Taj, and Joy, and had asked us to copy them down on our slates and take them to him for correction and punishment if necessary. I had copied four of the six terms and had earned the teacher's approbation. The boy in the next seat had also done well. Our duties for the hour were over, and that left us free to talk, in subdued whispers, though.

"What is your father's name?" he asked.

"I don't know. I call him Uncle."

"Is he rich?" the boy asked.

"I don't know," I replied. "They make plenty of sweets at home."

"Where does he work?" asked the boy, and the first thing I

did when I went home, even before flinging off my books and schoolbag, was to ask loudly, "Uncle, where is your office?"

He replied, "Up above," pointing heavenward, and I looked up.

"Are you rich?" was my second question.

My aunt emerged from the kitchen and dragged me in, saying, "Come, I have some very lovely things for you to eat."

I felt confused and asked my aunt, "Why won't Uncle . . . ?" She merely covered my mouth with her palm and warned, "Don't talk of all that."

"Why?" I asked.

"Uncle doesn't liked to be asked questions."

"I will not ask hereafter," I said and added, "Only that Suresh, he is a bad boy and he said . . ."

"Hush," she said.

My world was circumscribed by the boundaries of our house in Vinayak Street, and peopled by Uncle and Aunt mainly. I had no existence separately from my uncle. I clung to him all through the day. Mornings in the garden at the backyard, afternoons inside, and all evening on the front pyol of the house squatting beside him. When he prayed or meditated at midday I sat in front of him watching his face and imitating him. When he saw me mutter imaginary prayers with my eyes shut, he became ecstatic and cried aloud to my aunt in the kitchen, "See this fellow, how well he prays! We must teach him some slokas. No doubt whatever, he is going to be a saint someday. What do you think?" When he prostrated to the gods in the puja room I too threw myself on the floor, encouraged by the compliments showered on me. He would stand staring at me until Aunt reminded him that his lunch was ready. When he sat down to eat I nestled close to him, pressing my elbow on his lap. Aunt would say, "Move off, little man. Let Uncle eat in peace," but he always countermanded her and said, "Stay, stay." After lunch he chewed betel leaves and areca nut, moved on to his bedroom, and stretched himself on his rosewood bench, with a small pillow under his head. Just when he fell into a doze I demanded, "Tell me a story," butting him with my elbow.

He pleaded, "Let us both sleep. We may have wonderful dreams. After that I will tell you a story."

"What dreams?" I would persist.

"Shut your eyes and don't talk, and you will get nice dreams." And while I gave his advice a trial, he closed his eyes.

All too brief a trial. I cried, "No, I don't see any dream yet. Tell me a story, Uncle." He patted my head and murmured, "Once upon a time . . ." with such a hypnotic effect that within a few minutes I fell asleep.

Sometimes I sought a change from the stories and involved him in a game. The bench on which he tried to sleep would be a mountain top, the slight gap between its edge and the wall a gorge with a valley below. I would crawl under the bench, lie on my back, and command, "Now throw," having first heaped at his side a variety of articles such as a flashlight without battery, a Ping-Pong bat, a sandalwood incense holder, a leather wallet, a coat hanger, empty bottles, a tiny stuffed cow, and several other items out of a treasure chest I possessed. And over went the most cherished objects—the more fragile the better for the game, for, in the cool semidark world under the bench and by the rules of the game, the possibility of a total annihilation of objects would be perfectly in order.

Ten days after first broaching the subject Suresh cornered me again when we were let off for an hour in the absence of our geography master. We were playing marbles. Suresh suddenly said, "My father knows your uncle."

I felt uneasy. But I had not learned the need for circumspection and asked anxiously, "What does he say about him?"

"Your uncle came from another country, a far-off place . . ."

"Oh, good, so?" I cried with happiness, feeling relieved that after all some good points about my uncle were emerging.

Suresh said, "But he impersonated."

"What is 'impersonate'?" I asked.

He said, "Something not so good. My mother and father were talking, and I heard them use the word."

The moment I came home from school and flung off my bag my aunt dragged me to the well in the backyard and forced me to wash my hands and feet, although I squirmed and protested vehemently. Next I sat on the arm of my uncle's easy chair with a plate filled with delicacies, ever available under that roof, and ate under the watchful eye of my uncle. Nothing delighted him more than to eat or watch someone eat. "What is the news in your school today?" he would ask.

"Know what happened, Uncle?" I swallowed a mouthful and took time to suppress the word "impersonate," which kept welling up from the depths of my being, and invent a story. "A bad boy from the Third B—big fellow—jabbed me with his elbow . . ."

"Did he? Were you hurt?"

"Oh, no, he came charging but I stepped aside and he banged his head against the wall, and it was covered with blood, and they carried him to the hospital." My uncle uttered many cries of joy at the fate overtaking my adversary and induced me to develop the details, which always sounded gory.

When they let me go I bounced off to the street, where a gang awaited my arrival. We played marbles or kicked a rubber ball about with war cries and shouts, blissfully unaware of the passersby and the traffic, until the street end melted into a blaze of luminous dust with the sun gone. We played until my uncle appeared at our doorway and announced, "Time to turn in," when we dispersed unceremoniously and noisily. Once again my aunt would want to give my hands and feet a scrubbing. "How many times!" I protested. "Won't I catch a cold at this rate?"

She just said, "You have all the road dust on you now. Come on." After dousing me she smeared sacred ash on my forehead and made me sit with my uncle in the back verandah of the

house and recite holy verse. After which I picked up my schoolbooks and, under my uncle's supervision, read my lessons, both
the tutor and the taught feeling exhausted at the end of it. By
eight-thirty I would be fed and put to sleep in a corner of the
hall, at the junction of the two walls where I felt most secure.

On Fridays we visited the little shrine at the end of our street.
Rather an exciting outing for me, as we passed along brilliantly
lit shops displaying banana bunches, colored drinks, bottled pep-
permints, and red and yellow paper kites, every item seeming to
pulsate with an inner glow.

They both rose at five in the morning and moved about softly
so as not to disturb me. The first thing in the day, my uncle
drew water from the well for the family, and then watered the
plants in the garden. I woke to the sound of the pulley creaking
over the well and joined my uncle in the garden. In the morning
light he looked like a magician. One asked for nothing more in
life than to be up at that hour and watch brilliant eddying columns of water coming through little channels dug along the
ground. The hydraulic engineering for the garden was my uncle's
own. He had raised the ground beside the well to form a basin,
and when he tipped a cauldron of water over it, the column ran
down the slope and passed through to the plants according to
his dictates. He controlled the supply of water at various stages
with a little trowel in hand, with which he scooped up the mud
and opened or blocked the water course. I floated little bits of
straw or leaves, or picked up ants and helped them have a free
swim along the current. Sometimes without my uncle's knowledge I scooped off the mud bank with my hands and diverted
the water elsewhere.

I reveled in this world of mud, greens, slush, and water, for-
getting for the moment such things as homework and teachers.
When the sun came over the walls of the house behind our
garden, my uncle ended his operations, poured a great quantity

of water over himself, and went in dripping, in search of a towel. When I tried to follow him in, my aunt brought out a bucket of hot water and gave me a bath beside the well. Soon I found myself in the puja room murmuring prayers.

A perpetual smell of incense and flowers hung about the puja room, which was actually an alcove in the kitchen where pictures of gods hung on the walls. I loved the pictures; the great god Krishna poised on the hood of a giant serpent; Vishnu, blue-colored, seated on the back of Garuda, the divine eagle, gliding in space and watching us. As I watched the pictures my mind went off into fantastic speculations while my tongue recited holy verse. "Was the eagle a sort of airplane for Vishnu? Lakshmi stands on lotus! How can anyone stand on a lotus flower without crushing it?" From the fireplace would come my aunt's voice, "I don't hear you pray." I would suppress my speculations and re-cite aloud, addressing the elephant-faced god, "*Gajananam bhu-taganadi sevitam . . .*" for three minutes in Sanskrit. I always wanted to ask for its meaning, but if I paused my aunt would shout over the hissing of the frying pan (which, incidentally, was generating an enormously appetizing fragrance), "Why have you stopped?" Now I would turn to the picture of Saraswati, the goddess of learning, as she sat on a rock with her peacock beside a cool shrubbery, and wonder at her ability to play the *veena* with one hand while turning the rosary with the other, still leaving two hands free, perhaps to pat the peacock. I would raise my voice and say, "*Saraswati namastubhyam,*" which meant "O god-dess of learning, I bow to you," or some such thing. I secretly added a personal request to this prayer. "May you help me get through my school hours without being mauled by my teachers or other boys, may I get through this day unscathed." Although my normal day at school was peaceful, I always approached it at the beginning of each day with dread. My teacher was unshaven and looked villainous. He frequently inhaled a pinch of snuff in the class and spoke in a grating voice, the snuff having ravaged his vocal cords, and he flourished a short, stubby cane menacingly at the whole class every now and then. I had never seen him attack anyone, but his gestures were frightening, and I sat on my bench shuddering lest he should turn in my direction and notice me.

My life was precisely organized by my uncle, and I had little time to waste. When I emerged from the puja I had to go straight to the kitchen and drink off a glass of milk. This would be an occasion for my aunt to comment on my dress or voice. She would suddenly bring her face close to mine and examine my eyes. "What are you looking for?" I would ask, rearing my head, but she held it firmly between her palms and inspected until she was satisfied that there was no patch of dirt or swelling under my eyes. "Oh, I was mistaken, nothing," she would say with relief. "Anyway, you have grown darker. You must not roast yourself in the sun so much. Why should they make you do all that drill in the sun?"

Next I passed into the jurisdiction of my uncle, who sat leaning against a pillar in the hall with eyes shut in meditation. He said, emerging from his trance, "Boy, gather all your lessons for the day and put them in your bag. Have you sharpened your pencil? Cleaned your slate? Do you need anything?" In spite of my firm statement that I needed nothing, he came over, seized my schoolbag, peered into it, and probed its bottom with his fingers. It was surprising how lightly he could abandon his prayers, but he was perhaps an adept who could resume them at will, as his day was mostly divided between munching and meditation. He held up to the light a slate pencil in order to judge whether it could be used for just another day. He would sharpen its point on the stone floor, commenting, "You must hold it here and write, and don't bite the end; this can be used for a week more." It was painful to write with such a short stub; my thumb and forefinger became sore, and further, if my teacher noticed it he twisted my ear and snatched away the stub and made me stand on the bench as a punishment. I could not mention these problems explicitly, as I feared that my uncle might don his shirt and offer to visit my school in order to investigate. I had a secret anxiety lest he should ever appear in our school, as I thought that the boys might stand around and make fun of his girth. And so I had to manage with the stub as ordained. When he felt satisfied that I had used the pencil wisely, he would open his wooden cupboard, take out a lacquered casket with a dragon on its lid, and out of it a small cardboard box, and again from it a little package containing long slate pencils. He would take out a brand-new one and hesitate; guessing his intention, I would jump up and snatch it from his hand crying, "Don't break it, I want it full-length." Sometimes he gave it whole, sometimes he broke it into two saying, "Half is long enough." He then looked through my books page by page, and packed them securely back into the bag. He said from time to time, "Little man, if you don't read your lessons properly you will never count for anything in life and no one will respect you. Do you understand?" "Yes, Uncle," I said though not very clear in my mind as to what "respect" meant.

One evening I came home announcing, "They are going to photograph us in our school." My uncle, who had been lounging in the easy chair, sprang to his feet and asked, "Who? Who is going to photograph you?"

"My teacher's brother has a friend who has a camera and he is going to photograph us."

"Only you or others also?"

"Our class alone, not even the B section will be allowed, although they asked to be photographed too."

Uncle's face lit up with joy. He called Aunt and said, "Did you hear, this young man is going to be photographed tomorrow. Dress him properly."

Next day my uncle spent a lot of time selecting clothes for me, and my aunt gave a double rub to my face and groomed me. My uncle followed me about uttering several pieces of advice before letting me out. "You must never scowl even if the sun hits you in the eyes. You must try to look pleasant. You know in those days only girls waiting to be married used to have their photos taken. Nowadays everyone is being photographed."

When I came home from school that evening he asked anxiously, "How did it go off?"

I flung away the schoolbag to its corner and said, "No, nothing happened. He didn't come."

"Who?"

"Our teacher's brother's friend," I said. "It seems his camera has broken down or something like that, and so—no photo."

My uncle's face fell. Both of them had been waiting at the door to see me return triumphantly from the photographer. He murmured sympathetically, "Don't worry about it, we will find another photographer; only I thought you should not have taken out the blue shirt until Deepavali—never mind; we will buy you a new one for the festival."

My aunt said, "We could fold the shirt neatly and put it away until Deepavali. He has not soiled it."

"I sat very quietly today lest the clothes should be spoiled," I said, which was a fact. I had refused to play with my friends for fear that my shirt might get crumpled. This blue shirt was of a special kind; my uncle had bought the cloth from a street hawker, who assured him that the fabric was foreign and could not normally be acquired except through smugglers operating in certain coastal villages. Uncle bought three yards of the blue cloth after a whole afternoon's haggling, and planned to stitch shirts for me and himself. He had sent for an old Muslim tailor who had the original Singer sewing machine set up on the pyol of a house in Kabir Lane. He behaved extremely deferentially before my uncle and would not be seated even on the floor. My uncle relaxed in his easy chair and my aunt stood at the kitchen doorway and both discussed with the tailor various matters relating to persons, times, and places which sounded remote and incomprehensible to me. He kept addressing my uncle as his savior at the end of every sentence, and salaamed him. When the time came to take measurements my uncle stood very erect and muttered numerous instructions as to the length, cut, and number and kind (unbreakable, tin) of buttons that he favored, and so forth. "Note the measurements down properly," he said sternly several times, "lest you should forget and make a mistake; it is a rare kind of cloth, not obtainable in our country; can't afford to take chances with it, remember."

The tailor in answer avowed again his indebtedness to my uncle. "On the road that day if you had not—" he began.

My uncle looked embarrassed and cut him short with "Don't go on with all those grandmother's stories now. The past is past, remember."

"How can I help it, sir? Every morning I and my children think of you and pray for your welfare. When they gave me up for dead with vultures circling above and passed on, you stopped by and revived me, sir, although you had this baby in your arms . . . and you gave me the strength to walk a thousand miles over mountain passes. . . ."

My uncle said curtly, "Why don't you take the measurements?"

"I obey," said the tailor immediately, and proceeded to measure me. He was not only deferential but also patronizing in his tone. "Stand up, little master, otherwise you will blame this old man for any mistake that may occur. See how your venerable uncle stands erect at his age!"

He completed the measurements, noted them on a very small roll of paper, probably the torn-off margin of a newspaper, with a stubby pencil which he always carried over his ear, and departed after accepting all the advice given as they kept saying, "Remember he is a growing boy, make allowance for that; don't want him to feel suffocated in his new shirt after the first wash . . ."

The tailor left after uttering the only word of protest, "If master had bought just a quarter yard more . . ."

"Not at all necessary," said my uncle. "I know how much is needed, seeing that you are going to give me short arms, and no collar is wanted. . . ." The shirts came back stitched in due course and were laid away in the big trunk.

Next evening I came home gleefully announcing, "We were photographed today."

"Indeed!" cried my uncle. "How stupid of them when you were not ready for it!"

"Does it mean that you are going to look like this in the photo?" asked my aunt.

"It will not do justice to you," said my uncle. "They should have given us at least half an hour's notice, and then you could have . . ."

"Our teacher suddenly said, 'Come out, all of you, and stand in a line under the tree.' We marched out. A man came with a small camera, lined up all the tall boys first and all the short ones in the second line with our teacher in the center; and then he cried, 'Stand steady, don't move,' and it was over. Our teacher has promised to give a photo to whoever brings two rupees from home."

"Two rupees!" repeated my uncle aghast.

Aunt said, "Never mind, it is the child's first photo."

"I thought the class would be let off after the photo, but we were marched back for geography lessons."

My uncle thrust two rupees into my pocket before I left for school next day, cautioning me, "Take it carefully to your teacher." He sounded anxious lest I should drop the money or get robbed on the way. He stood on the front step and watched me go. I turned around a couple of times to assure him, "Don't fear, I will be careful," dreading lest he should suddenly don his shirt and decide to escort me.

For two weeks there was no sign of the photo. My uncle got quite agitated and asked every day, "What did your teacher say?"

I had to invent an answer each time as I did not have the courage to confront my teacher on the subject. And so I generally said, "The photographer has been very ill. But tomorrow positively we are getting it."

Ultimately the photo did arrive and we were given our copies at the end of the day. As I reached home I shouted from the street, "Photo!" which brought my uncle down the steps of the house. He followed me anxiously about while I took my own time to fish out the photograph from my schoolbag. "Such a small one!" my uncle cried on seeing it.

"His camera also was small!" I said.

They carried the print to a corner where a beam of sunlight streamed in through the red pane of a ventilator and observed it closely. Uncle put his spectacles on, but my aunt had to wait for her turn since they managed with a single pair between them. "Why can't we go out, it is brighter out there, and I won't need glasses?" she suggested.

"No," he replied firmly. "Inquisitive fellows all around—fellows ready to peer through the wall if they could, to learn what is happening here," said my uncle, passing on his spectacles and commenting, "Our boy has the brightest face in the group, but they have made him look so dark!"

I pointed out my enemies to them: "This is Suresh—always trying to kill me if I am not careful. This boy also is a bad fellow." My aunt's eyes met mine significantly at the mention of Suresh, who looked florid by the red light of the ventilator. "This is our teacher. He will not hesitate to skin alive anyone who is found talking in his class. The man who took the photo is his brother's friend. Own brother, not cousin. Suresh asked if he was a cousin, and it made my teacher so wild!"

My uncle counted the heads and cried, "Fifty? Two rupees each and they have collected their one hundred rupees! Not even a mount for the photo! They are robbing us in your schools nowadays!"

Next day when I was leaving for school my uncle said, "Come

home early. We will go out to the market. Have you any important lessons?"

"No, none," I said with conviction. "I will come home for lunch and stay on."

"Do you wish to come with us?" he asked, aiming his question in the direction of his wife in the kitchen. My aunt, with her years of experience behind her, flung back the responsibility of a decision on him, shouting from the fireplace, "Do you want me to go with you?" The man was cornered now and answered, "Not if you have things to mind at home . . ."

"Of course, I have asked that servant woman to come and pound the paddy today. If we miss her today she will not come again." She trailed off indecisively. This was a diplomatic game which, in spite of my age of innocence, I understood very well, and so I broke in, "Let Aunt come another day, Uncle. She will want a carriage to be brought and all that trouble," which was a fact; whenever she wanted to go out she would send me running to the street corner to fetch a jutka, and it was not always an easy job. Some days you found six jutkas waiting for fares under the margosa shade at the street corner, some days you couldn't find even one at a busy hour; sometimes the jutka drivers who knew me would tease and not take me seriously or pass disparaging remarks about my uncle, referring to him as "that Rangoon man" or mention incidents which I could not comprehend, and generally mumble and smirk among themselves at my expense.

My uncle added, "Quite right. We can walk to the market."

"Yes, by all means," said my aunt, much to everyone's relief.

We sallied out at three o'clock in the afternoon, having finished our tiffin and coffee. The main job for the day was to mount and frame the photograph. Uncle carried it in his hand delicately, enclosed in an old envelope, as if it were fragile and likely to perish at a finger's pressure. As we went down the street a neighbor standing at his door hailed us and demanded, "Where are you taking the young fellow?" He was an engineer who worked in some distant projects on the hills, coming home once in a while and then again disappearing from our society. He was a particular friend of my uncle, as they occasionally gathered for a game of cards in my house. He asked, "I am here for a few days, can't we have a session sometime?"

"Of course, of course," said my uncle without much fervor, "I will let you know," and moved on.

"Won't Aunt get angry?" I asked, remembering the arguments they had had after every card session. The card players would have been sitting around in the middle of the hall, demanding coffee and edibles, and playing far into the night. My aunt would complain after the company had dispersed, "Sitting there with your friends, you lock me up in the kitchen all day! What madness seizes you people when you touch a pack of cards, I wonder!" Worn out by her attacks, my uncle began to avoid his friends; the company gradually dwindled and disappeared. But it did not prevent them from dreaming about cards or luxuriating in visions of a grand session. Somewhere my uncle was supposed to have lost a lot of money through the card games, and my aunt was very definite that he should never go near cards again, although he kept saying, "We play only Twenty-eight, and not Rummy, after all, Twenty-eight . . ."

"Twenty-eight or forty-eight, it's all the same to me," said my aunt. "Fifty thousand rupees just scattered like waste paper, that is all! Sheer madness!" She was rather emphatic. My uncle, not being a quarrelsome sort, just accepted meekly whatever she said, and evidently benefited by her advice.

As we walked on I asked many questions. This was my opportunity to clear my doubts and learn about new things in life. I asked, "Why does not Aunt like playing cards? So many nice people gather in our house and it is so interesting!"

He answered, "It is very expensive, my boy, some people have lost all their fortune and become beggars. Gambling is bad.

Don't you know how Nala lost his kingdom?" And he began to narrate the ancient story of Nala. Cyclists passed, a herd of cattle returned from the grazing fields beyond the river, some very young schoolchildren emerged from the town primary school, the sun scorching us all. But my uncle noticed nothing while he unfolded to me the fate of Nala, holding me by the wrist lest I should be run over or gored by the cattle. I shrank behind him when we passed my school. I had skipped three classes in the afternoon and did not wish to be seen by my teachers or classmates. We could hear the voices from within the classrooms. Presently the bell for the three-thirty recess would sound and the boys would rush out to drink water at the tap or to make water on the roadside or swarm around the groundnut seller at the school gate. The headmaster was likely to prowl about to prevent the boys from fouling the road. It would be disaster for me to be seen by anyone now. Nor did I wish my uncle to get any ideas while passing the gate—such as stopping to have a word with my teacher. I quickened my steps and tried to divert his mind to other matters by suddenly saying, "Why did Nala lose?"

Before answering he paused for a moment to ask, "Is that noise all from your school? Why do they make all that row? Glad we don't live next door to your school!" Not wanting him to dwell too much on school matters, I trotted ahead of him, hoping to set the pace for him. But he remarked, "Do you have to caper like that? No, my boy, I could have given you a beating five years ago, but today I am deliberately slowing my pace." I paused for him to catch up with me. We had crossed the danger zone, gone past the school.

I asked innocently as we resumed our march, "What game did Nala play? Did he play cards?"

"Oh, no," Uncle said, "I am sure he would have, if they had invented playing cards in those days. He played dice." He went on to explain the game to me and continued the story. "The fellow played with his brother, but malevolent gods had got into the dice and affected his chances, and he lost his kingdom and everything except his wife and had to march out of the capital like a mendicant wearing only a loin cloth."

We turned to our right and took a shortcut through Kabir Street and were on Market Road. Not a busy hour, as the high-school boys were still not let off. Several donkeys stood about the fountain statuesquely. When the boys emerged from the high school, I imagined, they would shout and frighten the donkeys, provoke them in various ways until they ran helter-skelter, confusing the evening traffic. Street dogs dozing on the edge of the road would join the fray and give them a chase, and there would be a hullabaloo. I missed all this imagined spectacle and told my uncle, "We should have come a little later."

"Why?" asked my uncle and added, "You wish that you had attended your classes after all?"

"Oh, no," I said, and blurted out, "We could have seen the donkeys jump about." Even without this spectacle, Market Road thrilled me every inch, so full of life, movement, and activity. A candy peddler was crying his wares, sounding a bell. This man often established himself at our school gate, drawing out and pinching off portions of a pink, elastic, gluey sweet, stuck in a coil around a bamboo shaft. My mouth watered at the sight of it. I pleaded, "Uncle, please get me a bit of it!"

He suddenly looked serious and said, "No, no, it is dangerous to eat such stuff. You may catch cholera."

I said with bravado, "Not likely. He comes to our school every day, and all boys eat it, and also our drawing master. No one has suffered from cholera yet."

All that he said was, "I will get you something nicer to eat. Wait." As we passed a sweetmeat shop he said, "This is Jagan's shop. No harm in eating here. He makes things out of pure ghee." He stopped by a resplendently arrayed sweetmeat shop and bought a packet for me.

I swiftly unpacked it and asked out of courtesy, "Uncle, you want some?" and when he shook his head I ate it, and threw away the wrapper high up and watched it gently float down on Market Road until Uncle pulled me up, saying, "Look in front and walk."

The frame-maker's name was Jayraj. He had hoisted a sign-board which was rather pompously worded PHOTOGRAPHERS & PHOTO-FRAMERS, stretching the entire width of the outer wall of the market. Why he chose to display himself in the plural no one could say, since no one ever saw anyone except Mr. Jayraj in the proprietor's seat in the inner sanctum. Although there was always a goodly company on the long bench sticking out from his threshold, they were all his friends, well-wishers, customers, and general listeners as Jayraj held forth on his social and personal philosophy all day. Now he gestured to us to be seated on the bench while he went on gently hammering tacks onto the sides of a frame covered with a cardboard. Presently he looked up and greeted my uncle, "Doctor, where have you been all these days?"

I was surprised at my uncle being addressed as a doctor. Immediately I looked up and asked, "Uncle, are you a doctor?" He merely rumpled my hair and did not answer.

Jayraj took this occasion to look at me and say, "Brought this young man along, who is he?"

My uncle simply said, "He is my boy, our child at home."

"Oh, I know, yes of course, now grown up so!"

My uncle looked slightly awkward and changed the subject. He held out my photograph and asked with affected cheer, "Oh, here is this young man's photo which must be framed. Will you do it?"

"Of course, anything for you, sir." He looked at the photo with disgust. I thought he might fling the picture into the gutter that flowed copiously below the steps of his shop. His brow was furrowed, he pursed his lips, blinked his eyes, placed a straight finger across the picture, shook his head dolefully, and said, "This is how people cheat schoolboys nowadays. Underde-

velop and overexpose or underexpose and overdevelop. This is
what they do."

My uncle added fuel to the fire by saying, "Not even a mount
for the two rupees he charged!"

Jayraj put away the photograph and said, "Well, mounting
and framing is my duty, even if you bring the photo of a donkey's rear." While he paused for breath my uncle tried to say
something, but Jayraj didn't give him a chance. He said, "Here
I am in the heart of the city ready to serve our townfolk. Why
can't people make use of me instead of some tenth-rate camera-
meddler? I am open twenty-four hours of the day in the service
of humanity. I even sleep here when there is work to do, and no
factory act applies to me. I can't demand overtime or bonus, but
my satisfaction lies in serving humanity." He pointed at his
camera, a hooded apparatus on a tripod in a corner. "There it is,
always ready. If somebody summons me I respond immediately,
no matter what the subject is—a wedding, a corpse, prostitute,
a minister of state, or a cat on a wall—it's all the same to me.
My business is to photograph, and let me tell you straightaway
that my charges are more than moderate. I don't believe in doing
cheap work. I photographed Mahatma Gandhi when he was here.
I was summoned to Madras whenever Nehru was on a visit. Dr.
Radhakrishnan, Tagore, Birla, I could give you a big list of
people who were pleased with my work and wrote out testimonials spontaneously. I have locked them in the safe at home.
Any day you will be welcome to visit my humble home and
peruse them if you like. I don't mind losing all my gold, but
not the testimonials from the brilliant sons of our motherland.
I want my children and their children to cherish them and say
someday, "We come of a line who served the brilliant sons of
Mother India, and here are the tokens."

While this preamble was going on, his hands were busy giving the finishing touches to a wedding group; he was smoothing
off the ripples of glue on the back of the picture. He squatted
on his heels on the floor with a little workbench in front of him.

He held the wedding group at arm's length and said, "Not my business, so many committing the folly every week, the government looking on, while people howl about the population problem, but why can't they ban all marriages for ten years?" He packed the framed picture in an old newspaper, tied a string around it, and put it away. Now my turn. He picked up my photograph, studied it again, and remarked, "Fifty heads to be compressed on a postcard. Maybe they are only little men, but still . . . Unless you look through a magnifying glass you will never know who is who." He then asked my uncle, "Will you leave the color of the mount, frame, and style entirely to me or have you any ideas?"

My uncle was bewildered by this question and said, "I want it to look nice, that is all. I want it to look," he repeated, "particularly nice."

"I don't doubt it," said Jayraj, who never liked the other person to end a conversation. "Well, for the tone of this print there are certain shades of wooden frames and mounts suitable, and some not suitable. If you prefer something unsuitable according to me, it'll still be done. I will wrap it up, present it to you, and collect my bill; but let me assure you that my heart will not be in it. Anyway, it is up to you," he said challengingly. My uncle seemed bewildered by all this philosophy and remained silent. He looked apprehensive and wanted to know quickly the worst. The man had placed my photograph on his desk, weighting it down with a steel measuring scale. We awaited his next move. Meanwhile more people came and took their seats on the bench, like men at a dentist's parlor. Jayraj did not bother to notice his visitors, nor did he notice the crowd passing through the market gateway, shoppers, hawkers, beggars, dogs and stray cattle and coolies with baskets on their heads, all kinds of men and women, jostling, shouting, laughing, cursing, and moving as in a mass trance; they might have been able to pass in and out more easily but for Jayraj's bench sticking across the market entrance.

A very bald man came and gingerly sat down on the bench, announcing, "The trustee has sent me." It made no impression on Jayraj, who had picked up a length of framing rod and was sawing it off noisily.

My uncle asked suddenly, "When will you give it?"

Before Jayraj could muster an answer the bald man said for the fourth time, "The trustee has sent me. . . ."

Jayraj chose this moment to tell some other young man leaning on a bicycle, "Tomorrow at one o'clock." The young man jumped on his bicycle and rode away.

The bald man began again, "The trustee . . ."

Jayraj looked at my uncle and said, "It all depends when you want it."

The bald man said, "The trustee . . . is going away to Tirupathi tomorrow . . . and wants . . ."

Jayraj completed his sentence for him, "Wants me along? Tell him I have no time for a pilgrimage."

"No, no, he wants the picture."

"Where is the hurry? Let him come back from Tirupathi."

The other looked nonplussed.

Meanwhile a woman who sold betel leaves in the market came up with a basket at her hip and asked, "When should I bring the baby?"

"Whenever the midwife advises," replied Jayraj. She blushed and threw the end of her sari over her face and laughed. "Tomorrow evening at three o'clock. Dress him in his best. Put on him all the jewelry you can, and come early. If you come late the sunlight will be gone and there will be no photo. Be sure to bring two rupees with you. No credit, and then you can give me the balance when I give you the photo in a frame."

"Ah, can't you trust me so much, sir?"

"No argument, that is my system, that is all. If I want the betel leaves in your basket I pay for it at once, so also for what I do." She went away laughing, and Jayraj said, addressing no one in particular, "She has a child every ten months. Mother is constant, but not the father." His assembly laughed at this quip. "Not my business to question the parentage. I take the picture and frame it when ordered to do so and that is all."

My uncle asked all of a sudden, "Will you be able to frame and give me the photograph now?"

"No," said Jayraj promptly, "unless you expect me to stay on and work until midnight."

"Why not? You said you could."

"Yes, sir," he replied. "I said so and I will say so again, if you command me. Will you wait and take it?"

My uncle was flabbergasted. He said, "No, I cannot. I have to go to the temple," and he brooded over his inescapable routine of prayer, meditation, dinner, and sleep.

"It's five o'clock now. Your work will take two hours—the paste must dry. We must give the paste its time to dry. But before I can take up your work, you see that man on your side, whose scalp is shining today but once upon a time who had a shock of hair like a coir doormat," and he nodded in the direction of the bald man who was still waiting for a reply for the trustee. Jayraj continued his theme of bald pate. "About ten years ago one morning I noticed when he came to frame a calendar portrait of Brahma the Creator that he was growing thin on top; fortunately for us we cannot know the top of our own heads; and I did not tell him so that he might not feel discouraged about his matrimonial future; no one can question why or wherefore of baldness; it is much like life and death. God gives us the hair and takes it away when obviously it is needed elsewhere, that is all."

Every word that Jayraj uttered pleased the bald man, who remarked at the end of it, "Don't forget that I save on hair oil!" And he bowed his head to exhibit his shining top, at which I roared with laughter, Jayraj laughed out of courtesy, and my uncle smiled patronizingly, and into this pleasant and well-softened atmosphere the bald man pushed in a word about the business which had brought him there. "The trustee . . . ," he began, and Jayraj repeated, "Oh, trustee, school trustee, temple trustee, hospital trustee, let him be anything; I have no use for trustees, and so why keep harping on them?"

The bald man sprang to his feet, approached the edge of the inner sanctum, leaned forward almost in supplication, and prayed, "Please, please, don't send me back empty-handed; he will be upset, thinking that I have been loafing about."

Now Jayraj looked properly concerned and said, "He would think so, would he? All right, he shall have it even if I have to forgo sleep tonight. No more sleep, no more rest, until the trustee is pacified. That settles it." He said finally, looking at my uncle, "Yours immediately after the trustee's, even if it means all-night vigil."

My uncle repeated, "All night! I may not be able to stay long."

"You don't have to," said Jayraj. "Please be gone, sir, and that is not going to affect my program or promise. Trust me. You are determined to hang this young person's group picture on your wall tonight, perhaps the most auspicious date in your calendar! Yes, sir. Each unto himself is my philosophy. Tonight it shall be done. I usually charge three rupees for this size, Doctor; does it seem exorbitant to you?"

I felt startled when this man again addressed my uncle as "Doctor." My uncle considered the offer and said meekly, "The print itself costs only two rupees."

"In that case I will leave it to your sense of justice. Do you assume that frame and mount are in any sense inferior to the photo?"

Everyone on the bench looked concerned and nodded appreciatively at the progress of this dialogue (like the chorus in a Greek play) and my uncle said, "All right, three." He peeped out at the municipal clock tower. "It is past five, you won't take it up before seven?"

Jayraj said, "Never before eight."

"I have to be going. How will it reach me?"

Jayraj said, "I'll knock on your door tonight and deliver it. Maybe you could leave the charges, amounting to three rupees. Don't mistake me for asking for money in advance. You see that room." He indicated an antechamber. "It is full of pictures of gods, demons, and humans, framed in glass, ordered by people who never turned up again, and in those days I never knew how to ask for payment. If a picture is not claimed immediately I keep it for twenty years in that room. That's the law here. Anyway I don't want to keep your picture for twenty years. I will bring it to you tonight . . . or . . ." A sudden idea struck him. "Why don't you leave this little fellow behind? He will collect the picture, and I will see that he comes home to you safely tonight."

An impossible idea it seemed at first. My uncle shook his head and said, "Oh, not possible. How can he stay here?"

"Trust me, have you no trust in me? Anyway at the end of the day I will deliver him and the photo at your door."

"If you are coming our way, why do you want this boy to be left here?"

"To be frank, in order to make sure that I keep my promise and don't yield to any sudden impulse to shut my shop and run home."

"Until midnight?"

"Oh, no, I was joking. Much earlier, much earlier."

"What will he do for food? He is used to his supper at eight."

Jayraj pointed to a restaurant across the street and said, "I will nourish him properly. I love to have children around."

My uncle looked at me and asked, "Will you stay?"

I was thrilled. Jayraj was going to give me heavenly things to eat, and I could watch the procession of people and vehicles on Market Road. I pleaded, "Uncle, don't be afraid." I recollected all the dare-devilry of young men in the adventure stories I had heard. I wanted to have the pride of some achievement today. I pleaded with my uncle, "Please leave me and go. I will come home later."

Jayraj looked up and said, "Don't worry about him," and held out his hand. My uncle took out his purse and counted out three rupees on Jayraj's palm, saying, "I have never left him alone before."

Jayraj said, "Our boys must learn to get on by themselves. We must become a strong nation."

After my uncle left, Jayraj pushed away my photo onto the floor and took in its place on the desk a group photo of the trustee's. He kept gazing on it and said, "Not a very good photo. That Pictograph man again! So proud of his electronic flash! He claims he commands sunlight at his fingertips, but when he throws it onto the faces of a group before the camera, what do they do? They shut their eyes or open them wide as if they saw a ghost. For all the garland on his chest and all his pomposity, the man at the center and all others in the group look to me like monkeys surprised on a mango tree. . . ." The bald head kept swaying in approval. Jayraj constantly looked up from his work to make sure that the fellow was listening. I sat between them. Jayraj abruptly ordered, "Child, move over, let that man come nearer." I obeyed instantly.

This was my first day out, exciting and frightening at the same time. The world looked entirely different—the crowd at the market, which had seemed so entertaining before, was now terrifying. I feared that I might be engulfed and swept off, and never see my home again. As twilight came on and the street lamps were lit, I grew apprehensive. Somehow I felt I could not trust Jayraj. I stole a look at him. He looked forbidding. He wore a pair of glasses with thick lenses through which his eyeballs bulged, lending him a ghoulish look; unshaven chin and gray mottled hair covering his forehead; khaki shirt and a blood-red dhoti, a frightening combination. All his smiles and friendly talk before my uncle was a show to entice me. He seemed to have his own sinister plans to deal with me once I was left at his mercy. He had become cold and aloof. Otherwise, why should he have asked me to yield my place to the bald man? The moment my uncle's back was turned this man's manner had changed; he looked grim and ignored me. Where was the nourishment he had promised? I was afraid to ask. I kept looking at the restaurant across the road in the hope that he might follow my gaze and take the hint, but his hands were sawing, hammering, pasting, and smoothing while his tongue wagged uninterruptedly. Having promised me nourishment, this man was not giving it a thought. Suppose I reminded him? But I lacked the courage to speak to him. With unappeased hunger on one side, my mind was also busy as to how to retrieve my photo from this horrible man and find my way home. I had not noticed the landmarks while coming. There were so many lanes ending on Market Road. I was not sure which one of them would lead me to Kabir Street, and from Kabir Street should I go up or down? A well stood right in the middle of that street, and beside it the striped wall of an abandoned temple in which the tailor was supposed to live. One went past it and came through onto Vinayak Street somehow. Vinayak Street seemed such a distant dream to me now. Once some gracious god could put me down there, at either end, I could always find my way home. I was beginning to feel lost.

Jayraj paused for a moment to look at me and say, "When I promise a time for delivery, I keep it." Analyzing his statement, I found no hint of anything to eat. "When I promise a time . . . etc." What of the promise of food? What did "delivery" mean? Did it include eating? It was a worrying situation for me. I could not understand whether he implied that after delivering his picture to the bald man he would summon the restaurant keeper and order a feast, or did he simply mean that in due course he would nail my photo on four sides with wood and glass and then say, "That is all, now get out." When I tried to declare, "I am very hungry, are you doing anything about it? A promise is sacred and inescapable," I found my voice croaking, creaking, and the words in such a jumble and mumble that it only attracted the other's attention and conveyed nothing. He looked up and asked, "Did you speak?"

He looked fierce under the kerosene "power light" hanging from the ceiling, and the huge shadow of its tin reflector left half the shop in darkness. I had no doubt that he enticed people in there, murdered them in cold blood, and stored their bodies in the anteroom. I remembered his mysterious references to the room, and my uncle had understood. The wonder was that Uncle should listen to all that and yet leave me behind. Of course, if it came to it, I could hit him with the little rod on the work-bench and run away. This was a testing time, and Uncle perhaps wanted to try me out; hadn't they agreed that little boys should become tough? If he asked me in I should take care not to cross the threshold—but if he ordered food, but kept it as a bait far inside and then said, "Come in here and eat"—perhaps then I should make a dash for the food, hit him with the steel rod, and run—tactics to be accomplished at lightning speed. Perhaps my uncle expected me to perform such deeds, and would admire my pluck. Hit Jayraj on the head and run and munch while running. While my mind was busy working out the details of my retreat, I noticed that the man had risen to his feet and was rummaging among old paper and cardboard, stacked in the back room. When he stood up he looked lanky and tall, with long legs and long limbs as if he had uncoiled himself. Rather snake-like, I thought.

For a moment I was seized with panic at the prospect of combatting him. The bald man had edged closer and closer and had now actually stepped into the workshop, anticipating some excitement, the light from the power lamp imparting a blinding luster to his bald pate. Jayraj cried from the back room, "Impossible to get at what one wants in this cursed place, must set apart a day for cleaning up. . . . Ah, here it is." And he brought out a portrait in a gray mount, took it close to the light, and said, "Come nearer, the print is rather faded." They examined it with their heads abutting each other. I looked away. I realized

that while they were brewing their nefarious plan I should remain alert but without giving them any sign of noticing. "This
is the man; at one time the richest doctor in Burma. . . ." I
caught these words. Occasionally from time to time I turned my
head just to look at them and caught them glancing at me and
turning away. I too looked away, sharpening my ears not to miss
a single word; somehow I was beginning to feel that their talk
had something to do with me. Jayraj's loud and guffawing tone
was all gone, he was now talking in a sinister undertone. "Ten
doctors employed under him. But this fellow was only a chokra;
he sterilized needles and wrapped up powders and medicine bottles and cleansed the syringe; actually he must have started as
this man's [tapping the photo] personal bootboy. When the Japanese bombed Rangoon, these people trekked back to our country, leaving behind their palatial home and several cars and
everything, but still they managed to carry with them jewelry
and much gold, and a bank account in Madras, and above all
also a fifteen-day-old baby in arms. The doctor took ill and died
on the way. There were rumors that he was pushed off a cliff by
so-and-so. The lady reached India half dead, lingered for a year,
and died. The baby was all right, so was the chokra, all through
the expedition. The chokra, becoming all in all, took charge of
all the cash and gold and bank accounts after reaching this country, impersonating the doctor. That poor woman, the doctor's
wife, need not have died, but this fellow kept her a prisoner in
the house and gave her some injections and finished her. The
cremation was a double-quick affair across the river."

The bald man now moved back to my side. Jayraj had resumed his seat and was working on a frame. I still kept fixedly
looking away, feeling desperate at the prospect before me—a
total darkness had now fallen on the city, and there was the
hopelessness of getting any refreshment.

They continued their talk in conspiratorial tones all through.
The bald man asked some question. Jayraj replied, "Who could
say? I didn't know much about them. I think that the fat woman

must also have been there all the time and a party to it. I learned a lot from a servant maid who brought this picture for framing one day. I told her to call for it next day. She never came. So far no sign of anyone claiming it."

"The same fellow who sat here a little while ago!" said the bald man in astonishment.

Jayraj lowered his voice and muttered, "When I called him 'Doctor'—you must have seen his face!" and then they carried on their talk for a long while, which was all inaudible to me. I kept glancing at them and feeling their eyes on me all the time. Finally the tap-tap of the hammer ceased and he said, "All right, this is finished. Let the glue dry a bit. Anyway it must be said to his credit: he tended the child and brought him up—only God knows the full truth." He suddenly called me, held out to me the photograph salvaged from the dark chamber, and asked, "Do you wish to take this home? I can give it to you free." And they both stared at my face and the photo while he held it out. I had a momentary curiosity to look at the face of the man who had been the subject of their talk. The photo was very faded, I could glimpse only a mustache and little else; the man was in European clothes—if what they said was true, this was my father. I looked at their faces and noticed the sneering, leering expressions on them. I flung the photo back, got up without a word, and began to run.

I raced down Market Road, not aware of the direction I was taking. I heard the man shout after me, "Come, come, I will frame yours and give it to you, and then take you home." The bald man's squeaky voice added something to support his friend, but I ran. I bumped into people coming to the market and was cursed. "Have you no eyes, these boys nowadays!" I feared Jayraj might shout, "Catch him, don't let him get away." Presently I slowed down my pace. I had no sense of direction but presently noticed Jagan's sweet mart on my right-hand side this time and knew that I was going back the way I had come. My head was drumming with Jayraj's speech. It was agonizing to picture my uncle cheating, murdering, and lying. The references to my father and mother touched me less; they were remote, unconvincing figures.

Blundering and groping along, I reached the end of Market Road. People looked at me curiously. I did not want to betray that this was my first outing alone, and so sauntered along, tried to look casual, whistled and hummed aloud, *"Raghupati Raghava Raja Ram."* The street lighting imperceptibly dimmed and grew sparser as I reached the foot of Lawley Statue. The Lawley Extension homes were tucked far back into their respective compounds, no way of knocking on their doors for any help; nor could I approach the boys leaning on their bicycles and chatting; they were senior boys who might make fun of me or beat me. A vagrant lay stretched full length on a side away from others; he looked wild and dreadful, but he kept looking at me while others would not even notice my presence. I shrank away at the foot of this terrible statue, hoping that it would not suddenly start moving and march over me. The vagrant held out his hand and said, "Give me a coin, I will buy something to eat."

I turned my shirt pocket inside out to prove my statement, "I have no money, not a paisa, and I am also hungry."

"Go home then," he ordered.

"I want to, but where is Vinayak Street?"

It was a grave risk betraying myself in this manner; if he realized that I was a lost soul he might abduct and sell me upcountry as a slave. "I will go with you and show the way, will you tell your mother to give me a little rice for my trouble?"

Mother! Mother! My mind fell into a confusion . . . of that woman who died at Uncle's hand . . . I had all along felt my aunt was my mother. "I have only an aunt, no mother," I said.

"Aunts don't like me, and so go by yourself. Go back half the way you came, count three streets and turn on your left, if you know which is your left hand, and then turn right and you will be in Kabir Street . . ."

"Oh, I know Kabir Street, and the well," I said with relief.

"Get onto it then, and take the turning beyond the well for Vinayak Street, don't wander all over the town like this. Boys like you must stay at home and read your lessons."

"Yes, sir," I said respectfully, feeling intimidated. "Once I am back I promise to read my lessons."

The directions that he gave helped me. I came through and found myself at the disused well in Kabir Street. When I reached Vinayak Street I felt triumphant. In that feeling of relief, even Jayraj's words ceased to rankle in my mind. The dogs in our street set up a stormy reception for me. At that hour the street was deserted, and the only guardians were the mongrels that roamed up and down in packs. They barked viciously at first but soon recognized me. Escorted by the friendly dogs, wagging their tails and wetting the lampposts in their delight at meeting me, I reached my house. My uncle and aunt were on the front door-step and flung at me a jumble of inquiries. "Your uncle wanted to start out again and look for you," my aunt said.

Uncle lifted me practically half in the air in the sheer joy of our reunion, and asked, "Where is the framer? He promised to leave you here. It is past ten o'clock now."

Before I could answer my aunt said, "I told you not to trust such persons."

"Where is your photograph?"

I had not thought of an answer for that. What could I say? I only burst into tears and wept at the memory of all the confusion in my mind. Safer to weep than to speak. If I spoke I feared I might blunder into mentioning the other photo out of the darkroom.

My aunt immediately swept me in, remarking sorrowfully, "Must be very, very hungry, poor child."

I sobbed, "He didn't give me anything to eat."

All night I lay tossing in my bed. I kicked my feet against the wall and groaned, and woke up with a start from a medley of nightmares composed of the day's experience. My uncle was snoring peacefully in his room: I could see him through the open door. I sat up and watched him. He had impersonated a doctor, but it didn't seem to be a very serious charge, as I had always thought that all doctors with their rubber tubes and medical smell were playacting all the time. Imprisoning and poisoning my mother—Mother? My aunt was my mother as far as I could see, and she was quite alive and sound. There wasn't even a faded photo of that mother as there was of my father. The photographer had said something about money and jewelry. I was indifferent to both. My uncle gave me all the money I needed, never refusing me anything at any time. Jewelry—those glittering pieces—one had better not bother about. You could not buy candy with gold, could you? To think that the refugees from Rangoon should have carried such tinsel all the way! In my own way I was analyzing and examining the charges against my uncle and found them flimsy, although the picture of him emanating out of dark whispers and furtive glances, in the background of a half-lit back room, was shocking.

I needed some clarifications very urgently. My aunt, sleeping on her mat at the edge of the open courtyard, stirred. I made sure that Uncle's snores were continuing, softly rose from my bed, and went over to her side. I sat on the edge of her mat and looked at her. She had observed my restlessness and asked, "Why haven't you slept yet?"

I whispered, "Aunt, are you awake? I want to tell you something."

She encouraged me to speak. I gave her an account of Jayraj's narrative. She merely said, "Forget it. Never mention it to your uncle."

"Why?"

"Don't ask questions. Go back to your bed and sleep."

I could do nothing more. I took the advice. The next day Jayraj managed to deliver the framed photo through someone who passed this way. My uncle examined it inch by inch by the light from the courtyard, and declared, "Wonderful, good work, worth three rupees, surely." He fumbled about with a hammer and nail looking for the right place, and hung it finally over his easy chair, right below the big portrait of his ancestor on the wall.

I acted on my aunt's advice and never asked any question. As I grew up and met more people, I heard oblique references to my uncle here and there, but I ignored whatever I heard. Only once did I try to strangle a classmate at the college hostel in Madras who had gossiped about my uncle. Stirred by such information, sometimes I thought of him as a monster and I felt like pricking and deflating him the next time I met him. But when I saw him on the railway platform, waiting to receive me, the joy in his perspiring face moved me, and I never questioned him in any manner. After seeing me through the Albert Mission High School he had maintained me at a college in Madras; he wrote a postcard at least once a week, and celebrated my arrival during a vacation with continuous feasting at home. He had probably gambled away a lot more money than he had spent on me. It didn't matter. Nothing ever mattered. He never denied me anything. Again and again I was prompted to ask the question "What am I worth? What about my parents?" but I rigorously suppressed it. Thus I maintained the delicate fabric of our relationship till the very end of his life. After his death, I examined his records—not a shade of correspondence or account to show my connection with Burma, except the lacquered casket with a dragon on it. He had bequeathed the house and all his possessions and a small annuity in the bank to me and left my aunt in my care.